The Wrong Sort of Magic

ALEXANDRA ALAN

The Wrong Sort of Magic
ISBN #979-8-9922771-4-2
Copyright © 2025 by Alexandra Alan

Cover illustration by Libertad Delgado (@LiberLibelula)
Interior scene break and chapter illustrations by Alexandra Alan

Content Warning

Please note that this book was written by someone whose formative experiences were with '90s fantasy TV shows. It contains action, blood, and fight scenes, but there's also witty repartee and love.

The detailed list, for those who would like it:

Explicit sexual content, coarse language, descriptions of violence, depictions of blood, descriptions of anxiety and panic attacks, brief reference to an off-page animal death, death and grief, alcohol use, past parental death, emotional manipulation by a parent, explicit sexual content occurring in a work environment, references to nerd culture, dual POV, this is starting to look like a tag list, honestly I'm not mad about it, occasional vile puns, happy ending.

For all content warnings and heat levels, please visit the "Content" section of www.AlexandraAlan.com.

One

It was a perfect night for hunting demons.

Thin fog hung close to the damp pavement and grasped with flimsy fingers at anything that moved, while reflections of the thin, scythe-like moon glimmered in shattered windows and chips of glass lying on the concrete. Abandoned warehouses languished up ahead, corpses of steel and rust and broken bricks.

Pippa Beverly shivered in delight.

Not that she couldn't do this on a humid day with cottony clouds and an oncoming sunburn, but there was just something *right* about lurking through fog and gloom in pursuit of evil.

Pippa glanced at the blood trail in front of her and stepped over a puddle that still lingered from the day's earlier rain. Moonlight glinted off the surface, blood swirling through the puddle like oil.

Though the blood itself wasn't demonic—it belonged to the animal her quarry had taken as dinner—sourness squirmed in her gut as she passed through the remnants of foul energy hovering above the droplets.

She shivered again, though with much less delight.

When Pippa first began hunting demons, she'd been under the assumption that a demon's aura was something she could grow used to. Eventually, she wouldn't feel the awful twisting sensation of her body reacting to what should not be. Sure, the urge to vomit passed after a year or so, but the lingering discomfort never did.

Did the Ash Coven members still feel it?

Probably not. They likely had some ritual whenever a new witch was accepted: a little spell to calm the stomach against demon auras before the celebratory wine began to flow. Pippa would bet it would be a classy affair. There would be ties and lint-free dresses and cocktail napkins. And fancy cheese.

No Ash Coven protections for her, though. Pippa trudged through the night wearing old leggings, a loose sweatshirt with a hood pulled over her hair and a repurposed kitchen knife stuck in the pocket, and a pair of running shoes that tended to squeak at inopportune moments.

Everything was fantastic. Truly, just great.

If she weren't trying to be sneaky, she would have given a snarling, frustrated shout to let some of the anger in her body exist elsewhere for a second.

The day had already taken a massive, steaming dump: a shitty day at a shitty job, and a terrible, pointless meeting with the Ash Coven. To top it all, she had to worry about her shoes cooperating with her intentions to be silent.

If she had been accepted by the Coven, then she wouldn't have to think about said shitty job with equally shitty pay. Legal assistants had to make do with old shoes. Ash Coven members could buy themselves a new pair of non-squeaking shoes with excellent arch support and then take them out to the warehouse district on an inaugural hunt.

Being part of the Ash Coven would also mean that she wouldn't have to worry about asshole coworkers who had recently transferred.

Well. Just one transfer. Just one asshole.

Maxim Fucking Sheppard.

Ugh.

That probably wasn't the name on his license, but Pippa liked to pretend. He'd been at the firm for four months after having transferred from a larger one in New York. It must have been fancy, what with the wardrobe he hadn't gone through the effort to modify. Who had lapels that perfect? It was an affront to every single cardigan she'd thrifted and considered good enough for working a desk job.

Maxim. It was the sort of name that could perfectly accompany the question, "And which yacht would you like to take out today, sir?" The knot on his tie always looked like it had been arranged by a valet, which furthered the concept.

Every time he spoke to her, it was in sentences so brief and stilted they sounded like orders. She had never seen him smile. *Never.* When he asked for documents or paperwork to complete, he did it in a way that implied he was simply allowing her to fulfill her dream.

Pippa suppressed a wrathful yell again, instead strangling the cuff of her sweatshirt until the fabric creaked.

During today's meeting, she'd made the horrific mistake of sitting in his typical chair in the conference room. As far as she could tell, the foam didn't have an impression of his ass that made it better than the rest of the identical black ergonomic chairs in the room, but still, he had scowled at her until she moved. Not a single "Excuse me, but . . ." or "Sorry, do you mind if I . . ." He only stood glowering as if he had been given life by a mad scientist with overwhelming electricity bills. It was a glower that implied she was beneath him. She was inferior, not worth his time.

Then, hot off the heels of a warm drive in her old car that didn't even have a working radio she could blast to ease some of that anger, she'd met with the Ash Coven members and those exact same feelings of ineptitude returned with force.

She'd thought the interview with them this evening would be better than the last. Maybe they would have decided she had finally done enough to earn her place in their circle. Maybe they'd—

Movement along the top of one of the dilapidated warehouses caught Pippa's eye and she snapped her head up. She froze for long enough to realize it had just been a bit of moonlight shifting on a fire escape. Nothing more than a reflection. Her heart was slower to understand this and continued to pound frantically.

She wrestled the bitter thoughts away, rolled her shoulders, and breathed in the damp smells of old rain, rotting wood, and rusted metal. The magic in the surrounding air tickled her fingertips and brushed against her cheeks, calming her in the exact way that her mind never really could.

Comforted, she continued along the splattered trail. As long as she could reach out to magic and it could reach back, all would be well.

Pippa paused at the corner of one warehouse. Both the blood trail and the lingering energy stopped in the center of a derelict courtyard. Dead trees twitched in the breeze, their gnarled branches dripping with condensed fog. A soggy piece of cardboard, part of some long-gone distribution center, lay slumped against a bowed wall.

After a quick glance to make sure the courtyard was truly empty, Pippa stepped beneath the barren, twisted trees. She breathed in again. This deep within the warehouse complex, the fog rolled over her tongue and brought with it the sharp tang of rust. She shoved her baggy sleeves to her elbows, held out her hands, and closed her eyes.

Awareness bloomed slowly through her body. The moon dusted her skin with its pale light. Birds nested in high rafters, their heads tucked beneath their wings until dawn. A bat dodged between buildings as it picked off moths. From the north, a breeze dipped along the river before meandering over to pluck at the wisps of curling hair that escaped from Pippa's stubby braid. Rust prickled at her just as it prickled at every joist and beam and corrugated panel.

Just like the sort of prickle she'd felt when she suffered the disgusted frown at her worn shoes not an hour earlier.

Pippa curled her hands into fists.

"What else?" she had asked, unable to hide the desperation in her voice. *"What else do you want from me?"*

Elder Ranna had given her the sort of smile someone would give to a toddler asking for dessert at noon.

"We see all that you've done, Philippa," she'd said, *"and we're impressed."*

Pippa finished the elder's thought. *"But it's not enough."*

The other witches on the Ash Coven council had given pitying nods.

Elder Ranna smiled her same smile, though she added a patronizing tip of her head. *"Your acceptance is taking longer than most, since we must always consider the matter of your . . . family."*

"What does that have to do with anything?" Pippa had snapped. *"My father is long dead."*

"And yet alongside your Natural magic, you still have his power."

"I— But I've suppressed it. I haven't used it in almost two decades, and most of the time I forget it's there."

"It's in your blood, child," Elder Ranna said with a weary sigh. *"Although you might forget it, we won't."*

Pippa had actively forced herself not to scream. She'd put on a mask of indifference, crossed her legs, and leaned back in the stiff chair as if it were the plushest throne.

That was when Elder David had seen her footwear.

In the courtyard, Pippa clenched her jaw so hard that her teeth ached.

She'd hunted the streets every night since she was fifteen, chasing down monsters twice her size just to prove she was worthy of being part of the same coven who still saw her as a pair of bad shoes.

A sharp crackling pulled Pippa from her brooding. She opened her eyes. The dead branches of the courtyard trees were curling in on themselves, the smallest ones withering and twisting like they were being burned by some invisible flame. Bark burst into the air as one of the trunks split.

Shit.

Natural magic didn't much care about appropriate timing; it only knew how to listen.

Pippa forced her anger from her mind even as she frantically looked around to see if the noise had drawn attention to her presence. She urged the magic to silence, pulling back on it as if she were reeling in a net.

The branches shuddered and fell still, though several remained kinked at their ends.

Pippa ducked down beside a concrete planter and waited for the growl of some monster as it barreled around a corner or leaped from a building. But she only heard the sounds of the night: the soft rustle of wind, low calls of night birds, the grumbling creak of old structures.

She rose from her crouch and straightened her baggy sleeves.

What happened earlier today was unchangeable. All she could do was move forward, kill this demon, kill another, and another, and hope that someday, they would create a pile high enough to outweigh the other sort of magic she'd had no say in receiving.

To start, she had to find the trail.

Pippa shook out her arms and repositioned her hands. Breathed. There was the moon, the sleeping birds, the hungry bat. As she focused, she began to sense the demon's aura. All otherworldly creatures had them, and over the years, Pippa had compiled somewhat of a compendium in her mind. Succubi evoked the sensation of bare skin gliding across heated silk, ghouls were icy and bitter, wood fairies felt as fresh and clear as a summer rainstorm.

Pippa concentrated on this demon's presence. Thorns and grease. It crept along her skin and settled high in her stomach.

There you are.

She delved into that sensation and when she opened her eyes, a wavering path of murky red flickered along the concrete. The trail left behind by the demon's aura appeared dim where she stood but brightened as it passed through the broken wall of a warehouse up ahead. Easy enough to follow.

Broken glass littered the ground where she crept into the warehouse, and she rose to her toes in order to step cautiously between the shards. The building was silent except for a wet chomping sound that came from high up in one corner. She let her concentration drop, and the trail faded out of sight.

The thin moon did nothing to illuminate the warehouse. At her position by the door, she could see cobwebs floating through the air in front of her face, yet her eyes wouldn't adjust to the darkness, and the far half of the building remained pitch black. The large glass windows lining the walls were nearly opaque from dust and dirt. The stench of fresh blood wafted past her into the night and, combined with the stronger aura enclosing her like a shroud, made her regret eating so soon before her hunt.

Pippa swallowed hard in an attempt to keep her dinner in its place. She could ready an attack, but where would she aim it? And what exactly was she trying to hit?

Her fingers tapped the knife in her pocket as she thought. Different demons had different susceptibilities: a blast of fire might take out a blood-raged ghoul, but it would only encourage any number of other things. She just had to stay quiet. Maybe she could make a distraction to lure it outside, let her see it before it saw her.

If she could brighten the building, she could—

Right then, Pippa stepped on a chunk of brick, and her shoe let out a loud, farting squeak.

The chomping stopped. A beat of silence, and then the sound of something landing hard on concrete and sprinting in her direction.

Pippa grabbed on to a handful of nearby magic, twisted it, and hurled it into the air above her head. Light blasted out from a single point, but in her haste she pulled too little, and the light flickered out quickly. Yet in that brief flash, it lit up the demon long enough for her to see a sickly pale face, twin curved horns, and an impossibly large gore-streaked jaw unhinging wide.

She threw herself to the side and heard it smack the wall behind her. Its low snarl rattled through her bones.

"I do not like my meals interrupted, witch." The demon spoke in an indistinct, slow way that implied its jaw was still hanging loose.

Pippa couldn't see more than shadows. Adrenaline scalded her veins.

"Yeah?" she said. "I didn't know dog tastes better if you eat it all at once." She'd seen the torn collar, the little tag for *Billy*.

The demon hissed. "It was a stringy creature. Its hairs are stuck in my teeth."

Its voice twisted in disgust, and Pippa took advantage of the temporary diversion. She pulled more magic to her.

This time, when she hurled power into the air, light exploded outward and glowed bright and steady enough to illuminate the entire warehouse. Scattered bricks and beams littered the concrete floor, and the demon staggered across them as it threw one pale arm over its face. It wore a pair of sagging pants tucked into heavy boots. Its torso was bare, and though the demon's body was gangly, its stomach pouched in the sort of way that implied the size of its dinner. Two long spiraling horns curled along its scalp from its temples, and the pointed ears beneath them twitched backward in anger.

A Tro'grath. Before she'd been humiliated in yet another interview, the Ash Coven had mentioned that a new group of these demons had moved into New Hawkshead's underground several weeks past. They were known for their intelligence, but also their violence.

This one was young, since it only had a single set of horns. Older Tro'graths could have several sets sprouting from their heads.

More adrenaline trickled up Pippa's neck. Young demons were volatile. Even though they compensated for their lack of years and wisdom with rashness and stupidity, their strength outperformed that of their elders. She'd heard tales over the years of witches beginning fights with young demons under the supposition that "young" just meant "careless," only to become a cautionary tale for others.

Better be careful, then.

She let the magic around her flow over her hands, reveling in the strength it brought and the way it brightened the light overhead. The demon staggered and hissed at her like a cat sprayed with water.

"And what about the people you killed yesterday?" she said, surprised that she managed to keep her voice from trembling. "Were they pitiful too?"

It lowered its arm and blinked in the light. Something glimmered in its skin, and Pippa looked closer. Were those jewels embedded in its forehead? Two sets of eyelids shuttered quickly over milky pink eyes, and its pupils, like black pinpricks, settled on her.

It twitched its mouth in a grotesque parody of a smile. Red flecks adorned its bared fangs.

"No," it said. "They were delicious."

Pippa quelled her rising revulsion, even as magic continued to flood along her fingers. "The coven that protects this city can let an owned animal's death slide occasionally. But killing humans? You crossed a line when you ate them."

The Tro'grath snorted, then began to circle her in a wide arc. Those pink eyes fixed on her neck a little too firmly.

"Go on then witch," it said. "Tell me more about lines. You can speak of them as I gnaw on your spine."

Pippa frowned. "Gross."

That's when it lunged, spittle flying from its mouth, jaw open far enough to reveal the second row of fangs ringing its purpled tongue. The screech that burst from that awful maw was like the piercing agony of metal scraping against slate. Muscles bulged beneath its sickly skin.

Pippa was ready.

She forced the gathered magic out of her hands. It shot from her, spraying up and out in a wall of shining air that formed an arced shield. As the demon collided with it, the force rattled her arms.

The Tro'grath tumbled onto the concrete, its eyes wide. Black blood trickled down from a wound on its temple near one of its horns. It stared at her as if utterly shocked she would dare fight back.

Rage twisted the mottled lips into a snarl and it lunged for her again, but Pippa pulled on the magic, reorienting the shield to bring it down onto the demon. The magic crushed the Tro'grath into the concrete. She felt it writhe and twist beneath the magical pane, and she pushed down harder.

She didn't notice the demon had grabbed a brick to throw at her until she felt the impact of it on her shin.

Pain lanced through her leg, and she staggered with a cry. She scrabbled to keep the magic together, but she had been distracted for a second too long. The shield wavered, fractured, then fell over the demon as if it had been made of dust.

The Tro'grath erupted out of the shining cloud, all bared teeth and flashing claws. When Pippa turned to dodge, she landed on her injured leg. The blossoming bruise on her shin erupted into a pain so sharp that her graceful move became an awkward stumble. Claws raked across her sweatshirt, her skin saved only by the baggy bulging of the material.

She ducked beneath another swipe and pulled her knife from the sheath within her sweater, then propelled herself forward and embedded the blade in the demon's chest.

Different demons had different weaknesses, but she'd learned long ago that if in doubt, always go for the heart.

The demon let out a furious screech. When it scuttled away from her, she saw she'd aimed too high: the handle wobbled below the creature's shoulder, far from its heart.

It wrapped one clawed hand around the knife and pulled it from its body. Smoke wisped from the wound, and the Tro'grath gave Pippa a look somewhere between indignation and shock.

"You dare?" it said. "You dare to strike me with your fey-blade?"

If it was offended by being stabbed by her, it would be outright horrified to know the "fey-blade" was just a kitchen knife from a pawn shop doctored with a hasty spell to make it act like silver.

Despite her now-throbbing shin, or perhaps because of it, Pippa couldn't contain all of her laugh, and a small snort escaped.

The demon heard, and its face grew purple with fury. "You laugh, witch, the way a mouse laughs in the jaws of a beast."

It hurled Pippa's own knife at her, and as she flung her body to the side to avoid it, the demon sprung at her and raked its claws over her stomach. Two claws made it through the sweatshirt.

She cried out and pressed a hand to her midsection. Not mortally deep, but . . . deep. Blood welled beneath her palm and slipped over her fingers. Magic waited at her fingers, ready to pack into the wound and guide quick healing. She urged it along her arms and down her torso.

The Tro'grath's pin-sized pupils widened at the smell of her blood. It tipped its head back and howled in delight.

"My family will see what I do to you, and they will sing my name for lifetimes." Another one of those awful smiles stretched its lips. It pointed to the center jewel in its forehead, now glowing. "They will see."

The *hell* did that mean?

Pippa urged the magic to move faster. Already, the blood had stopped flowing from her stomach. Another few seconds and she would—

She barely managed to duck beneath the demon's swinging fist. Her head felt light from the triple impact of heavy magic, pain, and adrenaline, and her body wasn't moving as fast as it needed to.

The next backhand swipe caught her squarely in the chest. Pippa flew several feet across the warehouse, and when she landed, the scattered bricks didn't make for a comfortable landing. Two of her ribs snapped on impact, and her breath left her chest in a silent shout.

Snarling, the Tro'grath vaulted through the air and landed on top of Pippa. She threw out a hand and shoved against the demon's throat. Even though her muscles burned and her ribs screamed, she kept her arm extended while she tried to avoid its scraping claws. Her forearm trembled with the effort of keeping those gnashing teeth at bay. Saliva dripped from the demon's fangs and burned as it hit her skin.

The fangs were inching closer, and Pippa could easily imagine the feeling of them sinking into her neck. Claws dug into her side above her hip; hot, rotten breath filled her lungs.

A little thought brushed against her, breaking through the growing fog of fear: Natural magic required concentration and energy. With every second this fight continued, a little more of her abilities slipped away. She was already too tired. Too spent. If she became too exhausted to channel the magic around her, it might as well not even be there.

Yet there was that other magic, one that didn't need nearly as much focus and care as the magic she pulled and molded from the world around her. She only had to let this power out, and it would take care of everything.

No.

Pippa hadn't hidden away that part of herself for so many years just to give in to it now.

With one desperate pull, Pippa urged the world's magic up through her body, encouraged heat and fire, and sent it through the hand gripping the demon's throat. Flames shot from her palm into its skin, and with a scream, it arched its back in an attempt to pull away. Pippa brought her legs high and struck out with both feet, hitting the demon squarely in the chest.

It lurched off of her. Clawed fingers scrabbled at the shining blisters ringing its neck.

She tried to grasp more magic, but the demon was already preparing to lunge again. There wasn't time.

A piece of rebar, about twice the length of her arm, caught her eye beside her shoulder. She grabbed it, and when the Tro'grath leaped toward her, she used her entire body to swing the bar into the demon's side. It connected with a vibration that rattled Pippa's elbows, and as the creature tumbled onto the concrete, it let out a burbling screech.

Every limb ached, every muscle felt seconds away from collapse. She couldn't fight much longer.

Magic roiled in the ground beneath her back. It was there, ready to listen. Pippa called on it with her last scraps of energy and felt the concrete push upward in a wave that sent her staggering to her feet. Taking advantage of the momentum, she held the length of rebar tight and thrust it down so the rusted steel punctured straight through the center jewel in the Tro'grath's forehead.

Blood-smeared limbs spasmed. The demon's throat convulsed in a choked gurgle. One eye centered on Pippa, the pupil having contracted so small she could hardly see it.

"They will . . . come for . . . you," the demon croaked. Then, with a rattling breath, it fell still.

If Pippa had a dollar for every time some creature promised vengeance or death, she wouldn't have to be an assistant at a law firm. How nice would it be to have *payment* for all of this.

She had enough energy for one more bitter thought about the coven before her strength gave out and she sagged to the concrete and flopped to her back.

Pippa reached up to scrape her sweat-damp hair out of her face and, from the feel of it, managed to smear her own blood over her forehead and into her hair. She groaned.

Magic was slower to respond when she was so exhausted. Instead of racing through her body, it moved like cold syrup. But it still moved. Warmth oozed over her rib cage, side, and stomach, knitting bone together and closing her skin. It did best with fleshy injuries, and though her stomach and side would be closed by the end of the night, bone took longer to fully heal. At least it had done enough so she could breathe without her own ribs knifing a lung.

Pippa rolled to her side and forced herself to her feet. She still had more to do.

According to the Ash Coven, the citizens of New Hawkshead would riot if anyone saw a corpse like the one in front of her. No humans knew that the bus drivers and politicians and grocery clerks lived alongside creatures of myth and nightmare; she had to make sure that did not change.

Her legs wobbled slightly as she stood and held her hands over the Tro'grath's body. She focused on the flesh, the collection of blood and viscera that was an intrusion on this world. The magic hovering in the air flowed where she directed it, tweaking, changing, burning.

The Tro'grath's body withered on the concrete as if it were being consumed by flame from the inside. Skin burned red-hot momentarily before it turned to ash, and soon, the entire corpse was nothing more than a charred pile.

Pippa tried to call the wind inside to scatter the remnants, but after all she'd done, she could only manage the barest lazy breeze. A few clumps of ash twitched and then fell still. Whatever. If anyone came in, they'd have to look hard to find a pile of dust slightly darker than the other piles of dust.

She staggered from the warehouse into the moonlit warehouse complex.

"They will see."

The demon's words slunk back to her. She shook her head, then groaned and pressed a hand to her temple at the resulting headache.

A demon's dying promise didn't much matter now. And even if it did, she'd worry about it tomorrow.

Yeah.

Tomorrow will be a better day.

Tomorrow was going to be horrible.

Maxim Sheppard spun around in his home office chair before giving his computer a cold look. It was updating. The scurrying progress bar showed this wasn't going to be a lengthy update, but it had come at the exact moment he'd been in the middle of a flow, where any interruption threw him off track like a boulder in the way of a bicycle. He'd put the update off for too long and the computer had apparently decided that he was no longer trusted with decisions about its health.

He would have preferred to be at work on a computer paid for by the firm and updated by the IT department, but Ivanov, Barry, and Cruz had stringent rules about staff loitering in the building after midnight, for some reason.

Maxim thumped his palm on the chair's armrest. The new account was not his yet. By all rights, he shouldn't even have been working on it, and doing so must have been violating some-thing, yet he couldn't stop. There were numbers to check, finances to question, potential litigation opportunities to delve into. The announcement for who would receive the promotion wasn't going to come for another—Maxim checked his watch and frowned—fifteen hours. But if he was brought onto the account with ideas already percolating and a hefty base of knowledge already established, he would have nothing to worry about. At least for a few days.

He scoffed and made a half spin in the chair. He'd never been great at convincing himself.

The monitor's screen flashed and a new progress bar appeared, this one lacking the speed of its predecessor.

Maxim scrubbed a hand through his hair and gave his computer another withering look. At the bottom of the screen, a little number informed him that the update was at a very impressive two percent.

Maxim spun to face away from the monitor. His study was bathed in an eye-cramping blue glow. The room did have a light, one of those half-domed glass bowls with a nipple-like protrusion in the center, but it remained off. He'd planned to get a lamp to use instead of the overpowering overhead light, but four months into the condo's lease, he'd reached the point where no lamp seemed right, and the very prospect of picking one out sent him spiraling into a bad mood. There were simply too many options. The past week, he'd start scrolling on some elegant website only to hyperfixate himself into a cart filled with six different lamps and not actually liking any of them.

Maxim snuck a quick glance over his shoulder at the progress bar as if it were a child playing a game and would freeze if it saw him looking, and rubbed his temples with one hand.

The lamp was a distraction, of course. That was obvious. He was focusing on something he could control to keep his mind off of something he couldn't: the possible promotion. The possible raise, the possible change in his life, the possible sense of purpose.

With a growl, Maxim pushed off his chair and thumped into the kitchen for a glass of water.

He shouldn't think about any of that now. Especially since his computer was out of commission for probably the rest of the night (Morning? Day? Whatever), and the only end result of this spiraling would be a heavy layer of irritation and feeling like he'd swallowed a bag of eels.

The drink was cool and calming in his hand. He focused on the prickle of condensation, the tactile sensation of smooth glass and tickling beads of water. Outside the kitchen window, New Hawkshead's lights glittered. Not nearly as bright as he was used to.

New York was a city of gleaming beauty and horrible filth. It had an atmosphere to it, a tangible . . . well, he didn't want to say *aura*, because that was all hippie crystal-waving nonsense, but it fit. The city was a breathing, writhing mass of intoxicating toxicity. He loved it for that. In a city of eight million people, it was easy to blend in. Easier to find distractions. He could hurl himself headfirst into his work and it would consume him in a way that left no time for spiraling or hyperfixating on replacing tit-like lighting fixtures.

Here though . . .

Maxim sipped his water and made a face through the window at the small, charming, boring cityscape of New Hawkshead.

At the New York firm, he'd been treading water in a sea of other champions of humanity, being sapped of energy and motivation. He had made as much of a difference as a light bulb illuminating the Grand Canyon.

Here at Ivanov, Barry, and Cruz, though, he could make change. More importantly, he could make change that he could *see*. In the last four months, he'd had more interactions with the very people he was trying to help than he'd had in all his time at Prosten and Sons. The cases were smaller, the results not nearly as dramatic. Instead of multi-million dollar lawsuits that shifted a mansion and a pack of purebred Pomeranians from one soft hand to another, a day's success could mean a patient winning a case against their mildly negligent doctor, or a tenant proving their right to live in a rental without a gas leak. He'd been making a difference and even received a few Hallmark cards to show for it. But it still felt like he could do more.

Beyond the window, a distant searchlight marked the location of one of the more desperate car dealerships. He had done his research before arriving here, and aside from the occasional disappearance, murder, or wild animal traipsing through town, there was nothing notable. There had been some sort of newspaper-worthy event in a cemetery about twenty years ago that had ended with two dozen dead, which Maxim only remembered because it had sounded like the opening to a tabletop campaign, but it still paled in comparison to New York and its weekly horrors.

Maxim scoffed into his glass before taking a long swallow. One city was more memorable than another because of the number of homicides. *Way to be the stereotypical hard-hearted lawyer.*

Maybe he'd ask someone in the office if there was anything worth doing in town. Or out of it, even. A local might know of some trails, or a comfortable bookstore. It would give him the opportunity to get the hell out of his apartment and get to know the town that was now (at least according to his health insurance and driver's license) home. And, it'd be an excuse to talk to a coworker about a subject that didn't include the word "asset."

He could ask Pippa Beverly, one of the office's assistants. As far as he knew, she'd grown up in New Hawkshead and probably knew about the local interests.

Short, curvy Pippa Beverly. She had hair that, when it wasn't wrangled into a knot, came to her shoulders in molasses-colored curls. A slight overbite made her top lip a bit larger than the lower one. Her cheeks puckered with dimples when she smiled. She had such big eyes, too, so dark they were almost black.

Maxim frowned at the droplets clinging to the outside of the glass. He'd consider her quite attractive if she actually gave a damn about *anything*. The firm assisted the people in the community with problems they couldn't possibly solve themselves, and it seemed as if Pippa was the only one in the office who couldn't care less about any of it. She was distracted on the best of days and irritable on the rest. He wished that her indifference didn't rankle him so much, but every time he caught her staring through the conference table during a meeting as if her boredom could drill a hole through the mahogany, he wished he had a ballpoint pen to jam up his nose.

What else could *possibly* be prioritizing her attention? It wasn't his place to reprimand, though. He wasn't her boss, and colleagues didn't comment on the other's lack of professionalism.

Maxim drained his glass, then arranged it carefully in the dishwasher. He glanced at the clock on the microwave and let out a low groan, then raked both hands through his hair. If he stayed up any later, the circles underneath his eyes would have their own area codes.

After one last look at the computer's frozen progress bar and strongly resisting the urge to shut it down as punishment, Maxim stumbled into his bedroom, stripped to his underwear, and toppled onto the mattress. The sheets were crisp and cool, the fan overhead sent down a lovely, calming breeze, and crickets and distant traffic murmured melodies through the open window.

This room, with its natural white noise and the barest hint of chill, was typically enough to lull him into sleep.

Typically.

Most nights didn't come before a promotion. He'd pushed himself harder than anyone else at the firm, and tomorrow, he'd find out if all of the extra hours, sleepless nights, and caffeine migraines from diets subsisting only of coffee might finally turn into a job that would give him satisfaction.

So Maxim lay on his crisp sheets in his cool room and stared out of the open window at a town he'd barely gotten to know, and tried not to think about how his life was about to completely change.

Three

"And you're sure they denied you?"

"Yes, Mother," Pippa said into her phone for the eighth time in half as many minutes, fighting her irritation by fidgeting with the items on her desk. Clicking pens, picking some dust out of her keyboard, sliding her handwritten nameplate back and forth within its plastic holder.

Philippa Beverly, Kenzie from HR had written in a bubbly script. The *i*'s were dotted with circles.

"But are you sure?" Mary Beverly repeated. "Some of the Ash Coven members like to slur their words."

"No one slurred."

"Or maybe they were talking about the previous interviewee. You must have missed something."

"Mom." One of Pippa's eyes twitched as she stared at the paneled ceiling. Her ribs ached with the force of her sigh, and she idly rubbed her side. Although she felt much better than she had last night, a few twinges remained.

"They denied me," she said. "Again. They said it was . . ." She paused and glanced around the office.

Most of the associates' doors were closed, and those whose remained open were either pacing or flipping through depositions. The assortment of assistant desks in the center of the office space held only Pippa and Juliette Cohen, who had enveloped her as a friend shortly after starting at Ivanov, Barry, and Cruz. Geoff Davis—the third assistant—had just gotten up for another cup of coffee, and Jules was typing intently on her computer. Anything more than a cursory look revealed the words "Kirk," "Spock," and "throbbing."

Although no one seemed to be listening, Pippa kept her voice low as she spoke into her phone.

"They always say it's because of him. His power is in my blood, which makes my application take forever. It's impossible."

Mary heaved a loud sigh on the other end of the line, as if readying herself for a battle. "They'll change their minds. You have to keep trying. You're good at this, Pippa. Don't you want to have a career doing something you're good at?"

"Of course I do, you think I used to dream about proofreading emails when—"

Mary didn't seem to hear. "I don't think you'd want your father's faults to hover over you for you the rest of your life."

"Faults" was a weak term, considering what he'd done, but Pippa kept that comment to herself.

Mary continued. "They'll let you in. I know it."

"What if they don't?" It was the question that had been stabbing at Pippa for years. There wasn't much else in her life that she could confidently claim as worthy of a solid future; if she couldn't find success here, then where?

"They will."

Sometimes, she wished for her mother's optimism, even if it was just an overabundance of determination disguised as positivity.

Mary's voice grew gentle. "And until then, you're making New Hawkshead safer."

"Yeah." Pippa poked at her nameplate. The knowledge did give her some sense of duty, and purpose, and . . . hell, even pride. Every hostile creature she put down was one less murdered citizen. One less butchered pet. However, that never stopped her mother from—

"But you just have to keep trying."

Yep. From saying *that*.

The twitch moved from Pippa's eyelid to her temple, and she rubbed the spot hard with her thumb. She'd pulled her hair into a loose bun this morning, and as she massaged her scalp, several locks fell out of the clip and into her face.

"So what did you get last night?"

"A Tro'grath," Pippa said, so delighted at the change in subject she had to remember to keep her voice low as she recounted the fight. "But there was something weird. It had stones. In its head."

"Rude, Pip. I know they're demons, but there's no need to talk like that."

"No, I mean it had . . . jewels. In its forehead. Almost like a circlet, but in its skin."

"Oh."

"Yeah. Have you heard of anything like that before?"

Her mother made a "Hmm," and in her silence, Pippa could hear the warble of a television.

"I'll ask my book group."

Pippa's chair squeaked as she leaned back in it. "You have a book group?"

"It's online. We use videoconferencing. Pippa, I can hear your judgment."

"No judgment, just surprise." A little bit of judgment, as this was the same woman who had written every single one of her passwords on a piece of paper she kept within her folded laptop. But Pippa wasn't going to bring that up now.

"You have a book group that's all right with you asking about demons—"

A shadow moved into Pippa's field of vision, just enough in the periphery for her to see expertly hemmed pants and a set of shining black shoes.

"—that, uh, aren't in the . . . um . . . Player's Handbook?" she managed. The black shoes didn't seem to be going anywhere. "Hey, I gotta go, we'll talk more tonight." Her mother's confused squawks cut out as she ended the call.

Pippa plastered a friendly smile on her face and turned to the person hovering at the edge of her desk.

Her smile became a bit more forced when she saw who it was.

Maxim Fucking Sheppard.

Pippa had to crane her neck to look up at him. He really liked to loom. At about six feet tall, it came naturally to him, like he was a neolithic standing stone. With his wide chest and near-permanent glower, he only had to be cloned and aligned with the solstice and no one would be able to tell the difference.

"I'd like those printouts now. Please." His "please" at the end felt like trying to dab a bit of honey on a cactus to make it go down easier.

Pippa's smile became more forced. "Of course." She'd printed the files an hour ago and they sat on her desk, waiting patiently for this exact moment.

Maxim didn't go away when she handed them over. He flipped through the papers, checking each one. "The Burton case?"

"At the back."

"Ah."

He closed the manila folder, but then continued to loom as if he had something else to say. He had decently plump lips, the sort that could pull off a successful pout if they weren't always pressed into a thin line that hinted at unaddressed constipation. Now though, he was clamping down on the bottom one.

Was he . . . nervous? His hair wasn't quite as coiffed as usual. It was normally styled with the type of carefree tousling only achieved after twenty minutes of meticulous arranging in the morning, but today a few blond strands stuck up as if he'd been running his hands through it repeatedly.

Pippa's indignation hovered nearby, uncertain.

Was this the day she would find out if there was more to stony, yacht-ordering, cactusy Maxim Sheppard?

"You shouldn't be taking personal calls in the office," he said finally.

Never mind.

It wasn't as if non-workplace activity was forbidden; Pippa had overheard more than one lengthy conversation about some spoiled child's preference for a specific soccer team, or observed a game of table-tennis created with a makeshift net on someone's desk. For shit's sake, Jules was writing porn.

What Maxim had meant was *"You* shouldn't take a personal call."

Pippa bridled her anger and said, "Of course, Mr. Sheppard. Won't happen again."

Fuck, she hated calling him that, especially since he was only three or four years older than her. All that separated them was a handful of years and ninety thousand handfuls of cash that paid for a fancy degree.

Maxim's jaw twitched.

Before he could say anything else, Pippa slid into her secretary role in an attempt to urge the conversation into the type that encouraged him away from her desk.

"Do you need anything else? More depositions printed out?" *A colonic?*

"I— Uh, no." He walked away without another word. He couldn't bother with a "Thank you," or a "Good job, Beverly, I appreciate your work." Not even a slight nod.

Before he slipped into his office, Pippa fought the juvenile impulse to chuck her plastic nameplate at the back of his head.

Jules spun around in her chair and scooted over to Pippa's desk by digging the edges of her high heels into the carpet. She always dressed as if she were a lawyer herself: well-fitted blazer, pencil skirt, heels high enough to also function as weapons, her black hair pulled into a sleek ponytail.

Pippa thunked her forehead onto her keyboard, not caring about the alarmed chimes it created.

"*Jesus,* he has the social skills of a hornet," Jules whispered.

"Unhh," Pippa groaned against the space bar. At Jules's supportive shoulder pat, she straightened, then deleted the gibberish she'd headbutted into her open email. "At least he looked frazzled. Made me feel a little better."

Jules blew a soft raspberry through her lips. "If I were him, I'd be frazzled too." When Pippa frowned, she added, "Because of the— You forgot. About the dinner tonight. Seriously? The dinner where they're going to announce who gets promoted to senior associate and gets the entire Crossly-Williams account, and will basically be a private lawyer to the second-richest family in New Hawkshead?"

Oh.

Tonight, the entire firm—all thirty-odd partners, associates, assistants, and even the two janitors—would be attending a dinner to celebrate the achievements of the most tenured partner and reveal who would be rising to a higher level of snobbery.

Which was why Maxim had demanded more of Pippa than normal over the last month, asking for depositions and textbooks and taking on cases that would have broken someone who wasn't utterly desperate for the new title.

"Only forgot for a second," Pippa said.

Jules shook her head. "You'd think with three assistants, he wouldn't be riding you so hard—" She grimaced. "Sorry, poor word choice."

Warmth crept up Pippa's neck and settled by her ears. Even though she'd never seen Maxim when he wasn't wearing a suit and tie, she was pretty sure he was built underneath all that tailored black fabric.

Nope, nope. Pippa shook the images from her mind before they could fully unfurl. She was stressed after the conversation with her mother, exhausted from last night, and hadn't yet had her lunch, which were the only reasons the concepts of "hard riding" and "Maxim Sheppard" in the same sentence made her pulse quicken.

Jules appeared lost in thought. "I mean, I'm not one to speak on male attractiveness, but if you were to see him on the street, you'd have to admit he's nice to look at. Symmetrical."

"Not his nose," Pippa said. It had a bump along the bridge and was tipped slightly to the left.

"Yeah, but it's kind of rugged. Maybe he broke it saving a puppy."

Pippa had built a backstory that included a childhood accident of someone defending themselves from his bullying, which she liked a lot better than Jules's idea.

"What about his resting bitch face?" she said. "You have a positive spin on that?"

"It's mysterious." Jules arced her fingers through the air. "He's like an oyster you gotta crack open to get to the meat."

"Ew."

"What? It's a good metaphor."

"Because he attaches himself to any large moving objects, sucks out their joy, and smells like dead fish?"

The unamused irritation in Jules's face could have leveled buildings. "You're thinking of barnacles. Anyway." She flapped her hand, caught a chip on one painted nail, cursed, then flapped it again. "I'm surprised you're not trying to get in good with Mr. Oyster. If he ever makes senior associate and sees you as a, I don't know, a pal, it'll open up so many more opportunities for you. No more assistant. You could move up. Become an attorney yourself."

Pippa gave a noncommittal grunt.

"That doesn't appeal to you? Protecting the unfortunate, defending the helpless?" Jules arched one perfect black brow, then chuckled as she scooted back to her desk. "Wow. It's almost like you don't want to keep the city safe or something."

Pippa forced a laugh.

An incoming email chimed, and Pippa navigated to her inbox.

Burton Case is Missing a Page. Please Remedy.

She wrangled her groan into a heavy sigh. Her ribs didn't approve. There wasn't a missing page; she'd gone over it twice to check before collating it into a pile with everything else he'd asked for. It would be easier to reply to the email that he was incorrect, but much more satisfying to go the passive-aggressive route and print out another set, this time with numbered pages.

Sorry, trees, she was doing it for petty revenge.

Pippa looked over at Jules when the other woman gave a frustrated grunt and tapped her delete key in a forceful staccato. Jules spun in her chair and, using her high heels as traction assistance once more, scooted over to Pippa.

Jules leaned in. "Okay, so what's another word for 'cock'?"

IF THE DAY HAD been perfect, Pippa would have left work on time. She would have checked the clock hanging above the door to the break room, logged out of her computer, and taken the stairs, because it was only five o'clock and she needed to be at the restaurant at six, so why not get her legs moving? Jules would drive them over together and they'd laugh about all the genital euphemisms Pippa discovered on her phone.

The Ash Coven had a certain strictness about close interactions between members and the common public; mainly that they didn't allow it. Once Pippa was accepted (*if* she was ever accepted), she'd unfortunately need to prune some friendships.

So it would have been nice to have another drive, one more conversation, just a little extra laughter, that she would keep as a memory.

But alas, it was not to be a perfect day.

The clock above the break room read 5:45 by the time Pippa gathered up her belongings to leave. "One more email" had turned into a long rabbit hole of mismanaged documents and PDF viewer updates. By the time she shut down her computer, the rest of the office had already left.

Pippa stabbed the button to close the elevator doors behind her.

The red numbers ticked down. At least the building wasn't very tall; at least the elevator ride was short.

She eyed the sun as she left the building. Not for the first time today, she sent a few foul thoughts toward the person who decided to schedule what was essentially a well-catered meeting after work. Autumn was fast approaching and with each passing day, the darkness grew a little more demanding. Demons weren't very considerate of workplace social obligations. If she left the dinner early, maybe she could have enough time for a hunt or two while still being able to get more than six hours of sleep.

Ah, that was the dream.

She unlocked her car and slid over the hot upholstery, imagining how nice it would be to take off her awful, unsupportive flats, and her restricting pencil skirt, and the cardigan that, no matter the temperature, was either too hot or not warm enough, and collapse into her bed.

Pippa turned her key in the ignition. Turned it again. Pulled the key out, checked she was in the correct car, but, no: this was hers. It had the same scrapes on the dashboard, the same neoprene steering wheel cover, the same musty smell of old fabric and plastic.

Having to fight evil every night didn't leave much time for a college education, which, of course, most well-paying jobs in New Hawkshead required. If she had been accepted by the Ash Coven, their wages would be more than enough to buy something nice and functional and maybe even a little bit comfortable.

Pippa swallowed her bitterness and turned the key one more time.

Nothing.

She glanced at her phone. If she didn't leave in the next five minutes, she would miss the dinner. Which wouldn't be *horrible*, really, and everyone would understand the "car troubles" excuse.

The building's doors opened. Maxim Sheppard walked briskly out of them. He had a satchel slung across his torso and was digging in one of the pockets for his keys.

Of course he was the only other person from the firm still in the building. If she slumped down, maybe he wouldn't see her..

Maxim glanced in her direction, paused, then headed over to her.

Pippa twisted the key in the ignition several more times just in case.

"Something wrong with your car?" he shouted through her closed window.

"It just has a tricky start sometimes." Her smile was on the deranged side of overly cheery. "Thanks though!"

Maxim gave the front half of her car the same sort of look someone would give an old apple core. "I don't think that sounds like a tricky start."

"Nope! Got it! I'm good!" Pippa reached out to the magic floating about in the hot air. Magic was on uncertain terms with anything mechanical or electronic, but she was desperate. Her right hand was on the key and out of sight of Maxim, so she forced energy through the key, then through the starter, along wires and connection points until it reached the engine.

The car started. Pippa sagged into her seat. The only way her day could get worse was to have the universe substitute a laugh-filled drive in Jules's car with the uncomfortable silence of being trapped in a vehicle with someone who saw her as little more than a paper-fetching peon.

The engine gave a roar so powerful she could feel it along her spine, then it belched, sputtered, and died. A lazy stream of smoke emerged from one corner of the hood.

"I'll just take the bus," Pippa said around her heavy despair.

"If you take the bus, you'll be late. Come on. I'll drive you." He started walking to his car as if certain she'd follow.

Pippa took a deep breath and huffed it out through puffed cheeks. The door squealed when she opened it, as if the vehicle objected to being left behind.

"It's your own damn fault," she muttered before heading to Maxim's sleek sedan. Of course it was sleek. Of course it was fancy, and new, and appeared to be the kind of car above which birds wholly avoided perching.

After she got inside, her first thought was that the car smelled like him. A little sharp, a little citrus-y. Woodsy, somehow. But a pleasant scent—nothing like the cloying body sprays or colognes present in the office. It was . . . good. Disarmingly good.

Her second through fifth thoughts all revolved around how clean the car was, and how comfortable, and how it lacked even the slightest trace of human habitation. Pippa glanced around to try and locate a crumpled-up receipt burrowed in some deep recess or an abandoned grocery tote. Nothing.

She sent a sideways glance to the man beside her. He wasn't a demon; she knew that for certain. When he'd first transferred to the firm, she had pushed out with a dash of magic and groped around his aura for anything unnatural, but he was wholly human. There hadn't been a single magical speck in his body. No power, no hidden secrets. Nothing. He did have a warm aura though—comforting somehow, and spicy, like a bowl of hearty soup with a sprinkle of chili pepper.

Which made it that much more jarring when he'd opened his mouth.

Pippa uncrossed and then recrossed her legs. There was too much legroom. She didn't know what to do with it.

"Nice car," she said as they merged onto the freeway, if only to fill the car with something beside the barely-audible dulcet tones of news radio. She rested her hands on her purse, too nervous to touch anything lest she leave smears.

Maxim shrugged. This close, she could hear the crinkle of his suit as he did so. "It works."

His eyebrows drew together and a look eerily similar to discomfort crossed his face. "That's— That sounded callous. I'm sorry about your car."

"It's lived long enough," Pippa said. "If engines could talk, it would be letting out one shrill, sustained scream."

A short huff jerked Pippa's attention to Maxim.

Was he . . . was he *smiling*? She felt herself starting to gape and snapped her mouth shut. His smile wasn't large, really just a tip at the corner, but it was more than she'd seen before.

Maybe if she kept going on about her car, crack a few more jokes, she'd see that smile get larger. Would there be crinkles by his eyes? Creases in his cheeks?

Not that she cared. This was purely a scientific exploration.

Her phone buzzed in her purse, putting a pause on any further discoveries, and Pippa pulled it out to a message from Jules.

The Crown Jules: Okay but, like, how do they *work*

Pippa tapped out a response.

Pippa: How do what work?

The Crown Jules: Penises.

Pippa: What am I, your cock encyclopedia?

The Crown Jules: Yes, because you actually like them. Unless you don't?? Pippa if you've put me on for the past three years I swear

Pippa: I haven't put you on, promise.

The Crown Jules: Okay, well if that changes, I'd better be the first to know. SO precum. Tell me about it. Is it different than cum?

Nope, she couldn't talk about cum now, especially with Maxim sitting two feet away.

Pippa: Use an incognito search. Don't do images.

The Crown Jules: Boo. Also where are you?

Pippa: On my way. Are you working on your story at the dinner??

The Crown Jules: Yeah, it's boring as fuck right now.

Maxim drummed his fingers on the wheel. "You were, uh, talking about demons earlier?"

Pippa froze halfway through returning her phone to her purse. Panic raced along her arms and twisted tight in her stomach.

She'd been such an idiot to talk about her hunting at work. Why did she think no one would overhear?

Her thoughts tumbled around in her head, each one growing increasingly spiked. She could spin some story about how it was all part of a book. But what if he didn't believe that? What if he told someone else? The coven would come down on her for this, surely. Humans were like lambs, they always said. Brittle in both body and mind. Witches had to protect them from the demonic threat just as much as they had to protect them from the existential dread that would come from learning their nightmares lived right down the street.

Pippa braced herself and started an excuse just as Maxim spoke.

"It wasn't really what you—"

"I used to game, too."

Her excuse fizzled off her tongue. "Game?"

Maxim cleared his throat. "I mean . . . I assumed that's what you meant. I overheard 'Player's Handbook' and jumped to conclusions."

"Yes, yep, that's . . ." Pippa said, the words rushing out of her in relief. "That's what I was talking about."

She'd never participated in said game, since fighting pretend monsters always felt like taking her work home with her, but she'd seen enough online tidbits and references to grab for an innocuous-sounding name.

"My favorite character was a bard," Maxim said. "At least for the longest campaign." He huffed a short laugh. There it was again—that almost-smile twitching up one corner of his mouth. It was like seeing a crack in stone. "I had to really sing, and not just say I was singing."

"That sounds awful," Pippa said honestly.

"Not at all." His smile grew slightly and she caught a glimpse of his white teeth. "I used to love all of that. The adventure. Fighting evil."

How hard would he break if he found out the truth? Fighting evil was all well and good behind when it happened over books and dice, where the only threat was someone else's imagination.

"Sure," Pippa said, not managing to sound even partially enthused.

Maxim's smile faded. The stony countenance Pippa had learned to hate returned and covered any hint of emotion.

"But it was a long time ago. I was young." He shifted in his seat, and Pippa got the sense he was uncomfortable to have revealed this part of himself, as if she would think less of him upon the discovery that he used to have fun.

It was tempting to try and delve deeper into the man beside her, yet even though these new facets of his personality sat her perilously close to "not hatred," she wasn't getting paid to analyze his history.

Pippa watched the city flash past the passenger window.

They spent the rest of the drive in silence.

THE PARTNERS AT IVANOV, Barry, and Cruz loved anticipation. Dinner first and then the announcement before dessert. The firm would celebrate Doris Ivanov's innumerable accomplishments with gusto while at the same time basking in the anxiety of every associate waiting to hear if they were the one to be promoted.

Jules leaned over, chucking Pippa's shoulder and nearly making her choke on her pasta.

"So wait, he what?" Jules whispered.

"Gave me a . . . ride," Pippa said around a mouthful of penne.

Someone at the other end of the table shouted congratulations to Doris, then began to tell a meandering story about how she earned the nickname "Ironteeth."

"But why?" Jules hissed.

"What, so he saves puppies but can't let me in his car?"

"I implied that, at one point in his life, he saved puppies. Toss a dog in front of that man now and I bet he'd tell it to sign a contract before he pets it."

"He also used to play Dungeons and Dragons."

Jules pinned Pippa with an expression of such shock that a piece of unchewed broccoli fell out of her mouth.

"Oh, gross, Jules," Pippa said as Jules scrabbled for the floret in her lap and popped it back into her mouth.

"Whatever, I've seen you do worse."

"Please. When?"

"When you forgot your lunch and ate someone else's forgotten science experiment in the fridge. Don't you shake your head, I saw you. You sniffed the container, almost barfed, and then tried some of it."

"So? How's that a character flaw?"

"It isn't, and you're doing a great job of trying to derail this conversation." Jules shook her head in disbelief. "Mad Maxim is a nerd. Goddammit. I love nerds. This is terrible news."

"He used to play," Pippa said. "Used to. Really emphasized that part."

"Like that makes a difference. Once I know someone's tasted the sweet, sweet elixir pouring forth from the loins of geekdom, I gotta respect a little."

"You're still having trouble with that sex scene, aren't you?"

"No," Jules muttered unconvincingly into her wine glass.

Pippa sipped her own drink and glanced over to where Maxim sat. The restaurant had slid several large tables together to accommodate everyone, and he was between two other associates who were currently talking around him.

He had excused himself to the bathroom almost as soon as he and Pippa had arrived and returned with his hair looking as put together as it could with only water from the sink. More professional than the rumpled relatable mop of dark blond, not quite the magazine cover coif of previous days.

Maxim rolled the stem of his wine glass between his thumb and his forefinger while he sent a calculating gaze around the table. What turbulent thoughts battered his mind? What judgments was he passing upon his coworkers based on their food preferences or eating habits?

Pippa's attention snagged on the hand that held the wine glass. The slow spin of the glass stem between his large fingers would have been hypnotizing if not for her concern for the glass. With hands like those, she was surprised the stem hadn't already snapped in his grip.

He shifted and scrubbed one hand through his hair. For a brief second, dismay flared on his face at the realization that he'd wrecked whatever careful arranging he'd done in front of a bathroom mirror, and Pippa remembered that little almost-smile, the joy in his voice when he talked about things he'd once liked.

"How are you doing in the face of these discoveries, Pip?" Jules said, yanking Pippa's attention back to her side of the table.

Pippa smoothed her napkin over her skirt. "He might not be a total asshole. It's weird. I'm not sure how to feel about it."

"Good. We should feel good." Jules didn't sound as if she had convinced herself.

Idle chatter accompanied the bustle of plates being cleared away and the clink of refilled drinkware.

Daniel Barry pushed his chair away from the assembled tables and stood with all the care of someone who had discovered a decade ago which knee was the bad one.

The chatter ceased. It was time.

Pippa wished only slightly that she was excited about all of it, because that might make this speech more bearable.

Not all of Daniel's speeches were awful. He always began with a hearty thanks, followed with a reminder about any upcoming firm events (next Monday was Joclyn's birthday, and Michael would be bringing a cake from his nephew's bakeshop) then rambled about a topic in the way that implied he'd once attempted stand-up comedy.

"Wow," he said now. "Wasn't that delicious? The last time I saw such a gorgeous dish, I was getting married. And the food wasn't bad that day, either!"

Pippa joined the forced laughter and mentally began a list of the places she would scope out tonight. Last night, she'd gone as far north as Caldwell street, but maybe tonight she could head downtown.

"…thank you, I'm here all week! Nah, not really; no one wants me pouring wine. Anyway…"

There were rumblings of a few upstart succubi who'd set their designs on New Hawkshead's university and had taken full advantage of freshmen who were simultaneously high on gullibility and low on sense. She could give the demons a visit and make sure they understood the local laws. Succubi were some of the more easy-going demons, and confrontations typically ended in long conversations comparing bad sexual encounters. Plus, for some reason, they always made the best mixed drinks. Maybe it was the demonic magic.

After last night, Pippa could use an easy evening.

". . . but let's get to it. I know you're all on the edge of your seats." Daniel rubbed his palms together and grinned like a cartoon villain. "I know, I know—this isn't the usual way we announce promotions, but we all felt like tonight needed a little bit more impact than an email. Dana Crossly and Evan Williams have been this city's greatest champions. They've founded shelters, constructed low-cost clinics, and continue to shine a bright light on the injustices we here are all too privileged to experience firsthand. The associate who works with Ms. Crossly and Mr. Williams will have a direct hand in helping the people who need it most.

"So you all can understand why this announcement needs excitement! Pizazz!" Daniel punched the air.

Pippa hadn't ever thought a promotion should be treated in the same way as a film award, but maybe that was why she was only an assistant.

Daniel paused, looked around the room, and grinned again.

Across the table, Maxim's calm facade was believable except for the twitch in his jaw and the flex of his fingers, like they wanted nothing more than to fidget. He'd worried his lips so much they appeared rouged and slightly plumper than usual.

In one bright moment of empathy, Pippa could imagine how he must feel. She wasn't sure why it had taken her this long to realize what such a position would mean to him and to all of the other associates who had put themselves forth for consideration.

For Pippa, working at the firm had always been a way to pay bills. When she applied to Ivanov, Barry, and Cruz, she'd already had her sense of purpose, and if it involved a few more beheadings than board meetings—well, not everyone had the benefit of going home clean at the end of the night. But she knew her place in the world, what she had to do, and how she had to do it.

Maybe Maxim did deserve the title. Maybe it might make him a little more human, a little more bearable. A little happier.

Daniel Barry spread his hands and bent his knees as if bracing himself for a large wave. "We are thrilled to announce that our newest senior associate and header to the Crossly-Williams account will be . . ."

Roughly half of the people at the table held their breath.

"Reggie Cavatappi!"

Applause filled the room, along with a few whistles and cheers.

Reggie's smile seemed fit to break his face. He stood to accept another round of applause and began to shake hands with whoever stood nearby.

"Well," Jules said under her breath. "That was a letdown."

"Reggie's nice, isn't he?" Pippa said.

"But he's so boring."

Pippa turned to her friend. "You have a very strange set of ideals you admire in other people." Her palms were beginning to sting, but no one seemed interested in ceasing their clapping.

"I like 'em interesting. How is that a strange set of ideals?"

"Am I interesting?"

"Oh Pippin, my dearest sugar muffin of chaos. Of course you are."

At last, the eternal round of applause faded and was replaced by the constant murmur of congratulations and well-wishes and people rising from their chairs to congregate around him.

Someone started shouting, "Speech!" to which Reggie shook his head and then gestured in an "Oh, why not, I've actually been wanting to do this for months" sort of way.

It was then Pippa noticed Maxim's seat was empty. Thinking back, she didn't remember when he had left, but he certainly had not been in the line of other associates who gamely shook hands and accepted their defeat, like any reasonable adult would do.

She couldn't remember if she had ever gained a begrudging respect for someone only to lose it completely in such a short span of time.

"Do you think he'll ever make a speech, or will he just be swarmed by suck-ups and handshakes?" Jules said.

"I'll bet—" Pippa's chair started to vibrate, and after a very confusing second, she realized it must be her phone. Whoever it was could wait. She continued, "I'll bet you twenty bucks he ends up making the speech tomorrow in the office."

Jules wrinkled her nose. "Before or after nine?"

"Oh, before. Definitely befo—" She broke off as her chair vibrated again. A repeat caller, which, on Pippa's phone, wasn't typically benign. She fished her phone from her purse and unlocked it to two unread texts, two missed calls, and a voicemail from "Mamma B."

"Shit, I need to take this," she said as she scrambled out of her seat and tapped her mother's contact bubble.

"You're so rude right now!" Jules's conspiratorial grin lessened the chastisement.

Thankfully, the dinner had turned into a general milling about with Reggie Cavatappi looking disheartened that the whole "speech" shout had been taken more as a joke than a suggestion. Pippa dodged easily between chattering people.

"Oh, *now* you pick up," her mother said.

"I'm at a dinner. For work."

"Really? They do those? Are you going to have time to go out later—"

"Mom," Pippa snapped. "Please just tell me what's so important that you called. Twice." She trotted down a hallway, heading for a windowless door beneath a glowing exit sign.

"Oh. Right," Mary Beverly said. "The demon from last night. One of the ladies in my book group has a cousin from Portland, and she said a group of Tro'graths left there for the Northeast . . ."

Pippa emerged into a narrow alley. The sun had dipped behind the buildings across the street and cast the alley into dusky shadow. An overflowing dumpster sat along one wall, and wooden crates were stacked beside it.

". . . and she said . . ."

Movement in one corner sent Pippa's heart into her throat. Someone was sitting on a crate, their elbows on their knees and their hands scraping through their hair. She looked closer, recognized the hands and the hair and the person, and her alarm morphed into bitterness.

"Mom, I have to go."

"Pippa! I'm not done. She said that the jewels in the head—"

"I'll call you later."

"They mean that—"

Pippa hung up and started for Maxim Sheppard.

He glanced up at the sound of her approach. He'd unbuttoned his suit jacket and loosened his tie.

"Really?" she said. The venom filled her voice easily. "Reggie Cavatappi is a nice person. He has been nothing but kind to every single one of us in the office, from janitor to partner, and wishing him well was the absolute least you could have done. You couldn't shake his hand *once?*"

Maxim's laugh emerged sharp and bitter. "Why do you give a *fuck?*"

It was so unexpectedly vicious that Pippa was lost for a rebuttal. "I—" she managed before she let the rest of her sentence break apart in her shock.

His lips pressed together and he exhaled hard through his nose. "You don't care about this job. This firm. You don't care about anything we're doing, so why do you care how I react to utter, gut-punching disappointment?"

Maxim must have seen something in her expression. Bafflement, probably, and a bit of hurt from being cursed at in a restaurant alley. Leaning forward, he scrubbed at his head with both hands. His blond hair stuck up in a way that brought him a step away from rakish.

"Do you know what it's like to want to make a difference?" he said, more to the ground than to her. "To feel like if you could only get this one position, this one fucking job, you would find purpose. Fulfillment. And then it . . ." Another sharp sigh puffed into the crisp evening air.

"Yes." She said it again with more emphasis. "I know exactly what that's like."

Without realizing she had been walking toward him, she found herself close enough to see that his eyes were green, and as the setting sun filtered through a gap in the buildings across the street, the dying beam settled across his face and turned that green into a color so light they almost seemed golden.

How had she never noticed? Could office fluorescent lighting be that manipulative?

And the new softness in his features, had lighting hidden that as well? She swore the lack of tension in his brow and the absence of any jaw clenching was something previously undiscovered.

Maxim's lips parted around the beginning of a question—she could see it in the upward cant of his eyebrows—and Pippa found herself holding her breath.

Then his gaze slid off her to something at the opening of the alley, and the peaceful moment shattered. He surged to his feet and pulled Pippa behind him before she could utter a peep of protest.

"Stay behind me," he said in a display of unnecessary chivalry that had her rolling her eyes.

She thought about saying that she was more dangerous than any mugger that might try and accost them, but it was pompous and a bit douchey, and when she looked past his shoulder, she realized it wasn't at all correct.

The figure crouched in the alley's entrance was not a mugger. Not a human, either. It was the arms that really gave it away, since there were two extra. The face was wrong as well, with large, blinking eyes on either side of its head that were as red and shiny as marbles, and a vertical snapping mouth ringed with hooked teeth.

The creature was garbed in a pair of loose cargo shorts and a basketball jersey with "Hell's Outcasts" stamped in bright lettering. Additional holes had been cut into the fabric beneath the armpits for the extra arms. A pocketed bandolier lay across its narrow chest.

"What the fuck?" Maxim breathed.

Pippa could agree, for once.

"The shit, Charles?" she called out from behind Maxim.

The demon bobbed his head. "Hey, Pippa." It came out as more of a clicking chatter than any sort of normal speech, but that was mostly because of the teeth.

Occasionally, she'd get information from Charles about any new residents causing havoc or gossip of potential threats to the populace. The demon had straddled the line between ally and enemy, never drifting too far to either side.

Charles also never went out in public, and never in daylight. Being seen by humans was a fantastic way to get killed by an Ash Coven member. Or an Ash Coven hopeful. Something wasn't right here.

Pippa wriggled around Maxim, dodging his grip and ignoring his hissed, *"What are you doing?"*

"You're not supposed to be above ground this time of day," she said to the demon.

"Yea-a-h, about that." Charles tapped a set of stubby, curved claws on a bandolier. "Got a job I couldn't refuse."

A chill tickled Pippa's spine. "To do . . . what?"

"Someone wants you gone." He shrugged one pair of knobby shoulders. "Nothing personal."

"Yeah? Who paid you so well, then?" Magic hovered at her fingertips, ready to be channeled.

Charles shook his head. "Sorry, can't say. Signed a contract in blood. Some of that 'Say our name and your brain'll leak out of your nose or wherever' stuff."

"So they were rich."

"Rich enough."

"And there's no way I can talk you out of this."

If a face like Charles's could appear incredulous, it would have done so now. He shoved a hand into one of the bandolier's pockets. When he withdrew his claws, red powder was pinched between them. "I mean, I'll feel a little sad. You're not bad, for a witch. But you're still a witch."

Sharp teeth chattered in impatience. "Anyway. Burn, bitch."

With a clacking shout, the demon threw the powder into the air. It exploded into flames that shot toward Pippa like they'd come out of an ignited gas line.

Pippa forced magic out of her hands and battered the stream of fire, directing it upward, where it fizzled against the purpled sky.

More powder flew into the air, more flames engulfed the alley. Pippa kept them at bay with either redirection or scraps of conjured shield. The alley was growing hotter, and several small fires burned in the dumpsters and frolicked within the wooden crates.

Pippa had just gathered the power into herself, intending to use it to blast Charles across the street, when the demon threw three handfuls of purple powder out of the leather bandolier. Three long, whiplike tendrils lashed out at Pippa. She sent them flying with a quick series of magical punches, though one passed her face close enough to see the striations of power binding the powder and giving it substance.

If anyone inside heard the noise in the alley, they would surely come out to see. Couldn't have that; couldn't let anyone know.

For some reason, this thought set off a series of alarms in Pippa's head. She was forgetting about something in this alley, something that would—

The quick snap of a magical whip and the ensuing pain in her forearm broke the thread of that reflection, and she diverted all of her concentration to the demon before her.

Charles had a handful of the red powder, the same sort that he had thrown into the air to conjure fire.

"Do you think you'll taste good?" Charles said.

"Excuse me?" Pippa spat.

"Charred like this. Barbecued witch. Never tried it, myself." He reached his other three hands into the pockets and pulled out more powder, all of it red and shimmering like sand.

Pippa thought of shields and barriers, and an idea came upon her so suddenly that she almost staggered.

"That's disgusting, Charles," she said. She felt the magic around the demon quiver in anticipation of what she planned to do.

"Isn't that what you're good for? Why else would someone want to burn witches?" The demon flung out all four arms to engulf the alley in flame.

Right as Charles moved, Pippa tugged the surrounding simmering magic into a shield and enclosed the demon within a dome of it.

Flames arced around the inside of the dome like an apocalyptic snow globe, roaring and vile.

After the flames faded, she let the shield dissolve. A dark plume of smoke puffed skyward. When it cleared, Charles was nothing more than a charred pile on the concrete.

Pippa walked up to the body gingerly. It didn't move when she nudged it with the toe of her flat. Another pull on magic dusted the remains and scattered them into the street.

There was still that prickling sensation in her brain, of something forgotten that she really should not have let slip.

From behind her, there came a clatter and a low groan. Pippa whirled about, hands raised and ready to defend herself.

Oh.

Shit.

She had forgotten about Maxim Sheppard.

Four

He was dreaming.

Definitely dreaming.

Had to be dreaming.

If he wasn't, then it would mean he was imagining it. If he was imagining it, that would mean he would have to go back to therapy, and any appointment that began with, "How am I? Well, I watched a woman demolish a fucked-up moth-faced creature that threw fire. How are you?" would surely end with him on a high dose of medication and a schedule for when he could use the room with the television.

Maxim was in pain though, which wasn't a thing that accompanied either his dreams or his imagination. Around his midsection, some deep, awful ache radiated out to the rest of his body.

The first attempt to get up resulted in him falling back into a stack of crates.

Before he could make a second attempt, Pippa Beverly's frizz-framed face appeared in his vision.

"What . . . What was that?" he managed, even though putting forth the effort to say it made him feel like a locomotive was stabbing into his gut.

"Nothing," Pippa said, much too fast to be believable. She crouched beside him. Her gaze landed on his stomach, right where the pain was centered, and she paled.

That couldn't be good.

Maxim had other things to worry about.

"Was that . . . Did that thing call you a . . . a witch?" Why was speaking so difficult? "It— Magic. You did . . . magic."

"Nope," Pippa said, and he felt her tug his button-up out of his pants.

Buy me dinner first, Maxim thought, then mentally congratulated himself for not saying it out loud and coming across like a secondary, younger Daniel Barry.

With not a little effort, he pushed himself up onto one elbow and looked down at his stomach.

Big mistake.

As he'd watched Pippa fight the . . . thing, it had lashed out with long, barbed, whip-like knives. One of them must have caught him. *In* him.

That can't be good, he thought for a second time. *Those parts should be inside. Covered up. That's an awful lot of blood.* Rather inane thoughts, considering everything he'd just seen. His mind didn't seem capable of much more at the moment.

"Stop moving," Pippa ordered and pushed him prone on the concrete. There was panic in her voice and in the shake of her hands and the tremble of her lower lip.

Oh, he really hoped he wasn't going to die, but with an injury like that . . .

His blood was warm and slippery where it pooled beneath him. Another deep, aching pain spread through his midsection, though this one was a bit sharper and harder than the first.

Pippa had removed most of his shirt by now. She was kneeling in blood. That would stain her skirt. She should have put something down. Wasn't the concrete hard on her knees? Her hands hovered over his stomach and she closed her eyes in concentration. There was a long scrape along her forearm.

"You're hurt," Maxim said. "You should really b-bandage that."

When she inhaled, it was shaky. What was she trying to do? Didn't you need to apply pressure to these sorts of wounds instead of doing some weird hand-hovering shit?

Then he remembered: *Oh, magic.*

The air around her hands grew brighter, and little sparkles began to shimmer in the space above his stomach like a cloud of slow-moving glitter. Whenever he'd thought of magic, he'd always imagined it would be the fire-blasting sort of magic, not the 90s music video sort of magic. At no time in his life had he expected to learn that both were real.

Because this was real. It had to be.

His gut squirmed. It felt as if he'd become a mass of worms from his sternum to his hips. He urged himself to move through the pain and struggled to his elbows once more. Since Pippa was so engrossed with whatever she was doing, she didn't chastise him, and Maxim watched as his body bubbled and writhed. Organs sealed themselves shut, muscles re-formed, skin wriggled and spread over what was once a gaping wound. The new scar was a pale, gnarled patch, yet it looked as if the injury had happened six months ago instead of a few minutes.

There was a small spot by his navel that hadn't quite closed. Pippa's hands were shaking more now, her face scrunched with an expression that could have been exertion and could have been pain. Maybe both. Her jaw drifted open around a tight cry, as if she was trying to lift a weight too heavy for her.

Blood from her forearm flowed faster and dripped onto his crisp white shirt and his newly healed skin. Her temple shone with sweat, and curls of her hair clung to her cheek.

The spot closed, and the writhing in his stomach ceased. There was no more pain. When he prodded at the scar with a finger, his body felt just as it had this morning.

As soon as she saw him move, Pippa let out a choking gasp and her chin dipped almost to her chest, her shoulders rising beneath her flowered cardigan in deep, panting breaths.

Maxim couldn't decide what to say; he was filled with too many questions and too many statements of the obvious. *What did you do? You saved me. I would have died. How long has motherfucking MAGIC existed?*

He entertained a brief thought that he should go to the hospital, since that's what people typically did when they were slashed open, if only temporarily. What was the ideal way to explain that he just wanted to make sure all of his organs had grown back all right?

"Thank you," he said. The two words sounded hopelessly inadequate.

Pippa dragged her hair out of her face, then straightened and pinned him with her big brown eyes. Normally they were lovely and bright, but now they felt sharper than whatever magical blade had stabbed him.

"You can't tell anyone about this," she said. "No one." She sounded exhausted. There were bruised circles beneath her lower lashes, and her lips were pale and chapped.

Maxim nodded rapidly. Of course he wouldn't. He wished he had the faculty to tell her he'd already come to that conclusion, especially the whole bit about the medication and the room with the television.

Pippa rose to her feet and staggered. Maxim clambered upright with the intent to reach out and steady her, but he ended up reaching for the dumpster as he staggered as well. There was a lot of blood on the concrete. No wonder he was dizzy.

Pippa went toward the restaurant door. She gave her knees a hopeless look before tugging off her cardigan and using the inside to wipe off his blood, then wrapped it tightly around her injured forearm. Beneath the cardigan she was wearing a flouncy short-sleeved blouse, the cuteness of which clashed with Maxim's undying mental image of her roasting a demonic creature alive in its own magic.

"I have questions," was all he managed.

"Learn to live with them."

"But—"

"There's a law," she said to the door handle. "Rules. For people like me. You shouldn't have seen any of that. I shouldn't have..." She shook her head and grasped the handle, throwing her entire body into opening it.

"So?" Maxim said. "You can't just pretend that didn't happen. I can't."

The look she gave him froze his feet and a good amount of his healed midsection. "Don't make me wish I hadn't saved you."

Then she went inside. The door slammed behind her.

Maxim unfroze. He nearly slipped on his own blood on the way to the restaurant's back door.

Damn her, it couldn't end like this, terrifying threat aside. From the hallway, he could see her moving quickly to Juliette Cohen, leaning close to say something as she grabbed her purse.

Maxim heard Juliette's "Take you home? Thought you'd never ask!" and saw the wiggling of her eyebrows from where he stood.

He could also see how the second woman's expression sobered when she noticed Pippa's pale cheeks and the thin press of her lips.

Maxim took a step forward, not quite into the dining room. This didn't escape Pippa. Her eyes flicked to connect with his, and an icy chill crunched up his spine at the threat held within them.

She had mentioned law. Rules. How many had she broken when she'd saved him from bleeding out in the alley?

Juliette followed Pippa's glare. The witch started and ushered the other woman to the door, but not before Maxim overheard Juliette say, "Jesus, what *happened*?"

He glanced down, taking in the absolute wreck he had become. The crisp ironed button-up was open below his chest, the fabric stained with blood and some purple powder the same color as the whip that had stabbed him. His hands were coated in grime and more blood. He didn't even want to think about his hair.

A server turned the corner, and Maxim lunged for the bathroom door. One room, one toilet, one sink. Perfect. He spun around and threw the bolt.

The man in the mirror was a mess. An absolute, raw mess.

He did what he could with the sink and a stack of paper towels, and when he emerged, his hair looked slightly decent and he'd buttoned his suit jacket neatly over both the destroyed shirt and the large rip in his tie. If he left soon with a good excuse, it was likely no one would notice that he was experiencing a thrilling blend of existential dread, mild panic, and overwhelming shock.

He'd almost died.

He'd seen—

He'd watched a—

Fuck.

The time to think on all of that wasn't while walking up to Reggie Cavatappi and shaking his hand. It wasn't while telling him how much he deserved the new position. It wasn't while explaining that he'd spilled some wine and that was the reason for the stain on his cuff and jacket and *pants* and honestly, it was a *very* large glass of wine. It wasn't while excusing himself to the partners and the other associates saying that the meal had disagreed with him. Not any fault of the restaurant, he assured them. In all the excitement, he'd simply forgotten about his mild shellfish allergy.

Not until he'd slid into his car in the parking garage did he let everything pour out.

He began to laugh. It was too ridiculous. What would his college friends say if they knew that magic wasn't just relegated to stacks of books and twenty-sided dice? Cards, and video games, and fantasy movies?

He laughed until his ribs hurt, laughed until his breath came in rapid, jagged heaves that slid easily into hyperventilation.

Too much, too much, too much.

The familiar tingling in his hands pulled him out of his head and back to the car. He focused on the tingle, on the feel of the leather wheel beneath his palms. His breathing slowed. He focused on that as well, feeling the expansion of his ribs and the stretch of the new scar. One breath in, one breath out. Again and again until the whirling in his body calmed and settled.

A roar filled the garage as he started the car, and he began the journey home. Which therapist had taught him that process? The various counselors and psychiatrists all seemed to blur together in his mind, a single amorphous blob lobbing various bits of advice at him depending on the situation.

When had he seen the first one? Maxim followed that line of thought, since it was much easier to travel down while also having to focus on driving.

He'd been seven, probably. That sounded right. He had the faint memory of a kindly old woman conversing with him lightly while he played with plastic toys. The woman had offered him a wind-up dinosaur as she'd asked why he'd rather hide under an overpass than go to school.

He still remembered how the bumpy scales beneath his tiny fingers had grown slimy with his sweat at her question.

At least his coping mechanisms had improved in twenty-four years.

Maxim pulled into his garage without any memory of the drive that had taken him there. Now home and as safe as he ever was, the previous discoveries hit him with the force of a truck.

Monsters lived in New Hawkshead. Actual monsters. When he was younger, he would have given his left foot to know this, and probably would have foolishly walked right up to the creature, poked its shiny black carapace, and gotten his head ripped off for it.

He slapped the light switch in the kitchen. The sun had already set, and his reflection stared back at him from every window. Dirty, filthy, wrecked.

Clothes fell to the floor on his way to the bathroom. Normally, he would hate the thought of blood soiling the as-yet-unblemished carpet. After four months in the condo, every surface was just as clean as when he'd moved in. Tonight, he couldn't summon the energy or the mental capacity to care.

Maxim stepped out of his underwear and into the shower before the water was even warm. Blood mixed with dirt as it swirled into the drain.

And not only monsters had barged into his carefully constructed worldview.

Magic was real.

Witches were real, and Pippa Beverly was one of them.

Thanks to too many fantasy book cover illustrations undoubtedly painted by a bunch of horny men, Maxim realized that he'd always had a mental image of witches as scantily-yet-elegantly clad sorceresses waving about long sticks from which erupted great fountains of magic. (Thinking about it now, *totally* dick metaphors.) They were consistently posing in ways that implied they lacked internal organs, with metallic brassieres and expressions that foretold a sexy sort of doom.

Maxim slowed in the middle of scrubbing shampoo into his hair. And then there was Pippa. Her outfits were understated, her demeanor mostly innocuous. She was pretty. Nicely shaped. She filled out her skirts and floral cardigans in ways he absolutely should never admit to having noticed, and definitely never admit to having appreciated.

She was also terrifying.

This morning, he would have scoffed at the idea of Pippa being the danger someone could encounter in a dark alley.

God, of *course* she was distracted at work. Of *course* she didn't give a shit about being a legal assistant. Why would she bother with mundanities like dossiers, collated copies, and the specifics of personal injury when she could do *magic?*

Maxim finished rinsing his hair, then gave his body an extra once-over with the shower head in case any bits of the dark alley lingered on his skin in the form of dirt or expired vegetable scraps.

Yet . . . she had healed him. She had saved his life. In a world with demons and monsters and magic, there must also be some sense of good and evil, and if she had stopped him from bleeding out mere minutes after berating him, she must be on the side of good.

Right?

As he toweled off and emerged out of the shower stall, he nudged his boxers out of the way with his toes. They weren't bloodied or torn like the rest of his clothing, but he still considered them ruined, if only for the fact that he would forever associate them with a great amount of unpleasantness. Had he seen his spleen? What did that even look like? No. Best to try and forget completely.

Maybe he would burn his clothing from today. Shove it in the glass-enclosed gas fireplace and let the flames tear down the fabric into scraps of charred fibers and unhealthy chemical off-gassing. Or, to cut down on toxic fumes, he'd just stuff them all in a garbage bag and hope no one found its contents in a few years and opened a murder investigation.

He'd deal with that all later.

His reflection scowled back at him in the mirror.

Better. Still wrecked, but at least no longer filthy. The scar on his stomach snared his attention. About the size of his fist, it sat to the side and a few inches higher than his navel. He ran his fingers lightly over the weal, and when that revealed no change in sensation, he twisted his torso and arched his back so it shifted over his abdominals. There wasn't any pain; the only change was in the appearance.

Maxim understood he had a certain sense of vanity, and the sight of the new, large scar on skin that had so recently been unblemished sent a pang of disappointment through him.

Yet if given the choice between scar and death, he'd assuredly choose scar. He wasn't *that* vain.

He poked it again, as if it would encourage the patch to scuttle off. It was certainly not the life change with which he'd expected the day to end. He'd planned to come home, pour a glass of cele-bratory whiskey, sit and relax for all of thirty minutes at the most. Then he would dive headfirst into ideas he could pitch to Crossly and Williams so his first day with them would be as smooth and perfect as possible.

But in that thirty minutes of relaxation, he would finally feel that he had been heading toward something great. Soon, he would be helping the city and its citizens and making lives better. He would be proud of himself. Happy. Satisfied.

Instead of a promotion and an abundance of pride, Maxim ended his day with a vicious-looking scar and a whopping sense of unease.

He scrubbed away the remaining droplets that trickled over his body, carefully folded the towel, and hung it on its rack. On his way out of the bathroom, he kicked his underwear into the hall to join the scattered clothes, but caught by some unseen current from a nearby vent, they floated onto an end table and settled atop a squat, unlit candle.

Maxim grumbled, then plucked the boxers off the table and tossed it to the floor. Kicked it again for good measure.

About to continue to his bedroom, he lingered on the candle. An ex had given it to him years ago when they'd dated. It was one of those large ones, the sort that, without its three wicks, looked like a cream-colored wheel of cheese. Ciara had claimed that when he burned it, it would "help him find his center." Whatever that meant.

He hefted it in his hands and brought it to his nose. He always liked the way it smelled: citrus and cloves and a bit of cardamom. It was nice. Just like the miniature salt lamp another ex had given him with vaguely similar instructions. William had said all he'd need to do was plug it in, focus on the pretty orange glow, and try to chill the fuck out.

Unfortunately, chilling the fuck out was not one of Maxim's hobbies.

If he were seeing such things in someone else's house, he might wonder why they'd brought tokens of their past relationships and set them all on a little table like some sort of masochistic shrine to failed love. Sometimes it helped, though, to remember why they had left: apparently, he was too obsessed with what would make him feel complete to pay attention to who was around him.

What would either of them say to him now? He had fallen so far into the desperation of a potential promotion that he'd vilified himself to an entire office. Maybe not the entire office. Well. Most of the office.

Maxim set the candle back on its stand and scrubbed hands that now smelled like spiced oranges over his face.

His mind was already in a riot; there was no need to add regret to that as well. He needed exercise. Focus.

He threw on a pair of shorts and a sleeveless shirt, then thumped down the stairs to the punching bag that hung in the garage.

Night sounds made a desperate attempt to sneak in through cracks in the drywall: crickets, distant highway traffic, one lonesome coyote. Maxim drowned them all out as he rolled his shoulders, stretched his arms, and wound the wraps over his hands and wrists.

The bag thumped in response to his punches. He relaxed into the rhythm of burning muscles and prickling sweat. In the warm rush of exertion, his mind could lie back and let his body take over, channeling old lessons on form and flow and breath. The missed promotion fell away, as did the fanged moth demon that had stabbed him in the stomach.

A powerful kick set the bag swinging, and Maxim held it steady as he waited for his breathing to slow.

He couldn't shake the image from the alley: a woman swirling flames and shimmering air between her hands, manipulating the world around her.

It was as if he'd caught sight of an entirely new landscape through a kaleidoscope. There were pieces, little fragments of truth, and he could not settle until he saw the whole of it.

Maxim struck the bag again, and again. Each punch rattled another unknown along his arms and up into his head. What other impossibilities existed? Where would it all lead? Was it going to be too dangerous to find out?

One certainty stuck out through the growing jumble: he had to know more.

He and Pippa Beverly were not done with each other.

PIPPA STARED AT HER computer and tried not to think of how absolutely, unquestionably fucked she was. Someone cleared their throat in the office and she snapped her eyes up. For one horrible, short moment, she forgot she was on the tenth floor and beneath artificial lighting, and braced herself for a verbal attack by a berobed and furious coven member.

But no.

It was just Geoff, who appeared to have choked a little bit on his scone.

Pippa flexed her fingers on her keyboard. She tapped a sentence in an email, then deleted it, then tapped it out again. Then deleted it. Then dropped her head into her hands and groaned.

Demon's teeth, she couldn't focus.

When she woke up this morning, she'd entertained the thought that the day before had been a series of long, awful delusions. The fading scar on her forearm and the dark smudges under her eyes spoke strongly against that hope however, as did the long call with a tow truck service and a ride in to work on a particularly smelly bus.

As much as she would like to believe that Maxim Sheppard had not witnessed her using magic and killing a demon in an alley, it had happened. She had violated one of the Ash Coven's highest laws: respect and uphold the secrecy of the otherworld.

She couldn't think about this right now. Shouldn't. There were messages to write, queries to answer, and by focusing on the minutiae of this job, she could get through the day without crumbling.

It would have been easier if she didn't have to work with Maxim Sheppard.

Forever the interminable pain in the ass, he didn't seem to have been affected by her threat the previous day. She had expected him to keep his distance, maybe scuttle around her nervously, but even though he now knew she could turn him into a charred pile of woodsy-citrusy-smelling ash, he didn't seem to be able to stop staring at her.

While Reggie Cavatappi gave his speech at this morning's meeting (Jules accepted the twenty-dollar bill with a pleased "Aah!"), Pippa repeatedly glanced across the table to find herself pinned by golden-green eyes. Not an aggressive pinning, but Pippa still shifted under their intensity. Maxim looked at her as if he expected to see informative essays stamped in fine print along her hairline or along the bridge of her nose.

After ten minutes of this, Pippa nudged some magic so it clamped on his tie and cinched it more tightly around his neck. Not nearly enough to choke, but enough to make him start in his chair. He caught her glare, paled, and for the rest of the meeting, was at least more surreptitious with his attention.

She must have glared at him hard enough for Jules to notice. As they'd sat at their desks post-meeting, Jules had spun around to face Pippa.

"He's scared of you," she said. "He legit quailed. I've never even seen an example of that word in real life before. How do I gain this power?"

Pippa hadn't liked the emphasis Jules had put on 'power.' She purposely chose to not address it, and instead she shrugged, then mumbled something nondescript about throwing her drink at him and giving him a minor lecture after he'd stomped off to the alley like a child.

"Good for you," Jules had said. "Maybe he won't be so much of an ass on his next project."

Thinking of this earlier conversation reminded Pippa that his next project was actually her current project, which reminded her of the Burton case, which reminded her of the empty email sitting unaddressed on her screen.

She really should start that.

Dear Mr. Sheppard,

Attached are the files you requested. Please make sure to update your PDF viewer, as I believe that is part of the issue with viewing them.

Pippa Beverly

P.S. Stop staring at me like I'm hiding tentacles beneath my sweater. I am fully capable of melting your eyeballs without saying a word. Or waving a tentacle.

Ah yes, because emails post-scripted with a threat were the best kind of work emails.

Pippa frowned at her screen for a solid minute, then decided she needed a break, both for the good of herself and the good of the office. The building had a mini cafe on the ground floor;

she could do with something coated in powdered sugar. And something with caffeine. The effort of healing Maxim's severe injuries had left her with the same sort of head fog and groggy irritability that came along with a hangover, without any fun memories.

She grabbed her wallet and shoved her phone into her sweater's kangaroo pocket in case Jules finished her current chapter and wanted instant feedback, then made her way to the elevator lobby.

Her thoughts full of foamy, syrupy coffee beverages, Pippa skipped through the elevator doors as they began to close. Empty. Perfect.

"Wait!"

Pippa snapped her head up to see Maxim jogging across the lobby's shining tiles.

Shit.

"Oh no!" she said as she rapidly jabbed the "close" button. "The doors are closing too fast! Maybe you should take the stairs!"

Maxim shoved his arm inside and the doors bounced harmlessly off his fine gray sleeve. He charged into the elevator once the doors opened wide enough to admit him, then faced Pippa. Although he was breathing hard as if he'd sprinted from his office, his lips were pressed together in their traditional thin line.

"I'm getting coffee," Pippa said curtly. "I wasn't aware you wanted some that badly."

"We need to talk."

She aimed a glower at him and was very displeased when he failed to quail again.

"No we don't," she said, directing her glower at the closing doors instead. "I said all I needed to. Unless you want to be threatened a second time."

"What is happening here, Pippa?"

The utter desperation in his voice, as well as the use of her name, tugged at her. Whenever he'd needed to get her attention in the past, he'd usually just send her an email addressed to either "Ms. Beverly" or "Philippa." There were times when she'd assumed he looked it up in a roster every time he needed something.

"I don't know what you mean," she said.

"You— You know exactly what I—" Maxim made a low growl of frustration, and before Pippa could properly register what he was doing, he lunged in front of her and slapped the emergency stop button. The elevator coasted to a stop. According to the illuminated numbers above the doors, they'd made it a single floor.

Pippa let loose her own frustrated growl. "You're unbelievable."

"You're a witch," he hissed, as if someone outside the doors could even hear, and as if her being a witch was a perfectly valid reason for disrupting a large chunk of the building's elevator traffic. "I need to understand what happened last night."

"No, you don't. You have no right to be involved with any of it."

"You involved me! When you decided to kill a demon—"

"'Decided'? What a *great* way to describe that whole situation."

"When— All right, fine, whatever, *when you killed a demon,* because that's kind of the main issue here, you did it right in front of me. Did you just forget I was there?"

Guilt tugged at Pippa's stomach. "I'm insulted you'd even think that."

"You opened up a . . . a completely different world to me. And like hell will you convince me to lie down and forget about it."

There was an intensity to him she'd never seen before. This was not the same Maxim who had calmly and rationally paved the way for a winning case in a courtroom. It was not the same Maxim who had frowned at an incorrect coffee order, or talked about the differences in tie knots with a haughtiness that must have been inherited. His eyes were fiery, his skin flushed. Even his nostrils were flared. If he'd appeared more human the previous night in the alley when she confronted him, now he was *alive.*

Seeing him like this was both exciting and disturbing, though she couldn't quite unpack the reasons for either. It was a little thrilling, even; what else would make a flush stain his cheeks? Not at all the type of thought that was appropriate in a closed elevator with an agitated man she had to work with every day. Despite the thrill, her gut soured and her stomach twisted as if it were a caught creature.

Wait.

That couldn't be right.

No matter how the man irritated her, he'd never instigated nausea. Something was wrong.

"What else can I say to you? Is there any way . . ."

She tuned out Maxim's continued argument. The taste of bile burned hot and acrid in her throat. She focused on the air around her, on that twinge of *wrong,* how she suddenly felt as if the back of her neck was being tickled with a knife. It was coming from . . . She couldn't tell. Maxim was still talking.

"You're—And now you're pretending I'm not here." He rubbed his forehead. "Wow. All right."

"Shut up," she said.

"I— What?"

Before he could begin an offended rant, Pippa clapped a hand over his mouth and shoved him against the elevator wall. There was empty air below them, walls to the sides, and above—

"I need you to be quiet," she whispered.

After only a brief but muffled outraged curse, Maxim seemed to realize there was a change in her demeanor and didn't try to move away.

She was so much shorter than he was, and pressed up against him like this, she could feel the hard, strong lines of his body through his suit. It wasn't a good time to notice that, or the length of his eyelashes, or the thick arch of his eyebrows, or how soft his lips were under her palm.

Pull yourself together, Pippa.

There was definitely something above them. Whatever it was, its aura raked over her skin like coals. If not for the elevator muzak she might be able to hear more. A quick burst of magic through the speaker and a few sparks later, the only sound was the hushed rasp of their breathing: Pippa's slow and even, Maxim's emerging as erratic, warm puffs that brushed her knuckles.

In the silence, there came a soft *ping* from above the car, then the creak of shifting metal. More creaks followed, each one moving slightly across the ceiling.

Maxim settled his hands on her waist. A firm pressure, and although his touch caught Pippa off guard, it was a reassuring one. Was his first impulse really to hold on to her as if he could protect her? Was he being . . . *sweet?*

Pippa mentally shook herself and began to pull on the magic in the elevator's now stagnant air. She should be preparing magic, not suppressing a giggle over some pompous asshole's idea of chivalry.

Overhead, the creaking stopped, and for a lovely second it seemed as if it had all been one great overreaction. Then the entire elevator lurched and one of the illuminated ceiling panels collapsed as someone fell inside. Pippa caught sight of a bald head before she shoved Maxim farther into the corner. It wasn't a very successful action, since the elevator was just big enough for four people to stand comfortably or fifteen people to get very intimate with each other's deodorant choices.

Maxim pushed against her in his attempt to reach the person on the floor, who was wearing a maintenance jumpsuit and boasted a set of extremely hirsute arms. Maxim was oblivious to what was blindingly obvious to Pippa: this elevator hadn't been out of order and therefore no one up to innocent deeds would be atop it. Before he could wriggle out of Pippa's hold, the person stood, brushed debris off their clothing, and began to molt.

What was once a maintenance uniform sloughed off over scaled, ridged shoulders. The faded fabric fell along with a decent amount of pale, hairy skin, and pooled together around the intruder's hoofed feet like slime. The stench of sulfur and burnt oil filled the elevator.

Muscles crackled as the creature stretched and expanded, freed from the enclosure that had allowed it to travel unnoticed into the building. No horns adorned its head, but ruddy purple skin stretched taut over its skull and over the space where its nose should have been. Wide-set black eyes narrowed as they focused on Pippa.

No, not a person at all. This was only surprising to Maxim, who made a nervous "Umph?" into her hand.

Pippa disentangled herself from the corner and faced the demon with her arms spread wide.

Hold on, was she shielding Maxim? Oh, that wasn't a fun prospect, what with her hating him and all. In addition, "hatred" didn't feel like the right word anymore.

Fuck, no, why was she thinking about that when she was half an elevator away from a demon?

The demon snarled, revealing a mouthful of teeth that had been filed down into short little points, and pulled a blade from a scabbard at its belt. As long as Pippa's forearm, it gleamed green beneath the flickering fluorescents. The demon inhaled deep, and as its chest expanded, dark veins appeared under its skin as if the creature were a peeled plum.

"The witch," it said. Its voice was as coarse as two cinder blocks scraping against one another.

Without another word, it lunged.

Pippa drew a handful of magic into her and sent it out her palm, blasting the demon off its feet and into the opposite wall. The elevator lurched, and she tried not to think about the empty space beneath her feet. Close behind her, Maxim cursed; he didn't seem able to avoid such thoughts.

The demon recovered quickly, spinning about and hurling the fallen piece of ceiling tile at her, which she redirected so it glanced off the creature's ridged shoulder instead of cleaving her head from her body.

"Oh," Maxim said, his words high and strained, "you're not on a first name basis with this one?"

Pippa threw herself forward and pivoted so the demon's next swing was as far away from Maxim as the elevator's floor plan would allow.

"No," she managed. "Not"—she threw magic at the demon, then cursed as it dodged—"this one."

Purple skin, no nose, that hooked bump on the inside of its wrist: Boe demons were usually used as mercenaries by those who wished a dirty job to be done fast.

Sometime soon, she would have to ruminate on why she was a target for murder.

The green-tinged knife passed far too close to Pippa's stomach. In her haste to back out of the way, her slippered flat caught on the edge of the ceiling panel and she crashed to the ground, rolling just as the knife sank into the floor beside her. It caught, and the demon tugged on the knife until the muscles in its arms bulged.

The remaining lights in the ceiling flashed and threw out sparks that fluttered into the air like short-lived fireflies. Still lying on her back, Pippa pulled on those sparks, drew them in close, and nourished them until they grew.

Right as the demon yanked the knife from the mass of steel and carpet, she let the power loose. A blast of energy, white-hot and furious, erupted out of her hands and up at the demon's face and the ceiling above. The creature lunged out of the way with a shriek. The elevator lurched and wires screamed, and when the smoke cleared, Pippa saw that she had blown the entire roof off the elevator.

Her head swam with the effort it had taken to channel so much magic. She struggled to one elbow. The smell of burning skin filled the small space. The demon was on its knees, hunched and clutching its face. When it turned to Pippa again, those awful filed teeth were visible through a smoking hole in its cheek.

It paused then, looking at the corner of the elevator where Maxim was creeping along the wall in the direction of a metal beam that had fallen.

Pippa lashed out with her foot. She was aiming for its knee, but thanks to the respectable and restrictive pencil skirt, she instead struck one shining shin. Her heel instantly began to throb. The demon's attention was snared, at least. It whirled on her and grabbed her ankle, pulling her across the debris-strewn floor toward itself even as she kicked out.

The knife came up.

Maxim yelled.

She couldn't roll, couldn't dodge.

Pippa reached out to the magic above her head, and as the shining knife came down over her stomach, she grabbed that magic and pulled. She felt her body slide backward, yet despite it all, she hadn't moved far enough, so when the knife fell, it sank deep into her thigh.

And *oh*, the pain.

Pippa screamed, tears blurring her vision.

She had been stabbed before, of course, but by little switchblades carried by upstart fiends. This was different. This was horrible. This was as if a horde of wasps had swarmed into her thigh and been followed in by flames.

Through the haze, she heard Maxim yell again, followed by a heavy thumping. She had to focus. Had to return to the creaking elevator, even though every single inch of her body wanted her to float off into oblivion.

So she drew on that pain, used it to focus and lure herself back into awareness. She began to see metal walls, thin carpeting, the knife sticking out of her leg, the hilt flickering in the unsteady light.

And Maxim.

Pippa had assumed she would look over and see him in a crumpled heap. He had yelled, after all, and a yell like that didn't usually mean success.

It was with some surprise, then, that she took in what was happening: Maxim was upright, very much alive, and fighting the demon in a way that implied he was doing quite well, actually.

As she watched, he dropped beneath the creature's wild swing, used its own momentum to shove it face-first into a wall, then rapidly and repeatedly kneed a spot on its back where a human kidney would be.

Pippa gaped. Who the actual shit was this guy?

The demon, who did not have kidneys, shrugged off this attempt at injury. It wheeled about and barreled toward Maxim.

It dawned on Pippa that this was a fantastic distraction and the perfect time to char this creature into oblivion. Fighting the pain in her leg, she reached out to the magic around her . . .

And felt nothing.

She reached out again, harder. Nothing. Panic scoured her veins and whined in her ears as she tried over and over and over to feel the slightest brush of magic on her fingers. The world's power used to float around her, coursing along wind currents and nestling between bricks, ever present in the trees and the earth. She would simply nudge it with her intent and, as long as she had enough strength to channel it, it would respond.

The harder she pushed, the more she felt as if she was in a hastily constructed room trying to force her hands through the walls. Magic waited outside, if she could only find a way to get to it. If she could press harder—

Maxim had managed to avoid the demon's punches, but one quick jab caught him on the side of the jaw and he spun to the ground.

The demon's attention landed on Pippa, and she forgot everything about rooms and walls and lost magic as it stalked toward her.

She dragged herself backward, her stabbed leg useless and agonizing with the effort to move.

"I don't . . ." she said between pained gasps. "I don't suppose I can convince you not to do what you're . . . going to do."

"No." It stood over Pippa, one leg on either side of her hips. "And do not think to beg. I find it distasteful." It reached down with one long arm, grabbed her neck, and hoisted her into the air.

Pippa's scream turned into a gurgle. The demon's scabbed face wavered in her sight, and she scrabbled at the leathery hand with her nails in an effort to breathe. Its skin was too thick to do any damage. She needed more of a weapon than fingernails.

Ah.

She had a weapon, though retrieving it wasn't going to be pleasant.

The demon's fingers tightened.

Well.

Bright flashes appeared in Pippa's vision as her body slowly came to terms with the lack of air. Although it felt counterintuitive to stop fighting the hold on her neck, her hand dropped and her fingers found the knife hilt in her thigh. She grabbed it, squeezed her eyes shut, and pulled.

She would have cried out if she had any extra oxygen, and she would have collapsed if she'd been using her legs. Stars, taking the knife out hurt almost as much as getting stabbed by it.

The demon let out a short growl of displeasure. Pippa didn't know what it would try to do in response, and not wanting to find out, she summoned her remaining strength and shoved the knife into the demon's chest. The blade pierced between its ribs and into its heart. Boe demons had those, at least.

It dropped Pippa. She thudded onto the ruined elevator floor, her throat an aching, bruised mess. The demon staggered and stared at the knife in its chest, then collapsed, convulsing once before it stilled.

Maxim cursed from across the elevator. He staggered over, then fell to his knees beside her and began to strip out of his jacket.

Too tired to wonder what he was doing, Pippa lay in the rubble and embraced the simple joy of breathing. Now that the knife was out of her body, she should be able to—

Oh no.

Her head gave a throb of protest when she bolted upright.

Maxim reached for her shoulders, said something about how she should take it easy, but she ignored him. She still couldn't feel the magic. Even though she concentrated on those intangible, awful walls separating her from power, they held firm.

She looked over at the knife. It was covered with her own blood, the yellowish slime of the demon's blood, and whatever green tinge coated the blade. The green could have been a poison, designed to block access to her magic. Pippa swallowed back her nausea. If it was poison, it couldn't last forever, right? Her body would be able to process it, digest it somehow, and then it would wear off. Unless . . .

The other magic, the darker magic, the squirm that urged her to twist and pull and manipulate, lurked in a corner of her mind, alive and itching for her to use it. *Those walls might never dissolve,* it said. *Who will you be then?*

No. It would be temporary. It *had* to be. Panic fluttered within her gut like a captured hawk, all sharp talons and slashing beak. Maxim tightened his hands on her and pushed her to her back.

"Just . . . please," he said. He couldn't stop staring at the gash on her thigh. Which, when Pippa looked at it, looked rather bad. There was a lot of blood. Hadn't that been part of some first-aid training years ago? Leave the knife in so you don't bleed out? And with her magic gone, she didn't have the ability to heal herself. It was temporary, she told herself. It was going to be temporary.

Maxim wound his jacket around her injured leg, tying the arms together so it formed an impromptu bandage.

"I'll be fine," Pippa said, though she couldn't summon the energy to bat his hands away. "You'll ruin your suit."

"Not the first suit you've helped to ruin," he muttered. The uncomfortable look he gave her implied he hadn't meant to say that out loud. "I, uh—" He cleared his throat. "I'll manage. I have plenty."

"Fine. Next time I won't save you."

"I think you're running out of threats if 'not saving me' is the worst you can think of."

Pippa let out a halfhearted grunt. "Something tells me you'll ignore them anyway."

His lips twisted in something bizarrely smile-like. "My stubbornness might surprise you."

"No," she said, "It really won't."

Maxim settled on his heels and swept the back of his wrist over his forehead, then frowned at the residue he'd managed to wipe off onto his cuff. The fine fabric of his button-up used to be a crisp white; now it was smeared all over with grease and grime and what must have been her own blood. A bruise was starting to form on his chin from where the demon had hit him. There was a dark stain on his tie, rendering the classy geometric pattern into something more avant-garde. His once-coiffed hair had lost all of its careful structure, even going so far as to curl slightly where sweat had dampened his temples.

Before Pippa could question why she was staring, and why she was enjoying the staring, the broken elevator lurched down several feet.

Compelled by a million years of evolutionary instinct, Pippa grabbed for the closest solid object, which happened to be Maxim's thigh. When she realized the car wasn't continuing to fall, she snatched her hand back as if his thigh (firm, muscled, large, *Pippa, NO*) had burned her, though thankfully he appeared to be too distracted with his own wild grab for the nearest handrail to notice what she'd done.

"We have to get out of here," Maxim said.

"In a minute."

He shot her a look of confused exasperation, which Pippa ignored. In addition to the failing elevator, there was a nearly intact demon body she had to destroy first. She pulled herself over to the corpse and wrenched the knife out with a squelch. This was hers now.

She had to destroy this body, but without magic, there wasn't any ready way to do so. If she had a source of flame and a lot of time, that could work.

"We have to get out of here *now*," Maxim said before she could ask if he had a lighter, and ignoring her garbled protests, he grabbed her upper arms and pulled her to her feet. "I think you destroyed the brakes."

One look at the structure above the elevator reinforced his theory: several cables had already snapped, and what must have once been the brakes were now twisted clumps of metal.

Pippa's head spun with the effort to remain upright. She slumped against one of the walls and chose to simply watch Maxim as he struggled with prying the doors open. "Oh, *I* destroy your clothes. *I* destroy the elevator."

A long, miserable groan came from the twisted metal above them.

Pippa's alarm at the sound was much stronger than the exhaustion brought on by the dual loss of both magic and blood. The latter really seemed to be going for it, if the growing dampness of Maxim's improvised bandage told her anything. Like hell was she going to spend her last moments trapped in an elevator with Maxim Sheppard and a dead demon.

Newly energized, Pippa swayed toward the doors and helped Maxim grapple with them. With a grunt of effort on Maxim's part, and what surely must have been straining muscles unfairly hidden by shirt sleeves, the elevator opened.

The car had settled between floors; the lobby's doors were halfway visible through the opening they had just made. Maxim wrenched on one, and as it slid into the wall to reveal an empty lobby, the elevator shuddered and jerked down another foot. If one of them tried to climb out and was caught halfway between the lobby and the car when the elevator decided to plummet— No, best not to think about bisections today.

Pippa probably could have pulled herself up, if given enough time and also probably a stool; Maxim didn't leave her with the option. Grabbing her around the waist, he lifted her and tossed her into the elevator lobby like she was a professionally dressed and unprofessionally bloodied sack of potatoes.

She tumbled onto tiles hard enough to make new bruises blossom on her knees and elbows. The knife flew from her hand and slid across the floor. Halfway to grabbing it, Pippa turned and watched as Maxim pulled himself into the lobby, tucking his legs and rolling out of the way right as the elevator gave one last groan and disappeared from view.

Maxim's breath rushed from him in a gasping laugh. That "alive" Maxim Sheppard had returned, seemingly high from everything that had just happened.

A rumbling crash echoed up from the elevator shaft and startled Pippa out of her stare. She really had to stop doing that, no matter how alluring the unexpected rumpledness was on him.

She grabbed the knife, heaved her battered body upright, and limped toward the stairwell door. After a noise like that, the lobby wouldn't stay empty for long, and she needed to leave before someone ran in and asked questions; she wasn't in any state to fib convincingly.

What happened to the elevator? How did you get hurt? Why does Maxim look like he's just crawled through an air vent in pursuit of Alan Rickman?

Questions that would end in stammering and, truth be told, a good solid faint, which would then lead to hospitals, and that would not work for Pippa.

On the bright side, maybe a crashed elevator would be a decent substitute for burning the demon corpse. She would be optimistic about that part, she decided as she wiggled the knife into the impromptu swaddling around her thigh. Maybe it would all be fine. A seam ripped somewhere in the mass, and Pippa felt a little guilty, not that Maxim would want to wear the jacket anyway after all the damage she'd already done to it.

When she reached the stairwell door, she glanced back. Maxim didn't seem to be thinking about anything except the daring escape; he was grinning and looked a second away from letting out a joyful whoop.

Pippa paused with her hand on the door's push bar. She could leave him here, let him make up his own story and hope he wouldn't talk about demons and magic and accidental destruction. The idea didn't sit quite right with her though, considering how he had helped her. And how it was his suit jacket wrapped around her thigh that was preventing her blood from dripping all over the shining tiles.

No, she couldn't leave him.

"Maxim!" she hissed.

He glanced over, then scrambled to his feet and followed her into the stairwell.

After half of a flight of hobbling and biting her lip to keep from crying out in pain, Pippa began to think the stairs had been a terrible idea. For fuck's sake, there were two other elevators in the lobby—perfectly functional elevators—which, if taken, would have meant they would already be outside by now. Probably.

"How long until it works?"

She scowled at Maxim over her shoulder. He was hovering a few stairs behind her, arms slightly outstretched as if he expected her to fall.

"How long until what works?"

"Healing. The . . . uh . . . magic kind. What you did to me, and what I'm assuming you're doing to yourself right now."

A great heaviness pressed on Pippa's chest, and she missed the next stair, landing heavily on her injured leg with a yelp. She pushed away his attempt to steady her.

"It's gone," she blurted, then cursed herself for revealing it.

Maxim jumped down several steps and landed in front of her. "Gone? You can't heal your leg? Or you can't do magic?"

"Both. There was something on the knife." She limped along the length of one step so she could grab the railing Maxim wasn't currently blocking and used that to support her weight as she continued down the stairs.

"Pippa."

She ignored him.

"If you can't heal yourself, we need to get you to a hospital."

An entirely new sort of dread filled her. Sure, the situation might look terrible to someone not initiated to her lifestyle, but thanks to the incredible power of compartmentalization, she'd been expecting to go home, stitch herself up, then curl into a ball on the couch with a lot of hot drinks and wait out the time it took for the walls that separated her from her magic to crumble. Then she would heal, and then she would be fine.

She *would* be fine. She *had* to be fine. Maybe if she said it to herself a few more times, it would become the truth.

When she spun to face him, it set her head spinning as well. Pippa tightened her hold on the railing.

"No hospitals," she said, then gave him a look that she hoped didn't allow for argument.

It didn't work.

His expression hardened, and he was opening his mouth to argue when a door slammed a floor above them.

There was something fascinating about his rapid change from alarm to worry to exasperation in the instant before he charged forward.

"I don't need your help—" Pippa began.

Maxim caught her by the waist and lifted her off the ground, then with her pressed snugly against his side, he thundered down the stairs. At first, she was too startled (and a short moment later, too pained by the rapid jostling) to be properly impressed. She threw an arm around his neck just so she wouldn't feel entirely useless.

"We're going to my car," he said as he ran along a landing and thudded down another flight, skipping far too many stairs for Pippa's comfort, "and then straight to the ER."

She began to argue with that last statement, because there was no way in any of the hells she'd let that happen, when voices echoed around the stairwell from above and derailed all of her possible arguments.

Then, somehow, they were on the ground floor. Maxim kicked open the emergency exit and barreled out into sunlight so bright Pippa winced. They were heading across the pavement to his car.

"Stop," Pippa said. When he didn't, she elbowed him hard in the ribs, and with a "Gah!" he let her go. Her legs threatened to buckle as her feet met the asphalt.

"What are you doing?" he said, his eyes wide in disbelief. "You have to—"

"I just need to go home."

"You need medical attention!"

"No," Pippa snapped. A wave of fatigue threatened to bowl her over and, embarrassingly, she found herself holding onto Maxim's upper arm to steady herself. "I can't. I don't know how long I'll be like this. And if it comes back—" She stopped, then amended, "When my power comes back, and I'm hooked up to machines, or being observed, there'll be too many questions."

"But if you bleed out before—"

"No!" She curled her fingers into his arm. A vein in his neck pulsed with his frustration. She focused on that. "I need to get home. I'll be all right there."

For the first time since yesterday, she fully met his gaze. He looked at her as if he wasn't sure who was more insane: her, for denying help she desperately needed; or himself, for hesitating about providing it.

"Please," Pippa said.

He started shaking his head.

"If you take me home," she blurted before she could think of how terrible of an idea this was, "I'll tell you everything. Whatever you want to know. Ask any question and I'll answer it."

A muscle in Maxim's jaw twitched. "That's a shitty deal if it means you're going to die in an hour."

Pippa gave him a smirk she didn't fully feel. "I'm a witch. We don't die that easily."

He glared at the office building and tapped his index finger on his thigh in a rapid tic. Then his shoulders lifted in a heavy sigh, and Pippa knew he'd surrendered.

"Fine," he said shortly. "But this is a bad idea."

She let him sling one of her arms over his shoulders so he could help her to the car. Then she collapsed in the back seat and put all of her energy into proving him wrong.

Six

Maxim had never been a big fan of driving. Too many rules at odds with too many uncertainties. Maybe he would like it more if his life didn't depend on the knowledge and attention span of every other person on the road. He would definitely like it more if there wasn't a woman sprawled over the back who, when she wasn't apologizing for bleeding on the upholstery, was burning a hole right in the center of Maxim's carefully constructed sense of calm.

He blew through another barely red light. The steering wheel squeaked beneath his grip, and for the thirtieth time this minute, he glanced in the rearview mirror to make sure no flashing lights followed them.

His phone announced an upcoming turn. As soon as he'd started the car, Pippa had given him her address and he'd tapped it in with shaking fingers. Every time he glanced at the directions, he saw the red smear his bloodied thumb had left on the screen.

Pippa fell silent in the back. Panic punched into Maxim's stomach, and he risked a quick look backward. She was very pale. Her eyes were closed, dark lashes stark against her cheeks, her mouth slack.

"Fuck!"

A car had slowed in front of him, and only by slamming on the brakes did he avoid hitting it.

Pippa let out a startled warble, and Maxim felt her bump against the back of the driver's seat.

"Whattshappen?" she slurred.

"Traffic," he said, his throat tight. "You all right?"

"Mrhh. Yeah. You jus' gotta drive better."

Relief at her being alive clashed with the new panic of a near crash. He should have put a seat belt on her. Although, if he was getting into *should*s, he should have ignored her argument, he should have taken her straight to the emergency room, he should have— What, *not* followed her into the elevator? Let her fight that monster by herself, get stabbed, and then lie in a broken heap as the elevator car careened into pieces in the basement?

"They're moving," Pippa said.

Maxim frowned at the motionless traffic ahead. "What?" He twisted around but, seeing nothing unexpected in the back seat or out the windows, turned back to the road. She was alert, propped up on an elbow with her face screwed up in concentration. "What's moving?"

"The walls."

The traffic began to inch forward, and Maxim zipped around a delivery van. "What walls?" He didn't mean to sound so exasperated, though given what had happened today, he felt like he couldn't be faulted for any lack of finesse with his words.

"The . . . walls," Pippa said, as if it was self-explanatory. "They're moving. I knew they would, but there are cracks. They're . . . they're bowing. Bending. I think . . . whatever this is, it's not going to last much longer."

She sounded relieved, at least, and she was no longer slurring her sentences. If she was losing her connection with her sanity, then the one positive would be that she was going about it articulately.

The tires squealed as he turned a corner.

Even though he was now entangled in the sort of anxiety-inducing mess he usually tried to avoid, entangling himself in Pippa's messy, violent, fascinating life had been the right decision. As he'd fought a monster—an actual *monster*, not just a young asshole who expressed feelings with their fists—he had known exactly what he needed to do. Sure, he was terrified, and adrenaline was still tacky and sour on his tongue, but it wasn't the same sort of gut-twisting, finger-tingling terror that stopped him from acting; it was the sort that *made* him act.

And it had felt . . .

Good.

Disturbingly good.

The feeling of fighting real evil was grounding in a way that conscious breathing and tapping his fingers and mindfulness exercises never had been.

The apartment complex where Pippa lived wasn't in a bad part of town, but it wasn't in a great part, either. The landscaping consisted of scraggly bushes and trees so hemmed in by concrete and asphalt they looked one hot day away from withering into kindling.

Maxim careened into an empty parking spot in front of her building. She'd told him it was "E," though the only proof he was at the correct one was the faded silhouette of the letter left behind where a metal sign must once have been screwed into the exterior wall. The entire atmosphere made him more than a little uncomfortable thinking about his own condo, with its modern glass paneling, uncracked concrete walkway, and a front yard pulled straight from a magazine.

He helped Pippa out of the car, slinging her arm over his shoulders. The going was slow over crisped grass and exposed, gnarled roots. When she'd been in the car with him the previous day, she'd smelled of peaches. Her shampoo maybe, or her soap. A gentle breeze jostled her hair about and brought that same peach scent to his nose. Now it came along with sweat, blood, and the sulphury tang from the demon.

She was putting more of her weight on him. Her rib cage expanded in short, pained breaths alongside his own.

"I'm really tired, Maxim," she whispered.

The fear in her words crawled down his throat and nestled low in his gut. She hadn't actually seemed afraid up until now, and that stoked his own worries higher. Her apartment loomed ahead like some sort of bastion. As if changing locations would be the only respite they required, instead of intensive medical care and a backup force with earpieces and heavy weaponry in case any more threats against their lives arose.

He shifted his grip on the wrist Pippa had flung over his shoulders, squeezing it in a little pulse of reassurance. The small courtyard they were crossing was empty. Yet . . . what if something came after them now? With the combined attacks of last night and today, all logic pointed to an organized plan, the end goal of which was putting an end to Pippa Beverly. Any creature that attacked them here, in this crappy, sunny courtyard, wouldn't come up against any sort of meaningful defense.

That creature in the elevator had been fast. Strong. Maxim had sparred with people he'd secretly suspected of performance enhancers; he'd never encountered the sort that shrugged off every hit like his fists had been marshmallows.

As they walked, he glanced at windows and darkened entry-ways, dreading to see a curtain twitch or a curious face peek out around a corner. Part of him *wanted* someone to notice them, to run in their direction and ask if they needed help, then join Maxim in subduing Pippa so she could get the care she needed. And then he could call the police, tell them about the fight and—

And what, exactly?

A hamburgered demon corpse at the base of an elevator shaft?

Maxim's left eye twitched as he glared at the sidewalk in front of them.

Pippa tightened her hold briefly on his shoulders as they reached the stairs to her apartment. He supposed he just had to trust her; she had been a part of this world for a long time. The obvious way to move forward was to believe she knew what she was doing, even if he couldn't see the logic in it.

Pippa's keys were back in the office. Maxim bit back a retort when she wiggled one side of her door frame loose and pulled a spare key from behind it. It didn't seem like an especially secure hiding place and certainly wasn't a mark of fine craftsmanship.

She disentangled herself from him as soon as they entered, then promptly sagged onto a short end table by her couch.

"Thanks," she said.

The finalistic way she said that, with an "I'll see you later, goodbye!" very much implied, didn't sit well with Maxim.

He closed the door, then thought of demons and monsters and threw the deadbolt. Not that a single stick of steel would help much, but it felt a little nicer.

Pippa gave a soft, frustrated groan he was sure she hadn't meant for him to hear.

"I'm not leaving until I'm convinced you won't collapse and bleed out," he said in response.

She looked to be chewing over her thoughts, trying to figure out what would be the most likely thing to say to convince him she didn't need his presence. Nothing must have come to mind, or she was too exhausted to continue thinking, so she gave another long sigh.

"Just wait out here." Her legs trembled as she stood.

"While you do . . . what?"

"I have a sewing kit in the bathroom." She winced as she put weight on her injured leg, then began to wobble toward a short hallway. "I'll be a few minutes. Just read a magazine or something."

He watched her until she shut herself into the bathroom. The only light in the hallway was a warm slice beneath the door.

Maxim paced. He couldn't sit; his clothes were dirty and horrible, her couch was clean. He dragged his fingers through his hair and exhaled hard through his nose. Why was he even trying? She obviously didn't want him here. Had she lied about giving him answers just to manipulate him into taking her home?

His sigh emerged as a tight, frustrated growl. Well. He wasn't going anywhere until he was either convinced she was going to be all right or he'd figured a way to convince *her* that she needed help more than his meager first-aid training could provide. So he rolled his shoulders and looked around her apartment.

A witch's home, in his opinion, should have been dark and filled with enough incense to make him choke. Candles, too, or at least a lot of cast iron pots. Bundles of dried herbs would hang from a low ceiling next to skulls and shining glass bottles waiting to be filled.

He looked around the apartment and took in the floor lamp with just a bare bulb, the worn beige carpeting, and the messy stacks of papers sitting atop a chipboard table. With a note of embarrassment, he realized that with his heavy, smelly candle and fancy new age lamp, his home looked more occult than the home of an actual witch. She didn't even have a broom. Or— No, there it was in a corner of the small kitchen, modern and plastic with a mass of askew bristles.

A bookshelf made out of material a few generations removed from corrugated cardboard sat crookedly against one wall. Most of the books on it were paperbacks—Maxim recognized a few titles from his literature class in high school, though there were also some cookbooks, several guides to foreign countries next to a Spanish dictionary, and an impressive amount of what could only have been romance novels (unless *Eaten Right by the Duke* was another cookbook, which he doubted).

Along the top row, the books looked to be much older. This was what he'd expected: musty tomes no doubt filled with scrawling, handwritten tales and instructions. Scraps of brittle vellum jutted out from the leather-bound covers. He traced his finger over cracked spines, along gilded text swirled into languages he'd never seen.

He was in the midst of deciding whether it would be too intrusive to pull one book out and leaf through it when a loud yelp came from the bathroom.

Book forgotten, he ran down the hallway.

"Pippa!"

She cursed when he rapped on the door. "It's— Everything's— I'm fine!"

The hitch in her voice went a long way in convincing Maxim that things in the bathroom were exactly the opposite of fine.

"I'm coming in," he said, and when the door stuck in its frame, he shouldered it open to a surprised bleat from Pippa.

She sat on the closed toilet with her skirt hiked high. An upended first-aid kit lay scattered over the counter and the floor. Blood was smeared on the tiles and the bathtub rim. She'd removed his jacket; it lay in a sad, soaked pile by her feet.

Pippa held her injured thigh with one hand and a needle and thread in the other. She looked at him wide-eyed and pale, and Maxim cursed at himself for loudly barging in on someone who had just been attacked.

"You sounded like you were in trouble," Maxim said, as if an explanation of the obvious could be considered an apology.

"No, it's . . ." Pippa swallowed loudly, then glanced down at the impressive gash. "I just . . . I need to . . ."

The needle flickered in the bathroom's cool light. Her hand was shaking, and as she looked at her leg, her breathing became more unsteady, more rapid.

When she spoke again, it was so quiet that Maxim had to strain to hear. "I didn't think it was this big, and I've never—"

She swayed on the seat, and Maxim dove forward to catch her before she could fall off it.

"You having second thoughts about staying here?" he said, holding tight to her elbows.

Pippa shook her head so quickly that her hair tossed from side to side. "No," she added, as if the head shake wasn't enough. "Just . . ." She looked at the needle in her hand like it was a biting insect.

"Here," he said, dropping to his knees in front of her. "I'll do it."

She gave him a look of such disbelief it must have strained several muscles in her face. "Really?" She blinked. "Why?"

"You saved my life yesterday." He plucked the needle and thread from her slack fingers. "I owe you this, at the very least."

A strange expression passed over her then, as if she was pleasantly surprised. As if she had honestly believed he would have left when she'd implied he should.

"Have you sewn someone up before?"

"Sort of."

Pippa seemed to consider this. "Good enough," she said.

The tension left her and she sagged against the toilet tank. There was a surrender in that, a transfer of worry and anxiety, and Maxim girded himself so he wouldn't buckle beneath the weight.

"Probably goes against the finely crafted personality of 'office asshole,' I know," he said. A pair of nitrile gloves lay on the floor next to the spilled first-aid kit. Maxim rolled his sleeves to the elbows, tugged his tie loose, then pulled on the gloves. A little snug; at least they'd keep him dexterous.

Pippa smiled. Not as wide as the one she typically gave Juliette Cohen, but softer than any he'd seen before. "I won't let it leave this bathroom."

"Much appreciated." He swiped the needle and thread with an alcohol-soaked cotton ball and tried to ignore how her smile made him feel like he'd swallowed a bucket of hot tea.

"Don't think this is the normal thread for stitches," he said as he knotted it. It appeared to be cotton, and he was fairly confident that it would make any competent surgeon shriek in alarm. Maxim thought of how he was going to be stitching shut a wound that hadn't been disinfected or cleaned, and decided he'd ask for forgiveness later if they really did finish the day in the hospital.

"It's what I had," Pippa said. "Not in the habit of keeping sutures beneath my sink."

"Might want to invest in some."

Pippa snorted. "Next time I need an optimistic take, I'll know not to ask you."

"My takes are purely practical."

He hadn't realized he was smiling—barely, the slightest twist of his lips— until he saw Pippa staring at his mouth. She'd done that yesterday in the car as well, looking at his smile as if it were a rare species she wanted to catalog.

Maxim cleared his throat and settled onto the bathroom rug by her feet. He lay a hand gingerly on her thigh, keeping his attention on the three-inch gash instead of on the scalloped hem of her underwear, and pinched the wound closed. Blood welled up and trickled over Pippa's skin as she sucked in a sharp breath.

The first stitch was the worst. He didn't know if it would be better to announce the initial prick or to have it be unexpected, so when he slid the needle into her thigh without warning, he flinched almost as hard as she did.

Pippa held on to the edge of the counter, her knuckles whitening at the drag of thread through her skin.

"What did you mean by 'sort of'?" she said in a tight voice.

"Hmm?"

"You said you 'sort of' sewed someone up before."

"Oh, uh . . . yeah. I've never done this on the living." At her horrified expression, he stumbled on. "No, no— I mean . . ." He sighed, focused on the needle's placement, on keeping the string taut. "My roommate in undergrad was pre-med. While he was learning to suture, he'd leave his textbooks lying around next to whatever things he was sewing up. Orange peels, pigskin, rubber mats. It looked like fun. One thing led to another, and I was making little pigskin embroidery squares."

Pippa snorted. "Pigskin embroidery? Of what?"

"Flowers, bees, frolicking rabbits, the usual."

"Somehow I don't believe you."

Maxim smiled. "My embroidery journey ended when I tried to stitch a sword dripping in blood with some skulls at the base, and it ended up looking like an ejaculating cock and balls."

When Pippa laughed, she did so fully: flashing teeth, dimples in her round cheeks, the hearty bark of it echoing against tile. "You're not stitching a dick into my leg, are you?"

He glanced up at her. "I can if you'd like. But I charge extra for the ejaculation."

She snorted again, though a slight blush stained her cheeks. At first pleased she was gaining some color, Maxim felt his palms prickle in his gloves as he realized what he'd said.

"Anyway, I learned a bit about closing wounds. And here we are."

He must have hit a tender spot on her leg with the next stitch; Pippa choked a cry and squeezed her eyes shut, doubling her hold on the counter.

Shit. "If you want, I can add a little bit at the bottom so it also says 'Witches get Stitches'."

She barked out a watery laugh. "It's too bad you don't still embroider. I'd commission a hoop to hang in the hallway." Her laugh quickly turned into a whimper as he pulled the thread, and she pressed her lips tightly together until they were nearly white.

Desperate for something else to distract her, Maxim reached for his first thought.

"Tell me about magic."

Her breath hitched, and he cursed himself for his lack of tact. Hers was gone, and even though she'd seemed convinced it would return, it was obviously just as great a wound as the one on her thigh, if not greater.

"You don't have to—" he said as she began to say, "It's not that simple—"

"Sorry," Maxim said in the silence that followed. "You don't have to tell me now."

Pippa frowned at a spot high on the wall. "I've . . . It's just that I've never had to explain this to anyone before. Everyone who learned what I was, they already knew it all." She gave him a look that implied she was greatly regretting their agreement. Then she sighed, maybe remembering that it had been her idea in the first place. "I have no idea where to start."

Half of the wound was closed now, and rather nicely, he had to admit. But Pippa was starting to wilt again. He didn't want her dropping before he could finish.

"Then tell me what it is. How you use it."

"See, that's exactly . . ." She slid her grip along the counter's edge, leaving a long, red smear. "There's more than one type. Each one is different. I use the world's magic. What's around me.

I just . . ." She gestured aimlessly with her other hand. "I help it along. But there's another type with herbs and powders, mixing things and creating magic from that."

"Like the demon in the alley."

A flash of what looked like regret crossed Pippa's face. "Yeah. Like that. And there's another one with speech, or singing. Music, sometimes. Speaking things into being. And . . . one uses the magic in . . . people."

The way she looked at him quickly, gauging his reaction only to dart away, made him wonder how much of that last type she was leaving out.

Pippa's short speech seemed to have exhausted her, and he felt a little guilty for pressing. But he was almost done, and he didn't enjoy the idea of closing a wound on her if she was unconscious.

One stitch away from the end, Pippa exhaled heavily and slumped against the countertop.

"Hey," Maxim said, pinching her knee until she started and opened her eyes. "I need you to stay awake. Tell me more."

"About . . . what?"

"Magic exists, and demons. What about werewolves? They real?"

"Nah. No one turns into a . . . a big, hairy dog thing with teeth. Or if they do, they don't tell me about it."

"What else? Zombies? Ghosts? Mummies?"

"Are you just going through costumes you saw last Halloween?"

"Of course not. I haven't asked you if sexy pirates exist, have I?"

"True." Some of the pain had left her face, and she was smiling. A tiny smile, barely there, but he counted it as improvement.

"What about vampires?"

"Oh yeah, definitely. Dated a few, actually."

As he knotted the string and snipped off the extra, Maxim sent her an unamused look beneath his eyebrows.

She showed no sign that she'd been joking.

"You dated vampires?" Maxim said, baffled. "But they're evil. They're demons. Killers."

Pippa rolled her eyes. "I'm sure every one of your hook-ups has been well-thought-out and free of regrets."

He pinched his lips together. "Are you implying I fuck murderers?"

"No," she said slowly, "I'm implying that you might have fucked someone who made a few bad choices in their past."

"No one I've slept with has killed people."

"That you know of."

Maxim exhaled sharply. "I'd like to think I have higher standards than that." As soon as he spoke, he cursed himself for how rude he'd sounded.

"Oh, you can take your judgmental attitude and shove it," Pippa said, her posture stiffening and her skin flushing. "They're not as monstrous as you think. Don't look at me like that. I'm serious." She grabbed a washcloth from a neat stack by the sink and scrubbed at her hands. "Everyone makes mistakes, and if you live several lifetimes, you've just made that many more and have that much longer to feel guilty about them."

"Ah," Maxim said. Not the most eloquent way to express both understanding and contrition, and since he couldn't bring himself to say, "I'm sorry for assuming bloodsucking monsters aren't as bad as they sound," he settled for something else.

"So what are they like, if they're not monstrous?"

Pippa threw the washcloth into a corner. "Arrogant as fuck." A low laugh rolled out of her. "Imagine having two hundred years of confidence with no reflection to deflate it." She shook her head. "Exhausting."

"Wow. I feel betrayed by the media."

"'Sexy' sells better than 'douchebag,' I guess."

He set the needle on the counter and grabbed a washcloth from the pile. The hot water knob squeaked as he turned it.

If Pippa wondered why he felt the need to wipe off her leg, she didn't say anything, and just watched him run the cloth over her skin. He didn't remember the last time he'd bathed someone; it was distractingly intimate, even with the coppery bite of blood in the air strong enough in the air to taste at the back of his mouth. Maybe this was part of him repaying her. Maybe he needed to apologize for judging her previous partners. Maybe he just wanted to do it.

Caretaking, one therapist had said to him years ago, was tending to another person in order to make yourself feel better. He needed that right now. Yesterday, he'd discovered that demons were real and more horrible than he'd ever expected; today, he discovered that some of them were dateable. If gaining some sense of control and comfort over his life meant that he processed recent events with bare legs and a damp washcloth, then fine, sure, better that than some of his previous forms of self-soothing.

Maxim could hear Pippa's soft breathing over his head and the light drip of the faucet he hadn't completely turned off. Her sweater's wide neck dipped down in a shallow "V" and had shifted to one side. He found himself staring at the smooth skin along her collarbones, the gentle curve of her shoulder. As the washcloth skimmed her hip, the air grew warm against his neck.

It was pure insanity to become aroused in a moment like this, so instead of veering down that path, he began to talk.

"I had an ex who was really into them," he said.

"Into what?"

"Vampires."

"Ah."

"I mean, not the real ones. The fictional kind. Had hundreds of books on the shelf, every vampire movie, more than one *Queen of the Damned* shirt."

Pippa huffed a laugh. "She sounds fun."

"He," Maxim corrected.

"Oh, uh, sorry. I didn't— Sorry. I didn't mean to assume your . . . hrm."

She'd gone bright pink and was worrying her bottom lip, staring at the towel rack behind Maxim as if it had begun a fascinating conversation.

Her embarrassment was intriguing, so much so that he didn't want to leave the bathroom with her thinking he wasn't interested in her. That she wasn't his type.

It came upon Maxim suddenly that, yes, he was indeed very interested in Pippa Beverly. She was a mystery wrapped in a slouchy sweater; an intriguing bundle of frizzy hair, pretty lips, stubbornness, and the power to char him into oblivion. And fuck, the combination was just . . .

Hot.

"You could always ask me," he said in a low murmur.

Pippa caught his gaze and swallowed, the sound audible over the rasp of the washcloth. "So who do you, uh . . . go for?"

He could have spoken then about how long it had taken him to realize who he was attracted to, how strange it had felt to be the only one in his friend group who'd had a crush on both the Prom Queen and the Homecoming King. He could have spoken about how great New York had been for that—in a city so large and diverse, no one ever questioned who he went home with, not even the old woman who lived in the apartment next to his. She smelled like cats and mothballs and would give each of his dates an approving nod after asking, *"They being nice to you?"*

He didn't want to explain; he wanted to continue flirting. He wanted to stretch this moment with the washcloth lingering on her skin and her pulse a barely visible flutter at the hollow of her neck.

So instead, Maxim didn't bother to hold back his smirk as he said, "I go for humans."

"Wow." Pippa scoffed. "You fuck a few vampires and suddenly everyone's a critic."

Maxim tried not to analyze her expression too much. She looked pleased, though. Maybe a bit relieved.

"They're demons, aren't they?" he said.

Her look turned mischievous. "Yeah, but they're great at oral."

Maxim choked. "Sounds like a scene from a horror movie." Without rising from his position by her knees, he tossed the washcloth into the sink, then snapped off the gloves.

"No, no," she said, holding up a finger. "See, if they've been around long enough to learn the restraint to not drain your blood, that means they've been around long enough to get really good at giving head."

Maxim forced out a considering "Hm," instantly aware of how close he was to Pippa. His throat felt much too tight. He tugged at his tie only to remember he'd already loosened it. Oh, it was really quite wrong of him to imagine something or someone giving Pippa oral. How would she respond? What did she like? He gathered those thoughts close before they could fully unfurl.

Pippa snickered, and for a panicked second, he wondered if she had the ability to read his mind.

"Something funny?" he said in a calm voice he entirely didn't feel.

"*Queen of the Damned*," she said. "I just got that."

He laughed, more out of relief than humor.

Then Pippa's smile fell, her eyes widened, and she gasped. In pain? In shock? Maxim couldn't tell. Her hands fell to her sides as if all the strength had been sapped from them.

"What's wrong?" Had he fucked up the stitching? Was her leg becoming infected? Could that even happen so quickly? "What can I—"

Her whisper cut through his question.

"*It's back.*"

Seven

THE ENTIRE TIME THE magic-blocking walls surrounded Pippa, she had assumed they would dissolve slowly, like a trickle of water worrying away at a crack in limestone. Little by little, she would feel the world return.

Instead, one moment she was focusing on how the magic was off in the distance—hard to parse, but still there—and the next, the walls crumbled and the world crashed over her in a brutal surge.

Pippa gasped at the suddenness of it. She felt the sparkling pressure of the air, the low rumble of magic at her fingers and below her feet. Alive and vibrant, tangible enough that she could reach out and snatch handfuls of it if she wanted. And there as well was the reassuring nudge of Maxim's entirely human aura: comfort and spice and warmth.

She slumped forward onto him, surrounding herself with that aura, her forehead pressed tight against the curve where his neck met the broad sweep of his shoulder. The collar of his shirt had managed to retain some of its starch, and the sharp corner of the fabric tickled her nose. Harsh scruff along the edge of his jaw scraped along the curve of her ear.

Waves of magic rolled over her, bubbling up through her limbs and clustering around the wound in her thigh. As it battled whatever poison remained, the sharp, fiery pain of healing eased.

Pippa gripped Maxim's shoulders as if she could keep herself anchored by the warm, firm feel of him. The smell of his skin invaded her senses. Heated ginger, sour sweat, the earthy and deep blend that Pippa had begun to recognize as his. He sucked in a breath, and she felt it in the rise of his shoulders and the expansion of his rib cage, felt it in the squirming aura that grew even warmer.

With her senses amplified, with the smells and the feel and the nearness of him, it shouldn't have been a shock when arousal followed. It was a general sort of arousal, Pippa decided, and not because of the man she was slumped on. She slid her clutching hands from his shoulders down to a set of quite solid upper arms, and, all right, she could concede that he was a part of it.

A sound plucked at her awareness: high and pleasured, like it had come from a private browser tab she'd forgotten to close on her phone.

Oh, wait. That had been her. *She* had moaned.

Maxim's swallow was as loud as a thunderclap and just as startling.

Mortified, Pippa froze. Against her forehead, his neck grew hot. She cleared her throat, muttered "Sorry," and straightened without meeting his eyes.

"What just happened?" Maxim's voice held a tight edge to it, and it emerged a little more graveled than before. "What's back?"

Oh. She'd been so distracted by the magic returning, and then the ecstatic feeling of the magic returning, she hadn't realized how truly bizarre the whole scene would have appeared to him. Was she dying? Warning him of an upcoming attack? In the midst of a masochistic, pain-fueled orgasm? All three?

"The, um, the magic is back," she said. "It took me by surprise."

"So you can . . ." Maxim gestured at her thigh, and when Pippa glanced down, she realized her sensible skirt had ridden up all the way to her waist and her floral underwear were wholly revealed.

She let loose an internal scream. "Yeah, yep, yep," she said, and made awkward wiggling movements to start pulling the hem down her thighs.

Maxim cleared his throat and stared at the floor to his side, attempting to give her some form of privacy. As if she hadn't just lasciviously moaned on him a few seconds earlier.

"Is it working yet?" he said.

She assumed he had meant the magic, and when she replied in the affirmative, his attention snapped back to her thigh as if he couldn't help himself.

The sight was undoubtedly strange to someone unused to it. Even though the wound was smaller than it had been before the stitches, and it wasn't close to the size of the wound she had healed on Maxim yesterday, she could see flesh wriggling and reforming beneath the little lines of thread.

Pippa tugged her skirt's hem down to cover it. Stars, she had slumped onto him and moaned while her crotch was on display, and the only thing making it slightly all right was that he appeared to be just as startled by the whole situation as she was.

And that he seemed more interested in her healing wound than her displayed crotch.

So why was she a little disappointed?

"How are you feel—"

"When did—"

Pippa wasn't sure what form of magic made it so that, when two people sat in uncomfortable silence for any length of time, they always seemed to find the exact same moment to begin talking.

"I'm fine," she said, answering his interrupted question.

He leaned back and settled on his heels. It couldn't have been a comfortable position in those shining black shoes, which looked stiffer than she'd assumed his personality to be. Stoic and proud Maxim Sheppard, with as much personality and flexibility as patent leather Oxfords. Then he had gone and shown joy and worry and excitement and an unexpected softness completely perpendicular to the man she'd worked alongside for the past few months.

Maybe Maxim just needed a little breaking in before he became comfortable.

Pippa realized he had asked her another question and in answer, she had simply stared at one of the buttons on his shirt.

"Mmwhat?" she said.

Maxim set his hands on his hips and exhaled a small snort. "I'm baffled, really."

"Why, because I ignored your question?"

Now he crossed his arms over his chest, covering the button she'd focused on earlier. The rolled-up sleeves look was creating warm tingles low in Pippa's stomach, and although she'd been appreciative of the style before (because, come on, it implied the wearer was about to get into something *dirty*) it just really fit Maxim. Possibly because the rolled-up sleeves had allowed her to watch the flex and strain of his forearms as he'd stitched her leg.

That train of thought led to some mental acrobatics as she fought the urge to picture him naked. He'd been meticulous, considerate, and dexterous about pushing a needle into her skin.

There were parallels. Definite parallels.

Maxim sighed. The once-white shirt stretched tight over his shoulders, and Pippa tore her gaze away from the forming creases.

"I didn't ask you a question," he said.

"Then what—"

"I said, 'No, you can't possibly be fine, I don't believe you,' to which you responded by staring through me for a solid minute."

Pippa shifted on the toilet seat and winced when her thigh stuck to the warmed plastic. "I've had a hard day."

"I know!" Maxim said, exasperated. "I know that! So I want to know, are you all right? Are you going to be all right? Are you just tired, or are you going to collapse in a second from blood loss and infection, and . . . and, I don't know, just be lying on the ground half-dead if something with fangs and horns barges in through the front door?"

He was worried. It was as startling as it was confusing, until Pippa remembered how he'd whisked her out of the office and demanded a hospital. There was something in her head that continued to rail against the idea that he could be capable of empathy. Despite the concern he had demonstrated just today, the concept of him kept springing back to "Taciturn Dick" like it was made out of memory foam. But he was here. Concerned. Worried. Alarmingly endearing.

"I'm okay," she said, surprising herself with how gently it emerged. "Really."

Maxim's jaw twitched, and he tapped a finger against his bicep. Pippa was losing track of how many nervous tics the man had.

"I am." She caught herself reaching out to lay her hand over his to stop the fidgeting and instead redirected her movement to brush some invisible grime off her knee. "But, yeah. I'm tired. I have to direct the magic. I can't just relax and let it work, I have to channel it. Guide it. It's almost done though, and I'll be all better soon. Tomorrow it'll be impossible to tell I was hurt at all."

"Tomorrow." He tapped his finger faster. "And until then?"

"The apartment's warded. Nothing can get in."

"Was the office warded?"

"No." She should probably fix that at some point. Nothing had ever tried to attack her at work before; warding the building hadn't seemed necessary.

Maxim was silent for a moment, though the continued twitch in his jaw and the near incessant tap of his finger implied his thoughts were far from quiet.

"Do you want me to stay tonight?"

The question caught Pippa off guard. Not for the thoughtfulness of it, or the furthering of the whole "break him in like a shoe" metaphor, but for the images it conjured. Sleep-rumpled and sockless, he would sprawl his long body across her couch, an arm flung over his head and his face smashed into a decorative pillow. Or he'd join her in her bed. She would roll over on the mattress and into him, startle him awake, apologize, then get caught up in the feel of him and the smell of him and the taste of him and he would roll over in her bed and into her.

Her body thrummed at the thought of it.

No matter where he slept, she'd make coffee in the morning—the crappy kind, bought from a grocery store and slow-dripped into acidic oblivion—and maybe he'd give her another one of those lovely concerned looks over an old ceramic mug as he asked how she felt.

Like the look he was giving her now.

No, actually, that concerned look was fully due to the fact that she was once more sliding hard into fantasy instead of responding to his question.

It would be so easy to agree. Too easy. Which was why she couldn't accept. Yes, she'd promised him answers; that didn't mean she was all right with him delving deep into every one of the things she'd prefer to keep from someone who had no idea Boe demons didn't have kidneys.

"Why would you want to stay?" she said. "So you can poke through my apartment more? Find out all the things you think I'm keeping from you?"

Maxim frowned at the irritation she couldn't keep out of her voice, even though it was irritation with her own lack of restraint rather than with his proposal.

"You've lost a lot of blood," he said. "You're weak. That's why I offered. Nothing more."

Nothing more. Pippa mentally shook off the sting from that. "No need to worry about my constitution, Sheppard. I'm—"

"If you say 'I'm fine' one more time, I'll poke through your apartment until my fingers bleed."

It didn't seem conducive to keep reinforcing how she was not nearly close to death, and, if given a few hours to collapse onto a soft surface, would once more be able to legitimately threaten him with a good charring. Which, without a doubt, he'd shrug off and call her out again on the lack of creativity with her threats. It struck her then that his attitude was far too accepting of all of this.

Pippa leaned against the ceramic toilet tank. "The thing I can't quite understand is how fine you are."

He let out a soft snort. "Not the best compliment I've received, but thank you."

"No, you're . . ." She tried again, despite the flustered heat wrapping her throat. "You should be babbling. Panicked. Driven halfway insane from everything you've seen today and yesterday. You should be afraid of me. But you're not."

The muscle in his cheek jumped. She wondered (for a brief, confusing moment) how coarse his stubble would be on her lips if she was ever able to kiss that tic.

"I was," Maxim murmured, as if speaking to himself. "At first, I definitely was. A little afraid of you. Terrified of the rest. Magic. Demons. Monsters." He blinked several times, then stood and went over to the sink to wash his hands. "Then I guess the excitement won."

"Being able to fight evil, you mean."

"Sure. Maybe." He rinsed the lather off and grabbed a clean towel. "At the very least, getting beaten up by evil."

"Oh, I'm excellent at that part."

Maxim smirked at Pippa's thigh. "Yeah, I figured."

"I'll settle for having you be a little afraid of me."

"I was a little afraid. Past tense."

Pippa looked at him askance. "What changed?"

He rolled the towel around as if he could find an answer in the terrycloth. "I realized that you felt good."

She lifted a brow. "Not the best compliment I've ever received."

Maxim gave a low, short laugh, like it had been startled out of him. "I mean . . ." He lobbed the towel into the same corner as his ruined jacket. "I don't know anything about any of this." He made a broad gesture at what seemed to be the entire world, then sighed and leaned his hip against the counter. "But evil should make your stomach squirm, right? Or make the hair stand up on the back of your neck. All the cliches. It should feel bad. It should make you want to get away from it. Fight it, even."

He paused.

Pippa swiveled on the seat to face him. Her knee dug into the sharp wooden corner of the vanity, yet she ignored it in favor of her intrigue.

"I've never felt like that with you," he said. "Even when you were glaring scimitars at me from across the meeting table. Or when I asked you to print out hundreds of pages of things I ended up not needing, and you called me a bastard under your breath when I walked away."

"I don't remember doing that." She definitely did that, at least twice.

"You felt . . ." Maxim appeared to concentrate, searching for his next word. "Good," he said simply.

Hearing this shouldn't have given her the amount of relief it did. And it really shouldn't have made her want to preen. And it definitely, absolutely should not have tempted her to say the same back to him, because she remembered that yes, he had felt good pressed up against her during the various chaotic awfulness today. All tight and hard and—

"Thank you," she said, her words rushing out before she could fall into more of those thoughts. Then she realized she hadn't shown any appreciation for his hasty doctoring. "And thank you for your help. It looks better than if I'd have done it."

He nodded. "You saved my life. Figured a few stitches was a good place to start repaying you."

They fell into silence. Pippa unstuck her thighs from the seat yet again and struggled to figure out what to say. "Cool, thanks, see ya!" seemed callous; "You want to stay for dinner?" implied she had the energy to cook. Fatigue was settling over her like a blanket, swaddling her brain in cozy fleece.

To Pippa's great relief, Maxim spoke first.

"What will you do next time?"

"Next time?"

"When you lose your magic. When you get stabbed again."

Her relief faded as quickly as it had come. "I'll make sure to avoid running into knives."

"And if they run into you? Going to magic yourself an exoskeleton?"

"I can't do that."

Maxim pushed off the counter, his jaw working.

She didn't wait for him to continue. "When did I get stabbed?"

He frowned. "What?"

"What time? Do you remember how long ago it was?"

His nostrils flared in a frustrated huff, then he looked at his wrist in the universal gesture of someone who had forgotten to wear their watch. He shook his head. "Forty-five minutes?"

Well that was reassuring. Not that Pippa planned on getting poisoned ever again.

"See? That's not long to be magic-less."

"It doesn't take very long to be murdered."

"I'll take a self-defense class or something. I saw a sign for a place that gives a two-for-one discount on demon fighting."

Maxim inhaled sharply through his nose, like someone would do before putting forth an idea that scared them, then said, "I can help you."

Pippa scoffed.

"If you want. I mean it," he added to her continued skepticism. "I used to teach a few classes at my old gym."

"Self-defense against demons?"

"Self-defense, a little Krav Maga, some Muay Thai."

Pippa's laugh burst out of her. It was just so . . . excessive. "Gotta defend yourself against those New York lawyers any way you can."

"That's not—" He gave a short, low growl of irritation. "I'm offering to help."

"Why do you even care?"

For such a simple question, Pippa marveled at how effectively it made him look as if he'd been punched in the stomach. He should have a lot of experience with that, considering his extracurriculars. Yet she saw a bolt of panic in his expression, and when she thought of their conversations, his actions, his reactions, she stiffened in realization.

"Oh, I get it," she said. "This is how you endear yourself to me. How you dig your way into this life so you can get your rocks off living in a fantasy world."

Hell, of course this was why he was here. Bitterness twisted Pippa's chest into a tight knot. But this world was hers. It was who she was, how she'd lived. It wasn't something she got to choose for excitement.

"I'm not trying to 'get my rocks off'," Maxim snapped. "Whatever thrills I got from today were equally tempered by the horror of it." He gestured at her leg. "The blood of it." His sigh was so deep that it strained the topmost button of his shirt. "But this is . . . This could be how I can make a difference. If I can help . . . I don't know, the city? The world? If I can help you, then maybe I'll—" He cut himself off with a firm press of his lips.

How would he complete that? Finally be happy? Finally feel useful?

She thought of their conversation in the alley, before the panic and the demon and the flames.

"Do you know what it's like to want to make a difference?" Maxim had said then.

Guilt writhed in Pippa's chest. She sighed. "All right."

"Yeah?"

She tried not to let his excitement affect her decision. "Yeah. Sure. Teach me how to punch things."

"It's not just punch—" Maxim stopped himself against what must have been some soap boxy tirade he'd made before. He rubbed his forehead. "Okay. Great. We'll start tomorrow."

"We both have work tomorrow."

"We'll use sick time."

Pippa raised her eyebrows high enough to make her forehead twitch. "Are you suggesting blowing off work? You? The same guy who came into the office after getting dental surgery?"

"It was a crown."

"Half your face was numb. I watched you try and drink your coffee. It was hilarious."

Maxim gave an impatient grunt. "Then after work. I can come over. Or you can come over, or we can meet at a gym."

"I have things to do tomorrow night." Demons didn't handle themselves, after all.

"Saturday, then."

"Saturday." It'd give her time to keep healing, which she would greatly need if she was going to be wrestling with someone the size and weight of Maxim Sheppard.

Before that could lead to another unfortunate mental tangent of slippery skin and grappling bodies, he asked one last time if she was feeling decent enough to be left alone.

Then, with her promise to call if anything happened, which although nice enough of a gesture, was a little hollow, considering the potential circumstances that would necessitate it, he was gone. Pippa's apartment returned to its lovely, quiet state.

Exhaustion fully settled on her. She'd limped with him to the door, mostly to show him that she could move well enough to get around, and she now sagged onto her couch with a groan that would have impressed a bear.

Yet even so, the little kindled interest still flickered low in her belly. She shouldn't be looking forward to Maxim returning to her house. Everything about him, from his shining shoes to his college dreams of dramatic embroidery, proved that she should be sending him on his way instead of inviting him in for more.

Pippa let her head drop onto one of the couch's armrests. She had made a mistake. She had been caught up in the draw of returning a favor, distracted by muscled forearms and tousled hair and the firm grip of nitrile-covered hands on her bare skin.

She had let him in more than she ever expected, and now he was probably looking forward to the hundreds of questions he would ask that, because she'd made a promise when she was bloodied and delirious, she felt obligated to answer.

Pippa took a deep breath against the upholstery, inhaling dust and the lingering aroma of burnt sage from when she'd tried and failed to make herself a hasty dinner last night, back when her biggest problems were a sadly unfinished meal paid for by her employer, a broken car, and a man whose blood took far too long to wash off her hands. So caught up in worries about tow truck costs and how likely it was that Maxim might zip from office to office with the tale of his alley adventure, she hadn't paid attention as she stirred the sauce. When her attention returned to her kitchen, a brown sludge coated the bottom of the pan.

She inhaled the fabric again. Not just sage: burnt garlic, burnt cream, a bitter dash of burnt butter. Truly awful scents, but magnificent for the sole reason that she was alive to smell them. She was here, on her scratchy couch in her lonely apartment instead of existing as a smear at the base of an elevator shaft.

Pippa's phone vibrated from within the front pocket of her sweater. At first relieved it had managed to stay with her during everything, she let loose another sigh. She'd call back whoever it was later. It was probably Jules, asking why she hadn't come back from her coffee break, or her mother, wanting to finish their conversation from yesterday, and Pippa was much too tired to make any meaningful conversation.

But . . . oh *shit,* she'd left the office and then the elevator had practically exploded. If she didn't respond to a text soon, Jules would probably report her missing, or dead.

Pippa fumbled her phone, then brushed aside the notifications of sixteen missed calls and thirty-seven unopened texts.

I'm fine, she sent. *I'm home.* Then for good measure, she added a poop emoji.

She tossed her phone onto the couch cushion and watched the reflection in the screen shift as it wobbled on the edge of a pillow.

Fine. She'd been using that word so many times lately. She turned it over and around in her thoughts as if it were a smooth, heavy pebble she was trying to memorize the feel of.

The more she fiddled with it, the more it rang false.

Her stomach lurched as she realized that, no, she was not fine. Not at all.

She didn't know why it took so long for it to settle. Shock, probably. Wasn't that how it worked? Adrenaline kept her running hard and high until the chaos paused long enough for the brutal truth of what happened to hit her fully.

Her magic had left her. She had always considered it to be immovable, as reliable and constant as her own heartbeat. It was what made her special, powerful. Strong. But it had been taken from her, ripped out of her chest and flung far away, and all that remained was a shell that was brutalized and lost and useless.

A roiling sensation surged up through Pippa's throat and burst out of her as a harsh, racking sob. Tears tracked down her cheeks and she dug her fingernails into the padded armrest.

Don't fail, Pippa.

Be better, Pippa.

The phrases she'd once taken and twisted into inspiration to be stronger, more resilient, now swarmed around her like a flock of vultures—each one stabbed at her and reminded her how close she'd come to that awful, ultimate failure.

What you've done hasn't been enough. You *haven't been enough.*

The memory of the Ash Coven's recent words sunk deep and brought forth another heaving sob. The fabric beneath her face was damp as she pressed her forehead into the armrest.

Then magic brushed her fingertips, nuzzling her like an animal. Though she was exhausted, she pulled it close, taking comfort in the warm, sparkling feel of it. Her breathing steadied and her grip on the armrest relaxed as she floated in the reassurance it provided. Even if she couldn't access it, it would always be around her. It would always be there.

Pippa pushed herself upright and swiped her sleeve over her eyes. Wallowing was easy. She took one last lung-filling breath, stood, and made for the kitchen. She was hungry and filled with a blossoming determination. If she could conquer one thing today, she could at least make it edible.

PIPPA BUNDLED HER JACKET tightly around her shoulders and in-
spected the office building from her place by one of the maple
trees in the parking lot. Evening sun scattered through the fiery
leaves and danced on the concrete. Caution tape fluttered in the
breeze, tickling the boots of construction workers who stomped
through the office building's doors. She had worried herself into
a mostly sleepless night at the thought of returning to her job
only to learn that her worry had been unfounded.

This morning, she'd awoken to several missed calls from her
mother and a text from Jules that had arrived sometime in the
small hours of the night. She had glared at her phone screen over
a bowl of cereal. If she called her mother back, she'd have to tell
her about losing her magic, so she sent a brief text instead.

I'm alive, everything's fine.

Whether her mother believed her or not, that was a problem
for another day. Mary Beverly possessed no power of compulsion
other than the motherly sort, yet Pippa knew the moment that

Mary heard the fatigue in Pippa's voice she would want to talk about what had happened. And Pippa was not nearly comfortable enough with that yet. The knowledge that she could lose her magic meant that she could also lose her potential to become part of the Ash Coven, which meant losing . . .

It meant losing *everything*.

Before she could tumble back into those awful, spiraling thoughts, Pippa had punched Jules's number in.

Upon picking up, Jules's first reaction had been an extended, "What the fuuuuuuck."

"Hey, sorry. I should have—"

"You left your purse and your keys after you said you were going downstairs, and then a few minutes later we were all evacuated and if not for that fucking *poop emoji*, which, *really?* Philippa I would have thought you *died*."

"Kinda wish I had."

"You—" Jules's lecture had lost its inertia. "What do you mean?"

"Got a stomach bug. Like, the kind you can't really . . . go back from?"

"Ohmygod did you shit yourself?"

"Almost. I happened to be staggering out of the bathroom right as Maxim passed, and he offered to give me a ride home."

"That's good of him. I guess. Did you shit in his car?"

"Ew, no, Jules. No one deserves that."

"Some people deserve that. Anyway. Guess the email last night was a welcome surprise, huh?"

"Email?"

Jules had groaned loud enough to hurt Pippa's ear. "How are you so bad at keeping up? I swear. The elevator fucking exploded!"

"What?" Pippa had said. "R-really?"

"Yeah. The whole building was shut down the rest of the day, and the bomb squad was called in. The *bomb squad*. It was so exciting."

Pippa's stomach had dropped. "Did they find anything?"

"Oooh yeah."

At the ensuing conspiratorial chuckle, Pippa felt a cold sweat break out in her armpits.

"Turns out it was a malfunctioning brake line." Jules chuckled again. "Gonna be a huge settlement. Doris Ivanov is so pumped. You know the worst building to install defective safety equipment in?"

"A building full of lawyers?"

"A motherfucking building full of lawyers. Everyone's still working on the paperwork though, and there have to be some other inspections, so the whole place is closed until Monday. Your li'l tum-tum will have plenty of time to get better. You feeling okay now?"

"Mostly." Not a lie.

"Okay. Don't get up to too much trouble this weekend. I'd have you over if you weren't allergic to Bilbo so you could pass out on my couch and I could pamper you."

"Aw, thanks."

"Try and take it easy. Want me to bring you anything? Soup? Porn? Porny soup?"

Pippa had wrinkled her nose. "I hesitate to ask."

"It's just chicken and potato with all the potatoes carved into little boobs. You leave the skin on in tiny circles and that's what makes the nipples."

"Oh, that actually sounds really cute, Jules."

"I'll make some for you. I'll spend all afternoon with a stack of spuds and a paring knife if that'll make you feel better. If I'm feeling creative, I might try and sculpt a few vulvas."

"Ooh, tempting."

"They make the soup extra creamy."

At that, Pippa had snorted so forcefully her sinuses stung for almost a minute afterward.

Upon finishing the conversation, she had decided to go into work anyway and establish the wards she should have put up years ago, yet when she stepped off the bus, the complex had been swarming with day-glo vests and hard hats. A ward wouldn't be too effective if it was interrupted halfway through by a construction worker asking why she was gesturing wildly around the caution tape.

So Pippa had returned home, taken the longest nap of her life, then returned to wait out the workers' day.

The maple's branches creaked above her and she looked up quickly. Just a breeze; just old wood. She toyed with the handle of her spelled knife she'd stashed in her jacket pocket. It had been nearly an hour, and the workers were still carrying beams and rolls of wires and pouring over blueprints laid out on folding tables.

She longed to pull out her phone and continue her search for cars. Public transportation was beginning to chafe after just a few days, though she knew that if she started browsing, she'd get drawn down a hole that ended with staring at vehicles she could hardly afford.

Yet again, Pippa found herself dreaming of a hefty Ash Coven paycheck. There were other covens around the state that operated in a similar fashion to the Ash Coven, where members worked together to fight danger of the sort that would make the local police force shit themselves, but not all covens did so. Her mother was part of a small one that included half a dozen witches and warlocks who branded themselves as master gardeners. Instead of fertilizer and irrigation control, they modified fields with lightweight spells and a few well-placed charms. Growing up, Pippa had a childhood friend whose parents were in a small coven that focused on veterinary studies. The group's battles were with colicky horses and cats that had eaten shoestrings, and those battles were more than enough excitement.

The Ash Coven was old. Some of its members bragged about how some of the founders' names were carved into Revolutionary War memorials. Pippa personally doubted the veracity of some of those claims, but even if the dates were off by a few centuries, the Ash Coven would still be older than all the other covens in the state.

Those smaller covens typically functioned with their members acting as volunteers, but because of the Ash Coven's age and its predilection for taking advantage of the seers who had joined over the decades, its coffers were well-filled. Some might see it as cheating the stocks and illegal trading; Pippa saw it as a way to keep her apartment and avoid late-night bus trips while sleeping in every morning and not having to worry about whose turn it was to wash the dishes in the break room.

Maybe there were jobs outside of the Ash Coven like that, but in Pippa's experience, most of those took one look at her single semester of college and gave her a spiel about how she should "look for something more entry-level."

She'd tried in that single semester. Very hard. Yet night after night, she still had to follow blood trails and track auras and read through obituary pages for suspicious deaths. She would flip through flash cards as she rode the bus home, barely able to keep her eyes open after having fought for her life again. One day, a professor had asked her to visit during office hours and given her a lecture on how it was time to pick what was most important to her. He'd assumed she was out late doing normal college things, of course—drinking, partying, fucking—but his words stuck with her until the end of the semester, when she discovered how easy it really was to drop out.

She just had to learn to content herself with filing papers and sending emails and scrolling through used car websites as she tried to fall asleep.

As the sun flirted with the horizon, vehicles gradually began to filter out of the office complex. Finally, it was almost time.

The last of the construction workers ambled out of the building and locked the doors. He heaved himself into a truck, lit a cigarette, and drove off with music blaring out of his open windows. The blatant blue-collar stereotype was broken only by the boy band pop wafting down the street behind him.

Pippa waited another few minutes to make sure no one else emerged from the building, then hurried across the empty parking lot.

The north point would be the easiest ward to cast, so she did that one first, setting herself up in a patch of pea gravel beside an administrator's window. Magic leaped and flashed as she twisted it high to form a pillar. Tendrils branched wide, spreading and dividing like they were bolts of slow-moving lightning visible only to her. They rippled in the air and pulsed with a soft light.

Pippa let out her held breath. The magic stayed aloft, swaying gently as if it were affected by the same breeze as the caution tape.

She moved to the next spot, lifted her hands, and called the magic. When it rose up and reached out, the tendrils curled around the first ones, knitting themselves together from their highest point all the way to the ground. When that one was done, Pippa braced her hands on her knees and took several ragged gulps of air.

Creating a complete barrier that would keep out everything from the otherworld was difficult—creating a complex barrier that would still permit demons who'd disguised themselves so they could get jobs and afford housing was even more difficult. While manipulating power, she had to simultaneously hold the caveats in her mind: block malicious intent, block carnivorous or murderous appetites; but make an exception for the dread of an upcoming performance review or the irritation at seeing a meme-sharing chain email. During her college stint, she'd taken an intro class on programming and had been struck by how similar coding was to crafting magical barriers. Rules, exceptions, guidelines, and the occasional tension headache.

She straightened, stretched her back, then moved on to the next point, and the next. Each one was slightly more difficult to finish. As she moved around the building, it became harder and harder to lift her arms. Whatever strength she'd regained overnight and from her lazy afternoon and Jules's porny soup seemed to have gone. It was her own fault, really. When she'd healed Maxim in the alley, she had done more than was absolutely necessary. She'd closed his skin and fixed his organs, yet she'd also funneled her own energy into him in order to replace the blood he'd lost. He would have been fine, albeit a bit more pale and lethargic, if she had held back. But she had been so flustered, so terrified, she'd dumped power into him without thinking she might need it later.

Pippa wiped her forehead. She needed a break. A good, solid string of days where her biggest problem could be deciding what dumb show to watch.

Her last ward was at the front of the building. Magic didn't rise up out of the ground as it had earlier, instead feeling like she was tugging on an ornery child who refused to leave bed.

Pippa caught sight of the parking space Maxim's car had been in yesterday. Her thoughts flew backward and suddenly she was wholly consumed by memories. She was staggering across the parking lot, slumped into Maxim, her gut twisting at the absence of magic around her.

The air constricted within Pippa's lungs. Her hands trembled, and the magical pillar she'd been constructing shook itself apart and fell in a shower to the ground.

Her skin crawled. Though she glanced around frantically for any source of discomfort, nothing appeared. She became aware of how alone she was, how dark the sky had become. Long shadows scurried behind trees and along the lit corridor of the main road. The gravity of Pippa's situation struck her: she had been attacked twice in just as many days, first by an admitted hire, then by a demon whose type was known for being mercenaries. Something in the city wanted her dead, and here she was offering herself up to it like she'd crawled onto a platter and shoved an apple into her mouth.

The realization sent a bolt of new, desperate energy through her. She wrenched on the magic and arranged it in a hasty pillar. Where the other wards had lengthened and spread out as if they were lush trees, this one was scrawny and scraggly and shivered like it could be blown down by any strong gust. If not for exhaustion, stress, and the edgy feelings digging into her ribs like spurs, she would have tried again.

Not her best, but it would have to be good enough.

Pippa walked quickly to the doors and wiggled the air around the lock, twisting the latch from the outside. After the click, she slipped inside and into the stairwell, then began to ascend. Her pace was slow at first, more of a trudge, and with heavy reliance on the railing. What would be the point of rushing? It wasn't as if she had to chase her purse, or tackle her fleeing keys.

With every step, the stairwell felt larger. Her steps echoed against metal and concrete and seemed to multiply in the otherwise silent space. It was easy to imagine that she was being followed, the rumbling cascade of thuds precluding sharp fangs or long claws sinking into her skin through her jacket. Despite the fact that no magical auras prickled at her neck, and as far as she could tell, she was the only inhabitant of the entire building, she found her pace quickening. The faster she rattled up the stairs, the faster the echoes followed, and thankfully she reached her floor before she succumbed to the childish impulse to try and outrun her imagination.

Her purse was in the drawer by her computer. As she checked around, making sure she didn't need to grab anything else, she was struck by the eerie state of an office evacuated mid-workday.

Printed pages rested in neat stacks on desks, water bottles sat without their lids, the rest of Geoff's muffin grew more stale and sad and lonely on its little paper plate.

Pippa zipped her purse and left.

She checked the parking lot through the closed doors before sneaking out of them. A flick of magic, and the lock engaged once more.

The air was chilly and invigorating as she sucked it into her lungs. She imagined it flowing deep into her chest, washing away the exhaustion and the stress. She forced her imagination harder and tried to picture the crisp air strengthening her, as if she could build armor out of it and surround herself with power and steel, but as she made her way across the parking lot, all she felt was the cold.

A FEW MINUTES AFTER Pippa stepped onto the bus from the office, her exhaustion returned with force. Although the wound in her leg had closed, the healed muscles throbbed with every step. Wandering around abandoned buildings and fighting demons seemed about as alluring as stubbing her toe on an anvil. But because of the dual blow of her mother's pressure and that damned hypothetical Ash Coven paycheck dangling above her head, she couldn't just go home.

Since she had to do *something*, she decided to visit the university and the succubi who currently preyed there.

The Post-It note in her pocket had a short address given to her by a patron at the local bar: *Stillbrook Apartments, 90B.* The man had been young and already a few drinks deep, and when Pippa bought him a third, he'd told her sadly about a woman with ethereal beauty and a voice that sounded like sex. He'd blushed a little then. The woman had ignored his advances, hence the drinks. But he was hopeful. *Maybe,* he'd said with a dreamy, trance-like smile, *their paths would cross soon.*

Pippa had made a noncommittal "Hm" and bought him a fourth drink.

She stomped up a short flight of concrete stairs then scraped her shoes on a frayed doormat. The lighting was dim around these apartments, and she'd accidentally sunk into a patch of well-disguised mud on her way to the complex. She tightened her jacket around her shoulders, gave her shoes one more scrape, then pushed the doorbell.

An angel opened the door. At least, that's what someone else would have thought. The woman was tall, lithe, and had hair down to her elbows that was so blonde it appeared almost white. Her skin, where it wasn't covered by a short silk robe, was flawless and smooth; her smile was as warm and gentle as if it precluded a heavenly announcement.

But Pippa knew better.

"Huh," she said to the woman in the doorway. "Didn't realize you came back."

The woman leaned against the jamb with the sort of grace typically reserved for ballet. She pursed her wide mouth and raised one perfect eyebrow. "I simply couldn't stay away." Her words held a trace of a French accent, mostly in the consonants that lived in the back of her throat. She shifted. The robe slipped along her bare, smooth thigh. "Am I to be chastised once again?"

Pippa rubbed at her temple with the heel of her hand. "Yep, definitely. Thalia, you can't keep taking advantage of college students. They're dumb. You're a demon."

Thalia gave a grave nod. "Of course."

"So you have to stop it."

"At once." A pause. "Have a drink?"

"Yes, please." Pippa followed the demon inside and tossed her jacket and purse on a hook. At a sharp look from Thalia, she removed her mud-smeared shoes, though it seemed excessive for the state of the apartment. The carpet was stained in the entryway from decades of people ignoring the purpose of a doormat. Where the carpet ended, old linoleum curled up as it met the walls, which were painted a gaudy green that would have caused injury if there had been more light in the room. A young woman lay sprawled on the couch in her underwear, her eyes heavy-lidded and her fingers idly twirling a lock of her hair. She gave Pippa a raised brow.

"Who's this?" she said.

Thalia stood in front of the girl and crossed her arms. "You must go," she said. When she had been speaking to Pippa, her voice was even and lyrical—now Pippa felt threads of power weaving through the air with her words, soft as silk but just as strong.

The girl blinked quickly, glanced around as if in a trance, then dressed and walked out of the apartment.

Thalia sent a pretty frown at the door that had been left open.

Pippa sighed and swung it closed.

"You better not have charmed her to get her here," she said.

Thalia laughed in a clear, ringing melody. "Of course not. This is her apartment."

"You know what I—"

The succubus laughed again, her eyes sparkling. "I am allowed to joke, no? You don't need to worry. I only ever charm them to leave. They become infatuated, you see. I am the . . . the perfection to them. Wise, beautiful, forever beyond their reach."

Pippa slid onto a wobbling bar stool. "The perfection who lives in bad university housing?"

Thalia looked offended. "I do not live here. I told you, this is"—she gestured at the closed door—"her mess. I'd never settle for such a state. I'm shocked you would think so." She sniffed and glided into the kitchen where she pulled bottles out of a cabinet. "There are parties, and I am drawn to them. Tasty, succulent things. Sometimes I become too sated to move on. Sometimes I linger."

The aura surrounding Pippa now was warm and comfortable. Letting herself melt into it felt like she was sliding into a heated, blanketed bed. Pippa relished the sensation for a long minute. She felt . . . nice.

Thalia broke through her luxuriating.

"You are tired," she said.

"Did your succubus powers tell you that?"

"The bags under your eyes did."

Pippa glanced up at Thalia. She was leaning over the counter, propped up on her elbows and giving Pippa the sort of look a kind bartender would give a distressed patron.

"The past few days have been . . ." Oh *stars,* how was she going to finish that sentence?

Awful?

Confusing?

Deeply traumatic yet somehow honestly a little tiny bit nice because I haven't ever had anyone help me like Maxim has?

Pippa settled on a high, noncommittal whine accompanied by a shrug.

Thalia braced her elbows on the counter and placed her chin in her hand. "Ah." Her robe slithered over her skin as if it was made of something too intangible to be fabric. She gave a soft smile. "I'd better make you that drink, then." She shifted her robe into place, then grabbed a few glasses from a cabinet.

Pippa traced a crack on the counter. "Why didn't you tell me you'd come back to New Hawkshead?" The last time she'd seen Thalia over a year ago, the succubus had blown her a kiss from a departing car. Off to grand locations and grander lifestyles, and the anonymity only a huge city could provide.

Thalia paused before setting the glasses on the counter in front of Pippa. Her gaze flicked up and met Pippa's, the pale blue of her eyes seeming sharper than usual.

"Did they accept you?" she said instead of answering Pippa's question.

A weight settled into Pippa's stomach. "No." And then, just like always, she forced herself to add, "Not yet."

When Thalia looked all to the world as if she'd like nothing more than to shake Pippa by her shoulders, Pippa blundered on.

"I'm sure they'd be fine with me seeing you, though. You don't kill. You feed off orgasm energy. It's nothing like the type they worry about. You leave people sated and mildly hungover. I'm sure they—"

"Would still see me as a demon," Thalia finished. She pursed her lips. "Ash Coven members don't interact with demons. You might become . . ." She sniffed. "Biased."

"Is that why you didn't reach out to me? Because you don't approve of me?"

Thalia let out a frustrated sigh. "I rarely approve of what you want to do with your life. That doesn't mean I would ever disapprove of *you*. I . . . I would not want to get in the way."

Pippa reached out and grabbed Thalia's hands, then looked right into those pale blue eyes. "I will always want you to get in my way."

Thalia gave a very inelegant snort. "I will hold you to that, Philippa Beverly." Despite her air of nonchalance, she gave Pippa's hands a firm squeeze that lasted long enough to count as a hug, then began to pour liquor into the glasses. "So. The past few days . . ." She trailed off, then gave Pippa an expectant glance.

Pippa waved a hand. "I fought and killed a Tro'grath in a warehouse, then the next day got ambushed in an alley by a demon who I'd previously been on good terms with because apparently he'd gotten paid in, I don't know, diamonds. Killed him, but this guy I work with was also in the alley—"

"To try and kill you?"

"No, because he was pouting after not getting a promotion."

"Ah." Thalia swirled one glass, sniffed it, then added a dash from another bottle.

"Anyway, the guy got hit and I healed him, but he'd seen everything, so I had to threaten him, but the next day he kept hounding me for answers, because he's really into fantasy and magic and the fake idea of it all. But then we got attacked in the elevator by a Boe demon, and I got stabbed."

She briefly wondered if she should tell Thalia about the poison and temporarily losing her magic. Yet it still felt too fresh, too raw. Somehow, the very fact that it had happened remained coated in the stink of failure. The thought of telling Thalia made her stomach twist in embarrassment.

Thalia slammed the bottle onto the counter. "You were *stabbed*?"

"Just a little," Pippa said defensively. "Anyway, there was this whole thing with the elevator—"

"A 'whole thing'?"

"I'd accidentally blown out the brakes so we had to get out before it crashed—"

Thalia exhaled sharply.

"—then the guy and I went back to my apartment and he helped stitch up my leg."

The succubus rubbed one temple and gave Pippa a look of such exasperation that it must have pulled a muscle. "After you were stabbed. In a crashing elevator. Does he have medical training?"

Pippa ignored this. "He's a good person. More than I thought. He really wants to help, and even though he puts off this initial attitude of being a total asshole, he's actually kind of nice to be around. It's surprising."

Even more surprising was that she was looking forward to being around him again. Being *near* him again. A little flare of excitement crept up her neck when she remembered that he would be at her apartment by this time tomorrow.

Thalia laughed softly. "He is making you blush."

Pippa blinked. "I have no idea what you mean."

"I'm intrigued by who makes you feel like this." Thalia leaned forward. "Is he a warlock? A demon?"

"A human."

"Oh." The leaden disappointment in Thalia's voice could have sunk a barge. She shrugged in a trying-not-to-judge-friends sort of way. "At the very least, I'm relieved he's not another vampire."

"I've grown out of that phase."

"And we are all grateful. Have you fucked your human yet?"

No preamble, no segue.

Pippa did not want to think about fucking Maxim, even though her thoughts threatened to pounce in that direction like an excitable creature. His hands, his warm skin, the scrape of his jawline over . . . *No.* He was coming over tomorrow, and she couldn't think these sorts of things.

"And look," Thalia said with a devious smirk. "Now you drift away into fantasy at his mention. You must tell me something. It has been too long since I have felt such a sensation, and I wish to live vicariously through you."

Pippa cleared her throat and opted for a diversion. "Maybe you'd feel that way again if you stopped trying to seduce co-eds."

Thalia laughed, low and throaty. "Perhaps. I keep waiting for you to bring me someone of interest, Pippin, but you never do."

Pippa put her head in her hands and groaned. "How is that my nickname?"

"Because you are short, no? Like the curly-haired creatures in the books on your shelf."

For a brief second, Pippa wondered what would happen if she put Thalia and Jules in the same room. It might be funny for a few minutes, what with Jules's ensuing horror at barely landed culture references and Thalia's discomfort at inappropriate, prying questions about whether or not demons really did have forked tongues and how beneficial they were for cunnilingus.

Whatever amusement Pippa felt at the thought of them together crumbled in the wake of realizing that, no, Jules should absolutely not know about this world. She should not know about demons, and magic, and creatures that lurked in the cold, quiet places of her nightmares.

Though Thalia had no way of seeing what was in Pippa's thoughts, her wry smile hinted that at the very least, she knew the tortuous path they were taking. She didn't comment, and poured one last splash of alcohol into both glasses.

Thalia began to hum. Her lips parted around a delicate melody, and Pippa watched, transfixed, as the succubus swept her hands over the glasses. Long fingers stroked the air as if she were caressing bits of invisible cloth. She'd once pretended to be a fortune-teller, traveling with a circus through Rome and luring patrons into her tent with promises of futures told and past lives reawakened. It was all fake of course, since she didn't have that kind of magic, but the patrons didn't need to know that.

The way her hands moved, even when she'd demonstrated her act, had always reminded Pippa of weaving. Where Pippa pulled magic from her surroundings, Thalia took tendrils of it and stroked them into the shapes she wished.

Pippa blinked rapidly and looked away from Thalia's hands when she set them flat on the counter. She continued to sing, and rolled her shoulders beneath her slip of a robe, her eyes half-closed. Then she shook herself and magic dusted off her body and cascaded to the ground like powder.

With her façade shrugged off, Thalia became taller. Her shoulders beneath her robe were more angular, her fingernails closer to claws. When she tipped her head back and sighed, her smile held eyeteeth that were much sharper than they'd been before.

Her hair was the same white blonde, but her pale, flawless skin was now a striking red. Not bright, like the crimson of Jules's favorite lipstick, but a deeper red. A gentler red. It was the color of pomegranate seeds, of ripe cherries, of something full and heady and delicious. A blunt-tipped tail the same shade as her skin snaked out from the hem of her robe and twisted in the air as if stretching after a long confinement.

Pippa raised the glass to her lips and took a sip, then moaned. Was there bourbon in this? She hadn't been paying attention as the succubus had poured. The drink was so beautifully mixed that she could hardly taste the alcohol. Pippa gulped down half of it in an attempt to discern what had gone into her glass. Spicy, sweet, as smooth as the silk of Thalia's robe.

The taste lingered on Pippa's tongue. She closed her eyes, the robe's hem sticking in her vision. She could imagine it gliding nearly frictionless between her fingers. Where Thalia's robe was pale, Maxim's tie yesterday was a geometric clash of varying shades of navy. Not as soft to the touch, surely. She could almost feel that as well, how the patterns would rub her palm if she tugged on it. How it would crease and fold as she pulled him close enough for his warm breath to puff against her neck, and the tip of it would tickle her bare stomach.

Suddenly Pippa was shifting on her seat to try and ease a powerful ache that had manifested between her legs. Her breath shuddered out of her as if she were being squeezed.

She opened her eyes to see Thalia watching her with an excited smile. The succubus propped her red chin in both hands, and her tongue traced one of her sharp canines.

Pippa sent a glare at her drained glass. *Just . . . wow.* Classic succubus. She was probably getting a buzz off the lust radiating from Pippa right now.

"Rude," she said. "Charming my drink? *Really?* Because I haven't had enough to deal—" She broke off when Thalia lay a cool hand over hers.

"It was to help you," Thalia said softly. "You look exhausted, Pippin. It's strength. It's . . . nourishment. I thought you could use that more than alcohol."

If she focused, Pippa could tell that her head felt clearer, her limbs less heavy. Guilt washed over her at how she'd snapped at the friend whose only harm was in caring.

"So yes," Thalia continued. "A little bit of a charm." Then her smile returned. "Though your arousal is all your own."

Pippa tried not to look startled. She made a little "Hmm," and rolled her glass between her palms. Ice cubes clinked and swirled with the amber drink as they melted.

When she'd wanted to throw herself on Maxim yesterday, she'd been shot full of adrenaline and the exuberance for living that came with bumping shoulders with death. Having an attractive, attentive person practically between her legs had lifted that exuberance into full-blown arousal.

Now?

She had no similar excuse for fantasizing about him. There had been nothing threatening her in this apartment; the only nearby danger was a succubus with a commitment problem. Which meant that the reason she couldn't stop thinking about his crooked nose, his pursed lips, his rolled-up sleeves, and his flexing forearms was because she wanted him.

She wanted him.

Pippa sagged onto the counter, her knuckles pressed against her forehead. It wasn't a convenient realization. She'd already come to a tenuous acceptance of him learning a few more details about her world, and that was uncomfortable enough. She should be continually terrified of any additional knowledge he gained that might render him a panicked, broken mess instead of wondering what else might make his stern expression crack. How his breathing might catch, how his lips might part around filthy words she'd hardly dared to imagine coming from his mouth. How his gaze might settle on her differently if it raked down her naked body. Would his intensity remain then?

Heat crept up Pippa's chest and settled in a low pulse in her neck. It wasn't a leap to assume that his borderline dominating assertiveness might translate to fucking.

Before she could wonder any more about the potential lovemaking styles of Maxim Sheppard, Thalia chuckled. It wasn't the chuckle itself that wrenched Pippa out of her fantasies, but the thick, satisfied cast to it.

"Stop," Pippa said.

"Stop what?"

"Enjoying this."

Thalia kept smiling. "You offered me a free appetizer, it would be rude of me to not take it."

"I don't know why we're friends." Her skin still flamed from her thoughts, and she pressed her chilled glass to her neck.

"Because I make you nice things to drink."

"Ha," Pippa said wryly.

Thalia plucked Pippa's glass out of her hands and took it to the sink. She paused after setting it in the basin.

"I'm glad you came, considering," Thalia said.

"Considering how I'm flagrantly disobeying the group I want to be part of, or considering the rumors of my hellish few days?"

"Considering how your life is in danger."

"When is it not?"

The seriousness of Thalia's expression sent a chill down Pippa's neck. "Pippa, this is—"

"This is different? Is that what you were going to say?"

Beneath the silken robe, her red tail twitched like that of an irritated cat. "I didn't tell you before, but I already knew about the Tro'grath. The fight in the warehouse."

Pippa's hands grew cold. "What? How?"

Thalia sighed and crossed her arms over her chest. "There has been talk. Gossip. The one you killed was a prince, of sorts, from a highborn family new to the city. They didn't know all of our rules yet, or the Ash Coven's power over the city."

"And? I'm sure the rest of that family knows now."

"They do not appreciate witches ending the lines of their royalty."

"And that would be awful, if they knew it was me who'd done that." If any creatures had come to the empty warehouse after she'd left, all they would find was some scattered ash.

Thalia's tail lashed. "When a highborn Tro'grath comes of age, they have stones placed in their foreheads. The colors vary, I hear, depending on the family."

Ah, so that must have been what her mother had been trying to tell her. "All right, so I'll keep an eye out for others that have those and make sure I don't—"

"They are scrying stones, Pippa. Any Tro'grath in that family saw exactly who murdered their favorite offspring."

Her heart plummeted into her shoes.

They will see. They will come for you.

The demon's final words echoed in Pippa's head, raspy and snarled.

Stars. Charles's mysterious patrons, the Boe's presence in her workplace—all because she'd killed a demon with a powerful family.

"There's more," Thalia said.

Pippa let out a warbling laugh. "Of course there is."

"Word is going around that the Tro'grath family is working on something they're claiming will make you helpless. That will take away your magic."

Her mind whirled. It had worked; partly. Had the Tro'graths only known to make the poison to block her from the world's magic because that was what they had seen her use? They wouldn't spend time taking away magic that only existed in rumors. Why bother creating a poison to suppress what might as well not exist?

Pippa clenched the edge of the counter until a piece of chipped Formica dug into her palms. She needed to find the Tro'grath family and end them before they hired anyone else.

She inhaled slowly and gave Thalia a reassuring smile, since the succubus was watching Pippa like someone would watch a bottle of spirits at the edge of a fire.

"I'll figure it out," she said at last. "It'll take more than a handful of vengeful demons to finish me off."

Thalia didn't look convinced. "And what if this is what it takes? When will you find out your limit, Pippa?"

"At the same time everyone else does, I guess."

She glanced at the clock above the stove. It was getting late, and she still had a long journey of public transportation ahead of her.

"Thanks for the drink," she said honestly, then stood. Thalia's magic held fast; her legs were more stable than they'd been when she had arrived, and her feet hurt far less. The ache in her thigh was a foggy memory of what it had been before.

"Of course." Thalia was still looking at her as if she expected either an outburst or a breakdown and didn't know what to make of this forced cheer.

Pippa grabbed her coat and purse and slipped on her shoes.

"I'll let you know if I hear anything else," Thalia said. She'd reapplied her glamour and was once again the angelic-looking woman in a silk gown. "Be safe, please."

In response, Pippa gave Thalia a little salute before she left. Better that than a promise she likely would never be able to keep.

Nine

Despite Maxim's research, which amounted to roughly three hours of typing various iterations of "magic," "demon," and "witch" into multiple search engines, he was only eighty-percent sure he hadn't imagined the entire situation the previous day. If there was magic, actual *magic*, wouldn't someone have blogged about it? Wouldn't there be morsels of true information sprinkled among the aesthetically pleasing moodboards of candles and script-filled books? Surely if murderous, terrifying demons really existed, there would be some mention of them outside the context of late-night TV adaptations.

Maxim shifted his grip on the crinkling donut bag and the cardboard tray of coffee as he walked up the stairs to Pippa's apartment. They had originally agreed to meet in the morning, yet Pippa had struck his phone with one delay after another: she had to finish a few things; she had to take a trip to the store; she just needed to clean up a bit, since there was still blood in the bathroom.

Now it was late afternoon, and Maxim held a bag of stale donut holes and a tray of coffee that had been reheated in the microwave half a dozen times.

Pippa opened the door before he finished knocking.

"Hi." She said it in the voice of someone trying to be cavalier and failing. The *i* in her greeting didn't so much end as fade into nonexistence. She must have showered recently: her hair curled around her shoulders in dark ringlets. The collar of her loose T-shirt was damp, as if she'd pulled it on without fully drying off.

A droplet she'd missed glimmered at the crux of the shirt's low V, and Maxim fought the urge to catch it with the tip of his finger.

"I brought things," Maxim said lamely, after realizing he'd been standing in her open door without speaking. He lifted the coffee and bag in demonstration.

"Oh, you didn't have to—" She gave him a brief smile. "Thank you."

"The store was all out of frog hearts and demon brains, so I had to improvise."

Pippa wrinkled her nose. "Funny." She stepped aside and gestured for him to come in.

As he walked past her, he caught the scent of peaches. It was stronger now, lingering on her skin from the product she'd only just used, and there was a note of something tart as well. Apple, maybe. Or lemon. And beneath that, a sweet, heady smell that could only have been her.

He remembered the hints of those scents yesterday, and how they'd mingled with the acrid copper of her blood as he'd knelt before her in the bathroom.

"How are you feeling?" he said, turning to watch as she cast a roving look around the apartment complex then ducked inside and locked the door.

"Hmm?" She blinked at him.

"Your leg. And . . ." He gestured at her with the donut bag. "All of you, I suppose."

Pippa shrugged. "A little in shock, honestly."

He was about to commiserate and say that he felt exactly the same when he saw her lips twitch into a smirk.

"How so?" he said instead.

"I've never seen you in casual clothing." She gave his jeans, T-shirt, and unzipped hoodie an obvious once-over. "I figured when your suit got dirty, you just molted and grew a new one. Like a cicada."

"Keep bleeding on me, then. One of the new exteriors might have wings."

"Sounds like an incentive."

Maxim snorted. "When I'm redesigning my business card to 'Maxim Sheppard, Lawyer of the Skies,' I'll make sure to have you credited."

"Good. I take ten percent." A low chuckle rolled out of her, hearty enough to cause her shirt to shift over her chest.

Maxim kept his line of sight glued to her earlobe so he wasn't tempted to appreciate the thin fabric or her neck or the smooth, bare skin made visible by the deep cut of her shirt.

"It's a deal," he said.

Staring at her earlobe, he barely caught the flick of her eyes as her gaze traversed down his body, then snapped back up. He did catch her flush though, and the quick flash of her teeth as she caught her lower lip.

Pippa cleared her throat and spun toward the kitchen. "Want something to drink?" Her voice was pitched higher than before.

He followed her. She was barefoot, her pink-painted toes sinking into the plush carpeting, and she was wearing a pair of dark joggers that were loose around the thigh but tight on her hips and calves. He was staring. No, he was full-on ogling. *God,* what was wrong with him?

"I brought coffee," he said, "but I'm not sure if it's good anymore. I've microwaved it so many times that it might be sludge. I haven't checked."

"Sorry about that. I didn't mean to be out for so long."

"You're a busy witch," Maxim said. "I get it."

"No, I . . ." She faced him. "There were some things I needed to do. Leads to follow."

"Leads for what?"

Pippa shook her head. "It's not important."

He knew their arrangement was not the sort that lent itself to permanence. Maxim's position in her life—the demon-filled, magical, exploding, knife-y part of her life—was not that of a collaborator. Yet he still wondered how nice it might be for her to trust him, if she ever decided to do so.

He set his offerings on the counter. The narrow kitchen made up for its size with tall cabinets. Considering Pippa's height, he was surprised she didn't keep a stool handy at all times.

"I was being serious earlier, when I asked how you were," he said.

"I'm all right." The coffee was indeed rather sludgy as Pippa poured the contents of one paper cup into a mug. She frowned at it, gave Maxim an apologetic grimace, and poured the contents into the sink. "I'll buy next time."

"I don't care about the coffee. Does your leg still hurt?"

She rubbed at the spot on her thigh absentmindedly, then snatched her hand away. "A little. Barely." Her sigh stretched her shirt across her breasts and Maxim twisted to look at the crumpled paper bag of donuts.

"Are the stitches making it worse?"

Pippa shook her head. "I already took them out. Felt a lot better than they did going in."

A powerful sense of curiosity struck Maxim. "Can I see it? If that's not too weird." At her look of surprise, he continued. "Just to make sure I didn't fuck up the stitching too badly." It was almost entirely the truth. A great deal of his reasoning was that he wanted to see how the magical healing had concluded, and only a fraction was because he wanted to see her thigh again.

"Sure," Pippa said. She went over to her little table and sat in a chair, and as she began to wiggle the elastic cuff up her shin, Maxim sat in the chair next to her and chewed on his cheek. The cuff barely made it to her knee. She huffed in frustration.

"These are tighter than . . ." she muttered.

"You don't have to show me," Maxim said, suddenly embarrassed at the real risk of her breaking the seams on her pants to satisfy his prying. "I'm being nosy. It doesn't matter that much."

"No, no," she said, "you saved my life. You have every right to be nosy." She drummed her fingers on the table as if in thought.

"I don't know if that really means—"

Pippa stood and started undoing the ties at her waist.

"Uh, I— You—" Words rose up and lodged in Maxim's throat. Before he could attempt to say "Don't drop trou on my account, really," her pants slid over her hips and pooled around her ankles.

Pippa sat back down and shrugged. "I was basically like this in the bathroom yesterday," she said. "Same thing."

This was simultaneously the same and exactly the opposite. Yes, her thighs were bare, her legs fully uncovered, her underwear (navy blue without the scalloped hem that was on yesterday's pair) fully visible. Just like yesterday.

And yet so very unlike yesterday, Maxim was not panicked. Pippa's blood wasn't smeared over his nitrile-covered fingers. When he breathed deeply, the smells invading his lungs now were those of bitter coffee, burnt sage, and peaches. Calming smells. Grounding smells. No overwhelming punch of dread pummeled the pit of his stomach. He didn't have to force his hands steady out of worry he'd hurt her more.

No, he had to force his hands steady for an entirely different reason.

Pippa swallowed audibly. "Anyway. Um. Here." She pushed at her thigh and the thin, pale scar with her thumb. If she hadn't pointed it out, Maxim wasn't sure he would have known it was there. He realized he was leaning forward to see it better, and even reaching out, about to touch her. He drew his hand back and glanced up at Pippa.

"Do you mind if I . . ."

"That's fine." She huffed a short, breathy laugh. "Happened in the bathroom yesterday, too."

Wrong. When he touched her thigh now, there was no barrier enclosing his fingertips. He felt the barest ridge of the scar, yes, but he could also feel the warmth of her body and how her soft skin prickled into goosebumps.

The wound looked like an injury that had healed years ago. There were none of the deep ridges or valleys that adorned his own mangled stomach, yet as he pressed into her skin slightly, he felt a stiff seam of scar tissue. As someone who had been injured frequently over the years, he had a fair amount of experience with such things. Without thinking, he began to push harder in an attempt to knead out some of the stiffness.

Pippa inhaled sharply.

Maxim stopped at once. Even though he hated to do so, he snapped his hands to his sides.

"Sorry," he said. "Did that hurt?"

"Not— No. Um. A little. Maybe." She looked almost as flustered as when she'd moaned against his neck.

A very inopportune time to remember that. Maxim cleared his throat and straightened, pressing his spine into the chair slats and letting the dull edge of the wood bring his mind back to where it needed to be.

"It helps to massage it," he said. "To break up the scar tissue. Make it heal better. Hurt less."

Pippa arched an eyebrow at him as she wiggled the waistband of her pants over her hips. "So now you're a lawyer masseuse?"

"Soon to be a flying lawyer masseuse." He reined in his disappointment at her rapidly disappearing bare skin.

"Ah. Shame on me, I'd already forgotten." Her fingers were nimble as she drew the ties into a quick bow. "Well. Satisfied with what you saw?"

Yes. He absolutely liked what he'd seen. And he wanted to see more. God help him, he wanted to see her waist, her navel, the contours of her stomach, the dimple where her thigh met her pelvis.

"It's fainter than I thought," he said when he managed to wrangle these intrusive thoughts into submission. "I hope mine will fade like that."

Such was the force of Pippa's ensuing frown that a line formed not only between her eyebrows, but also in her chin.

"How bad does it look?" she said. Her eyes flicked to his, and in them, Maxim saw concern.

"Uh," he said, startled by this development. He'd of course seen her concerned before: when Juliette Cohen had shown up late to work after a car accident, looking paler than a sheet of copy paper; when Geoff Davis told the office he was leaving early to take care of his ailing dog; when the communal creamer had a note stuck to it stating, "Use with CAUTION."

The only time that look had been aimed at him he'd been bleeding copiously over the concrete. Since that was his only personal association with such an expression on Pippa Beverly's heart-shaped face, he resisted the impulse to check himself for a mortal injury.

"It's not horrible," he answered finally. "Just a bit—"

"Can I see?"

Their knees brushed as Pippa shuffled to the edge of her chair and leaned forward.

Maxim couldn't possibly say no, not when she was looking at him like that. He leaned backward and lifted the hem of his shirt over his stomach.

The warm light of Pippa's home gave the scar a certain realness that it lacked when he'd stood in front of his own mirror, as if part of him had hoped it was only a trick of the light in his apartment.

Pippa let out a distressed hum.

"That bad?" Maxim forced lightness into the question.

She scooted her chair closer to his, then leaned in and began to feel his stomach with all the professionalism of a dermatologist. Her fingers were warm and firm as she manipulated his skin.

"I didn't realize I'd left it this prominent," she said to his midsection. "I can make it less—"

Pippa broke off when she caught his expression. His desperate attempt to remain stoic and not at all aroused by how gravity tugged on the collar of her shirt and revealed the generous swells of her breasts must have come across as something darker.

She sat upright, pulling both hands to her lap. "I'm sorry," she blurted. "That was rude of me to just start groping you. I should have asked."

"Don't apologize. I was caught off guard." He gestured to his stomach. "Grope away."

Fucking hell. Maxim squeezed his eyes shut and gnawed on his cheek. Genius. Brilliant. Smooth as a goddamn kidney stone. But he took some small bit of comfort that when he opened his eyes, Pippa was biting her lip and staring at the button of his jeans. Then she blinked rapidly and seemed to collect herself.

"You're sure?" she said, even though she'd already started to reach out once more.

"Of course. What's a bit of scar palpating between consenting adults?"

Her laugh tickled the trail of dark hairs that led down from his navel. Then she was touching him again, and it took most of Maxim's concentration not to let his thoughts travel anywhere untoward.

God, she was close. Her nearness made his lungs hitch and his heart rattle into his sternum. He gripped the chair so tightly he was surprised the wood didn't creak. Despite all they'd been through together over the past two days, and despite the various states of undress in which they'd seen each other, nothing had been equivalent to a flirtation. One could not flirt while running for one's life.

So his fantasies of her hands traveling either up his chest or down into his jeans were ludicrous and awful and unbearably inconsiderate.

Yet Pippa's professionalism of earlier was gone. Where before she had prodded him as if he were a particularly interesting thing she'd found in a drawer, now she was letting her touch linger. It was slower, softer. She swept the pad of one finger down the ridge in the center of his abdominals, and even though the angle was not ideal for viewing it, he was sure she'd drawn her lower lip into her mouth.

Then Pippa started. An embarrassed flush spread over her chest and up her neck. "I'll help it along," she said quickly. "Make it lighter. Here."

She pressed her palm over the wide scar and as her brow furrowed in concentration, a stinging warmth bloomed in his stomach.

Maxim remembered how she'd healed him in the alley, and how close she'd looked to collapse right after.

"Pippa, wait." He rested his hand over hers and curled his fingers around her palm, pulling it gently away from his body. His shirt hem fell back into place, and the sensations ceased in an instant. "You don't need to do that."

She looked startled by his objection. "But—"

"Don't exhaust yourself for the sake of my own vanity."

As she looked him over like he was a riddle to solve, he realized he was still holding her hand. And even more, she made no move to withdraw.

Maxim found himself wondering what it would be like to suck her oft-bitten lower lip into his mouth and bite it himself. His fingers tingled with the urge to brush her wrist or the inside of her elbow and feel her pulse flutter. As he held her small, warm hand within his, the full force of that desire expanded outward with so much force he felt breathless.

"Are you sure?" she asked.

A second of confusion passed as Maxim mentally backtracked their conversation, then said, "I'm perfectly capable of making up creative and inaccurate stories to impress people." He'd simply meant to give her hand a light squeeze to reinforce his sentiments. But he found that his fingers slipped easily along the creases of her palm.

Her lips parted, and her gaze drifted down to his mouth.

"Oh?" Her monosyllabic question encouraged him further.

The inside of her wrist felt softer than anything he deserved to touch. He ran his thumb along the strong tendons, feeling the quick throb of her heartbeat.

"It could have come from a shark," he murmured. What was he doing? "Or a wannabe mugger." He'd come here to talk with Pippa, not try and seduce her. "Saving kittens."

Her eyes were darker when she looked at him. Perhaps his desire wasn't completely one-sided. He could lean forward, close the distance between them, feel her. All of her.

"Things seem to keep wanting to kill you, so you need all the strength you have already."

As soon as he said it, Pippa tensed, and the moment shattered like it was made out of ice. She stood with a swiftness that jerked her hand from his.

Maxim inwardly cursed. They'd been having a lovely moment that seemed like it was the kind to lead up to something, and he put his foot in his mouth and said . . . what? The truth? It wasn't a far-reaching truth, either. In two days, two separate monsters had tried to murder her. How was he being rude for pointing that out?

"I'll get you something to drink," she said quickly as she pulled a glass out of a cabinet. "I have some iced tea. Or I can mix up lemonade."

"Water's good." Fine, if she was going to pretend nothing had happened between them just then, so would he. What better time to start his questioning?

"So how do you fit in?"

In the process of filling the glass at the sink, she sent him a curious glance. "What do you mean?"

"The city. The . . . witch . . . uh, clubs. Are there clubs?"

"No." Pippa smacked the tap off and brought the glass over. "There are covens. I suppose they're club-like. There are benefits to being part of them. It gives you a sense of place. But you have to be accepted into one."

"Which one are you in?"

"None. Yet." Pippa plucked a mug out of the dish drain. "It's a work in progress," she muttered, then opened another cabinet and stood on her toes to peer at a shelf a good three feet above her head.

Right as Maxim was about to offer the assistance of his longer reach, she made a pulling motion with one hand and a tea box flew out of the cabinet and into her grasp.

It was strange—he could easily discuss magic with her, yet seeing her use it in front of him still felt as thrilling as the entire concept of it existing in the first place.

"What about brooms?" he asked. "What's the reality, ordinary housekeeping implements or mode of transportation?" He knew how dumb the question sounded. Her expression made him feel dumber for asking it. "A familiar, then. Have one of those?"

It was as if the question had been a demon itself for Pippa's reaction to it. She flinched, and the cardboard box tumbled out of her hands onto the kitchen floor. A fumbling grab prevented the mug from joining it and crashing over her bare feet.

Normally, Maxim would be spiraling into self-deprecating discomfort at having said so many inappropriate things, but now, he had literally no idea what he'd said that had apparently been so troubling. He remained standing and folded his arms over his chest.

"When you promised to answer my questions, I didn't expect to pick every one you hated answering," he said.

Pippa snatched the box from the floor and set it on a counter with the mug. "It's not—" She broke off and glared at the sink.

"What aren't you telling me?"

She bit down on her lip as if coming to some determination. Then she sniffed, turned to him, and mirrored his crossed arms. "I didn't plan on you knowing any of this."

Then why did you promise to share? he thought irritably. "I won't force you to tell me."

"No, you asked." She leaned her hip against the counter.

Maxim had the sudden impression that she was nervous about something. Her fingers drummed her upper arm in the same way he used to when he'd wanted to hide shaky hands, and her large inhalations were just like the ones he took when trying to slow a galloping heartbeat.

"I told you about the types of magic," she said. At Maxim's nod, she went on. "Natural, which is channeling the magic in the world. Chemical, with mixing powders, herbs. The sort that needs cauldrons. There's verbal, which uses spellbooks and words. Music, too, sometimes. The last one is called Reaper magic. Witches use it to control souls. Bodies."

"Sounds metal." Maxim went over her list in his head. *Verbal, somatic, necromantic.*

"It's not."

He pulled himself out of a lofty fantasy of writing a tell-all book titled "What Gygax Knew" to see a look of distress on Pippa's face. She seemed to be gathering her words, her courage, or both, so he let her move forward at her own pace.

"Reaper magic is . . ." She sighed and tugged on a lock of her hair. "It's manipulation of something that already has a will. The local covens don't look kindly on it. The one I'd like to be part of *really* doesn't look kindly on it."

"Is it dark magic?"

"What?"

"The evil stuff."

Pippa didn't comment on his brilliant word choice. She gave him a wry smile. "Any magic can be evil, depending on how it's used."

"You should put that on a mug."

She snorted.

"What does any of this have to do with familiars?"

Pippa turned so her back was against the counter, her profile to Maxim. At this angle, her overbite was more pronounced, the intense worrying of her lower lip more apparent. "Everyone has a soul. When we die, they go into a . . . a void. We return to the playground of the universe, I guess, if the universe has a cosmically infinite ball pit. A familiar is made when someone with Reaper magic pulls a soul out of that void, that space, and forces it into an animal."

Very metal. He didn't say that out loud, of course, because the entire concept was settling on him in a way that made his skin crawl. He'd always thought of death as permanent. Was it better or worse to discover that it wasn't quite so?

"I learned I had Reaper magic when I was eight. A bird had been hit by a car along the road outside our house. I ran out to it. In that moment, the magic in me understood what to do more than I did. I didn't realize what had happened, only that before, the bird was dead, and after I touched on this power, it was hopping around again. I'd only used Natural magic, and this was something wonderful and new. I was excited. Happy. Until the bird opened its beak and screamed."

"Jesus." Maxim tried to imagine how he would have responded to something like that as a child. Shit himself and cry, probably. "So this coven won't let you in because of something you did when you were eight? That sounds overly harsh. Why do you need to be part of this group?"

"Because they're influential," Pippa said. There was an edge to her voice that prevented it from sounding fully disheartened. "They have connections and funding, and every coven member gets a salary more than what a college dropout can easily find."

"Seems like they could overlook a childhood mistake."

Pippa swallowed harshly and reached for the tea box. Even from as far away as he was, Maxim could see the unsteadiness of her fingers as she ripped open a packet.

"Reaper magic is passed down through bloodlines. My father's was . . . powerful. He did some very bad things. To the city. To its people. It doesn't matter if I haven't used that magic since I was a child, the fact that I have it at all is enough reason for the Ash Coven to make my application process"—she sucked in a breath and sent him a pained smile—"difficult."

She was speaking more steadily. Maxim could easily imagine that these words had been bottled up inside her for longer than they should have been, and once released, each one came more easily than the one before.

"Shit. I'm sorry." Maxim took a breath. Then another. "When I was a child, I had terrible anxiety."

Out of the corner of his eye, he saw Pippa pause her tea preparation and turn to listen to him.

"I had panic attacks almost every day. No one was sure why. My upbringing was entirely ordinary, loving, and happy. But still, I'd slip into states where my palms would sweat and my stomach would churn until I vomited. I was bullied for it. Badly. Which then made the anxiety worse. That's how I got this." He rubbed a finger along his crooked nose. "The strongest kids in the grade cornered me on the playground. I hid the break well enough that when my parents noticed, it had already set."

He risked a glance at Pippa. She was looking at him intently, and even a little guiltily. No pity, though. He didn't think he'd be able to handle pity.

"That must have been terrible," she said quietly.

He faced her. "I know how it feels to have a part of you that you don't like. You feel that it could be better, should be better. But it's still you. It's who you are."

"Sounds like a nice way to think." There was a morsel of wistfulness in the way she said it. "Thank you, though. For telling me."

Maxim tipped his head at her in a way that played at light-heartedness. "Always happy to trauma bond."

She laughed. "Thank you for not fleeing, either."

"From what, tales of necromancy? Please. I've faced worse. Imaginary, of course. But worse."

Her smile didn't fade. "Is that why you learned so many ways to punch?"

"Yeah. It felt good to have a hobby that could help me protect myself. There's only so much damage you can do with a foam sword."

Confusion flashed across Pippa's face, but Maxim didn't feel like stories of the time he'd dabbled in LARPing would fit the atmosphere of her apartment. It seemed almost callous to follow up tales of woe with his own attempts at adventure.

"What about you?" he said.

Pippa had filled her mug with water and was holding her hand over the rim. "What about me what?"

"There must be something frivolous you like to do when you're not saving the city."

"A hobby?" She chuckled. "I like to cook."

"Because feeding yourself is truly the most frivolous hobby of them all."

Pippa rolled her eyes, then gestured to her crooked bookshelf. "I'm starting a collection of cookbooks. There are a few old ones, some I've bought off demons."

Maxim quickly reeled his thoughts back from wondering if *Eaten Right By the Duke* was in fact a cookbook. "From demons? Are you serious?"

"Some of them have really phenomenal ways to use butter. And their spice blends? Incredible."

Maxim chuffed a laugh. "Any favorites so far?"

Pippa circled her hand over the mug and pursed her lips in concentration. Maxim watched, fascinated, as the water in her mug began to steam beneath her palm.

"You wouldn't be able to pronounce it," she said at last. "There's a lot of gargling sounds in the languade. I'm pretty sure it's because their recipes are mostly cheese. The phlegm, you know." She gestured to her throat. "But I could make it for you sometime. If you'd like."

"I do have a hard time saying no to cheese."

When Pippa smiled at him, he was startled by the lightness in it. Her posture was more relaxed than it had been only a few minutes ago. The change entranced him. He wasn't sure if he'd seen this attitude on her before. He definitely hadn't ever seen the mischievous cast to her expression, the sort that put a dimple in her cheek and a glow to her skin.

Maxim stared. He had to. He stared at the steaming mug she took in both hands and lifted to her nose and at the gentle purse of her lips as she blew. The wanting within him filled his chest so swiftly and fiercely that he almost expected to explode.

Her eyes connected with his over the rim of her cup. Just for a moment, he wondered if she could sense the shape of his thoughts, and just for a moment, he wasn't sure if that would be so bad.

Under the weight of his staring, Pippa glanced down at her cup.

"Sure you don't want any tea?"

HE WAS STILL AT Pippa's table, a fact which left her with a curious mix of relief and suspicion.

The entire time she'd spoken of the magic that had haunted her entire life, she expected Maxim to turn around and exit through the door as fast as possible. If she were the one who had just learned about magic and was in the home of someone who openly admitted they were capable of necromancy, she would have run. Probably screaming. Definitely without looking back.

But Maxim stayed. He stayed, and he even fucking commiserated. In response to her opening up about the thing that most frequently kept her awake at night, he'd given her something of his own.

It all begged the question: *Why?*

They barely knew each other. Could a few days of conversation and danger really transform him from someone who could barely tolerate her presence into someone who cared what anguish she'd experienced as a child?

Maxim had sipped his water, and as he continued to ask questions, Pippa filled the glass as soon as it emptied so she'd have something to distract her from wandering thoughts of Maxim's recently exposed midsection as well as the feelings of attraction she'd discovered last night. Feelings which were rapidly strengthening under the bright wattage of camaraderie.

At least his other questions weren't as startling as the ones he'd already asked.

Are all demons evil?

Do we work with any?

Is Reggie Cavatappi one?

He seemed to accept the reality of demons having as much moral ambiguity as anything else in a world that spoke, lied, and cheated. If hatred could be in the little bodies of childhood playmates, then perhaps it wasn't a great leap to think that friendship could be in something with horns and a tail.

Maxim lifted his glass and paused before it reached his lips. His gaze was aimed at the water, but it was distant enough for Pippa to tell that his attention was elsewhere.

She took advantage of his distraction to look at him, taking in the creases in his forehead that had been etched into his skin from the intense frowning she'd grown used to over the past few months. The crinkles beside his eyes were shallower, as were the lines bracketing his mouth. Signs of a face more used to displeasure than joy. The long, crooked line of his nose as well as the little bump on the bridge sent a twinge to her chest when she thought of how she once assumed the old break had been from *him* bullying others.

Pippa could straighten it if he wanted, but she somehow knew he wouldn't take her up on the offer.

In grade school, her dentist had remarked on her overbite and suggested wildly expensive orthodontia. When Pippa had returned home with her mother, Mary had given her a consoling side hug.

"Don't worry," she'd said. "I can fix that with magic."

By the time Pippa realized her mother had been lying, she hadn't cared enough to fix it herself, especially since "fixing" would require intensive anatomical research and some very careful bone fracturing. She'd grown used to her body and considered its imperfections as the pieces of herself over which she could genuinely take ownership.

As Pippa looked at Maxim's crooked nose and late-day stubble, the creases in his forehead, the nearly invisible white scar in one of his earlobes from what could only have been a regretted piercing, the mangled patch on his stomach now covered by soft cotton, she saw someone who might believe the same thing.

She sipped her tea. It had cooled to room temperature, and she choked a little on the unexpected tang.

Maxim blinked rapidly several times, brought back by her noise, then drained his glass.

As Pippa reached for it, he held up a hand. "I'm good. Actually need to get rid of some. Mind if I . . ." He jerked a thumb in the direction of her bathroom and stood.

She fought a cringe. "Oh yes, um, of course." At least he was hydrated, thanks to her desperate attempts at busying herself.

The moment the bathroom door closed behind him, Pippa slumped in her chair. She scrubbed her face with both hands. *Fuck*, she could still feel him. The hearty spice of his aura hovered in the air around her, thrumming along her skin as if it were a tangible thing. His presence managed to overwhelm her even though he was across her apartment.

Pippa glowered at her cold tea, then grabbed the mug roughly and circled one hand over the top. Magic vibrated against her palm and the water began to swirl. This was one of the easiest and earliest tricks she'd learned. A bit of heat and a bit of patience. Far quicker than a kettle.

She had spent most of the day checking out possible locations of the Tro'grath lair. She even returned to the warehouse district and the courtyard to see if she could sense any lingering traces of the aura she'd followed before, but so many days had passed that the demon's trail was as faint as pollen.

By the late afternoon, she'd narrowed down her list to a few sewer branches and picked one at random. She'd climbed down a few feet, not wanting to completely ruin her shoes, yet the auras she felt had been benign ones: some rats, a raccoon, a bored ghost looking for entrances to old buildings.

When she'd arrived home after her sewer expedition, she'd felt the faintest hint of an aura hovering around her apartment. Not the thorns and grease of the Tro'grath; this one left a taste like burned steel at the back of her throat. It wasn't strong, and it wasn't that of a demon that was still close by, but it lingered in the air as if its owner had circled her home several hours earlier. She'd sensed it again after she opened the door to let Maxim in.

Pippa glanced at the empty chair and worried her lower lip. Despite all of his questions, she hadn't told him about the Tro'grath and the whole issue with the accidentally-on-purpose killed prince.

It would be a terrible idea. She'd known the man for four months and really only *known* him for a few days, yet she was certain that if she told him about any of her problems, he'd want to stick around to help her solve them. It was a thoughtful enough gesture for a broken modem or a clogged drain, but a horrible one for a hit put out by a murderous demon family.

Pippa rolled her shoulders and stretched her neck, then shook out the hand she held above her cold tea. A blend of irritation and worry had been building within her all day, tightening muscles she didn't know could cramp.

If only you knew a lawyer masseuse.

She took a slow, steadying breath, trying not to dwell on the memory of the firm pressure of his fingers on her thigh and how that strong touch might feel rubbing away every bit of her tension. The tea was beginning to warm under her hand, and gentle steam tickled her palm.

She'd dreamed about him last night. A chaste dream, unfortunately. Although most of it remained foggy, his blue tie and exposed forearms had made a prominent appearance. Neither were present today, and though she'd been a little disappointed at first by his different appearance, the faded sweatshirt and jeans gave him a softer feel. His hair was more relaxed as well, and lacked the expert carefree styling of both comb and product. Today, it was genuinely rumpled and likely wouldn't crunch in her hands if she grasped it. He looked wholly human, and perfectly relatable. This was the guy she could accidentally spill coffee on without worrying about the liquid seeping into his circuits.

The relatable aspect had crumbled when she'd seen him half-shirtless. He had a line—a legitimate *line*—between his abs, and they had been firm beneath her embarrassingly roaming fingers. There was a ridge along his hips as well, the sort Pippa briefly fantasized about tracing with her tongue.

How would Maxim respond if she licked him there? Would he groan? Gasp? Push her away because he was ticklish, or guide her down along the trail of coarse hair that dipped beneath his jeans? She closed her eyes, imagining how it might feel to brush her fingers against that hair. It was several shades darker than the blond on his head, and by the dusting that showed under the raised hem of his shirt, she'd guess it covered his chest as well. She could twine her fingers in it, pull him close. The stubble along his jaw would be a harsh rasp against her cheek and her neck and her breasts and her thighs, and she would grip his hair and hold him right where—

Boiling water splashed out of her mug and stung her palm. Pippa hissed in pain, snatching her hand away and cursing silently.

The bathroom door opened and Pippa urged her breathing to steady as she forced the fantasies from her thoughts.

Maxim had pushed the cuffs of his sleeves to his elbows (damn him), and his hair looked slightly more arranged than it had been earlier. A few dark, damp locks implied he'd used her sink as a styling accessory. Was it for her, or was it for whatever he had planned when he left her apartment? Pippa found her good mood twisting at the thought of him strolling into a bar with friends to chat up someone attractive and unencumbered by the wrong sort of magic. Or any sort of magic.

Maxim came over to his chair, though he didn't sit down.

"I have one last question." He shifted on his feet and shoved his hands into the pockets of his jeans. "I should have asked this earlier, but I . . ." One shoulder lifted briefly in a shrug.

Pippa sat up straighter. A frisson of excitement scurried through her chest at what question was making Maxim embarrassed, and even a little nervous. She wet her lips.

"Can you tell if someone is, I don't know, magical?"

She couldn't help but smile at him. He'd put on the same air of nonchalance as if he'd asked a very personal medical question "for a friend."

"I can," she said. "You can usually tell from an aura. If something is magical, there's a certain edge to it. A harshness."

"And . . . what's mine like?"

Pippa looked at Maxim with the most serious expression she could manage.

"Soup."

"Soup," Maxim repeated with a frown.

Pippa nodded. "It's warm. Kind of herb-y and savory. But there's a little kick of spice to it, like chili peppers."

It feels nice and welcoming and I've never felt another like it. Of course she didn't tell him that. It wasn't what he'd asked.

"There isn't any magic in it, though. You're one-hundred-percent normal."

Maxim gave a small nod. "Ah. I mean, I'd assumed as much, seeing as I'd gone this far in life without floating or burning anything. Still, might as well ask." He chuckled, though Pippa saw right through to the disappointment hidden beneath his forced smile.

How could he not have hoped just a little? If she had spent a life dreaming of magic and then discovered it was real, she too would have wanted to be part of it all.

"You do have power, though."

He glanced at her, eyebrows raised.

"You're very good at brooding."

Maxim's startled laugh came from deep in his chest.

"Looming, too, in case no one has told you so." She bit the inside of her cheek to keep from grinning. "Really. You're an extremely powerful loomer."

He pressed an open hand to his sweater, over his heart. "I'm flattered and honored that you recognize my talents."

Pippa dipped her head, her laugh making ripples dance across her tea. *Stars,* it felt good to just be with him. Just a few days ago, it felt impossible to mildly tease this man and have him *enjoy* it. Laugh at it. Smile at it with creases at the corners of his eyes and lines bracketing his mouth and a twinkle in his gaze that had her feeling like she'd been snagged somewhere beneath her ribs.

Maxim shifted, then rapped his knuckles on his hip. "I should probably head out," he said at last. "It's gotten late."

Pippa glanced out a window. The sky had darkened, and one of the courtyard lights flickered through the open blinds.

"I came over with a promise to help, and all I've done was bother you with incessant questions." He huffed a short laugh.

"They weren't incessant," Pippa said. And not all he'd done, either, but she wasn't about to say how thankful she was for the mutual touching or emotional sharing or even the stomach muscle appreciating.

"There's always next time. I mean, if you want a next time." He flashed her a smile that on anyone else would have been shy. On Maxim, with his rumpled hair, wrinkled sweatshirt, and crooked nose, that expression managed to look embarrassed, hopeful, and sexy.

It was a remarkably unfair attack on Pippa's restraint.

She turned the mug in her hands, and said more to it than to Maxim, "You can stay, if you'd like."

In her head, it had sounded thoughtful, like something a friend would say to another friend when it was late and the first friend worried about the second getting home safely.

Out loud, those innocuous words had emerged as flirty words. Sexy words. She hadn't planned for sexy words. If they had been actual objects, she would have scrabbled to catch them before they could land anywhere. Her armpits began to sweat.

"The couch folds out," she added quickly in a panic, yet when she glanced up at Maxim, she caught the tail end of that familiar, intense look on his face. His lips were parted, his eyes dark.

Then she blinked and it was gone, making her wonder if she'd imagined it had been there at all. He crossed his arms over his chest and one side of his mouth quirked in amusement.

"I thought by now you'd be sick of me," he said.

"It's late," she said defensively. "I don't like the idea of you walking alone outside. Dangerous things about." She did have some reason to worry. There was that strange aura to consider.

If anything were to follow him to his own house, he wouldn't have the benefit of the recently refreshed wards around Pippa's home. Or Pippa herself. She wasn't so proud as to think she could be the one barrier between Maxim living and dying, but she could at least be a speed bump.

As she closed her teeth on her bottom lip and waited for Maxim to speak, she found herself hoping he would say yes. His presence was enjoyable, exciting, and a perfect distraction for the recent stresses. Every little piece of him she discovered hinted at more she had yet to find.

Pippa almost expected Maxim to ask that if she was so worried, why couldn't she just walk him to his car, and was about to rescind the offer when he spoke.

"Sure," he said, with another one of those smiles that Pippa was sure would haunt her for several days.

Pippa lay in her bed and made a very solid attempt not to think about the man sleeping on her couch. She gripped her comforter where it lay over her chest and held still as if the barest movement would shake loose new fantasies or further encourage the temptation to shuffle out of her room and close the distance between herself and Maxim.

They'd ordered delivery for dinner and had eaten it together at the table. Maxim engaged her with small talk, almost as if he'd felt sorry for his earlier barrage of questions. They discussed some of the demon cookbooks on Pippa's shelves, though thankfully he avoided asking about *Eaten Right by the Duke.*

Maxim had helped her set up the fold-out bed. As they'd stretched the sheets over the mattress, Pippa had been struck by the way they'd wordlessly collaborated. It wasn't difficult to anticipate someone else grabbing one end of a blanket and pulling it taut, yet there had been an ease to it that was comforting. The kind of comfort that made her want to ask if he needed anything else before bed, pull him closer by his open sweatshirt, and give him a look that demonstrated exactly what she meant by "anything else."

She hadn't, though.

Instead, Pippa had given him an extra toothbrush, said good-night, and closed herself in her room. She'd heard the floor creak as he walked about the apartment, and each time a creak had sounded nearby, her breath had caught and her pulse raced as she anticipated a soft rap on the door.

Yet her door remained silent, and soon, all of the lights clicked off except for the one by Pippa's nightstand, and then that too went dark.

She didn't know what to do with all of this pining. All of her previous relationships had been shallow, transient things, since her lifestyle didn't exactly make room for brunches with a partner's friends and weekends with his parents. Of course, having dated vampires helped with that, since it was difficult to have a "where is this going" conversation with someone who had lived through the Renaissance. So she'd had flings, and passing dalliances, and a tryst or two. There hadn't been any of this . . . *yearning.*

Yearning was for high school or novels with tattered covers. She was an adult who could create flames and warp the fabric of her surroundings; why couldn't she bring herself to act on her desires?

What does he want from you?

Pippa tightened the grip on her blankets.

That was why.

That single question stopped her from strolling out into her living room, whipping her pajama top over her head, and joining Maxim on the thin, lumpy mattress.

Why had he wanted to stay? He'd said that he wanted his life to mean something, and that he'd wanted to help.

There were better, easier ways to do that, and most of them didn't involve assisting a witch who'd accidentally earned herself a death warrant. He could volunteer at an animal shelter. He could deliver meals. He could take up knitting and make hats for newborn babies.

Pippa flopped onto her side and grumbled into her pillow. If Maxim tried knitting, he'd probably end up with a misshapen cock and balls patterned into that, too. Her laugh came out as a soft snort. It was easy to picture him glancing up from a tangle of genital-shaped thread with a chagrined smile on his face.

It was irritating, truly, how attractive she found him now.

She remembered the thought she'd had several days earlier in the bathroom, and the mental image of Maxim sprawled on the couch returned with vigor. Before, she'd pictured him draped over the cushions with his face mashed into a throw pillow, his button-up shirt wrinkled. Now after having set up the fold-out, he was on the mattress, propping himself up on one arm with a long leg thrown out from beneath a blanket. Shirtless, his hair mussed, the low drape of a blanket teasing the shadows of his hips and pelvis.

A sweet, tight squirm formed low in her stomach. She caught her lower lip between her teeth and bit hard, hoping the flash of pain would lure her attention away from the building tension between her legs.

It didn't work.

The tactile memory of his fingers on her thigh rushed back to her, and her imagination took over, supplanting memory with fantasy and bringing his touch higher and higher until he was running the pad of his thumb along the elastic of her underwear, sliding a finger beneath the cotton.

Pippa caught her moan before it could emerge. Without realizing she'd done so, she'd slipped a hand down the front of her pajama shorts.

She shouldn't.

Not with him in the house. Not with him so close, not with the remote possibility that he might hear.

Desire wriggled beneath her skin and hummed in her ears. Her body felt wired and wildly tense.

Pippa huffed. She would just make sure to be quiet. She pushed her face into the pillow and shoved her fingers beneath her underwear, rubbing her clit with aggressive strokes that soon set her panting. This wouldn't be the type of orgasm to be dragged out until it grew into something bright and agonizingly great. This was just so she could sleep. Nothing more.

She rubbed harder, reached lower, curled two fingers into her pussy and pumped them in as far as she could. Big hands would be better. Thick knuckles, long fingers. He'd fill her until she shuddered beneath him and fell apart around him, until arousal covered his chin and she trembled against the vibration of his groans.

No, she shouldn't be thinking about Maxim as she did this. It was rude, especially with him here.

Pippa squeezed her eyes shut and recalled the last bit of porn she'd watched, where a petite woman was getting railed from behind by a guy who boasted the neck of a quarterback. That worked for a second. But then as her orgasm crept up her spine and cascaded through her limbs, the imagery shifted away from the actors and she climaxed to the thought of Maxim drilling into her as he bent her over the edge of her bed.

Mouth wide, she strangled her cry so all that emerged was a pathetic squeak.

She lay gasping, her sweat prickling along her thighs and behind her ears. In the dark, her hand still in her shorts, the full nature of what she'd just done settled on her like sludge.

What the FUCK.

She had to see him tomorrow. She had to work with him the day after. She had to walk out of her bedroom in the morning, offer him breakfast and bad coffee and the incredibly stale bag of donuts he'd brought and she'd forgotten to do anything with, and look him in the face while having to compartmentalize the fact that she'd gotten herself off to thoughts of him while he was sleeping in her home.

All because she'd been a little turned on.

Pippa grumbled and rolled to her stomach with her face pressed hard into her pillow.

But through the combined haze of her fading orgasm and her self-directed irritation, there was a new feeling.

No, a familiar feeling.

The aura from earlier was back. Pippa sat up, her heart hammering. She wasn't sure how long it had been here, since she'd been so embarrassingly distracted up until this point. She glanced at the drawn drapes that led to her balcony. At the back of her throat, she tasted burned steel and rust.

Nothing could come in through any of the doors or windows—the wards made sure of that. She'd spent hours this morning reinforcing ones that she already considered adequate, and they were currently strong enough to keep out the most determined otherworldly beasts.

Still, she focused on the magic latticed around the blinds and made sure it hadn't changed since her modifications earlier today. It pulsed strong and undamaged, vibrant in hues of green and yellow, twisting around as if it were made of electrified vines.

Nothing can get in, she repeated to herself.

But there was still something there.

Pippa scrambled off the mattress and faced the door. Between Thalia's drink and not having been injured in several consecutive days, her strength had returned fully. Magic swirled in the air around her, warm in her palms, thrumming and impatient for her to channel it.

As she crept toward the balcony, the aura grew stronger. The caustic, acrid tang flooded her sinuses and drew out tears she rapidly blinked away.

She reached out to the drapes with a shaking hand. When she pulled them back, would she see sharp talons, bristling fur, or another being she once thought to be an ally? Her mind conjured a pale, hunched, horned form that stared back at her through the double pane glass door. The aura she'd been feeling wasn't from a Tro'grath, but that didn't stop her from picturing it: milky eyes shining in the balcony light, twitching ears, a gaping fanged grin.

Her heartbeat felt thick in her wrists and neck.

Just open it.

Pippa grabbed one side of the drapes and flung them wide, her body tensed and ready for a fight, the magic blooming in her open hand ready to be hurled out.

Her balcony was empty.

The air stuttered in her lungs. She pressed her nose against the glass, squinting out across the small courtyards and rock-adorned landscaping tinted amber by the apartment complex's lighting. The aura was still there. When she slid the door open, burnt metal crawled over her tongue, but there was nothing in sight except for some bad landscaping and a scruffy rabbit. She stepped onto cold concrete, readying herself for a strike, or a shout, or any movement. Through her balcony's iron railings, she watched the rabbit shake itself and lollop into a sparse bush.

Nothing was here now, yet something had been, and perhaps she could follow it.

Just as she'd done among the warehouses, she closed her eyes, spread her hands, and settled her mind so awareness could follow. A chill breeze danced through the buildings before brushing along her bare skin. A honk sounded from the street, a foghorn bellowed out across the bay. Sirens from speeding ambulances wavered and chirped.

Pippa focused on the sensation of burnt metal until it felt tangible enough to grip, and when she opened her eyes, she saw a dark amber trail crossing between buildings and weaving through miserably stunted trees.

She glanced down, and her throat constricted.

Her balcony was saturated in it.

Whatever had left that aura had been here, right here, right where she was standing. It had lingered for long enough that its presence was smeared across her door frame and the cracks in the concrete. It had stood here, and it had waited.

Her sweaty hands slipped on the railing. Shadows shifted beneath the weak moonlight that fought to get through the clouds. The trail was strong. She could follow it easily. She flung one leg over the iron bar and was shifting her weight to slide over, tensing and preparing to soften the ground for a barefoot landing, when she stopped.

If she followed the trail away from the apartment, Maxim would be alone. He wasn't an infant, or a child, or any sort of person that needed coddling and protecting, but . . . well, all right, he sort of *did* need protecting. She'd had to do so once already. What if she wasn't in the apartment when a demon came again? Would he have enough sense to stay within the wards that guaranteed his safety? Or would he realize she was gone, charge out into the night, and get himself skewered by his own attempt at gallant defense? The idea of leaving a note came to her, followed swiftly by the realization that such a thing would do absolutely nothing to prevent him from following her—most likely, it would only encourage him further.

Maybe if she bound him to the apartment. Physically. Tied him to the fridge, his wrists cinched over his head, a knotted T-shirt as a makeshift gag.

The concept should not at all have sent a flicker of warmth over her skin. The hard ridge of the railing pressed against parts of her body still sensitive from earlier.

Pippa cursed, then wrung the iron railing and clenched her jaw. She didn't need illicit fantasies, not when she was already vibrating with the urge to drop to the ground and race after the thing that had invaded the space she'd considered safe. The flickering trail beckoned with the promise of revenge.

Maybe it beckoned too strongly.

Maybe that was the intention.

This entire situation could have been crafted just to draw her away from her wards so that something could ambush her in a parking lot, overpower her, and stab her with poisoned knives until her only retaliation was a few desperate hurled curses.

Pippa swung around and hopped back onto the cold concrete of her terrace, then slammed her palm on the railing in frustration hard enough for the vibration to rattle her entire arm. If it weren't for Maxim, she'd be sprinting across the complex, hurling magic at whatever thought it could spy on her without retribution.

The breeze picked up and drew forth goosebumps along her chest and arms. She curled her toes, now chilled as well. The aura was fading, the sour tang drifting away into the night.

As the trail dissipated and the air grew cold, Pippa's rationality returned. If it weren't for Maxim, she would have hurled herself over a second-story railing and chased after a mystery demon while wearing nothing but a camisole and a pair of sleep shorts. The demon couldn't have seen into her apartment; her drapes were the heavy, light-blocking sort, and had been pulled fully shut.

This was a lure. It had to be. A teasing, shining bit of distraction that hid the barbed hook beneath.

What waited at the end of the line?

A new chill spread over Pippa's body, this one entirely unrelated to the breeze.

Eleven

THE SHOWER WAS MUCH smaller than the one in Maxim's bathroom, and although he thought it would have made him uncomfortable, there was a certain coziness to the close walls and the fluttering floral shower curtain.

He'd managed to wake up before Pippa. He'd pulled on his jeans and shirt and hovered in the kitchen for a minute, wondering if he should make her breakfast. He was imposing on her home, dirtying her spare sheets, using her soap and her towels and her extra toothbrush. Yet assuming someone's meal preferences held a level of intimacy he wasn't sure she would expect, or even want. First a shower, and if she was awake by the time he emerged, then he'd ask.

Maxim rubbed suds over the back of his neck. The soap smelled like her. The instant the thought came to him, he frowned. Of course it smelled like her. She used it. Next, he'd be astounded by the fact that Pippa had been naked in this same shower. That she'd massaged shampoo into her hair from the cream-colored bottle sitting with a collection of other products in a hanging wire rack.

He suddenly became aware of the water droplets trickling over his skin like gentle fingertips. His eyes fluttered shut and he let himself sink into the bliss of heat and wetness and the slippery glide of his soapy hand over his chest. That bliss spread and tightened and when he glanced down, he was sporting a rather furious erection.

Maxim didn't need this now. He attacked his hair with vigor, as if he could scrub the thought out. He would simply ignore this boner until it went away, and if he had to scour his body with the pumice stone hanging from the spigot until he bled, then he'd do that. Because he couldn't take care of it here. Definitely not here. Not in Pippa's small shower stall where there was the slightest chance he'd get cum on her shower curtain, and where she'd definitely also been naked and wet.

Oh, he was in trouble.

It was far too easy to imagine her in here with him, her small hands splayed on the chipped ceramic tiles, her fingers curling and trembling, breathy moans puffing out of her with the rhythm of his thrusts.

He tipped his head so the water cascaded over his forehead and plastered his hair against his eyebrows, then scrubbed his face with both hands. This wasn't the sort of erection that would be content to drift out of existence after stopping by for a brief visit and then skip off with barely a glance backward. This was the angry, determined sort of erection, and it wasn't going any-where until he addressed it.

Maxim heaved a grumbling, defeated sigh. He lathered the soap, took his cock in hand, and made a valiant attempt to shove any feelings of guilt away. He was taking advantage of Pippa's hospitality and using thoughts of her to get himself off, and it was so goddamn fucking wrong, and he shouldn't be doing it, but he couldn't exactly step out of her bathroom with tented jeans and a raging hard-on and expect to be capable of conversation about what foods she enjoyed in the morning.

Of course, there was always the possibility that she might come in. She might need her toothbrush or an article of clothing out of her laundry bin. He'd hear the door squeak open. She'd say his name. There'd be a throaty edge to it, like she was asking a question she already knew the answer to. When she pulled back the shower curtain, he'd be facing her, cock jutting up proud and ruddy. Maybe his hand would still be wrapped around it so there wouldn't be any doubt about what he was doing before she entered.

Maxim's breath hitched and he stroked himself faster. She'd twist her fingers in his hair, hold on tight as he carried her across the room, then he'd dump her on the counter and fingerfuck her until her pretty lips quivered and her eyes rolled back in her head.

Thankfully, he missed the shower curtain when he came. The tiles were cold against his temple. As soon as the euphoria faded, guilt flooded in quickly.

It doubled when he had to rinse a few drops of his cum from her shampoo bottle.

MAXIM REALLY SHOULD HAVE gone home after that. It would have been the considerate thing to do. He'd just jacked himself off in Pippa Beverly's shower to thoughts of Pippa Beverly, and despite having made her breakfast (and cleaned all of the cookware after he was done), he still felt like he was hovering around the scene of his own crime.

She was quiet over her plate of scrambled eggs. Every time he caught her looking at him, she turned away with a swiftness that made him wonder if she somehow knew what he'd been up to.

"Thanks for this," she said suddenly.

Caught mid-bite, Maxim raised an eyebrow and made an inquisitive "Mmph?"

"The food. It's very good."

He swallowed a bit too much at once and cleared his throat. "The butter takes most of the credit."

"Ah. I'll make sure to thank it too."

"Great, um, good."

What the fuck is happening? The atmosphere at Pippa's table had all the uncomfortable hesitation that followed a one-night-stand, except without any of the tentative intimacy. Or post-coital bliss. After his night on her couch (at her suggestion), he'd assumed she wanted him around for either additional talk or the lessons he'd repeatedly mentioned.

Teaching a witch to punch had sounded reasonable in Maxim's head. Maybe a little fun, too, if he was being honest with himself. There could be surreptitious touches, flirting, that whole "Here, no, like this," bit where he'd stand behind her and position her arms correctly while standing very close. And if she appreciated his help with this, then maybe she'd want his help with more.

Hunched at Pippa's table with his perfect scrambled eggs sitting heavily in his stomach, it appeared as if he had assumed incorrectly.

Pippa hopped up from her seat, grabbed Maxim's empty plate, and brought it to the sink. She was wearing leggings today, and Maxim had to force his attention elsewhere so he wouldn't linger on the parts of her legs that had been hidden by the loose joggers from yesterday.

"I need to head out and take care of some stuff soon," she said.

Maxim looked over at the stiffness in her voice and frowned. "Of course. I don't want to intrude on your day at all."

Pippa blinked. "Oh, no, that's not—" She flicked the water off her fingers and gave him a contrite smile. "I didn't mean it like that. You haven't been intruding."

She was holding herself differently. Despite her smile and the warmth in her words, there seemed to be a tension winding through her body, one that Maxim had only seen when he'd approached her in the office with a task he knew she wouldn't want.

"Are you sure?" he said.

"Yes. It's just, after last night, I really need to—" She broke off suddenly with a startled expression and pinched her lips together, then turned to the sink and busied herself with the sponge.

He stood slowly, unease crawling up his neck. "Last night? What do you mean?" Had he done something wrong? Had he made her uncomfortable by having her basically disrobe in front of him so he could touch her? Had she not actually wanted him to stay the night, and her suggestion had essentially been just an empty offer because it had been the considerate thing to say?

But . . . no. She would have spoken up. He knew Pippa well enough by now. She wasn't the sort of person to make empty offers for the sake of appearance, and she certainly would have threatened him with some sort of magical injury if he'd overstepped in any of his terrible attempts at flirting. And the terrible, horrible, no-good, sweaty, steamy, self-indulgent shower was this morning, and not last night, so she couldn't possibly have been referring to that.

"What's going on, Pippa?" he said.

She paused and stared hard at the dish in her hands before scrubbing viciously. "It's nothing to worry about."

Ah yes, because those words always helped. Usually when someone said them, in that precise order, it meant exactly the opposite.

Pippa caught sight of whatever angst-filled look must have been overtaking Maxim's face. She let out a soft frustrated grunt and tossed the sponge into the basin with a slap. Her shoulders slumped in defeat.

"There was something here last night," she said. "On my balcony."

Well, he hadn't been expecting that answer, but at least it didn't include him.

"What do you mean?" he said. "Like a squirrel? Raccoon?"

"Demon."

His stomach dropped slightly before he remembered their conversation about demons pursuing all the same ventures as humans, and how being demonic wasn't an automatic brand of evil intent. "Why was it on your balcony?"

Pippa sniffed. "I think it was here to kill me."

Maxim's stomach fully dropped this time and chose to settle somewhere by his knees. "*What?*"

"My apartment's warded," she said quickly. "It couldn't get in."

"Why do you think it was here to kill you? And why—" He choked a little. "Wait, did it try to get in? Were you in danger? Were *we* in danger?"

"No," Pippa said, and shook her head quickly enough to set her curls bouncing. "It must have just stood there for a while. Maybe it felt the wards."

How was that better? Maxim's skin crawled at the thought of something lurking beyond Pippa's window, waiting for her to leave her apartment. For her to be distracted enough for one of the wards to lapse. Maybe that wasn't how they worked, but she hadn't exactly been forthcoming with the minutiae, and his context was a decade plus of impractical knowledge about how interrupted concentration affected spell casting.

"Is it still here?" He went to a window, wrenched open the drapes, and glanced out as if he'd be able to catch a demon mid-skulk. The sun shone brightly on the concrete. Birds flitted from one feeder-filled balcony to another. All appeared calm and idyllic.

Pippa came over to him. "It was only here briefly." She tugged the drapes out of his hand and fluttered them shut with a light laugh. "See? Told you. No need to worry."

"It's—" Maxim dragged a hand through his hair and exhaled hard through his nose. "I know I accidentally barged into your life. I know you probably still don't want me to be involved, but I am now, and something like this"—he gestured in the direction he assumed her balcony existed—"is the sort of important knowledge you share with a person who's slept on your couch and knows about demons and your . . . your sorcery!" His tirade ended as an alarmed, shrill whisper.

Pippa set her hands on her hips. "What did you expect me to do? Shake you awake, tell you there'd been a threat outside but it wasn't there anymore, and that's fine, go back to sleep Maxim?"

He pinched the ridge of one eyebrow in an attempt to dislodge the pain blooming there. "The alley, and the elevator, and this. Just tell me why things keep trying to kill you. Is your life always like this?"

"Are you having second thoughts about being part of it?"

No. He thought the answer immediately, but chose to glower at her in response.

Pippa sighed. "A few days ago, I killed a demon that had *connections.*" She said the word as if it were a sinkhole to avoid. "And now its family wants revenge."

"Ah, of course." Maxim flung his arms up in a dramatic shrug. "New Hawkshead wouldn't be complete without a demon mafia."

She gave him a look. "That's what I have to take care of today. I need to find out more. I've been looking for their lair—"

"Of course it's a lair," Maxim muttered.

"—and since they're pretty set on killing me, there's a bit of a time crunch."

He took in the light purple smudges beneath her eyes, the tired tilt to her forced smile. God, he'd been deep in stress dream about rooms filled to their ceilings with paperwork while she'd been wondering if tonight was the night she was going to die.

The awful reality of her situation struck him, and she'd shouldered it all by herself.

"Let me come with you today," he said. "Let me help."

She hesitated, and Maxim could almost see the thoughts swirling within her. And then a sort of clarity descended. Her expression shifted into one of disappointment and hurt, as if she had come to some awful realization.

"And there it is," she said.

"There what is?" Maxim said, utterly baffled at this change.

"Why you're here. Why you stayed. You want in on excitement, and you want my life to be what gets you your sense of meaning. The other day in the bathroom, you convinced me it wasn't your reason for being here, but that's exactly what's going on."

"No. No, that isn't true at all."

"Isn't it?" Pippa's throat worked in a harsh swallow. "You didn't give a fuck about me or my life until you learned I had magic. The moment you started treating me like I was a *person* was the same moment you realized I was more."

"That isn't true," he repeated. But it came to him then that, yes, it had been true. Or at least, it had appeared to be true.

But she thought that . . .

Maxim clenched his fists. He had to fix this.

"No." He stalked toward her. "I treated you as if you were someone who didn't care about what we did in the firm. I took your constant distraction as apathy, and it frustrated me endlessly."

Pippa narrowed her eyes at him. "So you—"

"I'm not finished."

She blinked, and a slight flush crept up her throat at his stern tone.

"Then I learned you had magic, and of *course* it made sense. Why would you give a shit about a law firm if you could . . ." He made a broad gesture that barely mimicked the way she conjured.

They were standing close now, their feet almost touching. Pippa had to tip her head back to look at him. She smelled like her shampoo and the butter from breakfast and the barest cinnamon from her tea. Maxim had to clench his jaw and hope the flash of discomfort would be enough to keep him steady against the urge to move closer until there was no space between them at all.

"Your power is amazing," he said once he'd steadied himself. "I can't lie about that. But even if you had as much magic as this carpet, I'd be thrilled to spend any time with you that wasn't in an office. I've gotten to know you and understand you and *like* you, and if it's taken magic and demons for that to happen, then so be it."

Pippa's "Oh" emerged as a little sigh that warmed the skin of his neck.

"Is that enough of a rebuttal?" he said. "Should I go on?"

"I won't stop you."

Maxim opened his mouth to continue, but noticed the puckish glint in Pippa's dark eyes and the way she was biting her lip to restrain a smile. He'd been about to tell her tender, revelatory things, and it was highly unfair to say "I think about you every night" when she'd hardly revealed a single morsel of what lurked in her own thoughts.

He had the sudden feeling of standing at the edge of something enormous. It would be too easy to give in to worries. Too simple to shrug off the wanting that had burrowed into him if not for the sense that if he took one more step into the unknown and uncertain, perhaps he wouldn't fall alone.

"Why did you really ask me to stay last night?" he said at last.

"I—" Pippa's lips drifted apart. The bottom one shone from when she'd bitten it, the white line from her teeth easing slowly back into pink. A tension grew between her brows as if she were struggling with some decision.

Then her breath hitched. She reached up slowly, almost as if afraid he'd spook, and lay a gentle hand on his chest. Through the thin cotton of his sweatshirt, the warmth of her palm sent sparks skittering along his skin.

Maxim had never thought that a single touch could be an answer in itself. He'd never thought a look could be an entire conversation.

There was hope in her eyes, as well as a cautious uncertainty that had him reaching out in turn to slide his fingertips along her waist until they tangled in her shirt's buttery-soft fabric.

One of them would have to speak at some point, surely. But Pippa's lips were parted and her fingers were curling into his chest and her gaze was fixed on his mouth. On his mouth. *On his—*

Maxim had fucked up a fair amount of everything in his life, but he at least understood this.

He eliminated the distance between them in a single heartbeat. His lips glided against hers as he cupped her nape and gripped her waist. She let out a soft, high moan and pressed herself more firmly into him. The air around Maxim felt alive and hot, and it churned along his limbs like a wild, excited thing.

He swept one hand up into her hair and through her curls—silken and thick between his fingers—then tightened his hold to tip her head and take her mouth harder. He worried for an instant that his enthusiasm would leave bruises, but she was being just as enthusiastic. She nipped at his lower lip, then threw her arms around his neck and pulled him down to her.

His tongue flicked against hers and she let out another one of those sweet moans. Her breasts were crushed into his chest and if not for his damn sweatshirt, then maybe he'd be able to feel more of their weight and warmth.

Pippa gave a little grunt of frustration. Maxim realized she'd been balancing precariously on her toes in order to reach him and was struggling to maintain balance. She was short. He was not.

With a grunt of his own, he lifted her off the ground, pinning her to him with an arm around her waist and another across her back. Too soon to grab her ass. Probably.

Pippa wriggled against him, but before he could wonder if lifting her wasn't what she'd wanted, she wrapped her legs around him, and he was practically forced to grab her ass in order to steady them both. Unfortunate, really, that. Two handfuls of an ass that had bounced and jiggled its way into more fantasies than he'd like to admit.

Oh god, he'd need a thousand self-indulgent showers after this. He squeezed her with both hands, reveling in the delicious give of her body and the sounds she made in reaction.

His skin prickled in a rush of pleasure as she dragged her blunt fingernails over the nape of his neck. She started to grind against him, and if she couldn't feel his erection through his jeans, he'd be shocked.

Pippa slid her mouth along the edge of his jaw and licked and nibbled her way to his ear. There was a spot, right beneath, that he knew would undo him.

She reached it and nipped the sensitive skin, and Maxim's head spun. He staggered to a wall just so his legs would be less likely to buckle.

Pippa met the wall with a solid thump, and Maxim pulled away to say, "Sorry, I didn't mean to—"

But she didn't seem to care. She interrupted his statement with a brief kiss, then tugged at the zipper on his sweatshirt.

"Take this off," she ordered.

He would do anything she asked, everything she wanted. Maxim kept her pinned against the wall by his hips as he yanked at the sweatshirt and threw it onto the carpet. He was overheating anyway.

Pippa slipped a little down the wall, and although she squeezed her legs, he had to push against her to keep her from falling. The motion settled his hips into the hot bliss between her thighs. Her head tipped back and she groaned.

Maxim took the opportunity to kiss along her neck. Her skin was achingly soft and her pulse fluttered beneath his lips. He would have been happy to stay there longer, teasing out little noises as he explored her, but she wrestled his T-shirt over his head and he had to lean away from her or risk getting strangled by its collar. As the shirt fell away, she let out a noise shockingly close to a growl.

"Fuck," she groaned. "I knew it."

What was she seeing? Maxim glanced down at his bare torso: coarse brown-blond hair over his sternum, the shadows from muscles, the ugly ridges of the scar. He looked back at her and realized she was staring ravenously at his chest and his stomach and his pectorals.

Oh, well that was flattering.

Lust beating a fierce tattoo throughout his entire body, he hefted her a little so she could also stare at his biceps.

Pippa's hands followed her stares and she swept her palms over whatever she could reach. "Too bad there aren't any lawyer calendars."

He frowned. "Lawyer calendars?"

Pippa nodded, continuing to take in his body like she would a buffet. "Like the ones for firefighters, but it'd just be page after page of Maxim Sheppard posing seductively with binders."

"Mmm." Maxim chuckled. "Sprawled on a plaintiff table, crotch hidden only by a gavel." He leaned in and nipped her earlobe.

Pippa's laugh warbled as she shuddered in his arms. "I'd buy it."

It was the silliest thing to feel proud of—that if there existed in the world a printed collection of outrageous photos of himself in various states of undress, this woman would want it hanging in her home.

"What about ones of you?"

"Me?" she slurred.

"If you can have sexy lawyer calendars, I'd like a sexy witch calendar."

Pippa snorted. "That would be attractive. Smeared in blood and running away from things."

"I was thinking more along the lines of straddling a broom. Bare-breasted in front of a fire. Getting bent over a cauldron." He punctuated the last part with a firm grind of his hips into hers.

Pippa whimpered. She crushed her mouth to his with such force that he "Mmf!"ed in surprise.

Their kisses were sloppy and desperate. The utter wildness with which he kissed her was a little embarrassing, honestly. Maxim considered himself, if not quite a master, at least extremely proficient in this act. He was well versed in the gentle tease, the quick lip bite, the small gestures and touches that were carefully curated to drive his partner into a state of trembling desperation.

But with Pippa, he was the desperate one. He didn't care about the coyness or the curated teases because he only wanted to be closer to her, to have her and take her and lose himself in her so utterly that he would no longer remember the definition of coyness or that it even existed as a concept.

He swept his hand up her shirt and cupped one of her breasts, feeling her pebbled nipple through the thin lace of her bra. God, he loved that he couldn't fully enclose her breast with his hand. He loved the soft weight of it and the sounds she moaned into his mouth when he brushed her nipple with his thumb.

With a sudden impulse, Maxim set Pippa on her feet. She swayed slightly and had to set her hands on his shoulders to steady herself. Her kiss-reddened lips parted and he could tell she was about to verbalize either a question or a complaint, but before any words came out, he dropped to his knees in front of her, his mouth achingly close to her pussy. All it took was a brief glance downward for her to understand.

"Oh," Pippa breathed. Her eyes had gone heavy-lidded.

Maxim slid his hands up the back of her thighs, skimming the curves of her ass and catching his fingers in the waistband of her leggings.

"Is this okay?" he asked, close enough for his breath to warm her through the fabric.

Pippa shuddered. "Yes."

She kept repeating it, again and again, as he hooked her waistband and dragged it low. The air tingled around Maxim, seeming to vibrate in tandem with the pulse that fluttered beneath Pippa's skin.

Yes.

Black fabric eased down her thighs to her knees. She was wearing a cotton thong and it was soft under his touch and wet between her legs.

Yes.

Pippa's fingers tangled in his hair, and he glanced up to see her watching him, her pupils blown and her eyes glassy. Her chest glowed pink above the low collar of her shirt and her stomach trembled with her ragged breaths.

Maxim kept eye contact as he pulled her underwear over her hips. Her grip tightened on his hair and he longed to surrender and drown in the pleasure of that feeling, but he watched her just as she was watching him.

He abruptly remembered their conversation in the bathroom over sutures, where she'd mentioned vampires and oral in the same sentence. Could she possibly be thinking that the only reason he was doing this was to prove something to her?

Perhaps. In that case, the best solution would be to stop her from thinking.

Maxim leaned in and covered her pussy with his mouth. He managed to hold her gaze for a long, sultry second, then gave in and let himself drown. She was all heat and salt and slickness. Her cries rang out above his head and he let them drive him onward. He took every garbled, slurred attempt at his name as further encouragement.

Pippa's legs shook as he slid two fingers into her. Her grip on his hair nearly rivaled her grip on his fingers and if he was any more erect, he'd—well, that wasn't possible. Setting his free hand on her hip to help hold her steady, he pumped into her with firm, languid strokes.

"I can't—" Pippa bit out around gasps. "It's— I—"

Maxim would have taken his mouth away from her and asked what she needed, but her vice-like hold on his hair kept him pressed firmly against her pussy. So he sucked, and licked, and urged out more of her gibberish.

When her legs buckled and she sank forward onto him, he finally understood what she must have been trying to say: *I can't stand.* He rocked onto his heels and guided her down on top of him so that instead of tumbling to the floor, she ended up straddling one of his thighs and holding onto his shoulders, his fingers still buried within her.

Now that their faces were at the same level, he saw the rosy flush to her cheeks and the soft shine of perspiration beading along her hairline.

Pippa gave him a chagrined smile and let out a short, huffing laugh. Maxim would have joined her, maybe attempted a suave and witty bit of repartee, but he was too taken by the sight of her. The feel of her. The puff of air from her laugh had made him aware of her arousal on his face, of the dampness around his mouth and on his chin.

Maxim had been on a rotating ride at a carnival once. Built like a drum, it spun faster and faster until he'd been pressed to the walls, utterly immobile and wholly helpless.

He felt exactly the same now: head light, pulse racing, the dual rush of fear and excitement battling as the world spun around him and he could do nothing at all about it. And even if it was possible to move, to tear himself away from this spinning bliss, he had no desire to.

Pippa flexed her hands on Maxim's shoulders. Her fingernails pressed firmly into his bare skin, and that whisper of pain brought him back to stillness, solidifying the floor beneath his body. His fingers were still buried within her, surrounded by her slick heat. She lifted herself tentatively off his thigh to settle down again, and again, until she was fucking herself on him.

"I thought of you last night," she whispered. "In my bed. Your fingers feel much better than mine."

Jesus. Maxim's entire body seemed to stutter.

He dragged his free hand through her tangled hair and cupped her nape. "Yeah?" he said. "I thought of you while I jerked off in your shower this morning."

Pippa's whimpered response could be bottled and sold as its own aphrodisiac. Maxim kissed her hard, wanting to consume it. She'd be able to taste herself on his lips and on his tongue. She tightened her hold on his shoulders as she rode his thigh, then gasped into his mouth as he crooked his fingers inside her. Each of her cries were muffled, but they were gaining volume, increasing in pitch, and he could feel the buzzing tension beneath her skin as if it were under his own.

He wanted to hear her come. Unobstructed, unmuffled. He wanted to see it.

Maxim pulled away from her mouth and gripped the back of her neck, pinning her in place as he fucked her hard. Her eyes widened briefly before they fluttered half-shut in pleasure. He drove in harder, faster. She quaked around him and her hold on his shoulders was no longer a whisper of pain, but a growl, a shout. He'd have ten half-moon welts on his skin after this, and he'd relish each one.

Oh, she was nearly there. Her lips drifted apart, that top plump one shining and nibbleable.

"I want . . ." she whispered.

"Yeah?" Maxim rasped. "Tell me what you want."

"Bite me."

He gave a surprised huff. "What?"

"Bite me," she said again, more urgently. "Hard. Anywhere."

He thrust into her once, deep enough to make her whimper. "I'm not one of your vampires, Pippa."

"That's not— I fucking know that." The crease between her brows deepened, and the desperation in her voice was almost palpable. "Please, I just like . . . Please do it."

Between the lust rampaging through his body and the urge to see her undone, he didn't have any remaining capacity to question her.

Maxim slid his hand from the back of her neck to the loose collar of her shirt and tugged it over her shoulder with the low pop of a breaking seam. He'd apologize for that later. He bit down on the soft slope between her neck and shoulder, feeling her skin give, tasting sweat and her summer-bright skin.

With his teeth fastened on her body and his fingers still pumping into her tight, perfect pussy, it seemed as if he was keeping her pinned against him, holding her still and doing as he wished. It was animalistic. Brutal. He would have felt guilty but for her throaty moan and the iron grip on his shoulders.

As Maxim bit down harder and gave an involuntary growl into her neck, Pippa came with a scream. She bucked against him even as he thrust into her. He wanted to feel her convulsions against his tongue. Against his cock. Oh, and how she would feel: hot and snug and silken.

Arousal fogged his vision and tightened his throat. Pippa's grip on his shoulders pulsed in time with the contractions squeezing his fingers.

Pippa's scream faded and soon she was just letting out broken whimpers. Her thighs twitched against his, the exhausted thrash of someone pushed past their limit.

He opened his mouth and released her, and before pulling back, he gave the spot he'd bitten a tender, soothing kiss as if to make up for the indentations he'd left.

The apartment's light played softly over the mark he'd left on her skin. Twin pink half-circles, the flat edges of his teeth obvious. Exactly the opposite of what she must be used to.

It took a second for the sight to settle, and when it did, it settled hard and sharp in the pit of his stomach.

Normally, he would have been relieved at the fact that he hadn't bitten her so she'd bled, but the visual display of his utter inadequacy struck him hard. Did Pippa's life, filled with demons and chaos and lovers with sharp teeth, have room for him? How the fuck did he expect to involve himself with her when he was so blatantly, utterly human? As she said, "one-hundred-percent normal."

He didn't belong in her world.

He didn't belong with *her*.

That single thought hit him with the force of a truck. A tingle began in his stomach, trickling slowly up to his chest.

He wanted her. In every single way. He wanted to see places with her, and explore weird monuments with her, and know how she looked when she woke up on a weekend. He wanted to date her. He wanted to go to dinner together where they'd pore over a menu and she would have to pick for him since he would get stuck on the number of options. He wanted a shared dessert, and an evening walk back to his place, a movie that would start out with some hand-holding on the couch and end with their clothes scattered on the carpet and her legs slung over his shoulders. He wanted to hear about her day and get her advice on his office concerns and gently massage the tension from her temples after she told him about whatever demon was giving her trouble at the moment.

It was all a fantasy though, wasn't it? To believe that he could shove his way into her thrilling life and think she'd be content with his boring date ideas and idle conversation and utter, pitiful, *normalcy*?

Pippa's attention darted down to his mouth a heartbeat before she threw herself at him, claiming his mouth in the way he'd only attempted to do earlier. Her tongue flicked his, then swept along his lower lip before sucking on it and nipping it hard, making heat flare in his groin.

It wasn't enough to distract from that damned tingle in his stomach, though. Now his hands were sparking too, as if he'd held them too close to a power grid.

Pippa fumbled with the button on his jeans and he wanted her to, he *needed* her to, but the tingle in his stomach was becoming a clench, and he couldn't . . .

He couldn't.

Maxim gently covered her hand with his own and halted the attack on his pants.

"Wait." He couldn't go further like this, with insecurities and grief and inadequacy buzzing around in his chest like a swarm of barbed insects.

Pippa pulled away as her fingers stilled, a questioning look on her face.

"I have condoms," she said. "In my room." At his silence, a rosy flush bloomed on her cheeks. She swallowed. "Which wasn't why you wanted to stop. Shit." She closed her eyes and gave a short groan.

Seeing her embarrassment, the twinge in his stomach eased somewhat. Sometimes he wondered if anxiety was a tangible, living thing, and when it recognized itself in someone else, it withdrew its claws in a display of camaraderie.

"Pippa." Maxim gave her a crooked smile intending to reassure her, and when that didn't ease the crease between her brows, he said, "I just think we're going fast." A funny thing to say with his fingers still inside her and her arousal soaking the fabric of his jeans.

"Ah. It's, uh . . . Yep. Fast." When she nodded, it was the sort of nod someone would give when they were agreeing for the sake of agreement. "Definitely," she continued. "I mean" —she cleared her throat and fuck, he was able to *feel* it inside her—"a few days ago, I was sure you hated me, so it's definitely an abrupt change. A total one-eighty."

As she chattered and Maxim heard the forced lightness in her voice, it slowly dawned on him that she might not think he wanted more from her. That he'd prefer to keep their interactions limited to some one-sided oral and hand things. It wasn't the most logical thought on either of their parts (even if hers was purely imagined by himself), and he was probably projecting his own insecurities on her (like he'd learned from another therapist after college), but he'd be damned if he left Pippa's apartment with her assuming he wanted nothing more from her other than what they'd just done.

He eased his fingers from her heat. Pippa shuddered, then cleared her throat and made as if to compose herself.

Maxim didn't want her to.

"Open your mouth," he said.

Pippa blinked at him at first, though she did as instructed.

He brought his hand up slowly, fingers shining and slick, and trailed them over her parted lips.

Her eyes darkened and her breathing quickened and she sucked her lower lip into her mouth before parting her lips even wider.

"I want to make something absolutely clear," Maxim said as he slid two fingers into Pippa's mouth, pushing them gently back and forth across her tongue.

She let out a soft, muffled moan.

He continued. "I want you. I can't stop thinking about you. Your body. Every single soft place I want to kiss."

Another moan, higher but just as muffled. She'd put one hand on his forearm, but it didn't seem to be out of a desire to pull him away. Her touch was gentle, almost seeming to keep him close. He slid his third finger into her mouth, mimicking the motions he'd done earlier to her pussy, watching as her lips glided over his knuckles as she sucked her own arousal from his skin.

His erection had flagged with the sudden burst of anxiety, but now as the anxiety retreated, his boner returned, hot and pounding, like the opportunistic monster it was. He'd address that situation at home.

"I lied," Maxim said. At Pippa's confused "Mmf?" he went on, "About going too fast. I don't think we are. There isn't anything I'd love more right now than to throw you onto your back and fuck you until neither of us could walk. But"—he spoke over her groan of approval—"that isn't what we're going to do. I want you to think about this all night, and in the office tomorrow, you'll stare at my fingers and you'll know how they feel and how deep they've been inside you. How they've filled both your mouth and your cunt."

Pippa's eyes fluttered shut and she melted onto him, the heat between her legs nearly searing him through his jeans. She gave his fingers one last suck that sent a tight ache all the way through his body, then he pulled out of her mouth.

She let out a humming chuckle, then swiped the corner of her lips with her thumb. "I'd wondered if you'd be just as bossy out of the office."

"I'm consistent."

"You're fucking hot, is what you goddamn are."

Maxim leaned back, searching for a smirk or any of that dry humor she often used, but he could only see genuine honesty. She had the soft, mussed look of someone who'd just been thoroughly fucked: a rosy, shining flush to her skin; her brown eyes darkened with arousal; her chest heaving (which *shit*, he hadn't actually caught a glimpse of yet).

He wanted to preen beneath her words and give himself up to the rosy wash of adoration. Yet with Pippa Beverly, that was far too dangerous. If he fell for her, it would only be a matter of time before she realized she really wanted someone who was just . . . *more.* Someone special. Powerful.

So instead of kissing her deeply and pulling her down to the carpet and saying and doing everything he longed to do, he slipped her shirt's collar back into place and helped her to her feet. This was good, he thought as they dressed and she reassured him that she'd be safe in her apartment. This was fine, he thought as he kissed her goodbye. This was all under control, he thought as he looked back at her doorway to see her biting her lip to keep from grinning, her shoulder pressed into the door frame.

Yet as he drove away, he tried to fight the feeling that he was leaving part of himself behind.

Twelve

Pippa sat at the conference table, kicked one foot out of her faux-suede flat to tap it on the carpet, and tried to focus on the current meeting. Kenzie from HR stood at the front of the conference room and flipped through her presentation. Kenzie had prepared a lengthy slideshow with zoom effects as well as coordinating pop songs, and it was highly rude to ignore something with that amount of effort, but how the hell was Pippa expected to listen to it over the vibrant memory of Maxim Sheppard diving face-first into her crotch?

A warm, tight ache bloomed between her legs and she shifted in the padded chair. That ache was part overwhelming lust, part tenderness from how he'd thoroughly done her over. His hands were large, and he'd been moving them with gusto, driving his fingers into her and working her orgasm from her like it had been his to take.

Pippa caught herself before she could let out a tight moan and wrangled it into a choke. She tugged at the knitted scarf she'd put on this morning to cover the lingering bite mark he'd left. Thankfully, the weather had turned chill enough that the scarf didn't look out of place.

"You good?" Jules whispered next to her.

"Mmhmm," Pippa whispered back. "Just, uh. Pollen." She tugged at the scarf again, fluffing it to make sure the pink marks on her neck remained covered.

"Right." There was something unnerving in Jules's expression, and something far too intrigued. Maybe that was the unnerving part. An intrigued Juliette Cohen was about as obsessed as they came; Pippa had never before met a person who had been able to successfully prophesize the entire third act of a movie from a single grainy image released a year before.

It was unnerving, sure, but also more than a little terrifying. When Jules discovered a secret, she treated it like a walnut. She rooted it out and pried it open and scooped out every morsel until there was nothing left but a shell.

Through their entire friendship, Pippa had been surreptitious enough about her other demon- and magic-filled life that Jules hadn't thought to investigate. Pippa hadn't acted suspicious, hadn't arrived at work with visible injuries that couldn't be explained away with a falsified habit of rescuing injured wildlife. All of her heavy, leather-bound books worked equally well as priceless heirlooms and "Oh this? I picked it up at a yard sale. Thought it looked spooky!" coffee-table displays.

The worst part about Jules's intrigue was that Pippa hadn't a single idea what she was intrigued by. The near-constant flush that stained her cheeks since she'd seen Maxim across the office this morning? Or maybe she'd finally put the magic-y tomes and the scrapes and the feigned illnesses together.

Pippa swallowed. Jules—damn her—gave her neck an intrigued look too.

Then Kenzie changed slides and background music, and Jules's attention returned fully to the front of the room.

Which meant that Pippa could return her attention to Maxim.

God, for the past four months he'd been the most frustratingly stoic and grumbly wall of emotional repression, and not twenty-four hours ago, he'd sunk to his knees in front of her and given her a thousand new fantasies. He'd attended to her with a desperation and an urgency that made her writhe in her chair just thinking of it.

And yet he'd stopped. Ordinarily, this would have made her pause and wait patiently. If someone stopped in the midst of relations, they had a good reason. But then he'd stuck his fingers in her mouth as he told her things far dirtier than she'd ever dreamed. And then had the gall, the absolute *gall*, to tell her that this was all in the name of teasing. Maxim was toying with her, making her his plaything.

It was arousing as fuck, but that didn't mean Pippa would just let that sort of thing go.

She glanced across the long lacquered table at Maxim. His arms were crossed over his chest, the well-tailored suit creasing in all the right places. For the first time in weeks, his hair was back to its immaculate almost-tousled style. All his attention was on the projected screen. His lips were pursed in concentration, and he wasn't even fidgeting. How unfair that he wasn't distracted in the same way as she was, that he had the capability to actually focus.

Not if she had anything to say about it.

The magic in the conference room was eager, responding readily as Pippa tweaked and twisted it into a tangible, invisible extension of her hand that she slid up Maxim's calf. He jumped a little and looked under the table with a confused frown, then returned to the presentation. Pippa touched again, and this time, Maxim frowned more deeply and glanced around the room. As his gaze landed on Pippa, his confusion shifted quickly into amusement, and he raised an eyebrow. *Really?* that eyebrow seemed to say.

Really.

She slid her extended touch higher, cresting the sharp edge of his knee, brushing over the swell of his thigh.

A dark flush peeked out over the top of Maxim's collar. He shifted in his seat, pinching his lips tight. Pippa felt marginally sorry for making him uncomfortable in a room of coworkers, so she paused in her advances, which was when he leaned forward and set his chin on his fist. It was a perfectly natural change in position, the sort that came with someone becoming more intrigued by the presentation's content at the front of the room. But as Pippa watched, he uncurled two fingers and brushed them in an absent sort of way against his lips. Those fingers. Those same fingers had been in her. In her mouth and her pussy. The realization crashed on her suddenly, and heat flooded her body.

He shouldn't be able to entrance her with such an innocuous gesture. She was the one with the magic and should have been the one doing the entrancing, but all Maxim Sheppard needed to decimate her was a hint of a satisfied smirk and some minimal gesticulations.

One side of his smirk twitched higher, and with the same amount of tease as if he were participating in a miniature burlesque performance, he uncurled a third finger and let it rest gently on his lips.

Dick.

Pippa collected herself, sat up straighter in her chair, and used magic to pinch Maxim's thigh hard enough for him to let out a startled grunt.

"Any questions?" Kenzie asked in a voice almost as bubbly as her handwriting.

Pippa started. The presentation was over. And, just like that, so was the game.

She had barely dropped into her own chair when Jules hurriedly scooched across the carpet to intercept Pippa from the other side of her desk.

"Okay," she said, in the sort of tone that implied there was either gossip to share or a secret to pry unwillingly from its host.

"What's up?" Pippa said, attempting nonchalance.

Jules narrowed her eyes. "Don't put on that act for me." She linked her hands together on the desk and leaned forward like a detective in an interrogation. "Something is going on with you. Ever since Mad Maxim gave you a ride to the dinner, you've been way too"—she made a circular motion with one hand, then immediately linked both together again—"fine."

"I've been way too 'fine'?"

"Yes!" Jules hissed. "There's been no complaining. No ranting. You haven't texted me at three in the afternoon to tell me that your feet hurt because of the stupid shoes you have to wear. You haven't been pissed at your mom for wanting you to get a better job."

"I'm still pissed at my mother for—"

"Well you haven't been telling me about it!"

Pippa patted Jules's hands. "Aw, sweet Juliette, are you feeling left out?"

Jules pursed her red lips. "Either something has happened that's made you extremely happy, or something has happened that's made you so wildly upset that your former problems are utterly inconsequential."

Pippa forced out a laugh, though it emerged as more of a wheeze. If not for the consistent lack of magical aura around Jules, Pippa would have thought the woman capable of telepathy.

Jules thunked her elbow on Pippa's desk and settled her forehead against the heel of her hand. "Or, shit, maybe it's both. Maybe you're upset with how happy you are."

Opening her mouth for a retort, Pippa caught the movement of a charcoal-gray suit over Jules's shoulder. Maxim was leaving his office. He strode over to the copier, set some pages in the tray, and leaned over it with his arms locked straight and braced against the sides.

It really shouldn't have been sexy. Making copies wasn't the subject of the average person's wet dream, but maybe that was because the average person couldn't picture the bare, muscled, shuddering torso of the photocopyist.

Her fingers clenched on the edge of her desk with the need to touch his body and feel the heat of his skin. She reached out again and swept magic up Maxim's sides. He stiffened at first in surprise, but then relaxed. As she moved along his stomach and up his chest, she spread warmth and pressure over his ribs and the broad planes of his pectorals. He dipped his head. His shoulders rose in a short, sharp breath and his knuckles whitened as he tightened his grip on the copier.

Tension built in her as she watched, just as it must have been building in him, the contact pushing them both toward some perfect finale.

"*Christ*, seriously? You're not even listening to me."

Pippa started and snapped her attention back to Jules. "I am! I'm unhappy. I'm the unhappiest."

Jules gave her the same look she would have given if Pippa had just declared that she'd grown webbed feet and wanted to try swimming across the Pacific.

"No you're fucking not!" She rubbed her temples with two manicured fingers. "God, I swear—"

"Beverly."

Together, Jules and Pippa turned to see Maxim looming at the end of Pippa's desk. He had a bored expression and a vaguely irritated tilt to his mouth.

Pippa swiveled her chair to face him. "Yes?"

He jerked his head toward the elevators. "I'm getting coffee. Come with me."

It didn't take an ounce of magic to feel the tension threaded through him, as if he were a cable one quick twist away from snapping. Had she crossed a line with all of the "touching?" They were at work, and even if their thoughts could travel down certain paths, that didn't automatically mean she was justified in acting on those thoughts.

"Yes, sir." It slipped out as an apology, as a reaffirmation that, yes, she understood she'd gone out of bounds in their workplace and had made him uncomfortable.

The reaction was immediate, at least to Pippa. Though his expression didn't change, his fists clenched at his sides and that tic pulsed once along the sharp edge of his jaw. She was beginning to love that tic. It said more about his state of mind than he likely ever would.

"You want me to bring you coffee?" Pippa asked Jules as she stood and brushed the creases out of her skirt. Her palms had begun to sweat during Jules's interrogation, and a quick glance down reassured her she hadn't left damp patches on the patterned imitation wool.

Nothing sexier than a sweaty witch.

"Nah, I'm good." Jules gave the barest purse of her lips. She glanced between Pippa and Maxim, her dark eyes far too calculating for Pippa's liking.

Before passing through the office doors on their way to the elevators, Pippa glanced back at her desk to make sure she'd logged out of her computer.

Jules hadn't moved away from Pippa's desk. Her eyes narrowed significantly. There was a brief, shining second in which Pippa thought that this was the end of the questioning, that by the time she returned she could think up an excuse that was simple and believable enough to put Detective Cohen's intrigue to rest. But then Jules's cherry-red lips fell open into an expression that was part delight, part horror, and part victory at having cracked open yet another mystery to reveal the juicy interior.

Well, *hell*.

That was a later problem. Pippa wasn't about to think about a Juliette Cohen confrontation when there were much more pressing things to consider.

She felt the heat from Maxim's body as they stood together in the elevator lobby, the tightness in the air hovering around them both in an oppressive silence.

One elevator was still out of order, its lobby doors covered in an "X" of yellow tape.

Was he frustrated with her? Mad that she'd distracted him from his work? Completely understandable, of course, but she'd just intended a bit of fun.

"Listen," she said. "I'm sorr—"

"They're taking too long." Maxim let out a low growl and made for the stairwell.

Pippa went after him, having to trot to keep up. "You don't want to repeat our last elevator adventure?" she said with forced levity.

"Which part? The stabbing, the near-death experience, or the explosive destruction of property?"

"Up to you, really."

It was hard to hear his scoff over the echoing ring of their descent. She had to skip steps in order to match his pace as he hustled down the stairs, his arms bent close to his sides and his dress shoes clipping against the metal treads.

Maxim paused at a landing and pulled a heavy door open, peeked inside, then shut it and continued down the stairs. Through the opening, Pippa saw stacks of boxes in an unlit hallway; the floor probably contained some company's product storage.

"What did you need to talk to me about?" she said, nearly out of breath from the quick pace. By now, she was certain that their destination wasn't Get Buzzed, which was too bad, because her "Frequent Fly-er" card was one punch away from a free latte.

Maxim didn't answer. He pulled open another door on another landing. The floor plan was a copy of Ivanov, Barry, and Cruz—a long hallway with glass doors at the end plastered in vinyl-cut names followed by acronymed degrees and certifications.

Maxim tugged open a door in the hallway, ushered her in, and closed the door behind him. A lock clicked into place. They were in a small, dusty room lit with a hanging bulb overhead. Spare filing cabinets stood along one wall, along with desk organizers, reams of paper, and a long-unused mop leaning against one corner. A closet. He'd led her to a closet.

Pippa opened her mouth to ask what exactly he'd planned for this expedition and then Maxim was pressed up against her back. His body radiated heat into her, his unsteady breaths ruffled the hair that had escaped her bun and curled on her neck. His woodsy citrus smell and the spicy warmth of his aura flooded her senses until she couldn't feel anything except him.

"Strange place for a performance review," she said. Her sentence ended on a gasp as Maxim's hands gripped her waist.

"I'm not your boss. I don't give you performance reviews." One large palm slid up her side, stopping just below her breasts.

She was going to combust. She'd spent all night thinking of him, thinking of this. Although, okay, maybe not here exactly, since her fantasies tended to involve more nudity and less discarded office furniture. After he'd left her apartment, she had replayed the afternoon through her mind over and over and smiled and whimpered and touched herself while she pretended he hadn't really left.

And now he was here, behind her, touching her, his chest shuddering against her back and his hands clenching on her body.

Pippa arched against him and when she did, felt the hard ridge prodding at her lower back. "I was all ready to apologize for teasing you like I did, but you've just destroyed any hope of that."

She felt his growl more than she heard it.

"The meeting wasn't the most ideal time."

"Oh?"

Maxim leaned forward to nip her neck above the scarf, and she bit back a moan.

"Mmhmm," he rumbled against the corner of her jaw. "You obviously weren't listening to Kenzie's presentation about appropriate workplace conduct."

Oops. "Neither were you, apparently."

"We're not in our workplace. It doesn't count."

Pippa tipped her head back and to the side, trying to lock eyes and give him an irritated glare. The moment she did, his mouth descended on hers. He gripped her jaw, pinning her as he slanted his lips and flicked his tongue into her mouth in a kiss so fierce that she felt it in her bones.

When they separated, that look was back in his eyes: the fiery, knee-buckling one she was growing to adore.

She twisted around, trying to touch him, trying to hold onto whatever she could, but he grabbed her wrists and held her still.

"No, sweetheart, you've done enough touching for now." In a smooth motion, Maxim spun her around and bent her over one of the spare filing cabinets.

She let out an "Ooh!" as her breasts were crushed against cool metal.

Maxim quickly covered her mouth with his hand to muffle any more sounds and they froze like that for a long second, her bent at the waist and his body pressed against hers as they waited for any commotion from the other side of the door.

"Can't have you getting loud on me, Beverly," Maxim murmured at last.

Pippa shook her head, but he didn't take his hand away. The fabric of his suit rasped gently over her sweater as his breathing quickened. He slipped beneath her skirt and started to trace feather-light circles on the back of her thigh. The tickling, teasing pressure of his touch on her bare skin made her stomach flutter in exactly the right way.

"Tell me to stop, and I'll stop." Maxim went higher. "Tap my hand. Or tap anything, three times, and I'll stop this." His voice was tight and raw and desperate, like he couldn't bear the thought of stepping away.

Good. She didn't want him to.

Pippa lay her palms flat on the filing cabinet and arched back until her ass was grinding against Maxim's groin.

He gave a sharp exhale, then nudged her underwear to the side and stroked skin already sensitive and slippery. He rubbed at her until she bucked beneath him, then pushed two fingers inside in a single thrust that brought his palm flush against her skin.

Pippa moaned into Maxim's hand, and even as he held more tightly to muffle her, he choked out a quiet "Oh, fuck" by her ear. When he began to move within her, she became nothing more than an electrified mass of nerves.

He took his hand from her mouth and, with a little tugging, the scarf slid off her shoulder into a puddle on the floor.

The filing cabinet creaked beneath the two of them as Maxim braced himself on his elbow, bringing him closer to her even as he sank his fingers deeper into her body. How easy it was to drown in the bliss of Maxim Sheppard's nearness and the heady, delectable smell of him.

In this cramped room, she wasn't a witch. She wasn't being hunted by monsters or haunted by things she couldn't control. She was just a horny, happy person getting fingerbanged by someone who was outrageously attractive. And sweet. And who was really quite silly, when he wanted to be.

"Fuck, you feel incredible."

And who said things like *that*.

Pippa's eyes fluttered shut and she curled her fingers into the scuffed metal cabinet.

Maxim kissed his way down her neck, but when he reached the slope of her shoulder where he had bitten her yesterday, he froze.

Just a little bit more of that, and she'd be ready to come. She arched against him in an effort to get his hand moving again.

"Are you okay?" he whispered.

She turned to look at him, confused. "Of course! I didn't tap anything accidentally, did I—"

"Your neck." He swallowed and straightened, and—*Nonono*—withdrew his fingers. "I shouldn't be able to see that mark. Something's happened to your magic again. Why didn't you say anything?"

The dual sensations of the sudden loss of pleasure and the uneasy squirm of being caught in . . . Well, not quite a lie.

"No, I, uh." This was something better discussed when one of them wasn't bent over a cabinet with their skirt fully up around their waist. She stood up and tugged her hem marginally lower as she turned to face him.

"Healing isn't automatic. It doesn't happen on its own."

Maxim waited for her to continue.

"And I . . ." She brought a hand to the twin pink semicircles. "I liked the look of this."

"Why?" That one rasped word was barely audible. There was a tightness to it, as if Maxim had to force himself to say it.

Because it felt like you were still with me.

It seemed like such a juvenile reason, as if she were a teenager wearing a hickey like a badge. It wasn't something she could say to a well-dressed man in a tie, even if his knuckles still shone with her arousal.

So instead, Pippa forced a light chuckle. "Maybe it reminds me of the things I like." She reached forward and grasped Maxim's tie, using it to pull him back toward her.

If he had been a book at that moment, he would have snapped shut. Muscles in his neck worked around his harsh swallow.

What on earth had she said? She'd thought that bit about "something I like" was flirty and might possibly imply what she was too embarrassed to say out loud, but here was Maxim with his jaw pulsing like he was chewing on his tongue.

"You know what else I like?"

"Hmm."

He'd gone back to stoic. How disappointing. Pippa backed up until she bumped against the filing cabinet, then wiggled and shifted to a seated position on top of it.

"I like you."

He quirked an eyebrow in such a minute movement that she wondered if she'd imagined it.

"I like this."

Maxim stepped between her legs and puffed a sigh through barely-parted lips, his attention darting between her mouth, her breasts, her bared neck, and her exposed and saturated underwear.

"I like you doing this." She took his hand and brought it to the heat between her thighs.

The air left his lungs in a strangled groan, and then he was kissing her again, one hand on her nape and the other rubbing and delving and curling into her so perfectly that her legs trembled.

A moan burbled up from Pippa's chest, and Maxim clamped his hand over her mouth, a little rougher than he'd done before.

She reached down between them and pressed her palm to the front of his pants, then moaned again at what she found there. She pressed harder, and Maxim gasped, tipping his head forward to rest against hers. His hips jerked into her touch and his breath tickled her cheeks.

How wonderful would it be to see him as undone as he had been able to do to her; to feel him quiver, to see him unravel.

Pippa said that, albeit much less eloquently, but only got a few words before Maxim blurted, "Oh, shit, sorry, what?" and removed his hand from her mouth.

"I want to suck you off," she repeated.

He hummed as she traced the curve of his stiff cock beneath his pants. "You really want that? Here?"

The enthusiasm of her nod loosed several strands of hair from her hair clip.

He leaned in, nipped her earlobe, and murmured, "Well then you'd better fucking come, Pippa."

An order she was all too ready to follow. Her fingers moved frantically right above where Maxim's were buried within her. Between the feel of him inside her and the demanding way he had said her name, it didn't take long before she was whimpering into the palm he'd clamped back over her mouth. Tension built hard and fast through her body, and every fierce thrust of his thick fingers pushed her higher and higher until she came with a bright flash of pleasure.

Pippa's limbs felt heavy and liquid, but she fought through it and even ignored the wobble of one knee as she slid off the filing cabinet.

She'd expected Maxim to be just as desperate for this as she, and it was a little surprising when she was the only one to fumble with his belt, the only one to tug his button free and wrestle his zipper into submission.

He stood silently, his hands resting gently on her upper arms and his jaw working.

Pippa paused. She bit her lip. Why wasn't he seeming as into this as he'd been earlier?

"The tapping thing can go both ways," she said softly. "If you're having second thoughts."

Maxim ran his thumb along her jaw and brushed it over her lower lip. "I'm not. Not at all." He was touching her far more tenderly than she would expect, considering how this closet encounter had begun. There was something reverent in the way he looked at her as she sank to her knees.

She glanced up at him before she fully lost herself in pulling at the waist of his unbelievably soft boxer briefs. In all the situations she'd imagined where they were arranged like this, none had ever included hesitancy. As she opened her mouth to get additional confirmation from him, he spoke.

"Are you sure?"

Something deep in Pippa's chest melted, and then melted further as he tucked some of her hair behind her ear. Here she was, inches from his dick, and he still thought to ask.

She rubbed the hard length of him through his underwear and sent up a coy smile. "I want to taste you."

A strangled groan escaped Maxim. It turned into a tight gasp as she dipped beneath the fabric and took his cock in hand.

Oh, he was nice. Thick and heavy and warm. But as nice as his cock was, with its flushed head and impressive size, his reactions were even nicer. He shuddered as she licked up the length of him. His trembling hand cupped the back of her head and he arched forward as if he could barely manage to stay upright when she tried to take him as deep as possible.

Such lovely, flattering reactions.

Pippa moved faster, stroked harder. She relished every single sound that came from above her. His hips bucked slightly as she flicked her tongue along a spot she would make sure to remember for later. It was tempting to draw this out, spend time learning his gasps and what little spots on his body set him shaking, but they'd already been in here for some time. Wouldn't want anyone to get suspicious.

Just as she'd done in the office, she sent magic sweeping up his torso, two warm extensions of her hands that traveled from his hips to his chest. They grazed his nipples and his pectorals, and right as they scraped his neck, he choked and shuddered and fell apart.

Pippa reveled in the glazed, startled look in his heavy-lidded eyes as she swallowed him down.

Maxim had braced one hand on the closed door, and as she stood and wiped her mouth, he ran his other hand down his face.

"You're merciless," he said.

She tucked his cock into his underwear, "No idea what you mean."

"It's not even noon."

"And?"

Maxim huffed a soft laugh. "And that means I have to force myself not to keep thinking about your mouth for the next five hours."

"I'm sure you'll manage."

"Yeah." Focusing on a point over her shoulder, he chewed on his cheek as if trying to figure out how to say something difficult.

Pippa swallowed, suddenly nervous. She tugged her skirt back into place and snatched her scarf from the floor. Big revelations after any sort of intimacy never tended to be ones that left her feeling bright and happy and free to revel in the recent orgasms.

"What are we doing?" he whispered.

Pippa's stomach sank. *Please let this not be regret.* She stepped close to him and put a hand on his lapel, feeling his heartbeat lurch under her palm.

"We're having fun." Her smile was far lighter than she felt. "Yeah?"

At least he smiled back. At least he placed a hand over the one she'd laid on his chest.

"Yeah," Maxim said, although there was something forced in his smile, too. "Yeah, we are." He cleared his throat. "Why don't you head back first. I need to get this"—he made a broad gesture to his body—"cleaned up."

Pippa unlocked the door, but before she could turn the knob, Maxim grasped her wrist and pulled her into a kiss.

It would be easy to assume that this was an ordinary "Well that was fun, bye for now" sort of kiss. She was about to leave the Closet of Debauchery, and Maxim was due in meetings for the rest of the day that were not the sort of meetings a lowly legal assistant would attend.

However, most parting kisses weren't this lingering, or gentle, and they certainly didn't involve the sudden intensity right at the end. He kissed her as if he was going to war tomorrow, as if he was trying to tell her a thousand things without speaking a single one. It was incredibly tempting to imagine what those things could be. Too tempting.

She left him behind in the closet and closed the door.

THE STAIR TREADS CLANGED as Pippa stomped up them, and it felt casually rewarding to make so much noise at the same time more unfortunate noise was happening in her head. Hell, what *were* they doing? She scraped her hair into some semblance of decency and frowned.

As she turned the stairwell corner, she'd tipped her head down to more carefully secure her hair in its clip, and only realized someone was in the hall with her when she saw the pair of shining black high heels set apart like their owner was about to start a fencing duel.

Shit.

"Oh hey!" Pippa said. "Heading to Get Buzzed?" The chipper note in her voice could likely be heard four floors down.

Jules crossed her arms over her chest. She was wearing a smart dark blazer over a button-down shirt, and Pippa chose to look at her rainbow cuff links instead of the excitement blazing in her eyes.

"You saucy bitch."

"Jules—"

"You illicit, saucy bitch." Her grin was on the edge of terrifying. If it got any wider, it would split her ears.

"Listen—"

"This is the best thing you've ever done. Seriously. Screw whatever you did to make Maxim all flustered and bloody in that alley— Oh my God did you bang him there too?"

"We didn't bang here either!" Pippa remembered where they were and pitched her voice lower right at the end, but "We didn't bang here" echoed through the stairwell.

"Pippin, you can't hide smudged lipstick from me. Oh come on, I've already seen it," Jules said as Pippa frantically wiped at her mouth. "If this wasn't so juicy, I'd be offended if you didn't tell me sooner. I mean I'm a little offended. I told you the second I caught Kenzie staring at my cleavage, and even though that's not nearly the same—"

The fine hairs on Pippa's arms stood on end. She tried to focus on her surroundings while ignoring Jules's continued rambling. There was a bad taste in the air, of burned steel and the sour tang of rust.

It was the exact aura that had been hovering around her apartment and had sat patiently on her terrace, then fled before she could see what had left it.

Her stomach clenched with the realization. The source of the aura was nearby, and it was fresh.

Pippa ran up the stairs past a spluttering Jules and paused at the door to the next floor. The sensation was stronger here. How had it gotten in? It must have been that last stupid ward she'd thought was simply good enough. It hadn't been, and something had snuck through it and was lurking on the other side of the door.

She jumped when Jules grabbed her upper arm.

"Seriously, I need to know. He's so . . ." Jules made a two-hand-ed gesture as if she were crumpling a ball of paper. "He's so Maxim. There's gotta be something you can share that'll make me hate him less."

"Jules, not now."

"Yes, now. You're already on a coffee break, and we're salaried. Have you been mouth-to-mouth? Mouth-to-crotch? Hand-to-crotch? How many did he use?" She held up a fist and began uncurling fingers. "Stop me when I'm right."

The aura behind Pippa crawled up her skin as if it were a living thing. Magic sparked in her palms and vibrated against her temples.

She had to take care of this, but Jules was no closer to leaving and had been continuing to count on her fingers. She held up all five and gave Pippa an impressed, "Really? Holy shit Pip, good for you!"

"Jules, go back to the office."

"Wh—" She scoffed, then spluttered. "Why?"

Deep inside Pippa, sitting cold and patient right next to her spine, the dark magic stirred. She could make Jules go away. It would be so easy, the magic whispered. She could turn around, sprint up the stairs in her cute shining heels, keep running until her feet bled.

She could make Jules stop questioning her. She could make Jules—

No.

Pippa clenched her jaw. "I have to shit," she blurted.

Jules blinked, her cherry-red lips parting in shock. "Uh?"

Goddammit, dammit, fuck. She was going to have to dig harder.

"Like, really bad. Like I need to use a bathroom on another floor bad because there's no way I'd be able to look anyone in the eye after the utter massacre that's going to come out of—"

Jules's expression was slowly twisting into one that blended concern and horror. "Okay," she interrupted. "Yeah, I get it." She started for the stairs that led up to their office, but just as Pippa grasped the door handle and was girding herself for what lay behind it, Jules turned back around.

"But in all seriousness," she said. "Pippin, my darling, you should really see a doctor soon. Your intestines sound jacked."

"Yep, on it." Pippa yanked the door open, then slammed it shut behind her.

Nothing attacked her. At least, not right away. Once the threat of either attack or Jules following her through the door had passed, she let herself relax enough to look around.

She was on the level Maxim had opened on their way down—the storage facility with stacks of product in corrugated boxes. Just like the other levels, it was a copy of the layout of Ivanov, Barry, and Cruz: a corridor with an elevator lobby, doors leading to closets in a long hallway, and a large office space at the end.

Unlike the other levels, instead of a cheerily lit set of double doors at the end of the hallway boasting the vinyl-cut names of those who worked within, a shape crouched in an empty doorway. Bone-like protrusions spiked down its back. It was bent so far forward that it was almost on all fours. It held one arm close to its torso, almost like a dog who had put one paw on a thorn, but this dog had a face like a skull and a jaw that didn't quite close.

The fluorescent bulbs overhead bathed it in blue-white, highlighting mottled fur-covered skin and puffs of smoke that rose up when it slapped a charred patch on a shoulder with a gnarled hand.

At least the ward had done *something*.

The demon uncurled with all the grace of a wolf trying to stand on its hind legs. Fully upright, it came to the top of the door frame.

It didn't have eyes. Whisper Hounds never did. Still, it stared Pippa down as if those empty pits could determine the brand of her sweater.

Magic swirled around Pippa's hands, and although it was excited and ready for her to shoot it out across the hallway, she kept it close. She wanted to make sure of something first.

"So," she said. "Guess you're here for me."

One tufted ear flicked backward. The creature let out a thrumming, twisting growl that moved through the air like a drumbeat.

A grating whisper filtered through Pippa's head.

IT IS NICE TO BE EXPECTED

She nearly staggered at the feeling of magic being forced into her brain. She'd gone a long time without experiencing a conversation with a Whisper Hound, and her body railed at the sudden sensation of snakes writhing between her ears.

Pippa fought back the dizziness and planted her feet on the carpet. "The last two I killed who were hunting me didn't give me any information about how much I'm worth. But I'm curious. Maybe I can put it on my resume."

The demon's lips—or at least what passed for its lips—curled at the corners.

YOUR KIND HAS HUNTED MY KIN FOR A CENTURY

THE BOUNTY IS WORTH NOTHING COMPARED TO THE JOY WHEN I BRING YOUR HEAD

WITCH

The last word speared Pippa like a tangible, sharp thing shoved into her temple, and the magic she had carefully drawn around her scattered.

The demon took full advantage.

As it lunged forward, it opened its mouth impossibly wide and a vibrating, pulsing wind blasted out from its jaws.

Pippa dragged power close and hurled it out, but the demon's attack struck her before she could fully aim. A heavy, shuddering force collided with her chest and sent her flying backward with a cry. She saw her own magical energy skew to the side and hit a stack of boxes that exploded into a riot of cardboard, shredded papers, and office supplies, and then she was tumbling across the floor, the air knocked from her lungs.

The low-pile carpet slid across her knees with the soothing caress of a cheese grater.

She rolled to a stop, her skin burning and her breath coming in short, desperate heaves as her lungs frantically tried to work again. The Hound threw its arms out to its sides in a slow, sinew-crackling stretch. The tips of its bony fingers glinted beneath the fluorescent lighting. They'd been dipped in a sickly, greenish lacquer.

Fuckfuckfuck, and that green was the same color as the Boe demon's dagger. At least she knew that the poison would only take away one part of her magic, but what if the concoction had been updated?

Panic flared up Pippa's spine. As she watched, she realized the demon's left arm didn't extend quite as much as the right, and it gave the barest flinch as damaged skin stretched taut.

That was the side to attack. Pippa just had to pull on enough magic to get to it before it came close enough to—

The door to the stairwell opened.

"Oh-h-kay," Jules said, one manicured hand resting on her hip. "I figured I'd bring some meds because I am the most wonderful, but what are you doing on the floor?"

Pippa's thoughts froze in an icy blast of panic.

The demon threw itself at the ground and slammed its clawed hands onto the carpet several times like a sprinter amping themselves up for a race.

Jules, who had stepped toward Pippa, heard the sound and turned toward its source. She opened her mouth to scream.

The demon charged.

Fury shattered Pippa's panic.

This demon did not get to come into her workplace, in a space she'd considered safe, and put the people she cared about in danger.

Magic roared through her body and shot from her hands. It blew past Jules like a gale, setting her hair flying and her blazer flapping before it collided with the demon and set it staggering backward. Pippa wrenched on the power to call it back to her, then spread it wide in a rippling pane across the hallway.

The demon hardly needed any time to recover. It charged again, but hit the magical barrier. Even though Pippa felt the impact as if it had been against her, the shield held.

"The FUCK is *that!*" Jules shrieked.

"Get behind me," Pippa ordered. She heaved herself to her feet, not taking her eyes off the creature on the other side of her magic.

For what must have been the first time in her life, Jules jumped to follow directions.

"Ohmygod," Jules said with a wheeze. "I knew you were a witch, but I didn't know it was like THIS!"

It took a second for that to settle on Pippa, and when it did, she gaped at Jules.

"You *what?* How could you possibly know?"

"I notice things, Pippa," Jules snapped shrilly. "I've noticed things for years. I've seen those creepy-ass books on your shelves, and I *know* you didn't just find them somewhere. I've overheard you talking to your mom. And you like to do this neat and fun thing to reheat your coffee when you think no one's looking. Well *I'm* looking!" Her eyes were wild and she looked to be mere moments from, as her writing would say, a "fearsome swoon."

The demon slammed a shoulder into Pippa's barrier. As the pane shuddered, she channeled more magic into it, making it thicker, stronger.

"Then why did you say anything?" Pippa said, spluttering against her shock. "Why didn't you ever ask me about it?"

"I wanted you to tell me!" Jules shrieked in the sort of high whistling tone that would have been audible to any nearby rodents. "I wanted it to happen *organically!*"

Through the wavering shine of the barrier, Pippa saw the Whisper Hound open its mouth.

She didn't have time to brace herself before a piercing, bone-jarring amalgamation of magic and words drummed into the shield, which flexed only briefly before it shattered. Shards of her own magic exploded around her like warm sparks. Jules cried out and covered her face.

Pippa frantically glanced around for anything that might be useful. Because of course, of *course*, she had been so swept up in the lusty excitement of the past few days that she had forgotten her life was constantly in danger. She'd left the house this morning with her mind whirling around Maxim Sheppard and his hands and his tongue when it should have been whirling around defensive spells and which cardigans would adequately hide ensorcelled weapons.

The few boxes that had exploded lay torn and ragged, their contents spewed across the carpet. The other detritus consisted of broken desk lamps, old and obsolete motherboards, and several pieces of what must have once been a desk chair. Pippa couldn't help but wish she worked in a knife factory.

The demon curled a lip at the fizzing scraps of magic by its feet, then charged once more.

Jules gave a hoarse, choking scream behind Pippa.

If she couldn't use anything in the boxes, then she'd have to improvise.

Channeling magic through steel and aluminum and carpet fibers, Pippa urged the floor up in a wave right as the Hound struck the ground. Floorboards cracked and carpet ripped as a tsunami of corporate pseudo-comfort threw the demon into the ceiling and drove its head into a fluorescent lighting fixture.

It was far too soon to feel victorious, but Pippa definitely had a strong desire to join in with Jules as she hissed, "Fuck yeah, GET IT— *Oh Jesus.*"

The demon crashed to the ruined floor beneath a cloud of drywall dust and broken conduit.

Pippa would destroy this building. Surely. Kill one demon who had a family with too many connections, and then before she knew it, she'd be responsible for leveling the entire Murphy-Eastman Office Park.

A bit of drywall and head-bashing wouldn't stop a Hound for too long, though. Despite all she'd done, the demon shook itself off and stood easily.

Pippa raised her hands and began to back up, herding Jules down the box-lined hallway away from the danger.

Her skin started to burn. She looked down, frantic, only to see that her skin looked completely normal, but it didn't change the sudden, desperate feeling that she needed to strip out of it. The drumming surrounded her, scalding and oppressive.

Words speared into her thoughts.

POOR THING

THE GIRL WITH TWO MAGICS WHO USES ONLY ONE

"F-fuck you," Pippa gritted out.

More pulses of words, like thumb tacks pushed one by one into her mind.

HOW SAD TO SEE THE DAUGHTER OF HARBINGER SO HOBBLED BY HER OWN CHOOSING

"Don't you call him that." God, that awful name. That stupid, pompous, supervillain name. The demon either didn't hear her or didn't care, and more words were shoved into her thoughts.

I HAVE CHANGED MY MIND

I won't get joy from killing you

You're like a broken animal needing to be put out of its misery

Her skin screamed, and a tight burning agony began along her limbs, racing up her arms to settle in her head and pulse steadily behind her eyes. Something tickled her upper lip and she tasted the rusty bite of her own blood. From behind her, there came a whimper and a thump as Jules collapsed to the floor.

Pippa focused on the magic around her and forced her hands higher, pushing energy out through them. A pitiful light leaked out, so sad and small she was a little surprised a comedic farting noise didn't accompany it. She was tired, distracted by the continuing beat of pain on her skin and in her head and whatever part of her body she tried to move. She wanted to curl up by herself in a ball on the ruined floor and sob.

But she wasn't alone.

Behind her, Jules was on the floor, wracked with an agony she didn't understand. Because of Pippa, she was in danger.

The same anger from earlier burned bright and blinding within her, encouraging magic to flood into her body. It settled in her head, mending and binding and healing, even as it swarmed around her hands. She pulled on the magic in the air, the magic in the broken floor and in the walls and in the succulents that sat sad and over-watered on the floor above.

The demon strode forward and cocked its undamaged arm back, poisoned claws glinting in the light as it readied a swing at Pippa's neck.

She gave the magic one last urgent pull, then threw it forward. White-hot energy flashed from her palms and hit the Whisper Hound directly in the throat. It staggered and gurgled, and in an instant, the pain disappeared.

Relief cascaded through her. She called on more magic to strike again, and again, and when the demon opened its mouth, she aimed right at the back of its throat. The demon choked, bringing both clawed hands to its neck.

A heaviness brushed her shoulders. She couldn't keep hurling magic at it forever, and as soon as she slowed down or grew even more tired, it would be ready to use those claws.

Pippa ran forward, ignoring a sharp pain in her ankle and the ache in her scraped knees. She snatched a broken lamp from the floor as she passed it. It was a heavy desk lamp, the kind with a wide metal base to help balance a long, arched stem. There was no bulb or shade, but it felt good in her hands and it felt even better as she swung it base-first into the demon's jaw.

Both arms rattled with the impact. The Whisper Hound stepped back and one foot caught on a piece of exposed conduit that had fallen from the ceiling. One more blow to the jaw knocked the demon onto its back.

It snarled and swiped at her from the floor, but the swipe was desperate and uncoordinated, and she was able to throw herself out of the way.

Another swing from the lamp base impacted the demon's head, and Pippa yelped as the vibrations nearly shook her elbows apart. If she had an hour, she could possibly do some damage, but that one swing felt like it had hurt her more than whatever she'd done to the demon.

What she would have given for anything sharp.

The demon had fallen next to the box of old motherboards that had split open and lay scattered around broken ceiling tiles and fluffy bundles of pink insulation. Pippa snatched one motherboard, raised it high, and with magic swirling in her muscles and giving her every last bit of strength she could muster, she drove the plastic board down onto the demon's neck.

Black blood splattered onto her face and the demon convulsed a few times. She drove the board down again just to be certain.

Pippa's attention snapped to Jules, who had pulled herself halfway upright, bracing her hands on the carpet. "Are you okay?" Pippa said. "Are you hurt? Can you—" She drifted off as she caught sight of Jules's expression.

Disgust.

Horror.

She could deal with that look on anyone else but Jules. After all the years of their friendship, she'd be the one to end it with a revelation that the magic Jules had thought was neat and fun was actually something to fear. Something to loathe. A weary ache bloomed at the base of Pippa's rib cage and her throat grew tight. Anyone but Jules.

"Jesus *fuck*," Jules snapped, though she sounded winded. "You do all that shit with the goddamn sorcery and fuck up all of that"—she gestured to the destroyed floor and ceiling—"and you don't carry a goddamn *knife* with you?"

"I—" Pippa blinked. "Uh . . ."

"That's disgusting." Jules let out a short, high laugh before she slumped against the wall. "God, you're cool," she muttered as her legs gave out and she slid to the carpet.

Pippa struggled to stand and go to her, but from the other side of the door, she suddenly heard the rapid clang of footfalls on the stairwell.

Everything she'd just done had been loud, destructive, and of course people would have heard and were sprinting to investigate. Everything around her could be explained through a freak accident with shoddy workmanship except for the partially decapitated demon lying at Pippa's knees.

Shitshitshit.

Pippa pulled on the magic, though in her state, it wasn't quick to respond. Her shoulders ached, her ankle was certainly sprained, and as she held her hands over the demon's body, she realized that the motherboard had cut deep into her palms.

The commotion was coming closer. She needed to get rid of the Whisper Hound's body before anyone saw it. Anyone other than Jules, of course. Oh, and Maxim.

Hell, with all of the people she had inadvertently revealed the otherworld to, maybe she should just leave the body and let the Coven give up on her once and for all. Maybe Geoff would win some succubi over with a plate of muffins.

Maybe another day.

With a guttural cry of exertion and the feeling that she was hoisting a boat anchor out of a tar pit, Pippa gave the magic around her a final, exhausted pull.

The demon's body smoked under her hands, embers spreading and flaring along skin and beneath sparse fur. It sank into itself as ash settled and sifted over ceiling detritus right as the door flew open and several people ran in.

Pippa didn't recognize most of them: the barista from Get Buzzed who was wearing an apron stained with coffee, a few people in suits, and a custodian who instantly shouted, "Get a first-aid kit!" to someone who hadn't yet made it out of the stairwell.

Her head was swimming. She tried to tell them to take care of Jules, to pay attention to *Jules*, but no one listened. They surrounded her and told her to lie back and keep still, that an ambulance was on its way, that she would be all right. A voice to her right demanded to know what had happened, and then another voice to her left shouted that the building was obviously falling apart, and what was next, asbestos?

Everything was too loud and too close. She could stop it, though. The darker magic wriggled awake. It would be so easy to have everyone be quiet and leave this floor and forget what they've seen.

She could do it.

She could be more than a broken animal, a half-functioning witch.

No one would be hurt, no one would be the wiser, and when someone found the destroyed hallway, they would scrounge up conclusions that didn't involve Pippa whatsoever.

But with one pull of that magic, it would mean all those years wasted. She had spent so long pretending it didn't even exist; if she used it, she'd be no better than her father. Than Harbinger. Her stomach pitched and threatened to empty.

Over the bobbing heads of the three people now clustered around her, she saw someone else come through the door. Blond hair artfully rearranged, sharp jaw, furious eyes, crooked nose.

Pippa let out a cry of relief, and the barista beside her grabbed her arm, thinking she was in pain.

Entirely the opposite. She saw Maxim Sheppard, and he saw her, and she wanted to sob with the absolute, total rightness that flooded through her because now, everything would be okay.

Maxim charged forward, squeezing between the people clustered around Pippa.

"I'm fine," she told him as he nearly dove down to get to her. "I'm fine." The bruised ligaments in her ankle were already mending, and if anyone around her looked closely, they would have been able to see the cuts on her palms knitting together beneath the bloody smears.

Maxim's lips were pressed in that firm, delectable line. "You—"

"Is Jules okay?" Pippa interrupted. "Maxim, is she okay?"

"She's here?" He glanced over his shoulder as Jules used the custodian to pull herself bodily to her feet. The poor man was at least a half-head shorter than she, and he staggered in surprise.

"How did this happen?" the barista said to the pile of debris.

Pippa hoped no one noticed how quickly she aimed an intent look at Jules. Unfortunately, Jules was one of those who did not notice.

"The ceiling fell," Pippa said before Jules could cheerily tell everyone how amazing it had been to watch Pippa decapitate a demon with old computer parts. "We heard a cracking sound above us and it just dropped."

"I think I'm gonna barf," Jules said as a contribution, and the custodian stepped as far away as possible. She'd gone pale and was shaking, and someone in the crowd mumbled a sentence that included "shock."

Pippa scrambled upright, pushing past the person trying to apply bandages to her hands, and took the place of the grateful custodian.

"Hey," she whispered. "You okay?"

Jules gripped Pippa's shoulders and closed her eyes tight. Pippa used the contact to push crumbs of healing magic into her, settling her stomach, calming her panicked pulse. Her breathing came slower and she nodded at last.

"Yeah. I'm good." Without opening her eyes, she went on. "But we're going to talk about this, right? You're not going to keep changing the subject when I ask you, and you're not going to pretend it didn't happen? Because—*shit*, Pippa, I saw all of it, and—"

Pippa made a soft "Mmmm!" to silence her, then sent up a quick, silent apology to her own future self. And then, another apology for opening up to someone who wouldn't be able to accompany her into the Ash Coven life. "No one can know what happened here. Lie your ass off, fake amnesia, whatever it takes. Please, just . . ." She took a slow, unsteady breath.

And then for the second time in her life, she said, "I'll tell you everything later, I promise."

Somehow, it didn't feel any easier to say it.

Thirteen

Maxim was quiet in the car as he drove. Pippa had expected something, whether it was a question or a demand or a concern, but after he'd asked about the demon that had attacked her and Jules and she'd assured him that, yes, she was—mostly—undamaged, he might as well have been a chauffeur for all the chatter he wasn't making.

He'd stuck right by her side as the building was evacuated due to "structural concerns." He'd hovered nervously nearby in the parking lot as she and Jules had given their statements and as the EMT checked her for head trauma. She'd been able to explain away the black demon blood as grease from a damaged pipe. She was pretty sure the EMT didn't believe her when she'd said the blood on her palms was a different type of grease, but without any visible injuries, he'd had no choice but to nod.

Despite Jules's state, she was also deemed well enough to only require an ice pack to her head and a shock blanket, but not well enough to drive, so Kenzie volunteered to take her home.

Jumped at the chance, really, which had Pippa wondering if hers wasn't the only case of inter-office canoodling. And with the HR representative, too, which—

"Am I taking a right or left here?"

Maxim's question jerked her back to the car and the reason why he needed directions.

"Left."

The blinker was a low, soothing *tock, tock, tock* against the silence, punctuated by the creak of Maxim's hands on the steering wheel.

"What was it?" he'd asked as soon as they'd gotten in the car. Pippa hadn't needed him to elaborate. She told him about the Whisper Hound and its verbal magic, how the hallway ended up the way it did, and Jules's revelation that Pippa was horrible at keeping any sort of secret.

And then, Pippa had told him where she was intending to go. He'd less volunteered to take her there, and more simply assumed. She had been too tired to argue.

He'd seemed tense though, in the same sort of angsty, brooding way she had come to expect from him before she'd gotten to know him so much better. It was as if a wall had slid into place. Not a heavy wall, or an impenetrable one, but a little of his warmth felt cut off from her.

Pippa aimed the air vent away from her damp hair. They'd stopped by her apartment just long enough for her to shower, scrub the dried blood off, and change into her nicest sweater and skirt.

The Ash Coven didn't appreciate dishevelment. Plus, if she could make her appearance as put-together as possible, maybe her emotional state would follow. Eventually.

Her throat felt too tight, so she fiddled with the air vent again. She should have gone to them sooner. Getting attacked in an alley hadn't been anything out of the ordinary, especially since it wasn't the first time a demon had admitted to receiving money in exchange for killing her.

But the responsible thing would have been to go to the Coven after getting attacked at work by a demon who'd been armed with a poison it knew would incapacitate her. The first time, that was. She chewed her lip and glared out of the window.

Going to the Coven felt like defeat. It meant admitting she couldn't handle her own problems and hoping that a group of people in a musty-smelling room who had more connections and more power than she did would be able to fix the shitty situation she'd wrangled for herself. Of course, if she hadn't been so goddamn proud and had gone to them earlier, Jules Cohen's biggest issue this week would have been wondering how to make an alien/Spock/Kirk threesome sound believable.

Oh, Pippa was tired. Only the steady beat of dread kept her from slumping against the passenger door during the drive.

"Thanks for taking me," she said. "You didn't have to."

"Yeah. Of course." Maxim's voice was soft, almost encouraging. "This was the place you've been wanting to join, right?"

She sighed. "Yeah."

"And they'll help you?"

"That's the hope."

They were coming up on the Ash Coven's building, a three-story Victorian house surrounded by a picket fence, because the Ash Coven really, really liked "aesthetic." A few blocks ahead, the roof's black iron finials were becoming visible.

What if someone glanced out a window as they parked? What if they saw Maxim? What if they asked questions?

"Turn here," she blurted.

With an, "Oh, okay?" Maxim slowed and turned onto a dirt-paved alley, moving carefully around the potholes. "Do you know what you're going to say?"

"Say?"

"To make your case to them." At the growing look of dread that must have been on her face, he reached over and patted her thigh. "Well. Good thing you have a lawyer with you."

Any other time, his goofy smirk would have made her laugh, but now it just rankled.

"You won't be with me," she said. "Just park here." She jumped out of the car as soon as he rolled to a stop. "I'll meet you later."

"Pippa!" Maxim called after her, throwing his own door open with enough force to thump into the dumpster he'd parked alongside. "Goddammit— What the hell is going on?"

The rusty-red shingles of the Coven's building showed in the distance behind a stand of palm trees. Pippa's palms were slippery and there was a sour taste in her mouth. What if she couldn't convince them? What if they somehow knew that she'd involved others?

"Pippa," Maxim said again, though softer this time. She felt his hand close around hers. "It's fine if you want me to wait in the . . . lobby, or—I don't know if they have a waiting room. Whatever. I can be wherever you want me to be."

She tried for a slow, steady breath that ended up emerging as a choke. "I don't want you here at all, Maxim."

His hand slipped from hers.

"You weren't supposed to know about demons," she said, "or magic, or me, or any of this. I told you that there were laws. If the Ash Coven knew I've been associating with you, involving you, they'd never let me in. They'd make it impossible for me to ever—" Her throat seized around that last word and she swallowed hard.

Maxim stayed silent, and when she looked back at him, his forehead was creased, his mouth in a tight frown.

"What happens if they accept you?" he said. "Say they let you in. Say you become part of this club."

Frustration simmered beneath Pippa's skin at his snappish tone. "It's not a—"

"You're not allowed to associate with someone like me. Isn't that the rule? Someone— What did you say the other day? Someone who's 'one-hundred-percent normal.' So if you get in, what then? Do we just . . . stop? Do we work day after day and pretend there's nothing at all between us?"

The sinking feeling in her stomach was made heavier by her growing dread. She knew where this conversation was headed, and she hated it.

"If they accept me, I wouldn't be working at the firm anymore."

The moment she spoke, she knew it was the wrong answer. She watched her words settle on Maxim and twist his expression into one of despair and disbelief.

"So this entire time you knew that this"—he gestured between the two of them—"wasn't going anywhere." His lips had paled drastically with how tightly he'd been pressing them together. "I was convenient. Someone to drive you around and, what, help you *get off*?"

The last words emerged as a snarl.

Frustration simmered under Pippa's skin. She twisted to face him, her shoes scraping in the dirt and making dry dust puff into the air.

"No! Of course not!"

She adored him. She loved his brain and his humor and his hapless attempts at small talk. She couldn't think of what she would rather do than have him come with her and stand by her side as she knelt before the people who controlled her future. And honestly? She'd been so swept up in the thrill of getting to know him and learn what happened behind the walls he'd so carefully built around himself she had forgotten that, yes, if she were to be taken in by the Ash Coven, she'd have to cut out the non-magical people in her life.

Fuck, this was too much. Everything was too much, and too confusing, and the sky was too sunny, and her head felt like it was trying to decide whether to burst or melt.

Yet . . . maybe she hadn't forgotten. Maybe part of her had thought that the Ash Coven's acceptance was so outlandish that having a relationship full of intimacy and honesty and shameless bliss was the option more likely to come true.

And if they didn't accept her? She thought of the satisfaction she'd have once she knew that she was *part* of something important. She thought of what it might be to feel fulfilled. She thought of a bare patch in a cemetery that no landscaper had ever been able to fill with grass.

"I need this, Maxim," she said. Her throat burned and her eyes stung with tears that threatened to fall. "If they accept me, then it means that I'm . . . worth it. Despite what my father did. Despite the magic I can't bear to acknowledge. I can't do anything else. I'm not good at anything else."

"That's bullshit!"

Pippa flinched at his snarled curse. "I need this!" she shouted through the strangling tightness in her throat. "You have no idea what I'm constantly fighting against. His magic fucking *haunts* me, Maxim, and you can't even begin to understand how it—"

"I'd know if you'd TELL ME!"

She'd never seen him bellow before. She'd never seen the cords in his neck strain so hard she was afraid something within him would break. There was a fierce desperation in his yell, but as big as it was, it was also fragile. That little piece of him snuck in through her anger, and it forced her to talk.

"He was . . ." Pippa searched for the word before remembering their conversation during a car ride when she'd seen the first glimmer of the true Maxim Sheppard.

"He was a villain. Evil. Like one of the monsters you'd play against in your games. Twenty years ago, he pretended to be some rich asshole giving away free shit. He drew a small crowd of people and used Reaper magic, the same magic that I inherited, to make them kill each other."

Maxim had frozen, his lips drifting apart and his green-gold eyes fixed on her. His anger had dissipated, but seeing his shocked expression only fueled her own.

"He did it for absolutely no reason. He wasn't trying to make a point, he wasn't trying to accomplish anything, he did it just because he could. Most of them didn't even have anything sharp. He made them use their house keys, or branches, or the own fucking fingernails. The Ash Coven was . . ." She cleared her throat. "They were able to take him down. From what my mother tells me, they made sure nothing was left of him. Even came up with some story about drug overdoses to cover it. There's *nothing left*."

A breeze tickled her skin, and she realized her cheeks were wet. How awful it was to still be capable of mourning.

She clenched her jaw and swiped the sleeve of her sweater over her tears. "That's why I want to be part of this *club*, Maxim. If I can be something else, why wouldn't I take that opportunity?"

"Because he isn't who you are!" He wasn't yelling, but entreating. This was the voice of the lawyer coming through, the one who used his silver wordplay to twist opinions like she twisted magic. "I'm so sorry you had to go through all of that. But just because you have that same magic, it doesn't mean you're the same person. It doesn't—" He broke off and stepped closer to her, and when he spoke again, he was softer. No longer the lawyer, but the man who had helped her, who had made her laugh as he stitched up her leg so she wouldn't feel quite so terrified.

"He may have been evil," Maxim said, "but that doesn't mean the magic was."

A short laugh burst out of Pippa, so bitter that she was a little surprised it hadn't blistered her throat on its way up. "Were you listening to what I said? Do you think magic capable of . . . of *that* would ever be anything but evil?"

The last word barely made it out. Her neck felt tight, her hands hot. How could he even think that? He had no idea what that magic felt like. He had no idea what it could do. It was manipulation and destruction, death and horror.

Maxim stepped forward again and he rested his hands on her upper arms. "You told me that any magic can be evil, depending on how it's used. Doesn't that mean any magic can be good?"

The sunshine was too bright, the air too thick. It dawned on Pippa then that no matter how hard she argued or shared horrible stories or tried to show him that the world she inhabited was nothing like the idealistic and adventurous one he'd painted in his mind, he would never understand. All of her frustration and anger bubbled higher and filled her ears with a shrill, sharp whine.

There was no way to make him understand.

Yes, the power inside whispered. *Yes, there is.*

The air grew quiet and Pippa's thoughts slowed into a cool stillness. He had to understand.

Pippa closed her eyes and let the Reaper magic rise to the surface. It thrilled and surged within her like some excited thing finally leaving a kennel, and it brushed against her fingers with the gentle softness of velvet. She felt its giddiness as if it were her own. Giving into it was a blissful release. The sun grew less blinding and all of the tension in her limbs eased.

Pippa looked at Maxim, and through the lens of the magic, she saw him as he might have appeared to the Coven: weak, human, so very, very malleable. He could be clay in her hands.

"Do you really believe this could be good?" When she spoke, she heard an echo of her own voice, lower and softer, and it lingered on her tongue like honey after she spoke.

Maxim took a step back as his expression turned into one of confusion.

A wooden fence lined the alley. With the barest push on the magic, she forced Maxim's legs to stagger backward. Another push, and his body hurled itself against the slats. The entire structure shook with the impact. Maxim's eyes were wide and panicked; his chest heaved and sweat beaded at his hairline.

Satisfaction nestled warm and sticky within Pippa. *Good. Let him see. Let him know.* This was who she was. She'd warned him, and he hadn't believed her, and here he was, wholly helpless.

Without taking a step closer to him, she pinned his arms to his sides. "This magic can make you do anything, Maxim," she said. "It can tell you to walk into traffic. I can twitch my fingers and stop your heart."

She could feel it within him. Warm, red, and galloping beneath his sternum. Each of his heartbeats seemed to pulse within her, along her veins, under her skin.

"What do you think?" Pippa spoke louder, and the words rang in her own ears and resonated through her bones. "Is this *good*?"

The magic was as heady and thick as syrup, and just as sweet. She felt strong. She felt unstoppable. A roar was growing in her head, like a windstorm, or a crowd shouting in one, unbroken chant.

She could dive within him and submerse herself in his thoughts until he wouldn't know what was his own mind and what was hers.

Through the gooey haze of her own power, she felt Maxim's heart lurch into a frantic, rabbiting pace.

He was terrified. Of her.

The power instantly soured in her mouth. Pippa wrenched on the magic and tugged it back inside her, shoving it down hard to where it had sat patiently all these years.

That deafening roar stopped. After the chaos, the silence was unbearable. A wave of nausea passed over her and she staggered backward, biting back the urge to vomit.

What had she done?

What the *fuck* had she just done?

Maxim was standing still against the fence. His shoulders rose as he sucked in quick, shaking breaths.

Every time Pippa had thought about using that magic, she realized she'd assumed something horrible would happen afterward: a Coven member would pop out of the air in front of her with a screaming proclamation, or her skin would explode, or the ground would fracture beneath her shoes and she'd drop hundreds of feet into a fiery, sucking chasm.

But as she stood in the dirt, nothing around her hinted at what she'd just done. Birds chirped above her head and a squirrel chittered in a backyard. The sounds of steady traffic made a leisurely journey down the alley. Everything was back to being bright and lovely and perfectly suburban.

It was terrible.

Because of a brief moment of frustration, everything she had worked so hard to maintain had crumbled. Her one solid defense against the Coven's hesitation to let her join them had just vanished. How could they let her in now, if she'd been so eager to let the magic swarm through her and control someone else's soul?

But it wasn't just someone. It had been the man she'd come to care for, who had trusted her, and believed in her, and wanted to follow her into a coven's home so she wouldn't feel so alone.

Pippa would have preferred the screaming Coven member. She would have preferred the chasm.

When Maxim finally moved, he brought a hand to his chest, over his heart, as if assuring himself that it was still beating.

"Was that to show me?" he said. There was a bitter snap to his words, like he'd broken them off just to slice at her. "Prove that I'm too weak, that I'll never fit in with what you are or what you do?"

Pippa was too stunned to respond. That hadn't been it at all, and she started to respond only for Maxim to interrupt.

"I already know." He adjusted his tie, though she could see that his hands shook. "I'm already very well aware that this is just fun for you. Nothing more. You didn't need to give me a demonstration to reiterate it."

A thousand arguments spun around in Pippa's head, and instead of being able to pick out a single good answer, she just felt dizzy.

Maxim began to walk toward his car.

Wait, no, wait, shit, fuck.

Pippa's head spun faster. "This is who I am!" she shouted after him. "You didn't . . . This is what haunts me. Every day. You told me to tell you. And I did."

He stopped and sent an incredulous expression over his shoulder. "You didn't fucking *tell* me."

No, she'd shown him, and somehow, she'd thought that would be better.

"Wait, Maxim . . ." she called after him.

He turned back to her, his face stony.

He was leaving, she knew this. And after what she'd done, there was nothing she could say that would convince him not to go.

"Be careful," she said, her voice far more meek than she'd have liked. "Please."

Maxim worked his closed mouth. That little muscle pulsed in his jaw, the one she'd never had the opportunity to kiss away.

"Why?" he said, his voice cold and sharp. "Everything is after you."

She stood in the alley after he left, and watched as the dust settled on her scuffed shoes.

The Ash Coven's entry hall had creaking wooden floors and thick rugs that looked older than the house. Behind a reception desk, two arcing staircases curved along the wall and joined at the second level, their balustrades carved like lions' feet.

Every time Pippa walked into this damned building, she expected it to smell like an old attic, but there was only a sterile bland scent that wouldn't have felt out of place in a hospital.

She'd wiped her face to the best of her ability on the short walk over and managed to get her breath steady so she wasn't shuddering with the will to hold herself together and not melt into a puddle of tears and snot in the middle of the crosswalk.

The man behind the reception desk looked up as she approached. His expression soured.

Did he know? Could he tell from her face or her aura? But no—if he had known she'd used that magic, he wouldn't be regarding her like she was a damp leaf someone had brought in on the bottom of their shoe. There was no horror, just haughty irritation.

"I'm here to—"

The man gave her a look that cut her off. "They know." He tucked a lock of shoulder-length red hair behind his ear and tapped out something on his keyboard.

Pippa swallowed. "They know I'm here, or they know why I'm here?"

The receptionist flicked another look at her and continued to type.

She didn't have to wait long. Right as she dropped into a leather chair (also with claw-foot legs, because, *consistency*), there came the sensation that she'd been snared by a fishhook, and the line was drawn taut. Not a painful feeling, but certainly uncomfortable enough to notice.

Pippa stood and followed the pull, and the prickling lessened. When the Coven elders were ready to see her, there were never any announcements, or name-calling, or "They're ready for you, Pippa." They simply beckoned with magic.

She nodded at the receptionist as she passed, who, in response, fully ignored her.

The pull directed her to the staircase. On her way up, she surreptitiously tried to wipe her dust-covered flats against the plush burgundy runner pinned against the stairs. By the time she reached the top, they looked better, however the runner did not.

Maxim would love this place. He'd pause to remark on the ornate frames along the walls: the landscapes and impressionist paintings with little brass plates at the bottom boasting names from art history textbooks. He'd point out the mahogany stair treads and wonder what magic had banished the creaks and the scuffing from floors that were surely older than New Hawkshead itself.

"*What the fu-u-ck?*" he would stage-whisper to her at the sight of the mummified hand in a glass cabinet at the top of the staircase. He'd point at it and give her a look of such intrigue and horror that she would have to stifle a laugh. She would explain that it was rumored to be the hand of the first witch in New Hawkshead, who had founded the Ash Coven and set them on their current path.

"That's disgusting," he would say. Then, *"Do you think it's ever been used to flip someone off?"* And she'd laugh again.

With every additional thought of him, a pained ache joined the Coven's pull in her chest. She thought of his joy, and the warmth of his body, and how his smile had felt against her skin. She thought about how he'd always thought the best of her and desperately wanted to help in any way he could, and the ache grew sharp, curving barbs and tightened around her heart.

Not now.

She couldn't think about any of that now, so she shoved the feelings deep and focused on the magical pull that was calling her to the door at the end of a long hallway. It swung open as she reached it.

Although she had gone through this exact door last week, Pippa stepped into a room that looked completely different. Before, it had stone walls and castle-like decor. Tapestries had hung at odd intervals against chipped sandstone. A suit of armor in the corner had witnessed all of Pippa's humiliation, and it had probably judged her sneakers just like Elder David had.

Now, the walls were papered in a soft, floral print and lined with bookshelves. More framed paintings hung on any bit of wall unoccupied by books, and a sepia-tinged globe on a thick iron stand sat beside a heavy desk.

The Coven liked to change the rooms every few months. In Pippa's opinion, the entire purpose was to show off how much power they had and how much free time to use it. This room looked like someone had image searched for "old library aesthetic."

Elder David, the man, the legend, the asshole in the flesh, sat behind the desk, staring intently into a clear ball the size of a baseball.

Pippa opened her mouth to speak a greeting, and Elder David, without looking away from the ball, held up a finger as if to say, "Shut up, what I'm doing is more important than you are."

Pippa forced her anger out alongside a slow, controlled exhale through her nose, and perched on the edge of the only other chair in the room. The pull in her chest had entirely disappeared so she instead focused on the swirling patterns in the rug at her feet. Roses, vines, little white flowers along the borders that must have been stitched by hand.

There came a low click behind Elder David's desk, and as Pippa glanced up, one of the tall bookcases swung into the room and Elder Ranna strode through the new doorway.

God, of *course* they would have a secret bookcase door. It was excessive and atmospheric and if Pippa had control over creating a room, she would fill it with secret passage entrances exactly like that.

Elder Ranna twisted a hand and spoke a few lilting words, and a chair matching Elder David's appeared in front of her. She dragged it across the floor, not seeming to care about the scratches she left in the parquet, and sat beside Elder David with an air of irritation that she had to be here in the first place.

Elder David straightened, then covered the glass ball with a slip of silk. "If you're wanting to talk about your application again," he said without preamble, "then I'm afraid we don't have anything more to tell you."

Pippa swallowed. "That's not why I'm here."

Elder Ranna gave Pippa what she must have thought was a kind smile. "It's a beautiful day out. Surely there's somewhere you'd rather be than in this stuffy room."

It was meant as a light joke, a self-deprecating comment about a room they'd intentionally designed themselves, and that managed to make it all that much worse.

"I came here because I need help."

Pippa watched the two elders' faces as she told the story of the warehouse, the Tro'grath, and the ensuing hit-demons, leaving out any mention of Maxim or Jules. She expected surprise, if not empathy, so when she finished and the two expressions of the witches behind the desk looked exactly the same as when she'd entered, the first little spark of concern flared within her.

She'd already thought this meeting wasn't going to go the way she hoped. Now, there came the creeping feeling that it was about to go worse than she'd anticipated.

Elder David's eyebrows furrowed into a position that tried to imply concern. "And the corpses? Were they taken care of?"

Any thought that they'd be worried about—heaven forbid—the health of one of their potential coven members vanished.

Pippa shifted in her chair. The leather creaked under her thighs. "Yes. All three were destroyed without any incidents."

The two elders sighed in relief, their stony faces relaxing. Ranna sent David a pinched smile and a nod.

In turn, Elder David leaned back in his chair, crossed his arms over his chest, and asked Pippa, "Then why are you here?"

Why was she here? Were they fucking *serious*? Pippa clenched her fists in her lap.

"I'm here because in the past week, I've been attacked three times, two of which were in a public building that was filled with non-mages. I've been sought as a revenge killing, I've been *hunted*, and multiple times, I've barely been able to—"

"But you *were* able," Elder David interrupted. He unfolded one arm to gesture where Pippa sat in her chair, silently vibrating with rage. "Obviously."

She didn't want to say this. She hated to say this, but she steeled herself and said it anyway.

"I came here for help."

Ranna gave her another one of those kind-adjacent smiles. "You've been doing just fine on your own, Philippa. As Elder David said, you've been able to handle everything you've encountered."

Vibrating with rage was no longer good enough. Pippa surged to her feet and let the rage flow free. "So it's fine if I kill demons for you, but the second I ask for help, I'm denied?"

Elder David held up a hand and lowered it as if telling her to lower her volume. Either that, or instructing her to sit back down. Pippa wasn't sure which she hated more.

"We never told you to go after the Tro'grath, Philippa," Elder Ranna said. "You did that entirely on your own."

"I followed a lead! It had *killed people*," Pippa said vehemently. "Was I supposed to just let it—"

"You're not *supposed* to do anything," Elder David snapped. "You are not a part of this Coven. What you do in your free time is entirely up to you, which means the consequences are entirely yours as well."

It was bullshit. It was awful. Everything she'd done to try to earn her way into the Ash Coven was apparently something she'd chosen to do in her "free time." She was completely, wholly on her own in a situation that had nearly cost her her life multiple times.

A liquid heaviness spread up into Pippa's throat. Her lungs burned with the effort to not scream.

"At the last application meeting, you said you appreciated everything that I've done."

Elder Ranna made a face that implied she'd completely forgotten she'd said that. "Oh, well, it's true," she said. "We do appreciate it." Another one of those shitty, false smiles plastered itself on her mouth. Her eyes were as warm and kind as that of a dead fish.

"We appreciate it," Elder David repeated. "We didn't direct it."

A thought came to Pippa then, like a last, desperate argument after the debate had ended. "One of them had a knife. With a poison on it. It blocked my magic from me for almost an hour."

No point in telling them about the Reaper magic being unaffected; that wasn't exactly a conversation she wanted to start.

Elder David sighed, though Ranna leaned forward, intrigued. "Can we see?"

Pippa nearly sagged with relief. She might be able to convince them that the threat she was facing was worthy of Coven assistance. "Yes, of course, it's . . ."

At home.

She wanted to drop to the rich carpet and melt into the fibers. The knife was in her apartment, wrapped in a plastic bag inside an old shoebox so she wouldn't accidentally touch it. If there was one thing—*one thing*—she forget today . . .

"I don't have it with me right now," she finished lamely.

"Bring it in when you can," Elder Ranna said, although her fake fucking smile was far louder than her attempt at placation. "We can do some tests, see what the poison is." She didn't believe the knife existed. Elder David certainly didn't, what with his expression hovering between annoyance and boredom.

But still, there was hope, even if it was just a splinter. She held onto that hope as they asked if she had anything else to say, and clutched it close and firm as she bowed her head in goodbye.

But before she closed the door behind her, she heard Elder David's exasperated groan, and that splinter was just a splinter, nestled under her skin and aching.

There was a small bathroom in this hallway that she'd used to compose herself after a meeting before, and she managed to hold herself together until she entered and locked the stall door.

Pippa collapsed onto the toilet seat and screamed silently into her palms. She just had to keep going, fight through this frustration and the groans and the false smiles. They were right, in a way; she had managed to handle all of the attacks in some fashion (maybe not *well*, but she wouldn't be here in a bathroom fighting tears if she *hadn't* been able to handle it). The knife would help. Once she brought it back, the Ash Coven would be able to see that there was an honest, genuine threat—not just to Pippa, but to anyone who used Natural magic in New Hawkshead.

The bathroom door swung open and two women entered, chattering to each other. Pippa recognized the low rasp of Elder Ranna, although the other, higher voice belonged to someone she'd never met.

"...doesn't sound like there's much to it, but it wouldn't hurt to see," Elder Ranna said. "Who knows? The warlocks down in the basement would love to have something to do. If there even is anything."

The woman with the higher voice chuckled. "*If* there is even anything. She just keeps coming back. It'd be funny if it wasn't so sad."

Pippa's stomach lurched in that awful, sinking mortification of knowing exactly who the two women were talking about.

The stall next to Pippa opened and a pair of heels clacked inside. From within, Elder Ranna chuffed. "Harsh words, Colette."

"I don't know why you don't just . . . keep her out." Colette sounded as if she was standing at the mirror and opening her mouth wide to fix her eye makeup. "Why even let her in the building? It's not like she'll ever wear Ash robes."

Pippa clenched her jaw so tightly that pain shot through her teeth. Should she say something? Announce her presence? No, then they would stop talking. And no matter how close she felt to vomiting, something told her that this was a conversation that she needed to hear to completion.

"Well no," Ranna said. "But she's just trying *so hard.* All we need to do is give her the thin hope that if she keeps going, she might get in. Which, of course, won't happen."

"That magic," Colette said, in the same way someone would say, "that cockroach." "Could you imagine how it would *look* to have her here?"

"I know. Awful. But meanwhile, she's been doing wonders on the local demon population. The Coven's duties have been halved. More than halved, actually. It's been so nice. I've gone to the cabin, oh—what, it must be three times last month? You should come with me next time."

"Is the kitchen done?"

"Almost. We're still waiting on the marble."

"Oh, Ranna, you know how I feel about kitchens."

"You hardly cook."

"That's not the point. If anything is unfinished, I just feel . . ." Colette made a sound that implied she'd shuddered.

It would have been amusing in a different situation that this world-rattling conversation was happening between one woman adjusting mascara and another relieving her bladder while Pippa sat, shaken, on a toilet that likely cost more than her monthly rent.

Pippa's vision swam before her as she listened to Ranna flush and wash her hands, all while she prattled on about stainless steel appliances and whether or not the arches in the hallway fit the *feeling* of the rest of the house. The two women left, and then it was just Pippa, alone, feeling like all the air in the bathroom had vanished.

So it had never mattered. None of it. Every late night she dragged herself back to her apartment covered in sewer stink and demon blood, every bit of joy she ignored in favor of working, of *hunting*, every second spent at a job she used only to scrounge a living in a life that left no time for anything she really, truly wanted.

It had all been absolutely, extraordinarily useless. She had spent every year since she was fifteen focused on pleasing this building of pompous assholes in the hope that they'd forgive her for something she'd never done.

All this time, only one person had fully believed in her. One person had wanted to help her, and she'd repaid him with horror.

She needed to apologize to Maxim. She needed to find him, but she'd never been to his home, and had no idea where he lived.

And even if she did, how could she even think he'd want to see her after how she'd treated him?

Pippa sat up straighter and ripped off sheets of toilet paper to soak up the tears. That hurt was too much to focus on right now. In this moment, she needed to get the hell out of this shithole of a bathroom and this shithole of a building which could have served as a witchy daytime sitcom backdrop. There would be no more desperate attempts to work her way into a place she'd never truly felt comfortable.

Pippa stood and smoothed the creases from her skirt. She needed to refresh Mary's wards anyway, and while she was there, they were going to have a conversation.

She strode out of the bathroom and down the hallway. A new Pippa Beverly emerged from that toilet stall, and she was *mad*. This was her rebirth. Kind of an underwhelming rebirth, but didn't all great realizations happen in a bathroom in some fashion?

Before she left the Ash Coven for the last time, she made it down a few stairs, then paused, trotted back up to the landing, and twisted magic around the sacred and preserved hand so only its middle finger remained extended.

Fourteen

The cursor on the empty email blinked in an accusatory way. It felt judgmental, like the repetitive tapping of an impatient foot.

Maxim glared at it and dragged his hand through his hair. His eyes felt raw and the screen seemed much too bright. He'd tried to sleep last night. Genuinely tried. Whenever something truly awful had happened in his life, it had always seemed less awful the next day. So he'd turned on the peaceful salt lamp, listened to soothing ambient sounds, and had a cup of tea that tasted like fermented grass—everything he could think of that wasn't drugging himself.

When those didn't work, he'd cracked open his medicine cabinet for his first sleeping pill in months.

It had helped, in a way. He'd gone to sleep.

Unfortunately, the pill hadn't done anything for his dreams. He dreamed of rotting demons and bloodstained sidewalks and wounds that wept black tar. He dreamed of a cardigan-clad witch who slid her hand between his ribs and squeezed tight. He'd jerk awake, his heart pounding in his throat, before slipping into a state of half-wakefulness where he'd float until the darkness dragged him right back under.

It had been one of those mornings where he'd watched the sun rise with the exhausted, delirious idea that if he projected enough hatred upon it, it would get uncomfortable and return to its place beyond the horizon.

Maxim scrubbed at the nape of his neck and stood to stretch out his cramping lower back. At least he wasn't at work, surrounded by people asking about his unkempt hair and the atypical creases in his suit. After the elevator "failure" and the hallway "collapse," the entire building had been deemed a structural hazard. Ivanov, Barry, and Cruz had sent out a memo that they'd gotten a few rooms in one of those rent-an-office spaces for a few weeks, but those who could work from home were welcome to do so.

Therefore, no one but Maxim was able to see his sweatshirt and his gym pants and the purple circles smudged beneath his eyes.

His computer chimed with an incoming video call.

Maxim had the sudden sensation of combined adrenaline and hope, where it felt like his stomach had been punched up into his brain. He lunged for his computer, desperate to see her name on the screen. He'd see her face. Her smile. She'd tell him that . . .

That what? The hope fizzled. That she'd given up all of her life's aspirations just so the two of them could keep dating?

But the name on the screen wasn't the one he'd wanted. Maxim let out a sigh, then sank into his chair and connected the call.

Juliette Cohen's face appeared on his screen. She looked to have called him from her phone, and was holding the camera close enough to her face that Maxim could see the individual hairs of her eyebrows.

He got as far as saying, "How are you feel—" before she interrupted him.

"Shit, hold on." Her phone was jostled around, and Maxim briefly felt motion sick before it stabilized. Her background had changed to that of trees and sunshine. "Okay, here we— Uh, wow," Juliette said. She squinted and brought her phone even closer to her face. A fine crease formed in her forehead.

Maxim frowned. "What?"

"You look like garbage."

He glanced down at himself. His sweatshirt was clean and free of holes, though the logo claiming that he was an honors student at "R'leah University" had started to fade.

"Your face, Max."

His frown deepened at her nickname. "What's wrong with my face?"

Juliette's sigh was heavy enough to cause a crackling static over Maxim's speakers. "You look like you haven't slept all night." She paused, and her bright red lips quirked at the corners. "Which has only gotta be good, right?"

If his frown got any deeper, it would attract exploratory submarines. "What are you talking about?"

Juliette leveled an unamused expression at the camera, and muttered something that sounded like "Can't believe he's got a damn law degree." Then, emphasizing each word, said slowly, "Because of all the fucking. Speaking of which, where is she? Can I talk to her? She keeps pushing my calls to voicemail, so I know she's not dead. Although if the two of you were going hard enough that you look like *that,* maybe she might wish she was."

Maxim gaped at the screen. Maybe this was why he'd never had a decent conversation with Juliette Cohen. As her words sunk into his brain, he fought past the delicious images of Pippa sprawled in his bed, sweaty and content. He clenched his jaw and his stomach twisted.

"Hold on. You were attacked yesterday, and you watched someone do *magic*, and all you can think to ask me is if me and the person who did the magic have been fucking?"

For a long moment, Juliette stared at him, blinking slowly, before shouting a frustrated "Yes!" so suddenly that Maxim jumped.

"What is wrong with you?" he said, exasperated.

Jules pursed her lips and looked somewhere behind her phone. Her expression turned thoughtful. "I bet this is my way of coping. You know? You learn that shit is super fucked, like—I mean, you always knew there was something weird with the world, but then you find out that it's really, *really* weird, so you obsess over something that's comforting and distracting." She shrugged and flapped a manicured hand. "Anyway, if she's not conked out in your bed, put Pippa on please."

"She's not here," he snapped. "Sorry, I need to get back to work." He should probably have continued to ask how she was, or if there was any update from the firm about the building, but every cell in his body was screaming at him to run away from this conversation and nurse his wounds in solitude.

"Oh weird," Juliette murmured, as if she hadn't heard the second part of what he'd said. "She said she wasn't coming in today, so I'd just assumed she was with you."

A leaden weight dropped inside Maxim's chest. Had she been accepted into the coven, and this marked the start of her culling her previous life? First him, then Jules, then her job. He sagged in his chair and let the despair cover him like a cold blanket. Could he have salvaged any of it? If he'd said something different, or done something different. If he'd been more open with Pippa about he'd begun to feel about her, maybe she would actually be sleeping down the hall.

The tips of his fingers began to tingle, and the top part of his chest felt just a bit too tight.

Jules must have seen Maxim's expression. He glanced up at his monitor to see that she'd narrowed her eyes and was leveling a mild glare at her screen.

"What did you do?"

"What did *I* do?" He opened his mouth to tell her that her friend had—

What had Pippa done, actually? Backed him into a fence and made him fully understand the power she was terrified of using? Forced him to realize that there had never been any talk of commitment or a long-term relationship and any attachment had been only on his end? He rubbed his face again. Now his hands were tingling. His breath was coming quicker, his heart hurling itself into his diaphragm.

"Right," she said. "Normally, this would be the moment I'd tell you something toxic like, 'If you hurt her, I'll hurt you.' But I feel like Pip's got it under control."

Maxim let out a laugh, as dry and brittle as an old leaf. "Yeah."

Jules was still watching him, head cocked and a strange expression on her face. "Are you doing okay?"

Oh how he hated that question. There had never been a situation where someone had asked it, in the same genuine way that

Juliette Cohen was doing now, where the honest answer was ever anything but "No."

The room was starting to spin around him, and he realized he'd been staring at the corner of his monitor without blinking.

This conversation was deeper than he'd ever had with Jules, yet they still hadn't gotten to the point where he was comfortable succumbing to a panic attack in front of her.

Maxim forced a tight smile and said, "Yeah, I'm fine. I'm sure she'll get in touch with you soon." Then he disconnected the call, powered off his laptop, and crawled from his office chair onto the floor where he flung out his limbs and lay splayed, breathing shallowly as he fought the urge to remain perfectly still as if the anxiety were a predatory dinosaur whose vision was based on movement.

The carpet was rough on his cheek.

Focus.

Short and loop pile, it smelled like dryer sheets and dust and feet. *Ugh.* He had to clean it soon.

Nope, focus.

If he looked closer, he saw the little color variations within each whorl of the clustered fibers. Taupe and charcoal, tawny brown and cream. Every deep breath pushed his chest into it. His stomach and his shoulders, too.

Maxim needed to talk to someone. It struck him then that he hadn't spoken with anyone outside of work since he'd moved to New Hawkshead, and the urge to hear a familiar and friendly voice became suddenly overpowering.

His phone was in the kitchen though, and after a moment of focusing on that damned dusty carpet, he felt able to push himself to his feet and slouch out of his study.

He'd call William. They'd only dated a few months, but once they realized there was no spark, they slid into a friendship that had held fast over the past decade. Will had never been much for phone calls when he could easily communicate through a simple and immaculately spelled text, but right now, Maxim wasn't in a texting sort of mood.

Will picked up after three rings. "Hey!" he said, lengthening the word until it became its own melody.

His enthusiasm surprised Maxim. This "Hey" sounded much less like a greeting of "I'm about to tell you I'm busy," and a lot more like "Oh thank fuck, I was starting to worry you ran off to join a commune."

Will went on. "I was just thinking about you. Old Birdneck treating you okay?"

"New Hawkshead."

"But don't you like my version better?"

There had always been something so soothing about Will's voice. Low and melodious, it was a radio DJ voice, or an audiobook voice. Whenever they'd studied together in college and test anxiety began to rise, Maxim would ask Will to read passages from textbooks out loud. Even now, he could feel his blood pressure dropping. He sagged against the kitchen counter, then decided that wasn't good enough and slid down to the cold tiles.

Maybe Will had magic. Hadn't Pippa mentioned verbal power as one of the types? There could be a spell weaving right now on the other end of the line, soaking into Maxim's bones through his phone's little speaker. If that was so, when would Will decide Maxim wasn't worth keeping around?

God, he hated how easy it was to slip into the warm lap of bitter pessimism. He pressed his forehead into his knees and stared at the heathered fabric of his sweats.

Will gave a short, tinny chuckle. "By the sound of your silence, I can tell you're so very impatient to tell me about all of the amazing things in your life."

"Yeah," Maxim said in an exhale. "It's . . . Things have been better."

"What's on your brain?"

"Getting in over my head, disappointing myself, fucking up relationships, falling for someone who never had the intention of falling back. The usual."

"Hmm. You should probably stop doing all that."

Maxim groaned and hoped Will could hear the thunk of his head against the cabinet door. "Thanks. I knew I called you for a reason."

"Use the salt lamp I gave you. Just stare at it for a bit, it might help—"

"Center me?" Maxim finished along with Will. He scoffed. "No, thanks, but I think my life right now needs something more impactful than a bowl of glowing pink rocks."

He heard Will sigh, slow and long. "What did you want from this call, Maxim?"

Coming from anyone else, Maxim would have assumed that his defensive snapping had earned him the recipient's annoyance and impatience. But Will knew him too well for that. Sometimes, all Maxim needed was a little direction and a reminder that *he* was the one who'd called.

He pinched the bridge of his nose.

"What would you do if demons were real? Hypothetically."

A surprised laugh rolled out of the speaker. "What a weird hypothetical question."

"Just pretend. Like . . . vampires. What would you do if they were real?"

Will hummed thoughtfully. "I mean, I'd be pumped. Remember that shirt I used to have?" He laughed again. "I don't know. I guess I'd worry about what it meant for the world. I'd wonder what malevolent forces were in place that had managed to keep them secret for so long. I'd wonder how ignorant the rest of us were who had no idea they existed. And, well, selfishly, I'd wonder what it would mean for me. I'm not sure how I'd be able to wrap my brain around it all without breaking."

Leave it to Will to have eloquent, thoughtful answers to Maxim's dumbest questions.

"And what if you found out that you were dating someone who had dated them?"

There was a pause, and another hum. "I'd be fucking flattered. I mean, I wouldn't be surprised"—Maxim snorted at this—"but I'd think that there was a reason they'd want to be with me. Besides my ruggedly handsome physique and my excellent hypothetical communication skills." He paused. "I have to be honest here, though."

Maxim swallowed, anticipating a question about if he'd had a recent medication change or was experimenting with hallucinogens.

"It feels like you're mining me for a new character backstory or something. Did you find a group to game with out there?"

"Yeah," Maxim said, relieved. "Yeah, I did. Some people from work."

"Right, because nothing says fantastical and emotive creativity like a room filled with lawyers."

"We can't all be stuffy history professors, Will."

"Of course. Some of us have to be stuffy lawyers. What's the difference between a lawyer and a vampire?"

Maxim smiled, caught off guard. "One's a cold-hearted blood-sucking monster and the other's a vampire?"

"Oh. That's actually better than what I had."

"What was yours?"

"'There isn't a difference'."

Even though Will couldn't see him, Maxim rolled his eyes. "You've got the start of a great joke collection."

"'Start'? Please. I already have tomes." There was a pause, then Will said, "You know you can call me any time, right? Whenever you feel like this. Or whenever you're happy and just want to have someone to be happy with."

Maxim traced the edge of a tile with his toe. "Yeah, I know."

"If I'm teaching, I can always call you back later. I'd rather you leave gruff messages every few weeks than call me once a year with your head completely tangled up."

In this sort of state, gratitude didn't come easily, but having a friend like Will made it easier.

"I will. I promise," Maxim said.

"Excellent. It's an agreement."

"Little do you know what you've agreed to. I've got an entire library of sound effects downloaded, so I have the power to make my voicemails sound like I'm calling you from a farm. Or a tavern. Or a cave."

"Oh Maxim," Will said, surely smiling and shaking his head, "I would expect nothing less."

After they hung up, Maxim plugged in the salt lamp and let it light the hallway in a soft glow as he gathered his dinner together. His stomach no longer roiled and his hands felt steady and solid. Thinking about what Will had said, he frowned.

Why hadn't his brain broken from all of this? It wasn't doing *excellent,* but here he was, standing in front of his stove and toasting garlic while vegetables baked. Nothing burning, nothing forgotten on the counter top to spoil, nothing crisping into carbon. Except for last night, he'd been sleeping well even with earth-crumbling knowledge thrust upon him.

He suddenly remembered his conversation with Jules. *"You always knew there was something weird with the world, but then you find out that it's really, really weird, so you obsess over something that's comforting and distracting."*

Maxim stared at the little drops of oil bouncing around in the pan.

He knew that when faced with a stressful situation, he tended to focus all of his attention on something else. And, as was tradition, he'd been hyperfixating on Pippa's life and troubles and all of the ways he might be able to help her in order to distract himself from the existential dread that lurked around the corner. He had immersed himself in the world of fantasy and peril as an escape from the real world only to discover that the real world was more fantastic and perilous than he'd ever expected. It was bigger than he'd ever dreamed, and so much more horrific.

He'd felt like he'd belonged in that fake world of fake demons and fake monsters, but in this real world, it was yet another lash striking him with the knowledge that he didn't fit in. Just like when he was a kid, how he'd desperately wanted to be happy or carefree or able to go to a birthday party without taking four hours to decide what present to bring. He didn't have power, or anything special, and no matter how much he wished it, he'd never—

One piece of garlic shifted and sent a large drop of oil flying through the air and onto the back of his hand. He hissed in pain and pushed the skillet off the burner, cursing as he ran his hand under cold water.

And Pippa . . .

He clenched his hand under the faucet. He'd been using her. That's what it was. He'd always wanted to see himself as someone who *helped.* Ever since he was old enough to crack open a book about swords and sorcery, he'd imagined himself as a hero—someone who would make a difference, even if it was from behind a desk or at the front of a courtroom.

But he wasn't the hero. Pippa was. He'd wanted to help her, and had fooled himself into thinking that it was the way he'd find his own happiness and satisfaction. That her success would be his, and at the end of the day, he'd be able to fall asleep to the knowledge that he had helped the city, albeit indirectly.

She'd been right when she'd accused him of doing exactly that before, and he'd been a stubborn asshole to not see it sooner.

Maxim bent over the sink, his elbows on the hard counter and his head pressed firmly into his forearms.

He should have just talked to her about everything. He should have been honest with her instead of lashing out with his own insecurities and telling her that it might be better for her to *not* belong. Of all people, she knew what it was like to be an outsider, an observer pressed against the glass desperately wanting to find a way inside.

Maxim set his jaw and straightened. He wasn't going to let things end like this. He cared for her. No, that wasn't quite right. He loved her.

A wave of dizziness crashed over him, and he had to brace himself on the edge of the counter.

That's why this all hurt so much. It wasn't just rejection, it was the knowledge of unrequited *love*.

Fuck.

He needed to see her. Not to try and change her mind about choosing the coven over him; that was her decision alone. But even though he'd messed up, what they'd had together deserved more than to be unceremoniously discarded.

He scarfed his food and strode down the hallway to scrub some of the sleeplessness from his skin. Just as he had told himself so many days before, he and Pippa Beverly were not nearly done with each other.

Fifteen

PIPPA STRETCHED HER NECK, and her upper back gave a satisfying pop. She'd been whirling about in the kitchen for hours, accompanied by a long-cooled mug of tea and forcibly peppy music blasting from her computer.

Demonic auras still hovered around her apartment, but they weren't the solid, vibrant ones of a recent or lengthy visit. They were keeping an eye on her, watching her movements. Fine, whatever. Let them. Her wards were refreshed and solid. Nothing was getting in.

She'd barely managed to type out an email last night saying she was taking the following day off before she collapsed in a messy pile on her bed, somehow simultaneously exhausted yet unable to keep the day from replaying over and over again.

In a single day, she had destroyed a relationship, upended a friendship, and had enough gut-punching realizations to leave her winded and directionless.

Visiting her mother yesterday had gone about as well as Pippa had expected.

"They've been manipulating me," she'd said as a greeting when Mary had opened the door.

Mary's thick gray hair was tied in a braided crown around her head. She had a short sprig of rosemary pushed into a lock above one ear, and dirt smudged her cheekbone and the tip of her pointed chin.

Pippa had been ushered inside and was offered a freshly-picked apple. The duplex smelled like cinnamon and anise, and steam rose from a large simmering stock pot on the stove.

"The demons?" Mary said. "I've been trying to tell you, they're royalty—"

"And they have scrying stones. I know."

Mary had given a little frustrated huff, then muttered, "Glad to know you're having conversations with *someone*."

Pippa pretended not to hear. "No, it's . . ." She'd rubbed some dirt off the apple's shiny green skin and took a bite. Sharp and sweet. Perfectly ripe. Between more bites, she told the story of visiting the Ash Coven and what she'd overheard in the bathroom.

"They used me," Pippa said. "It was awh ah jhock—"

"What?"

She swallowed some apple. "It was all a joke. They strung me along. It's finished, I'm finished with them."

"They could have been talking about someone else. Are you sure it was you?"

Pippa gave her mother a look that had Mary raise her hands defensively.

"All I'm saying is that—"

"No." That same resoluteness, the one that ended with her flipping off the Ash Coven with their own sacred relic, warmed in Pippa's chest. "I'm done."

With excessive gingerness, Mary had sat on a creaking wicker chair at her table. "Are you sure? You have strong magic, Pumpkin. Strong enough for you to do something big, and they would be a way for you to do that."

The apple soured in Pippa's mouth. She'd set it, half-eaten, on a napkin on the coffee table. "I know how strong it is. Shouldn't that be even more of a reason for it to not be puppeted by a coven who doesn't give a shit about the person it comes from?"

"But . . . what else would you do?" Mary's face had twisted in genuine concern. "What else are you—"

"Am I good at?" Pippa finished for her, unable to stop the snap in her voice.

"That's not what I meant." It had been Mary's turn to snap. "Do you think I'm happy to see you in that job you hate? I know how much potential you have, and I can see how it hurts you not to live up to it." Her expression had softened, and she'd come over to Pippa, reaching to her in the tentative way that suggested she wholly expected Pippa to snatch her hands away.

Pippa grasped back, feeling potting soil and the paper-soft texture of her mother's palms.

Mary had sighed. "Pumpkin, if I had the magic you did, I'd feel like I could do *anything.* I don't want you to look back in twenty years and curse yourself for sitting back when you should have charged forward."

Pippa looked at her mother's brittle smile and saw a woman who had been through horrors. Mary had picked up the pieces of their shattered life by herself, and did her best to lead Pippa along while the ghosts of memories, mistakes, and regrets fluttered behind them.

"If you think I can do anything, could you trust me to find my own way?" Pippa squeezed fingers that had begun to bend with the very beginnings of arthritis. "I'm a capable witch, Momma."

Mary had nodded. A dimple creased in one tanned cheek. "I know. I'm sorry I made you think I didn't know."

Pippa wrapped her mother in a hug. "I'll figure it out. Somehow."

"Of course you will." Strong gardener's arms squeezed Pippa right back. "One more thing, though, Pippa."

"Yes?"

"Answer your damn phone when I call you."

After refreshing the wards around her mother's home, a quick run to the grocery store left her with a considerable hit to her bank account, but a truly excellent range of possibilities for her day. So instead of thinking about Maxim's eyes and hands and laugh and smile, she thought about flour-to-water ratios and what herb best complimented cheddar. She made a pan of mini quiches and a tray of gooey brownies, and was currently waiting for the icing to set on a platter of intricately decorated lacelike cookies.

Pippa tapped the handle of her spoon against her lips in thought. She could invite Jules over and, while plying her with treats, do the knowledge dump.

She could invite Maxim over and ply *him* with treats.

Please forgive me. Have a cookie. I'm a monster, but I'm a monster that makes a perfect pastry crust.

The knock at her door startled her into dropping her spoon. It could be the Ash Coven, come to tell her that they'd made a mistake and she would be accepted immediately. It could be a neighbor asking her to turn down her music.

Or it could be Maxim.

Where once the first option would have been the one to get her pulse racing, now it was the latter. She would have no idea what to say to him. Part of her hoped that she would come across as aloof and suave, as if she were completely unaffected by it all. But another part dreaded that *he* would look just that way, as if nothing they had done or experienced or talked about had stuck with him.

So when she opened the door to see Maxim Sheppard standing on her doormat, her brain shorted, leaving her capable of only stunned silence. Light stubble shadowed his jaw, and the sleeves of his shirt were pushed to his elbows. Weary smudges lay beneath his eyes and accompanied an expression that fluctuated between determination and hope. He was *here,* and he seemed like he was the one who needed to apologize, which didn't really make sense, but she figured she'd get to that in a minute.

Maxim slipped his hands into the pockets of his jeans, and Pippa was drawn to the shifting muscles in his bare forearms. The rumpled state of his hair made her want to sweep her fingers through it and tug until he groaned. Oh *God,* and she was wearing sweatpants and hadn't bothered with any sort of bra and her hair was a tangled mess, and here he was, just…effortlessly glorious. Then she remembered how she'd treated him, then realized he was waiting for her reaction to him turning up at her door, and in a desperate attempt to say something, she let out a choking gasp that sounded like she'd inhaled a bug.

Maxim's expression grew tortured, as if he'd interpreted her choke as one of outrage.

"I'm sorry," he blurted. "I shouldn't have . . . I'll go." He turned and made for the stairs.

"Wait, Maxim." Pippa had unknowingly reached out as if to grab onto him. She pulled her hand back. He was here. *Here.* He couldn't possibly leave now. "Do you— Would you like a brownie?"

He paused, one foot on the landing and the other on the step. His head was down, angled just right for Pippa to see that thin press of his lips and the furrow in his brow and the tight squeeze of his lashes against his cheeks. Quintessential turmoil. Pippa hated to be the cause of it.

But Maxim stepped back up to the landing and came to her door.

"Yeah," he said. "Okay."

He followed her inside, and Pippa closed the door in a gentle way that she hoped came across as "No point in leaving this open" instead of "You're never leaving, I'm about to magic you into oblivion."

Maxim faltered, then blinked. "It smells amazing in here."

"It's the butter." She gave him a quick smile, though disappointment pricked her when he didn't return it.

He didn't say anything else, and Pippa occupied herself with navigating the kitchen and the trays of pastries and desserts cooling precariously on upside-down dishware functioning as improvised trivets. The brownies were warm to the touch but had chilled enough that their surface cracked as she sunk a knife into the pan. She scooped one out and deposited it onto a plate. A little drizzle of a melted chocolate chip stretched across the plate, and before she realized she'd done so, she'd swiped at it with her thumb then licked it off.

When she turned to hand Maxim the plate, he was staring at her mouth, his brows drawn together and gaze intense. He blinked rapidly, then cleared his throat and took the offered plate with a swiftness that startled her.

It would have been easy to glide back into that mindset where she reveled in his reactions. Easier still to let satisfaction settle on her because of that involuntary stare, the taste of it as rich and sweet as the brownie she'd handed him.

Pippa tried not to watch him as he bit into it, but she did so anyway. A flash of white teeth, the barest flick of his tongue to catch a rogue crumb that lingered on his lower lip. He chewed slowly.

She waited until he swallowed, then blurted, "I didn't think you'd want to see me again."

Maxim frowned at her. "What? Why?"

"Why?" A half dozen barely formed words tumbled out of her. "Because of the alley. What I—" She set her palms on her cheeks and pushed up until her eyes squeezed shut, then took a breath, laced her fingers in front of her stomach, and looked at him directly. "Because I used that magic on you. Because I manipulated you and took control of your will and did exactly what I promised myself I would never do. I unleashed evil on you, Maxim, and I'm sorry. I'm so, so sorry."

It had all come out in a rush and had left Pippa feeling winded. She wasn't sure what she expected in response, but it wasn't Maxim Sheppard frowning down at his half-eaten brownie. And he wasn't looking at it—he was looking through the plate, his concentration inward and not on anything in her apartment.

"When I first found out that you were a witch," he said at last, "I thought of old book covers. The dramatic fantasy ones, painted by people who liked horror and whirling colors and chaos."

He never said what she thought he would. Pippa's hands disentangled and fell to her sides. But she did know the covers he was talking about.

"And boobs?" she added.

At last, a sliver of a smile made its way past Maxim's stoicism. He tipped his head in agreement. "Cleavage aside, they all had a sense of fear. Of power and destruction. And when I first saw your magic outside the restaurant, I wasn't able to connect that at all with you. It felt like I should be able to, but I couldn't."

He fell silent, and Pippa's guts twisted as she suspected where this train of conversation was headed.

"And the other day, when you . . ." He pressed his lips together and frowned. "You looked like those illustrations. Power surrounded you like an invisible wind and you glowed with it. You could destroy."

Before she could shrink into herself even more, he continued.

"But even like that, even when I should have been terrified out of my life, I felt your magic and I felt *you,* and you were still good. That magic was still you. The power gripping my arms and holding tight to me had the warmth of your skin. And it smelled like peaches. The taste in my mouth was just . . . you."

Pippa felt dizzy. Elated. Dizzier.

There came the tic in his jaw, and a slight shake of his head, an embarrassed twitch of his lips. "Plus, someone who makes desserts this good"—he finished off the brownie in another bite—"can't possibly be evil."

"Hansel and Gretel would like a word."

He gave her a look. "Let me know if you suddenly have the urge to bake gingerbread."

Pippa huffed a laugh through her nose.

"Did you use the, uh . . ." Maxim jerked his head at her bookshelf.

"No, these are just ordinary." She hadn't had time to visit any shops for Quillgluth extract or fairy wings, so her demon cookbooks sat unloved and unused on the shelf.

Pippa glanced down and rubbed a crumb of chocolate off her knuckle. She wasn't sure how to begin saying what she wanted to say, so she decided to just start.

"The coven will never let me in."

Maxim sighed and set his plate on the table. "I'm sorry I said that to you earlier. It wasn't right. I know how much it means to you that—"

"No." She bit her lip. "I overheard some of them talking when I was there. They've never actually intended for me to become part of their house. They've been using me to do their work for them, but still see me as something that, I don't know, *taints* their image. No matter what I do, I'll never be good enough for them."

Maxim's look of outrage felt nice, and she let herself appreciate it even though she was long past that point herself.

"*Jesus,*" he snarled. "Are you serious? What are you going to do? We can go there right now. There must be some litigation that can pull their assholes through their necks." He paused, considering. "Maybe there's a spell that can do that, too."

Pippa shook her head, though a little snort escaped her. "It's not worth it. And it's better this way. I'd been so caught up in needing to be a part of the Ash Coven that I never stopped to ask myself if it was something I even wanted."

She risked a glance at him, and though the outrage was gone, his intensity wasn't. She felt it snag her by the sternum and she wasn't able to look away.

"You were right," she said.

Maxim closed his eyes and raised a finger as if he were a musician paying close attention to a quiet note. "What was that?"

Ass. If not for the hint of a smirk at one corner of his mouth, she would have said the word out loud.

"You were right."

He tipped his head back and let out a groan far too close to orgasmic for the situation. "God, that feels good."

A sweet squirm low in Pippa's belly sent heat flooding up her neck. She shifted, hoping that it would calm her body, because she wanted to see that look on his face and hear that phrase and feel that groan rumbling against her skin and *hell* why was she such a mess right now?

She wrangled her thoughts and said, "It shouldn't have been on me to fix it all. It never should have been."

Maxim sobered and nodded. His expression was one not of pity, but of understanding. Maybe, if she looked close enough, a little bit of pride, too. *I'm glad you figured that out,* said with nothing more than a dip of his chin.

He gripped the back of one of her chairs and leaned forward, a casual stance that also reminded her of a sprinter preparing to launch.

"While we're on this subject." Maxim sighed and gave her a chagrined smile. "You were right, too."

Pippa couldn't resist. She let out her own breathy moan, a high "Aaah" that darkened Maxim's eyes. "Say it again."

The chair creaked in his hands, and he gave her that look again, the one that made her feel like she was the dessert handed to him on a plate.

What revelation would he share? Pippa's pulse lurched beneath her skin, her body excited and nervous all at once.

Then he cleared his throat and shifted, his attention wholly on the table in front of him. "I've been thinking of my time with you as a way to give me what my job doesn't provide. You accused me of it before—twice, actually—and both times I'd been too fucking stubborn to see it."

Well, that wasn't the revelation she'd hoped for. The taste of sugar and chocolate soured in her mouth.

"So that's the only reason you—"

"I'm not finished."

Although he didn't raise his voice, intensity laced his tone and the look he pinned her with. Pippa blinked, startled by the sudden heat it instilled.

"The other day, when I was here last, I stopped you because I was scared."

Pippa stayed quiet and let him finish at his own pace. Memories of him on his knees and his mouth working feverishly threatened to overwhelm her, but she dug her fingernails into her palms and kept them at bay.

"The more time I spent with you, and the more I learned about everything you live with, the more I wanted to be part of it. It was the excitement that I'd always wanted and the fulfillment I've felt I needed. I was forcing myself somewhere I didn't belong, and it wasn't right of me."

"You were scared of not belonging?" Pippa let out a high, short laugh. "It's funny, I can't think of anyone else in this room who might have been going through that *exact same thing*."

"No, that's not what I—" He swallowed and took a deep breath as if he were preparing to dive into treacherous water. "I'm not magical. I'm not special. How could I compare to anyone you would want to be with? I was scared that I would fall for you, and you would never fall back."

Pippa noticed that her mouth had fallen open in her shock, and she snapped it shut. "Are you serious? I don't think that at all! Can't you believe that you're nice to be around? Enjoyable, even? *God*." She dragged her hands down her face. "I never wanted just a fling with you, Maxim. I like being with you. I like talking with you, and arguing with you, and do you know how *obnoxious* it is to suddenly realize that seeing you is the best part of my day?"

Maxim was staring at her, the slightest crease between his brows. It looked like he was fighting with a smile and losing.

"Then why did you keep the mark on your neck?" he said. "It reminded you of what you like. Something that I couldn't fully give you."

Oh, *that's* what he'd been thinking? It made a certain sense once she remembered the vagueness of what she'd said in that closet, when she'd intended to be coy and flirty and had apparently instilled a lingering sense of self-doubt.

Pippa let out a frustrated groan. "Goddammit, Maxim. I kept *your* bite mark on my neck because it reminded me of *you*. Because I love—"

She broke off. There were a thousand ways to end that sentence without leaving her exposed and raw. A quick readjustment could send her on a tangent far away from words she wasn't sure she was ready to say out loud. *Because I love knowing that someone might see your mark on me. Because I love how straight the welts from your teeth are, did you have braces as a kid? Because I love scarves.*

Pippa had spent enough time recently dancing around the edges of honesty.

"*. . . You,*" she finished in a whisper.

Maxim strode toward her, swept her into his arms, and kissed her harder than she'd ever been kissed in her life, consuming her gasp like it was nourishment. He tasted like chocolate and sweetness and *him.*

The stubble on his chin and upper lip scraped at her skin, but she didn't care. She wrapped both fists in the soft collar of his shirt, and she tugged him down in an effort to keep him as close as possible. When she slid one hand up his nape and dragged her nails along his scalp, he gave a little groan, perfect in its desperation.

Maxim turned them, and Pippa felt the edge of the table dig into her ass. Suddenly, the kiss turned soft. Tender. He pulled back slightly until their lips barely brushed, and he brought both hands up to gently frame her face.

This was impossibly sweet, charmingly divine. Pippa no longer felt her feet on the floor or the weight of gravity or the temperature of her apartment; all her senses were overwhelmed by him. Hard muscle, thick hair, the citrusy, heady smell of his skin.

Maxim flicked his tongue along her lower lip and cradled her jaw in his palms, tracing the curves of her ears with his fingertips. She was on the cover of a bodice ripper. That's how this felt. She was in the climactic windswept scene of a movie, with a dramatic cliffside in the background and soaring orchestral music.

"I'm going to need you to take off all your clothes," he whispered.

And that would be the exact dialogue in one of those scenes, too, Pippa was sure of it. She smiled against his lips. "And here I was thinking that I'd been experiencing the pinnacle of romance."

"Nudity is romantic."

Still smiling, she grabbed the hem of her t-shirt, but as she lifted it, she paused.

"Actually, no." She stepped back out of Maxim's reach and walked around the table so it stood between them.

He looked concerned until he noticed her smirk.

"Here's the thing," she said, putting on an air of serious analysis. "Once I get my shirt off, you're going to jump me. You're going to see my tits, which are admittedly incredible. You're going to lose your wonderful horny mind and do all sorts of things to me on the carpet or the table or against the counter."

"Don't forget the couch," Maxim said. "Also maybe a wall." He followed her, stalking around the table.

"Exactly," Pippa said. "And while I admire your creativity and can-do attitude, we've already done things in the living room. And in a closet. When I fuck you, I want it to be somewhere comfortable."

The look Maxim gave her could have leveled entire buildings. His eyes were dark, his cheeks flushed, his hands clenched as if readying to grasp her as soon as she was in reach. The same part of her hindbrain that told her she wanted snacks and a warm fire and a place out of the elements was telling her now that, really, the floor would be just fine, actually, because she needed him driving into her hard, and she needed that *now*.

Despite the growing haze of lust, Pippa walked backward toward her bedroom with the hope that she would look suave and sexy and not bump into any walls.

"So," she continued. "Here's the deal." She delicately lifted the hem of her shirt until it was barely beneath her breasts, and Maxim's expression told her that he was making a solid attempt to rip off her clothes using only the power of his stare. "We're going to my bedroom, and you can't touch me until we get there."

Pippa slid the shirt over her head, then tossed it away. Goosebumps tickled over her breasts and her nipples tightened under the dual intimidation of her apartment's chill air and Maxim's guttural exhale that sounded very much like both a curse and a prayer.

"You're ruthless," he managed. He followed her as she made her way down the hallway, and whipped his shirt off without breaking stride. His chest heaved, and muscles flexed in his upper arms and shoulders as he hurled the shirt to the floor.

Pippa's thoughts stuttered and her backward shuffling slowed. Maxim was within reach. She could just touch him. She could just *grab him.*

He even loomed effectively while turned on. Not surprising, of course. The normal intimidating size of him held an additional thrill because she was the entire object of his attention. He wasn't looming over her with his thoughts a thousand miles into depositions or witness statements. Here, he was absolutely intent on her. The carpet could turn into moss, or a swarm of bees would burst from an air vent, and he'd still be training that razor-sharp gaze on her. Well, her and her tits.

Maxim still came closer. His collarbones were level with her nose and she imagined briefly how he'd react if she surged forward and dragged her tongue along the ridge of each one. She'd snake her fingers through the golden-brown hair over his sternum, tug at it until he gasped.

But she'd made a decision, and for fuck's sake, the bed was so close.

Pippa tutted. "We're not even through the doorway yet." Then, because she'd never been able to resist mild torment, she cupped her breasts, flicked her nipples, and reveled in Maxim's unraveling. "Come on, now. Think of my poor body. Think of all the rugburny possibilities this hallway will provide and all the joint pain you'll—"

Maxim interrupted her with a low growl that managed to travel all the way down her spine. He scooped her up, carried her through the doorway, and dumped her on the bed like a sack of laundry.

Pippa would have felt some outrage at that if she hadn't become a giant bundle of nerves and lust. He followed her onto the mattress and then buried his face in her chest, letting out a groan that was equal parts relief and ecstasy.

She couldn't help but giggle a bit, and when Maxim pulled back, he was wearing a chagrined smile. He didn't stop touching her, though. Her breath hitched at the whisper of his knuckles along the swells of her breasts. Her nipples tightened into sweet, sensitive buds when he circled her areolas. Although she wanted to do the exact same to him, to stroke and pinch and lavish attention on the parts of him she'd not touched yet, this seemed to be something that Maxim needed.

His expression was heartbreakingly reverent, and Pippa felt her throat grow tight. It struck her then how absolutely ridiculous it had been that she'd ever thought he was only wanting to be with her because of what excitement she might be able to bring to his life. That he saw her as a character from a thrilling story and by association, he could pretend to be in that story as well. Someone who thought those things would not be looking at her as if he were memorizing her, tracing her curves and assuring himself that she wasn't about to dissolve in front of him.

Maxim let out a short sigh, then buried his face in her breasts like he wanted to set up residence in her cleavage.

Pippa arched against him and gripped his hair, keeping him close as he licked and sucked and nipped at her until she writhed beneath him. He attended to every freckle, each stretch mark. Her entire body felt hot and tingling and far too tight. From below, she heard a muffled voice that sounded very much like "God, your tits are perfect."

"Maxim, I need more," she said in a breathless whimper. As he rose up to kiss her, she reached down between their bodies to his belt in a wild fumble that brushed the ridge of his erection.

He let out a choked gasp and bucked into her, grinding against her hand, which then pressed her fingers firmly against her clitoris. Pippa cried out at the pleasure that flooded up her spine, but it wasn't enough. Not at all.

The elastic waistband of her sweats suddenly felt as confining and awful as a cage. She struggled with the fabric until Maxim noticed and finished wrestling them off, taking her underwear with them and sending both into a pile on the carpet.

He came back to her in an instant, mouth on hers and stroking thick fingers between her legs, just as hard and fast as she needed. The rasp of his jeans on her inner thighs and the raw slide of his stubbled jaw along her chin were her only anchor; if not for the slight flash of pain, she'd be drifting up through the ceiling and into the sky.

As Maxim slid two fingers into her, she cried out and held tight to his shoulders, his skin hot under her grasp. Oh, she could never get enough of this. Not of his breath coming in quick puffs on her neck, or the wickedly dexterous motions that stretched her and flicked against soft, slick parts that made her legs spasm.

But still.

"I need you," she slurred. "I need all of you. *Please*."

He rolled to his side and whipped his belt open, and before he'd fully undone his zipper, Pippa was yanking his jeans off. Or, at least, trying to.

"You could have made this easier and worn breakaway pants," she said, tugging on the cuffs that had become stuck on Maxim's surprisingly bony ankles. She could use magic to help remove them, but knowing how little she'd be able to concentrate on directing it, she'd probably end up disintegrating the denim completely.

"You know," Maxim said, "that was my first thought when deciding what to wear here." The jeans were turning inside-out and one foot finally popped free. "I was planning on giving an impromptu striptease on your counter and buying a sparkly thong printed with 'I'm sorry'."

Pippa took a brief second to really appreciate that visual, then mentally filed it away for the future. "At least then I wouldn't feel like I was shucking you like a corn cob."

Maxim's moan was fake and exaggerated and still managed to make her mouth dry. "You say the most arousing things."

After one last yank, the jeans fell defeated to the ground and the only remaining piece of clothing between them was his underwear—soft, likely expensive, just so very *him*. Her fingers hovered at the waistband as she battled with the dual urges to either ravish him or to take things slow and savor every second.

As if he could see the pattern of her thoughts, Maxim sat up and leaned forward. He dragged his hands up her thighs, his thumbs barely brushing where she wanted him, and as Pippa let out high whine, he gripped her hips and looked at her intently.

"Pippa," he said, his voice low and rumbling. "I want you to shuck me. Shuck me hard."

She pounced on him and pushed him to his back. His underwear came off much easier, bless it, and once she'd hurled it away, she straddled his hips and let herself stare.

His skin was soft and hot beneath her hands as she slid them up his sides, over his chest, along his neck. She'd never enjoyed how bright the light was in her bedroom, and it had forever irritated her that she could see the dust that collected in corners when the intent to clean had not been as strong as the intent to eat or sleep or do a thousand more important things.

With the brightness, she could see every bit of Maxim's body that had been hidden before now. The flushed length of his cock demanded her attention, and it was lovely, sure, with its ruddy head and shining tip, and it jerked in the most delightful way when she brushed it with the back of her hand. There were other parts of him that were just as satisfying to explore: the ridges of muscle above his hip bones, a faded leaf tattoo at the top of one thigh, a half dozen little moles scattered along his rib cage.

Pippa traced each part of him just like he'd done to her earlier. And just as she had done, he lay still and let her. His skin tensed beneath her fingers and his breath quickened as her fingers brushed his flat nipples and trailed over the coarse hair that led down the center of his stomach. She reached the rippled skin of the scar, still pale and as large as her palm, and she stopped.

He didn't seem to react as much to her touch here. She'd tried her best to heal it fully, yet was there still numbness? Lingering damage that she hadn't been able to heal that day?

Pippa pressed her palm to the scar. "Why won't you let me heal this for you?" It had happened because Maxim had been in the wrong alley at the wrong time. He had nearly died surrounded by splintered pallets and puddles of restaurant wastewater.

Maxim gripped her hand, pulling her attention out of her head and back to the fact that he was fully naked and sandwiched between her thighs.

His mouth quirked into a little half-smirk, though his eyes were serious. "Maybe I like it," he said. "Maybe it reminds me of you."

He let out a grunt of surprise as Pippa pounced on him again, kissing him hard enough to send them both to the mattress.

Maxim swept a hand through her hair and kept her pinned close against him as he delved between her legs once more. She moaned into his mouth, trying to buck and get him deeper, closer.

Oh, she was through with waiting. Pippa reached out to the magic surrounding the nightstand by her bed and pulled on the drawer. Yet magic required concentration, and her current focus was on dexterous fingers and soft lips and a very firm dick currently poking at her stomach. What she'd intended to be a gentle tug to slide the drawer open instead bloomed out of her control.

The entire drawer wrenched out of the nightstand and crashed into the opposite wall, spilling its contents across her floor.

Shit, fuck, whatever. Pippa flicked the magic and a condom flew into her hand.

Maxim peered over the edge of the bed and gave a raised eyebrow to the toy collection rolling and bouncing over the carpet.

"I thought witches didn't use magic wands?"

"I will walk out on you." The threat was a lot less believable when she was actively ripping open the condom wrapper.

"We're in your home."

"I'll bequeath it to you. Mazel tov on your new rent, Mr. Sheppard."

He was hard beneath her hand as she rolled the slippery latex onto his length, and his chuckle caught in his throat as a garbled groan.

Pippa rose to her knees and aligned him with her entrance, then dragged the head of his cock through the slippery mess her body had made of itself. Her head tipped back at the beautiful pressure. She'd put a hand on his chest to steady herself, and now she felt his breathing shudder and his heart hammer against her palm. She eased down slightly, barely, not nearly enough. Then again, and again, until he slid in deep.

Scalding pleasure raced up her spine at the tight fullness. She wanted to close her eyes, lose herself in every sensation. But even more than that, she wanted to watch Maxim as she took him.

He looked enraptured. According to his expression, her pussy was life, and death, and everything delicious and exquisite. Muscles jumped in his arms as he held onto her hips, and when she began to move, he said her name in a way that melted most of her body below her navel.

So Pippa moved faster, harder, her ass smacking his thighs and her breath coming in high, cracking moans. Her skin was hot and tingling and with every buck of her hips, pleasure bloomed higher and higher until it burned hot at the base of her skull.

Maxim rubbed her clit with the pad of one large thumb, and the heat crested so high she could hardly breathe. He pushed harder.

Oh . . .

There.

Her orgasm swept through her in a bright, searing wave. She cried out, holding onto Maxim's shoulders as if he could keep her tethered. Little skittering aftershocks pulsed along her legs and through where her body stretched tight around him. Her breath slowed, and she drifted back to the room.

"That was ridiculously hot."

Pippa let out a laugh that was more of a wheeze. "Wh— Ah, really?" She dragged a hand over her forehead. Sweat had dampened the hair by her ears and along her nape, and she felt a drop trickle between her breasts.

But when she looked down at Maxim, the level of lust in his gaze quickly evaporated any of her doubts. She bit her lip.

"So," she said. "What do you want now?"

He sat up, leaned forward, and took her lower lip between his teeth, tugging slightly and making her gasp. His chuckle sounded far too self-satisfied.

"I want to fuck you, Pippa," he murmured. "I want to fuck you *hard.*"

"Well I'd really like that too, but I'd also like to know if we're already doing away with the 'shuck' joke, or—"

She let out a squeak as he fluidly rolled them over. His hips slid along her thighs and his weight pressed her into the mattress. He guided himself back into her and started to thrust slowly, building his pace until he was drilling into her and fully driving the thoughts out of Pippa's head.

His sweat-slicked skin moved between her knees and slipped under her hands. She tasted salt on her tongue when she sucked his neck, then reveled in the way he groaned as if he were falling apart in the best way.

"I need you to come again." His voice was a desperate, broken growl.

"I need that too," Pippa panted, reaching down to her clit.

"Do you know how much I've thought about you coming on my cock?"

She wasn't capable of much more than an inquisitive sounding whimper, so she did that, though she did touch herself harder.

"So many times. Too many times. And now I've felt it, I can't get enough. I want you to come until you can't stand." He was beginning to sound breathless. "I want— I want you to be exhausted and sweaty and . . . filthy. Then I want to clean you up and— Fuck, *fuck,* just start all over again."

Oh stars. Pippa quickened her fingers into brutal strokes as her orgasm crept up slowly through her toes, then sent her careening off the edge. This one was bigger than the first. Lights danced behind her eyelids and she cried out, arching her back against the bed. She squeezed her legs around Maxim's hips to keep him close, keep him deep, and every one of his merciless thrusts drove her even higher. She was weightless and breathless and bodiless.

Maxim slowed. As the fog cleared from her senses and the ringing faded from her ears, she realized she'd been digging her nails into his back. There was a red welt on his shoulder where—*oops*—she'd bitten him without realizing. If he'd noticed, it didn't seem like he was about to say anything. The hard fuck had become something else. He cradled the back of her head and gripped her thigh, holding her leg high against him as he rocked into her.

He let out a shuddering sigh that tickled her neck. "You feel— *Shit,* you feel incredible."

That spicy, herb-y sensation of his aura surrounded her in a comforting haze. It was strange, in a way, to simultaneously feel so at peace, so connected with someone, and wholly out of her mind with arousal. Or maybe this was what happened when you said "I love you" and meant it.

"Maxim," she whispered, and he rose up high enough so he could meet her gaze. His weight was braced on his straightened arms and it did some distracting things to muscles now just out of reach of her mouth.

She wanted to say something perfectly sweet or outrageously hot, but when she saw his flushed cheeks and kiss-swollen lips and rumpled hair, she ended with, "I love making a mess out of you."

Well, that was kind of both.

He huffed a laugh through a crooked grin. "You're very good at it." Then he began to move again, kissing her jaw, her neck, his breath hot puffs against her skin.

Every nerve in Pippa's body still buzzed from her orgasms. With each of Maxim's thrusts, the parts of her that were tight and tender and aching grew hotter, brighter. She was unfurling. Dissolving. Her jaw ached from being caught around her silent scream, and she arched into him and held onto his arms so that she wouldn't completely shake herself apart.

Maxim's pace grew more rapid and a guttural groan rumbled in his chest when she clenched around him. His eyebrows were drawn down and—oh, there—the tic in his jaw. The tic that meant he was holding himself back somehow, trying as hard as he could to keep it all together.

Exactly the opposite of what *she* wanted.

Pippa pulled him down to her, then pressed a kiss to that tic. It pulsed beneath her lips and her tongue before she brought her mouth to his ear and whispered, "Give it to me, Sheppard."

His exhale began as one of surrender, then twisted and shuddered into a low groan. He pounded into her with a vigor that set her breasts bouncing and the bed frame rattling against the wall. When he came this time, it was louder than she'd expected: a broken, choked cry let out without the worry of being overheard.

They lay together after, Pippa sprawled on top and her sweaty cheek pressed to Maxim's sweaty chest. She lifted her head to look at him.

Maxim's eyes were closed, his long blond eyelashes resting flush against his cheekbones. The corners of his mouth twitched after a second as if he could feel her watching him.

"I'm not sleeping," he said, a little defensively.

"You could if you wanted to." Pippa settled her hand flat on his sternum and rested her chin on her knuckles. "I wouldn't think any less of you for needing a nap after fucking my brains out."

Maxim gave a soft laugh. He shifted beneath her, settling with one arm bent behind his head and the other slung over her back. His fingers traced light circles around her shoulder blades.

"I don't need a nap. A breather, maybe. A short moment of respite."

Pippa couldn't hold back her smile. "*A moment of respite*? What era have you traveled to? Are you going to besmirch my reputation next?"

"I've been expanding my literary cuisine."

"Incredible." She rose onto her elbows. "You know, if you're suddenly into historicals, I do have this book about a duke you might be interested in reading."

"How do you know I haven't read it already?"

Pippa scoffed. "Right."

Maxim continued, his expression serious. "You don't know what I skimmed when I was desperately trying to sleep on your couch." He gave her ass a swift, soft smack, and Pippa yipped in surprise.

A little part of her said that she should get dressed and check around the apartment complex for any lurking demons. But not right now. The bed was soft, the warm man beneath her silently begging her to test his refractory period. Probably. She'd oblige in any case. The outside world, with its horror and danger, seemed far, far away.

Pippa pressed a kiss to his chest. Soft at first, but as soon as she tasted his skin, she wanted more. She flicked her tongue along the plane of one pectoral, then glanced up to see his eyebrows raised and an amused smirk crinkling the corners of his eyes.

"It's the strangest thing," Maxim said dryly, "but I *swear* your intentions right now are less than honorable."

Pippa smiled against him, then began a slow path down his body. "Let's get filthy."

THEY COLLAPSED INTO THE bed eventually when exhaustion and contentment proved more overwhelming than the need to make new discoveries, several of which included Pippa's toy drawer.

Pippa hummed contentedly and shimmied closer to Maxim. She couldn't properly move her legs anymore, and her head felt packed with warm, downy fuzz.

They'd given themselves a hasty cleanup, then crawled beneath the covers together, Maxim's arm draped over Pippa's waist and her ass pressed tight to his stomach. His breathing had already slowed and he made a sleepy, snuffling sound against her hair. This was perfect. Everything was perfect.

She smiled into her pillow and fell into a sleep so deep she didn't even smell the smoke when it came.

Sixteen

THE ALARM PRICKED THROUGH her dreams first. It hovered on the periphery like a screaming mosquito that bobbed closer and closer to her neck. It couldn't have been more than a few hours since they'd fallen asleep. Why was her alarm going off *now*?

If she could just reach out to grab it, crush it in her hand and grind it into silence—

Someone was shaking her shoulder. A loud voice in her ear yelled her name.

Pippa struggled awake with a snort. The alarm was louder, sharper. As she fought through the fog of sleep she realized that the sound wasn't the buzzing squawk of her alarm clock but the high scream of a smoke alarm.

She surged upright and yanked the chain for her bedside lamp. Smoke made the air hazy and left an awful, acrid taste at the back of her throat. But there were no visible flames, no ominous glow. Not yet.

Pippa scrambled out of the bed. Maxim was already pulling on his jeans, and as she wrestled with her own pants, he glanced down the hallway.

"I don't think it's your apartment," he said. "But we have to go. Right now." He tossed her shirt to her from the floor.

Getting dressed was so much more difficult when her brain was screaming at her to flee. She found herself caught up by little, inconsequential things: her socks didn't match, which would mean her stupid squeaking sneakers would fit differently. It was getting harder to breathe. Adrenaline pricked at every inch of her skin and sent her stomach lurching high in her chest. Everything seemed important and nothing seemed important. Her shirt was on backward. *Where was her phone? Her keys?* The shirt was a V-neck, which would look absolutely *ridiculous.*

"Pippa!" Maxim pulled her out of her spiraling thoughts by literally pulling her from the bedroom. When had he put on his t-shirt? *Her books.* She thought of old pages crisping in flames and a pang shot through her.

The floor was growing warm under her socked feet. Another smoke alarm began to go off, and from the apartment below, she heard the soft hiss of the sprinkler system activating.

As they ran through the front door, she had a momentary thought about whether or not she should lock up behind them, but now flames glowed in the slats between the stair treads. There came the sound of breaking glass and something large collapsing right as she and Maxim made it to the ground floor.

They were both coughing, and two paramedics hustled them away from the building. An extremely impressive response time; Pippa would have to write an email to . . . someone. She couldn't quite think of who that would be at the moment.

The paramedic who had grabbed Pippa held her shoulders with a cool, firm grip and steered her to the back of an ambulance, where he sat her down and wrapped a flimsy Mylar blanket around her. It seemed extremely excessive, but she wasn't going to object. Maxim coughed and tried to shrug off his own blanket. The paramedic beside him tucked it closed.

What the fuck had happened? Her downstairs neighbor didn't smoke. He was standing in the crowd gathering in the courtyard, and even at this distance she could see the blank, empty look of utter shock on his face. Had there been an electrical fire? Was it just luck that her own outlet hadn't shorted at the wrong time?

Pippa looked back at the complex and the bright horror that had once been home.

The fire was spreading to her own floor despite the desperate defense of the sprinkler system. She hadn't ever thought she was attached to her apartment: it was cramped, not especially well-lit, and there was a spot on the carpet that, no matter how often she cleaned it, had a stain and smell that hinted at illicit pets at one point in the apartment's life. All of it had always just been "good enough."

As she watched smoke barrel out of the open door, she realized that perhaps she'd grown more attached than she'd thought. Although it hadn't been perfect, it had been hers. It had been where she'd flopped onto the couch after wandering dirty streets and smelly demon haunts. Endless nights of coming back to that couch, that bed, that kitchen, thinking of that space as just a transitional one. Somewhere to recover before it all started again. She'd stared up at old stains on the ceiling and daydreamed about a time when she could look up and see something beautiful.

Pippa fully admitted she didn't know much about house fires, however she didn't think that they exploded into being this quickly, especially with modern safety regulations. The apartment complex wasn't that outdated.

Unease wiggled at the back of her brain. Something about this was wrong.

She had turned to Maxim with the intention of telling him just that when an aura crawled across her skin like a swarm of insects. *Thorns and grease.* It transported her back to a dark warehouse, a late night at the docks, a gore-flecked jaw opening wide.

There was a Tro'grath demon nearby. Now that she was focusing, a second aura distanced itself from the first: acid and burnt oil.

The unease in her skull unfurled and spread through the rest of her body. This fire had been completely intentional, and it was spreading so quickly because it had been made to do so.

No hostile demons had been able to get inside her apartment, but judging by the near-constant auras hovering around the building, they had tried. And since they couldn't get in . . .

Just like unwanted vermin being eradicated from a field, Maxim and Pippa had been flushed out.

She had to get Maxim somewhere safe, somewhere warded and fortified with—*fuck,* with anything. Boarded-up windows and seventeen locks and maybe a mastiff.

"I'm going to give you something for the shock, okay? Your blood pressure is really high."

Pippa barely heard the paramedic talking. For a fraction of a second, she wondered how exactly he could tell her blood pressure since he hadn't done anything except wrap a blanket around her, but that didn't matter right now.

She turned to Maxim. "Did you get your keys?"

He patted a pocket, then nodded. The movement made his Mylar blanket fall to his elbows, and he shrugged it back up. "Why?"

The two auras were twisting her intestines into knots. Oh, this was so bad.

She stood, turning to the paramedic to say that they were both fine, not to worry, they just needed to go somewhere quiet to calm down, but the words froze in her mouth. There was something off about the man's face, as if his muscles were lagging behind his intended expressions.

He was holding a syringe. Before Pippa could flinch away, he jammed it into her upper arm and depressed the plunger. A horrid burning sensation flared in her arm and spread through her body.

"Hey!" she shouted at him, trying to pull her arm out of his suddenly painful grip. The Ash Coven had always impressed the importance of never doing magic in front of the populace, but what were they going to do? Not let her in? Again?

Pippa reached for the magic around her to blast this asshole away from her, but . . .

It wasn't there. Nothing was there. She'd thrown herself into what she'd expected to be a comforting embrace only to instead fall through empty, dark air. Glancing down, the syringe still had a little of its contents: an awful, sickly green liquid.

Shock slammed into her, and everything within Pippa froze. The taste of bitter metal coated her tongue. Where before in the elevator she had sunk into the numbness and the disbelief, now she exploded up through it. She'd been manipulated and her apartment had been destroyed just so she could be ambushed by two demons wearing flesh disguises. And she didn't have her magic. Again. *Not fucking again.*

She wound back her free arm and punched the paramedic full the throat, nearly throwing herself to the ground with the force of her swing. As he staggered back, she yanked the needle out of her arm and threw it at him. It bounced harmlessly off his chest.

"What the hell?" Maxim yelled. "Pippa, what are you doing?" He was suddenly at her side, Mylar blanket pooled on the asphalt.

Where she'd punched the disguised demon's neck, the skin was hanging loose as if it had been stretched out. Little tendrils of magic flailed uselessly in an attempt to keep the shell attached, but it had not been designed to withstand any sort of impact.

The other demon grabbed Maxim and hurled him through the open ambulance doors, his body crashing into the cab's barrier. A gurney ricocheted into a wall of cabinets with an ear-shattering crash.

Pippa cried out and looked desperately at the crowd at the apartments. Surely someone had heard. Someone could help. *Anyone* could help. Yet every single person was intent on the flames, and the roar of the growing blaze must have smothered all other sounds.

Her second punch wasn't as successful.

The demon anticipated her lunge and easily dodged, then picked her up as if she were a bag of garbage to be disposed of and threw her into the ambulance. She fell bodily onto her side, her elbow digging between her ribs and forcing the air from her lungs.

The demon that had stabbed Pippa ran around to the driver's seat while the other climbed into the back of the ambulance along with them and slammed the doors shut.

The world lurched as the van squealed into motion, and Pippa rolled into a spilled pile of boxed gloves and intravenous tubing.

Just out of arm's reach, Maxim was struggling to sit upright.

Disentangling herself from latex and nitrile and plastic, Pippa inched her way over to him. Something was sticking to her forearm. As she tried to swipe it away, she realized it was a bit of the skin from the demon's disguise, and she forced down the bile that nudged at the back of her tongue before wiping her arm on her jeans.

There was a squelching sound from the cab. Even through the wall, she could smell the sulfurous stench of the now undisguised Boe demon.

"Hate this," the Boe demon shouted from behind the wheel. "Hate it." There came some garbled snarling and the ambulance lurched hard to the left, followed by more garbled snarling.

Pippa reached out and closed her fingers around Maxim's wrist. His eyes focused and connected with hers. The hair at the edge of one of his temples shone dark and damp with blood. Not a lot, but the fact that he didn't seem to be able to *stay* focused on her was worrisome.

The demon in the back of the ambulance with them barked out a grating laugh. The Tro'grath, then. It rolled its head as if stretching, and the fake skin separated around the neck and began to slough to the floor.

"You were hired for it," the Tro'grath said. "Think it matters if you hate it?" Skin, hair, and navy uniform fell off as if it had all been a fragile shell. "The family gave you money to bring them, and if it means you have to drive, then it means you have to drive."

So they were to be brought to the family of the prince. As revenge? As a meal? Both?

This Tro'grath was an older demon than the one Pippa had killed in the warehouse. Two sets of horns swooped back from its forehead and its pale skin was covered in scars. It still wore the uniform pants and the heavy black boots. The demon raised long arms over its head in a stretch, then brushed off a scrap of skin and blue fabric that clung to one shoulder. The gems in its forehead, laid out like a mockery of a coronet, glowed a soft pink.

The ambulance squealed around a corner, hurling Maxim into a cabinet and hurling Pippa into Maxim. His arms came up reflexively to wrap around her. Even though they were captured by demons inside a death box barreling along what felt to be the Autobahn, she breathed deeply and buried herself in the homey, thyme-y savory feel of his aura and felt *safe*. They would be all right. Somehow.

A glance behind her showed that the Tro'grath hadn't been bothered at all by the rapid swaying of the ambulance. It had kept its footing, shifting its weight easily.

Pippa prodded gently at Maxim's head. "Are you okay?" she whispered.

Maxim let out a short breath. "Yeah." He winced as the ambulance rattled over a bump in the road. "I wouldn't be offended if you offered some of that healing magic, though."

Bitterness pooled in Pippa's stomach. "They jabbed me with that poison earlier. I don't— I can't do anything."

Maxim closed his eyes and tipped his head against hers. His exhale stuttered as pain mixed with despair.

She remembered their conversation days before.

What will you do next time?

She'd had the opportunity to figure out what she'd do if she was attacked again, and instead of accepting the help offered to her, she'd made the decision to shoulder it on her own. Accepting help was as bad as *asking* for help, and if she had asked for help, that would mean she wasn't able to handle everything she was trying to do: protect the city, earn her place in the coven, prove herself to a bunch of people who—shockingly—didn't give a fuck what she did.

Frustration and fury twisted about inside Pippa's chest. She could have done a lot of things differently. *Should* have done a lot of things differently. But none of that mattered, because right now she was without her magic, and no amount of self-pity would fix that.

The Reaper magic twitched inside her, wriggling and impatient. Maybe it could help. She'd only used it once though, twice if she counted the accidental familiar creation, and she was hardly able to say with any confidence that she could control it. And what if it exploded out of her control? What if she hurt Maxim again? No. She'd find a way without it.

There were plenty of drawers nearby; one of them must have something sharp enough to use as a weapon.

Before she could slide herself over to the wall and surreptitiously pilfer, the ambulance slammed on its brakes and she and Maxim were thrown around once more. The sudden stillness felt simultaneously like a relief and a menace.

The driver's door slammed shut, and a second later the back doors squealed open. Humid night air filled the ambulance.

She'd expected chaos, sirens, some sort of uneasiness that represented the situation they were now in, but all she heard was the unnerving normalcy of crickets and the calming rush of distant traffic.

The Boe cracked its neck and gave Pippa and Maxim a disgusted sneer. "Let's just kill them now, save ourselves the trouble. Bring the bodies."

Pippa's spine grew cold and her fingers dug into Maxim's arm. She'd use anything she could find to defend them: a roll of gauze, a pen, a needle.

The Tro'grath rumbled a snarl. "They want her fresh. You'd like to be the one who brings them cold meat?"

Well that was . . . not quite a relief, but it gave them more time. Since the poison was injected this time, it might not wear off as fast as what had been on the knife, but she just needed to wait for her body to break it down. If they could stall the Tro'grath family for long enough, then they might make it out of this.

The Tro'grath bent over and grabbed Pippa, wrenching her arms behind her back as it heaved her out of the ambulance. She lashed out with her feet and struck the demon's shin with the back of her heel. *Shoes. Shoes would have been nice.* The demon hissed in pain at the same time Pippa did, then grabbed her ankles and slung her over its shoulders as if she were a deer being brought to a hunter's table.

Perhaps it was too accurate of a metaphor.

The Boe grabbed Maxim by one leg and dragged him out of the ambulance toward a large sewer grate, not pausing when Maxim thudded onto the ground with a shout. He swung at the demon, but his movements weren't as snappy and quick as she'd seen before, and it almost seemed as if he had to move his limbs through syrup.

Pippa squeezed her eyes shut and threw herself against the thick, greasy walls blocking her from magic. Was there a crack? A gap? Could she feel a tickle against her fingers, or was it just her imagination?

She snapped her eyes open as the world grew suddenly weightless. The Tro'grath had jumped into the sewer entrance, and above her, she saw the Boe holding the grate with one hand and Maxim's leg with the other. With a quick movement, it slung Maxim over one of its shoulders, then climbed down the metal ladder and set the grate back in place.

The tunnels were cleaner than she'd expected. Although she was loath to admit it, Pippa had been inside her fair share of sewers. This, by far, was the least disgusting. It smelled as if it had been constructed for a subdivision that had not yet been built. In the darkness, she felt a damp cave-like chill, and smelled concrete and animal droppings and a bitter musk that hinted at some sort of habitation, but nothing close to the nose-singeing rankness of wastewater.

Small things to be grateful for. If she were to die, at least it wouldn't be alongside the scent of excrement.

Something clanged down the tunnel, and the Boe growled.

The Tro'grath chuckled. "Watch your head."

Another growl, though this one sounded far more irritated.

Information trickled back to Pippa from some of her reading after the first Boe attack. Their night vision was about as good as a human's, so it would have just as much difficulty seeing in this tunnel as her. Since she could barely make out glints of metal and puddles of watery moonlight, the Boe must have been following them by sound.

She'd read other things, too, but they were somewhere in her head, locked away behind adrenaline and panic and fear.

Together, they reached a larger open area. The Boe let out a frustrated snarl, to which the Tro'grath carrying Pippa called out a few words she couldn't understand. There was a scuffling, the drag of something heavy, and then little electric lights came on around the perimeter of the area: a sizable space that would have served as a junction for multiple tunnels. The demons had dug into some of the side walls to expand it into a larger place to gather.

Pippa hardly had time to take in her surroundings before the Tro'grath swung her down onto the concrete. Gasping in pain, she was unable to do more than roll when the demon shoved her into a corner with one clawed foot. Maxim thudded beside her with a grunt.

His face was twisted into a grimace, and dirt puffed in front of his face as he coughed. Pippa pulled herself over to him and grabbed at his wrist, his arm.

"Maxim," she whispered. "Are you—"

The Tro'grath let out a shrill cry as more demons emerged, their skin pale in the dim yellow light. A ring of softly-glowing stones were on each of their foreheads. One of them seemed more frail than the others, and it put most of its weight on a crooked cane. It had three sets of horns, all long and twisted, as if they had been growing for centuries. One thin arm held a book bound in mottled, dark leather.

Pippa made a quick count of the demons milling about. Six Tro'grath demons and a Boe. Still overwhelming for a witch without her magic and a mildly concussed lawyer, but not so overwhelming as to be utterly and completely impossible. Just mostly impossible.

The demons circled each other, then began to lunge in play fights and shriek like a pack of jackals after a successful hunt. None of them paid any attention to Pippa or Maxim. The two of them were the meat left in the corner.

Maxim had closed his eyes, and Pippa shook his shoulder. When he looked at her, she gently swept his hair back from his forehead. The blood at his temple was tacky and beginning to mat, so at least the wound had closed.

"Can you move?" she asked. "Are you all right?"

Maxim nodded, though it made him wince. "Head hurts a bit. I'll be okay."

"Are you sure?"

He gave her a wry look. "No." Then he swallowed and pushed himself closer to her. "What do we do?"

Pippa took a deep, filling breath. "My magic will come back eventually." She spoke in a whisper barely above silence, unsure how much the Tro'grath demons were able to hear over their cavorting. "We have to stall them somehow. Or just . . . hope they let us sit here for that long."

"And if they don't? Start preparing our own kidneys for dinner?"

His words set off a flare of recollection within Pippa. "Boe demons. The, uh, the one that's different from all the others here, like the one that was in the elevator at work. They have a gland under the arms kind of like a kidney. Hit it hard enough and they might not go down, but they'll be hurt."

"So, what, we fight our way out?"

"If we have to."

Maxim nodded slowly. "What about the horned ones?"

"Tro'graths are fast. Their teeth are sharp, and they can unhinge their jaws. Silver burns them, but I don't have anything with it."

"What else?"

Pippa bit her lip in thought. "See the glowing gem in their forehead? The central one is a bit more fragile than their skull, so aim there if you need to hit them."

Maxim nodded again, then winced and tenderly prodded at his head.

"Maxim—"

"Do you see anything we could use against them?" Although still pained, his expression held a certain determination. He was never going to admit that he was too hurt to fight back against whatever death awaited them in this sewer. Maybe it was the attitude she should adopt as well; what had grim surrender ever done for anyone?

"No," Pippa said. "But I haven't—"

The old demon rapped the cane on the concrete floor until all of the demons grew silent.

"I know we have waited long enough for this," the demon said in a raspy croak. "So I will not talk overlong."

Shit. Pippa shared a look of dread with Maxim.

The demon continued to speak. "Our prince was unjustly killed, his body defiled by witchcraft. That witch, that putrid offender of our ways, is here now. And we have been given a bounty. The witch has come along with an additional extra bit of flesh. Whatever shall we do with them?"

She didn't know that Tro'grath demons could laugh, and now she never wanted to hear it again. It was part jeer and part cackle, as dry and sharp as an old, broken bone. Jaws slackened and teeth shone in the dim light, and she turned away from the sight of drool dripping down from one demon's open mouth.

There was nothing around them but concrete. Concrete, and rubble left from when this area had been roughly expanded.

Pippa nudged Maxim and jerked her head at a chunk of rock as large as her hand. And there, a length of galvanized steel conduit only a few feet away.

"Consider this my gift to you," the old demon said. "A welcome to our new home. Let us consecrate it in their blood."

The demon closest to the corner where Maxim and Pippa sat took a step toward them.

Maxim began to breathe faster and deeper. He gave Pippa a quick, short nod, and that was it.

They moved at once together, Maxim grabbing the rock and surging to his feet as Pippa threw herself at the conduit pipe. Her hand closed around cold metal, and even though she was still on the ground, she swung it as hard as she could at the nearest knee. The pipe impacted the Tro'grath with a sickening crunch, and the demon screamed in alarm.

Another shriek came from behind her, and she risked a glance over her shoulder to see that Maxim had smashed another Tro'grath in the forehead with the rock. The demon staggered backward, the center gem in its forehead crushed.

The other demons let loose a series of awful, discordant screeches. It felt fitting then, to be in a cave. For a second, it seemed as if she were in the darkest corner of hell, surrounded by the furious damned. The ground seemed to shake with the volume of it all.

Pippa urged herself to her feet and as she rose, she swung her section of pipe at another demon. It dodged easily; they were expecting an attack now. She barely managed to dip out of the way when it swiped at her with its claws. When she swung again, the end of the pipe clipped a demon's rib cage.

It was all so futile. The pipe in her hands wasn't light, and each swing caused the muscles in her arms to burn, and with every additional miss, it became harder to bring the pipe back up to try and block the downward swipe of demon claws.

Something glowed in the cavern, and Pippa glanced up. The older demon had discarded the knobby cane. It held the tattered book open in one hand as it raised the other over its head. As it rasped out a series of grating words, crackling blue light coalesced in its open palm. Then, just like the demon was throwing a baseball, it sent the magic flying out at Pippa.

She threw herself to the ground and the magic collided with the wall behind her. A sickly warmth radiated out from the wall, making the back of her throat burn. Chunks of concrete dug into her palms. She could smell blood, somewhere. Maxim yelled her name but it sounded muted.

A demon leaped for her and she kicked at it as hard as she could. Her heel impacted a soft demon belly and it doubled over, wheezing.

Pippa scrambled upright. Faster than she could even see, the Boe appeared before her and grabbed her shoulder, digging sharp claws into the flesh around her collarbone. Her eyes watered at once.

Armpit.

With a yell, she swung the pipe up and sent it hard into the Boe's armpit. It seized, arching backward in pain. The grip on her shoulder released immediately, and Pippa staggered backward into the reach of a waiting Tro'grath.

Claws raked across her back, fully from her neck to her waist. Pain followed—a bright, acidic bite that seared her veins. She cried out as her muscles locked in shock. She couldn't move, couldn't think. Her vision flashed white and she tasted bile. But she could hear Maxim to her left, hear him yelling and attacking and *still fighting*. A memory came to her then of him in the elevator. Battling every screaming nerve in her body, she spun around and struck up with her knee, hitting the Tro'grath fully in the stomach.

The old demon barked words from its ancient spellbook, then hurled out more magic. Pippa saw it too late this time. She wouldn't be able to dodge this.

But it wasn't directed at her. She watched as the bright magic left the demon's clawed hand, speared through the air, and impacted Maxim in the chest.

Everything froze.

No.

NO.

A lock of his hair blew in some unseen breeze as he collapsed to the ground.

Pippa didn't care about the demons or the magic or the hot blood flowing down her back. She dove to where Maxim lay. She didn't have to feel for a heartbeat or breath to know that both would be absent. Something deep within her knew.

No, the Reaper magic knew. There was nothing within this body to control.

Fury, anguish, *rage*. She was burning from the inside, breaking apart like blinding-hot metal heated past its limit. Her vision swam and wavered.

She'd promised herself she wouldn't use the Reaper magic. She'd kept it inside to protect her family, to protect Maxim. But now? None of it mattered.

The Reaper magic knew what to do, and Pippa let it come. In the sunlight and between rows of trees in a peaceful neighborhood, she'd let it sniff the air. It had stretched, moved around and brushed up against her before she buried it deep enough to pretend it no longer existed. Now, she let it consume her.

Pippa dug her fingers into Maxim's shirt and screamed. Her lungs felt infinite. As she screamed, it began to reverberate around the room, becoming layered and frantic. Concrete crumbled from the ceiling and rained down around her like little hailstones.

The demons surrounding her all stepped back, but that older demon came closer. The stones in its forehead reflected the glow building once again in its palm.

Magic raced beneath her skin and surged out around her as she stood. Chips of stone dug into her feet and an aching throb began in her heels. She looked up at the Tro'grath and it stilled, the thin muscles in its arms bulging uselessly. The magic curled around the demon and dug into the pale body.

Pippa's senses bloomed. The demon's heart lurched as it sensed the new intrusion. Blood slithered through its veins in a thrum that matched its quickening heartbeat, and thick tendons pulled and stretched. Lungs inflated around rich air, bones as solid and white as obelisks stood powerful within a construct of meat and viscera. In this body was strength, energy, *life*. Everything that the demon had destroyed in Maxim, and all that it no longer deserved to have.

Everything that she now would take.

Pippa yanked on those strong bones, those unyielding tendons, and with a yell of exertion, threw the demon bodily into the wall with a horrid thud. Chunks of concrete thundered down onto its body and she felt its life dim and then go out, like a candle sputtering against a gale.

One of the younger Tro'graths charged at her, and she twisted on its body, its mind.

I am not your enemy, she thought to it. *They are.* She could sense its resistance through the joints straining against her command, then there was a give and a cool relief, as if she had been pushing her fingers through the velvety skin of a peach. Suddenly, the demon was attacking the other demons around it.

This power felt raw and right. She had thought she wouldn't be able to control it, but there wasn't any controlling it, no more than she could force her mind to wake in the morning or tame the curl of her hair. It just *was.* She encouraged it, and it followed her intention.

The Boe demon ran at her. It froze when she held up a hand, though the motion sent a new wave of pain into the puncture wounds in her shoulder and the deep gouges in her back. Her own strength was beginning to wane; the Boe was overflowing with it.

Pippa found the source of that strength and grabbed it. Energy flew from the Boe, and as she directed it to her back and shoulder, she felt the stolen life force knit her skin together and replenish the blood she'd spread over the concrete. Her back felt whole once more, the pain gone.

The Boe choked, then crumpled bonelessly.

The younger Tro'grath had finished off the last of the other demons. It stood as if thinking, a chunk of something red and dripping held tight in its maw, its claws covered in gore.

Pippa tensed. She had been distracted with the Boe and her hold on this young demon had loosened completely.

It blinked at the bodies around it. She would have thought the demon would show remorse for having killed its family, or even shock, but instead it simply seemed irritated. Its milky eyes landed on her and narrowed. With a loud, wet gulp, it swallowed the meat in its mouth and made the smacking motion of a toothless octogenarian after a caramel.

Christ, she didn't want to think about what it had just gleefully eaten.

It smiled at her then, a horrific widening of an unhinged jaw.

She would be dessert, that smile all but said out loud.

But Pippa knew the feel of the Reaper magic. Right as the demon lunged for her, she twisted its body into a vicious angle, pushing harder and harder until she felt a little *pop.* The Tro'grath fell slowly and crookedly.

The Reaper magic settled against her, calm and satisfied.

It was quiet except for the roaring in her ears and the magic's soft thrum beneath her skin. She was the only living being in this room. Bodies surround her, broken and horrific, and she would have felt victorious except for the one at her feet.

Pippa crouched to touch Maxim's cheek lightly. His skin was still warm and soft. A sob rose up from the deepest part of her chest and burst from her in a fractured, awful cry. None of this was right; none of it was fair. They had found each other, actually *found* each other. And it had all been ended by magic. If he hadn't come with her, if he hadn't come over . . . If—

She curled over him, her tears dampening his hair. She thought of fairy tales and fantasy novels and pretend games and how if Maxim were here, he'd have had a thousand ideas for what to do.

The Reaper magic settled around Maxim like a blanket of fog, surprisingly tender after what Pippa had just made it do. As it lay against him, she felt his body, his muscles, his bones. There was a slight laceration on his forehead from their time in the ambulance that had since knitted shut. Beneath that, his skull was unbroken. Other than bruising and a few scrapes, his body was uninjured. The magic had only banished his soul.

In which case . . .

Pippa swallowed and sat up straight, rubbing the tears out of her eyes. She thought back to when she had made her first familiar. She had pulled a random soul out of the ether and into a body. What if she could do the same with Maxim's? His body was fully capable of accepting his soul, if she could find it.

There were about a thousand reasons why she shouldn't do this, but were any actual *genuine* destroy-the-world reasons?

The coven would definitely never let her in after this. Not a problem at all.

Her mother would be royally pissed. Well, it wouldn't be the first time.

She might do it wrong.

That gave her pause. If she didn't do this correctly, then she would be damning some innocent person to a life of horror and she would lose Maxim forever.

And if she didn't do it at all? Then she would still lose him, and spend the rest of her life wondering what would have happened if she had tried.

Pippa sat on her heels and forced her mind to calm. When she had first made the familiar, she had felt the barrier between life and death and dipped her fingers inside. Now, it wouldn't be enough to grasp blindly and hope she could find the exact soul she needed; she would need to force herself in completely.

She closed her eyes. Maxim's hand lay in hers and she squeezed it tight, then submersed herself in magic and slipped through into death.

Seventeen

He was dreaming.

Definitely dreaming.

Had to be . . .

Had to . . .

No, that didn't quite work anymore.

Dreams had a fogginess to them, an ethereal quality that even if his brain told him they were *real*, the rest of his body claimed the contrary.

This didn't. It was crisp. Vivid.

But unlike the last time he thought he was dreaming—lying in an alley, soaking the concrete, staring at a discarded piece of lettuce that stubbornly clung to the side of the dumpster by his head—where he existed now lacked the visceral weight of *life*.

Maxim looked around. He stood on a vast expanse of shining black marble. Above and around him, sparks burned like rapidly growing trees and shone so brightly that they reflected off the stone. In the bright flashes, he caught the silhouettes of ruined houses and ancient castles. Shapes of people formed around him and wisped into smoke like blown-out candles. Stars exploded in endless fractals that grew into insectoid legs and then dissolved.

Who knew the afterlife was *metal.*

Maxim caught sight of a particularly alluring tower whose wobbly walls and crenellated roof seemed likely to contain whimsical secrets. He began to walk in its direction, but paused with one foot lifted.

There was something he was forgetting. That probably wasn't the correct word. Forgetting was accidentally leaving a memory behind. It was getting up with his gloves still on a bench, or letting the face of a childhood playmate soften and fade with time.

This was harsher. There was a fracture deep in his chest where he'd once felt whole, but now it was as if something had been forcibly ripped from him.

He put a hand to his sternum and pressed hard. It was strange to expect the familiar sensation of bone and flesh and a thrumming heartbeat and instead touch only a muddy warmth.

When he glanced down, he frowned. He was blurry. Faded. If he bent forward, he could see the sharp edges and arched vaults of architecture through his stomach.

There was an eerie calmness to death. An unexpected emptiness, too. He'd expected to at least see a distant ancestor or the class hamster from fourth grade, but the landscape seemed barren and even the humanoid silhouettes floated away and out of reach as if they were hesitant to come too close. A few reached out with spectral fingers before darting backward like scared cats.

Was it him? Was he the problem?

"I could feel you."

Maxim choked and spun around. "Pardon?" He hadn't heard anyone come up behind him, although in this place, would a footfall even register the same? It was reassuring at least that he wasn't here by himself. This was what he expected: an afterlife with actual life in it, not just hints and teasing outlines.

The man who'd spoken was shorter and slighter than Maxim. He too looked faded, as if his skin and his hair and his plaid flannel shirt had been diluted. He stared at Maxim harder, seemingly unaware that his abrupt statement could have come across as awkward and inappropriate. Unless that was just the way of things in death; who had time to care about tact in a place like this? They could have met before though, and Maxim had just forgotten. Maybe that was it. The man did seem oddly familiar.

"Her magic," he continued. "It's in you." His dark eyes ticked down and he stared at Maxim's stomach and the scar hidden behind his clothing.

Unease prickled up the back of Maxim's neck. The non-air around him suddenly felt colder, the non-sky a little darker. A swirling figure drifted past where the man stood and reached out only to snatch its arm back as if it had spotted a venomous snake.

"What do you mean?" Maxim said slowly.

"It's easy to recognize." The man flashed a short, wistful smile. "A parent never forgets."

For all the lack of sensation in this space, Maxim's body must still have contained blood. It turned to ice as it raced up his spine.

Fuck. This was him. The murderer himself.

And of course, that was why the man looked familiar. He had Pippa's overbite and her molasses-colored hair that crested in a wave over his high forehead. His eyes, though large like hers, were closer to black and lacked the warmth Maxim had come to love. There was an unnerving edge to him too, as if he wanted to be moving but had been forced to stand still.

Maxim fought an overwhelming urge to put more distance between them.

"I was so proud of her when she first showed her potential," the Devil in Plaid said. "Even as a child, she was powerful." He spoke of his daughter as if she were a collectable trading card. The pride in his voice jarred with the lack of any emotional weight.

"When you 'left'?" Maxim raised an eyebrow. "Funny way to describe what happened." He expected an argument on that at least, but the absence of a reaction felt far more jarring than any anger or frustration.

"What's she like now?" Those dark, empty eyes bored into Maxim's.

"Happy," Maxim found himself answering. "She's clever and capable. And she's happy."

Her father made a face. "Her magic," he pressed. "Is she strong? Can she use my magic?"

What the fuck is it to you? Maxim wanted to ask. Before he could open his mouth, the space around them shifted and Pippa's father appeared next to Maxim. As Maxim took an involuntary step backward, a strong hand wrapped around his wrist. The grip was stronger than expected. Colder, too.

"Magic leaves traces," her father said. "Every type. It's like a fingerprint." He was looking at Maxim with a fresh excitement that was somehow worse than the apathy. His gaze tripped around Maxim's torso and settled around the middle of his chest. His smile widened. Behind his even teeth, the inside of his mouth was black. "And she's used it on you. She has it." He let out a long sigh and tipped his head back to grin at the inky sky.

Maxim wrenched his wrist free. Pippa's father didn't seem to notice or care.

"Why does it fucking matter?" Maxim finally snapped. "You won't see her again. We're both dead. It's not like death has visiting hours."

Oh, that hurt more than he'd expected. It was shocking enough to die, it was something else entirely to realize *he* would never see Pippa again. He'd never watch her laugh or bask in the way her face glowed when she said she loved him. Every thought he had of their possible future together and every idle fantasy of how it might look paraded through him: nights on the couch after dinner and slow, sleepy makeouts; waking up together and playing chicken with who would make coffee first; coming home to a place that the two of them had made together.

None of it would happen. Ever. Where once such thoughts had felt like nourishment, now they struck him like they'd been barbed. The emptiness in his chest grew and erupted out of him in a shuddering gasp he tried valiantly to contain because like hell was he going to become emotional in front of Pippa's evil dad.

Her father remained oblivious to any of these brutal realizations. He gave Maxim that appraising look again, as if he was deciding whether or not a pig was fat enough to sell.

"If she's used magic on you," he said, "enough to leave a trace as strong as there is, she must care about you." He spoke slowly and deliberately, like speaking to a child. "And if she has my magic, then . . . Well. She'll find you."

The absolute arrogance of this man made bile (just the memory of it, surely) rise in Maxim's throat. This single person was responsible for everything in Pippa's life she regretted, and every part of herself that had caused her misery. He'd caused such pain and here he was, speaking about her as if he *knew* her.

Pippa's father smiled again. He stayed smiling until Maxim reared back and punched him full in the face.

It was a hard hit. Darkness puffed out around her father like black pollen. He staggered backward, and when he straightened, his face was misaligned slightly, his nose crunched inward.

Maxim felt slightly guilty. Not that he'd caused this, but that it was him doing it in the first place. This was Pippa's father; she should be the one punching the shit out of him.

Her father let loose a scream of rage and swiped at Maxim. Maxim dodged the fist easily, yet power shot out from that outstretched arm and clung to him like an ooze. He felt his guts squeeze and cramp, his muscles seized, and every bone in his body begged him to curl into a ball.

The intrusion was similar—as when Pippa had done this, he had the same sensation of someone else's presence under his skin. Even though she'd been angry and desperate, her touch was still soft. She was catching a bird but holding it gently enough to keep it still without damaging a delicate body.

Her father's magic was nothing of the sort. Maxim felt the sickly creep of rot, the burn of coal, the taste of rusted iron. He was a bird to be crushed and squeezed until it bled.

The smile was gone. Cracked lips pulled into a snarl.

Maxim fought past the agony in his guts, striking out again anyway. His knuckles impacted jawbone and the memory of pain radiated up his arm.

Pippa's father was becoming blurrier. Angrier, too. His face contorted with fury, his jaw hanging crooked and his eyes as dark and empty as glossy stones. The blackness within his mouth trickled out over his chin.

The grip on guts and bone and muscle tightened. That awful rot filled Maxim's nostrils as his body was yanked upright and held still with his arms at his sides.

"She told you, didn't she?" Pippa's father said. He dragged his plaid shirt sleeve over his nose and mouth, spreading the greasy black ooze across his cheek. "She must have. How I came to be here."

Magic wrenched Maxim's hand up to his neck so his own fingers reached clawlike for his throat.

Yeah, Maxim knew. Under this sickly power, people had been forced into violence they didn't understand. They'd been used like puppets until their puppeteer was . . . well, he didn't much know that part. Killed, decidedly, but the details had been vague.

Maxim closed his eyes. Maybe he should have asked Pippa for more information; something in the way her father was looking at him made him think the same was about to happen now.

What would happen if he died while already dead? Would his soul be destroyed completely? Would he shatter into the ether? If Pippa came looking for him—not that she would, not that she *should*—would there be anything to find?

His hand closed on his throat. The pressure of his fingernails dug into the spot where his pulse would have once thrummed.

This sucked.

This really, really sucked.

He imagined that he heard Pippa calling his name. It sounded far away and muffled, and he wondered if it was just some sick trick of the universe that now, seconds before his permanent dissolution, he'd hear her calling to him from the world of the living.

He'd take it.

His hand tightened and he braced himself for whatever horrible wrenching agony would . . .

She called his name again. It was louder, closer.

Right as he wondered if this was not, in fact, his imagination, Pippa's father sucked in a sharp breath and released the hold on Maxim.

Maxim fell to his knees and watched as the man before him looked around wildly, prodding at his jaw and his smashed nose.

"She can't . . . She can't see me like this," he gasped. The air around them both wavered, and then he was gone.

The smallest hope flickered in Maxim's chest. If he could hear her— If her father could sense— Maybe she was—

A silhouette moved out in the starry blackness. Where the others had been meandering and aimless, this one moved with purpose. It had a familiar shape, too.

"Pippa?" he said, almost afraid to say her name out loud in case it would cause that growing hope to be blown out.

The silhouette was running to him.

Then she was there, stumbling to a halt in front of him, beautiful and exhausted and happy and *holy shit* she was *here* and the moment he wrapped her in his arms he felt that missing chunk of himself slot into place. If he was to dissolve, perhaps it would be like this: infused with so much joy he would explode.

She hugged him back, strong arms around his waist, the pressure solidifying her existence here. It sounded like she was crying, but it could also have been him.

"Hey," he said to her. "So I think I met your dad?"

Eighteen

She'd fallen through a veil. It had felt like drifting through the finest spun cotton, each strand tender against her face. She had pushed forward blindly at first and charged through dark landscapes and silhouetted crowds. There was too much surrounding her. Thousands—no, hundreds of thousands—of auras had spun past, battering her with the smell of roses, the acrid tang of vinegar, and the soft brush of down.

But *there*. A hint of spicy warmth. Pippa had pushed forward, clawing her way through a maelstrom of mist and thorns and stardust. The warm sense of his aura fluttered around her. It was faint, but enough for her to follow.

She'd called out his name, over and over again. More than once, she thought one of the silhouetted figures gestured in the same direction of his aura. Sometimes they pointed, yet sometimes they seemed to be shaking their heads or slashing diagonally with their arms as if discouraging her to go further.

It had just been her imagination, surely.

She'd come closer, and closer, and then finally she saw the outline of his shoulders and nose and she broke into a run, not stopping until she was holding him as tightly as she could. It didn't feel quite right, since he was more pressure and aura than anything of substance. There was a bit too much give when she squeezed. He didn't complain, so she kept doing it.

"You're here," Maxim said into her hair, her neck, against her lips. "*Fuck,* you're really here."

Pippa couldn't quite believe it herself. She'd opened her mouth to say just that when Maxim pulled away.

"We need to leave," he said.

The urgent tone of his voice punctured the giddy relief at finding him, and it took several long seconds for what he'd said earlier to drift back to her.

"Because of my father?"

Maxim nodded quickly and glanced around. "He was here. He's here, he's creepy as fuck, and he knew that you'd be coming for me." When he made eye contact, his expression held an earnest terror that made chills race over her skin. "He just . . . *looked* at me and saw that you'd used the Reaper magic on me and—" Maxim swallowed. His hold on her upper arms tightened. "Pippa, he saw it and he was *thrilled.*"

Because she'd used his magic.

She'd used *his* magic.

Oh stars, what had she done?

For the first time since she'd come to this place, she looked around at the crumbling buildings and dark apparitions floating in her periphery. Everything appeared faded and dim. Sounds were muffled, as if she was hearing them with her head swaddled in a quilt. There was no breeze, no movement of air, just an empty cold that pressed on her skin.

And Maxim. She couldn't quite *feel* him. While she still sensed the overwhelming presence of his aura, there hadn't been any warmth to his body. She could see through him as well, structures squatting in the distance that shouldn't be visible through his shirt and his jeans and his handsome, worried face.

Yet her own body was solid and tangible, so far removed from the landscape and people around her. She was breathing. Living.

Pippa knew exactly how it felt to not belong somewhere. When her coworkers chatted about their weekends at the country house or their "ridiculous families" that included an uncle with a rock tumbling fascination or a grandparent who spent too much on bingo, Pippa had the sense she was trapped behind glass and only able to view it all at a distance.

It was wrong for her to be in this place. She was an intrusion, and she shouldn't have come, but she did anyway. Life was sacred. Death was as well. Right on the heels of using that dark magic, she'd made a mockery of the natural order. Just like her father.

What had she done?

Her limbs turned leaden. Her legs buckled, and the ground rushed up to her. It should have been bruising and hard on her knees, but she only felt a gentle pressure as if she had been kneeling in mud.

"Pippa?" Maxim sounded worried. Muffled, but worried.

Sorrow, as thick and sludgy as tar, crawled through her stomach and adhered her knees to the ground.

A thought came to Pippa then: maybe it would be better to *not* go back. It was a trickle of a thought, barely bold enough to grab.

But in this world, this landscape without weight or air or breath, that thought grew heavier.

Pippa looked at her hands, the empty sky, the shadows and the mist swirling between. "I'm . . . I'm like him." How could her breath hitch when there was no air to catch on? "I used his magic to manipulate. I used it to *kill*. I—" A sob was building in her chest and it burned her throat as she tried to fight it. "I'm here. I'm disrespecting life. Death. All of it."

Maxim lay a hand on her back. There was no contact, just warmth. His aura strengthened around her and she closed her eyes at the rightness of it.

"Why did you come here?" he said. He was crouching at her side, one elbow resting on his knee.

Pippa blinked at him. "To— What do you mean? I came here to find you. To bring you back. It's wrong though, I shouldn't—"

Maxim grabbed her hands. She wished she could feel it.

"You didn't come here to be like him, Pippa," he said. "I'm going out on a limb, but when you said you used that magic to kill, I'm assuming you used it to kill the demons in the sewer that kidnapped us."

"I— yeah."

"Same demons who hired others to hunt you down? Who were a genuine danger to everyone in the city?"

She nodded.

Maxim stroked his thumbs over the curves of her wrists. "There's something fundamentally different between wanting to cause pain for the sake of *pain* and what you've done."

"What did I do?" She hated how small her voice sounded in this space.

The corners of Maxim's mouth twitched. "You helped the city. You saved people. And you came here because you love someone so much that you'd ignore death to follow them. It's both highly impressive and deeply, *deeply* flattering."

Pippa's laugh was watery. When he squeezed her hands, she squeezed back.

"And," Maxim continued. "For what it's worth, that person loves you just as much. But, you know, doesn't have the power to transcend mortality for it."

A giddiness surged up through her chest like champagne. "Hell of a time for a love admission," she said.

Maxim shrugged. "If I can't say it in an eerie land-of-the-dead hellscape, when could I?"

"Before you'd traveled to an eerie land-of-the-dead hellscape would have been nice."

He huffed a laugh and smiled at where their hands were joined.

Pippa stared at the way their fingers, transparent and opaque, laced together. The visible contrast between them and the absence of warmth on his skin sent her joy skittering away like a kicked animal.

"I want to bring you back," she murmured. "I don't know if I should." It hurt to think the words. It hurt even more to hear them out loud.

"I'd give you advice, but I don't think I'd be able to be impartial."

She caught the tail end of a wry smirk when she glanced up at him. "Maxim—"

He pursed his lips. "Ignore what you *should* do. What do you think is right? What do you feel is right?"

What would feel right would be a handbook, or a syllabus, or someone wizened and stern hovering over her shoulder to tell her what to do.

In their absence all she had was herself.

Pippa closed her eyes. Of course Maxim would want to come back with her. She wanted that as well. Yet how could she fly in the face of death and manipulate a soul while still condemning her father for having done the same? Even when she'd done this before as a child and brought the bird back to life, the consequences had been both horrifying and chastising enough to stick with her for so many years.

She usually shied away from that memory. The human scream, the wide-open beak, the small beady eyes rolling in terror.

Now, it gave her pause.

That soul hadn't been willing to return. She'd sunk her fingers into the afterlife and tugged blindly, yanking a random soul into a bright and unexpected world without even thinking.

This was different. Maxim was aching to come with her and be deposited back into a body that was uninjured except for a few scrapes and bruises.

She would do it. *They* would do it. Determination set a new lightness in her. The air didn't feel quite so cold; the sky didn't seem quite so dark.

Pippa gripped his hands and stood, tugging him up as well. "Bringing you back would be against the laws of nature."

His face fell and he nodded in understanding. "I underst—"

"Maxim," she interrupted before he could go too far. She rested her hands on either side of his face, holding him still so she could summon every bit of sincerity to say, "Nature can suck it."

A startled laugh burst from his chest, not as loud or resonant as it should have been. "I love you," he said around a sigh.

Stars, that was lovely to hear. And the way he said it, too—easy and earnest, as if the words were already comfortable.

A sudden chill crept up the back of Pippa's neck. About to ask Maxim if he felt it too, she froze. His posture was rigid, his expression twisted into a mask of fear.

In that moment, she became aware of a new aura infiltrating the space around her. This one crept through her senses as if she'd put an old penny and moldering leaves beneath her tongue. Copper with a hint of rot.

"Hello, Philippa."

A man was standing away from them like someone who was too nervous to join a group of people mid-conversation.

There had been no photos of her father that survived into Pippa's young adulthood. It had taken a few years for Mary Beverly to find them all, and when she did, she left behind voids in picture frames and collections of printed-out memories. An entire person had been physically ripped out of the past. Pippa would find an elbow occasionally, or a few fingers lingering outside the jagged border.

He'd died when she had been young enough to have forgotten how he looked. And yet, as he stood in front of her, she still recognized him. She caught some of her features in his face and it turned her stomach to know she shared that much more with him.

Her father smiled. He was smudged around the edges, as if someone had gone over him with a few short scrubs of an eraser.

Pippa swallowed the dryness in her mouth.

His smile split his face. It was a little too wide, a little too white. "I'd hoped you would be like me, of course, but I'd never—" He took another step toward her, then frowned when Pippa retreated, keeping the same distance between them.

"Philippa," he said in a chastising tone. He'd said that before: she'd been five and was standing above a broken window, shattered glass surrounding her bare feet.

He didn't approach her further, yet as he looked at her, something shifted in his expression. The sharpness faded and transformed into a familiar warmth.

There was the man who tucked her in at night. The man who hugged her when she fell, who laughed at the uncoordinated wave of her chubby toddler's arms.

"I missed you, sweetheart," he said. "I know it's been hard without me. But we're tough. We're so alike, honey. More than I ever knew."

"Bullshit."

He frowned at that, and Pippa wasn't sure if it was because of her foul language or the venom with which she'd spat it out.

"If it's been hard, it's because of you," she said. "You left a stain on my life. The only reason it was hard was because you'd been there in the first place."

He jerked as if he'd been slapped, though it seemed to Pippa that he wasn't hurt by what she said, but startled she'd had the gall to say it in the first place. Any veneer of the doting father dropped in an instant. His narrow jaw clenched, and his upper lip twitched.

"Do you know what they did to me when they found out about this magic?" he said through a snarl. "The Ash Coven tore my soul from my body and scattered what remained into the wind.

They made an example out of my corpse. What do you think will happen to *you*?"

Pippa wanted to laugh. "The Ash Coven didn't do that because they found out about your magic." It was all so silly that she laughed anyway. It came out hard and sharp. "They killed you because you used your magic to entertain yourself."

Her father's look hardened. The sense of his aura tilted into something more charred, an acrid smoke that burned the roof of her mouth. "It doesn't matter," he said. "You have my magic. You're *using* it. You've accepted it."

She shook her head. "No, we're—" She huffed a laugh. "Sorry Dad, I already had this conversation with someone who matters."

"You'd ignore your *blood*? I *made you*, Philippa."

Pippa frowned at that. No, actually, he hadn't. Far more than his presence during her early years, her life was a product of everything else she had welcomed into it. She thought of having tea with her mother, laughing at bad TV, succubus-spiced drinks, meeting Jules in the apartment courtyard with Bilbo waddling behind them on a leash and every day-brightening comment from someone who smiled at the sight of a basketball-sized black cat taking a stroll. She thought of Maxim's determination and his crooked nose and how he could give his whole self to wanting to make something better.

She opened her mouth to correct the egregious misconception her father had just made, but realized that it didn't matter. Why should she defend herself to someone who saw her as nothing more than the magic he'd given?

Pippa turned to Maxim. "Let's go," she said again.

Movement caught her eye. Her father had tensed his fists, and black smoke trickled out from between his knuckles.

"No," he said simply. "You won't be leaving. Not like that."

There was a clench at her back as if someone was squeezing her spine. She wanted to move, she *needed* to move, but she couldn't. Panic lanced through her guts. Was this how Maxim had felt when she'd used it on him? An awful immobilization that came from another's will taking over and settling in? Pippa wanted to vomit. That awful aura flooded her sinuses and stung the back of her throat.

"You're not being thoughtful at all, Philippa." Her father twisted his hand, and Maxim cried out. The clench along Pippa's spine tightened until it sent pain radiating down through her legs. "I'd hoped Mary would have raised you better."

How *dare* he speak her mother's name and try to use their relationship as manipulation.

Fury bubbled up through Pippa, and the Reaper magic's hold on her limbs twitched uncertainly.

It was easier to control here. Maybe it was more at home in a world only occupied by souls. When she wrapped her thoughts around it and forced the tendrils of magic away from herself and Maxim, the magic bent more easily to her intentions.

Her father's eyes were wide as he lunged at them.

Pippa pushed with the Reaper magic. There was no heartbeat to feel, no muscle to guide, but his soul was solid enough.

He froze, his limbs straining against the magic holding him in place. He would break free. That was obvious. Pippa could feel the Reaper magic already buckling against her father's willpower. Was this to be her future? Spending eternity trading magical violence in the afterlife?

Fuck, they had been so close. If only they left earlier. If only she'd found Maxim sooner. If only—

A wisp of energy brushed her fingertips. Not the Reaper magic; this was lighter. It was faded, just like Maxim and her father. She pushed hard on the Reaper magic holding him in place and let her awareness drift just enough to feel this new power in the cracks between the old stones and the wisping exhales of long-dead plants.

Natural magic.

She hadn't bothered looking for it because of the poison, yet it seemed that had no bearing here. There was no body to poison, after all.

Pippa pulled on that magic. It began as a trickle, but the more she called, the more came until it was rushing through her hands, pouring out of the stars and cobblestones and air and wrapping itself around her father to contain the black smoke now billowing out of him. He tried to lash out with the Reaper magic through Pippa's barrier and only managed to send a pitiful swat her way. She batted it aside easily.

Her father's yells took on a new desperation. "You're here *because* of me! *You need me!*"

Pippa leaned forward into Maxim's aura. It was chicken soup with a dash of chili powder. It was coming home after a cold day to comfort, love, laughter, and perfection.

"No," she said to her father. "I really don't."

Her father screamed, his jaw too loose and his eyes too big, right before the magic and the smoke closed around his face.

"Goodbye, Dad." Pippa wrapped her arms around Maxim and that spicy, happy warmth, then threw herself backward through the mist and empty space and crumbling monuments to where her body knelt on cold concrete.

The air slammed into Pippa. It smelled far too beautiful for an unused sewer. The damp concrete and rusting iron might as well have been perfume and roses. She was back. Fully back.

Every part of her felt the swift, breathtaking swoop of relief, although her knees ached from the hard press of stone. She was still holding Maxim's hand. His skin was growing warmer and she saw the slow rise and fall of his chest.

Pippa barely breathed. She only attempted this once before, and even then it had been a fraction of what she'd just done. She tasted blood and realized she'd bitten her lower lip too hard.

Maxim's eyes snapped open as he gave a choking, dry gasp. His brow was furrowed and he seemed confused. He looked around wildly.

"I'm here. Please, it's—" She didn't know what else to say. Her throat was too tight to speak, anyway.

Maxim's gaze landed on her and as he focused on her, he stilled. He appeared the same: the bump on the bridge of his nose, the stubble at the edge of his jawline, those beautiful green-gold eyes. He blinked, and his hand tightened on hers.

"Pippa?"

She threw herself onto him with a sob, and his arms came up around her, pressing her close.

"Oh thank fuck." It came out very damp and muffled by his neck, and she wasn't completely sure he could even hear her.

Maxim gave a weak chuckle, made weaker by Pippa's full weight pressed onto his chest.

"That was . . ." he said when she finally straightened. His breathing was ragged and uneven. He blinked rapidly, as if to clear images from his vision. "I think we just beat *death.*"

Wet laughter burbled out of her and she squeezed his hands. *Stars,* she loved him. This wonderful, ridiculous human who, despite having gone through the ordeal of being brought back from the dead, was still coming up with possible quotes for throw cushions. Untethered, the Reaper magic let her feel him completely—the warmth of his soul up through his hammering heart to the steady rush of air in his lungs.

He leaned close and pressed his forehead to hers, and she held him tight, reveling in the sensation of the wild pulse racing through his body.

And it was because of *her* magic. Not bad, not evil, not her father's. This was hers, through to its core. As much as it was her anger, it was also a product of her love. Her joy.

Slowly, her other magic returned. It skittered along her forearms, almost bashful, before trickling into her. She closed her eyes and basked in the tingling at her fingertips, the fullness of the world, and the warmth of the man beside her.

For the first time in a long while, Pippa felt whole.

All she'd needed was the right sort of magic.

Epilogue

Three months later

Maxim's apartment felt much better with someone else living in it. He finally bought a new lamp for his study, and after quite a bit of Pippa teasing him about it, he convinced the landlord to purchase a ceiling sconce that didn't look like a tit.

Pippa had been able to salvage some of her things from her apartment, although they still smelled a bit like smoke. Some of her books on demon cooking fit nicely on the bookshelf next to his books about fake demons. Many books had turned to ash, so Maxim gave her a stack of new ones as a housewarming gift. It turned out that *Eaten Right By The Duke* had been part of a series. She'd already finished all of them except for the last one, *Matey'ed Right By The Pirate*, which in Maxim's opinion sounded like the author was running out of steam, though by book fourteen it was understandable.

Right after Pippa had moved in, she'd started looking for another job so she wouldn't feel uncomfortable about currently fucking one of her coworkers. She found an admin job on the floor below, so they were able to have lunch together every day and listen to books on the drive to and from the building. She'd joked about having another closet tryst, but both of them had decided that the comfort of their bed (*their bed*, oh it felt nice to say that) was far better than the thrill of a potential HR nightmare. They also had the kitchen, and the couch, and on one highly uncomfortable occasion, the back of his car.

Sometimes, Maxim dreamed he was floating in emptiness. He'd fall asleep and suddenly the air would be like silk against him, brilliant light flashing into his eyes. He'd see ancient civilizations and beautiful landscapes, strange faces barely visible behind a swirl of dust. Then he'd wake up with sweat slick and hot on his neck and in the darkness of their bedroom he'd wonder for a split second if he'd ever truly left.

Every once in a while, usually when he was tired or fretting about something, he would see a shadow that lingered a little bit too long for it to be a trick of his sight. He hadn't told Pippa about it yet. She knew, though, in the concerned look she gave him every time he'd flinch at a shape hovering just at the edge of his vision.

He wondered if there might have been consequences when she brought him back. If the coven who'd ostracized her knew about what she'd done—the killed demons, the Reaper magic, *him*—they hadn't sent any word about it.

Pippa was working on starting her own coven. It was very small, and right now only included her mother and Jules, but more were coming. She was close to convincing her succubus friend (which was a combination of words about which Maxim still felt a bit incredulous), and seemed optimistic.

Jules had taken the new world of magic and demons about as well as Pippa thought she would, and was so beyond thrilled to be included that she had to be threatened into secrecy. Maxim wasn't sure what would happen when Jules finally met the succubus, and he was simultaneously anxious and delighted for the day he'd experience it.

Pippa had also been learning embroidery. He showed her all of the basics he remembered, which were not much, and she used videos and experimentation to figure out the rest.

She was sitting on the couch now, her jaw set in determination. Her yelps and curses were becoming less frequent as she worked on needle control.

Maxim looked over her shoulder at her hoop. Crooked letters were scrawled in black thread across the bottom. Above the words, she'd stitched a stylized needle and spool of thread surrounded by sparkles and cartoon stars. The needle was too thick and quite phallic, though he didn't mention anything. The top of the spool also looked a bit like a vulva, but he wasn't going to mention anything about that either.

Pippa caught him looking.

"What do you think?" She held it up to him so he could read it better. "I want to put it in the bathroom."

Witches Get Stitches.

He leaned in so he could kiss her. "It's perfect."

Author's Note

When I started writing this, it was supposed to just be about magic, monsters, love, and smut. The amount of time it took me to realize that both characters were inspired by my own experiences with anxiety is embarrassingly long. I'll never share exactly how long. (Kidding, it was Chapter 9.)

Hey, they say to write what you know.

I've had anxiety for most of my life. Like Maxim, it didn't have a horrible or traumatic reason for existing; it was just there. My little gremlin. It accompanied me everywhere I went and always had helpful tidbits to share, such as "If you make a mistake in this piano recital, every single person in the audience will remember it for the rest of their lives," and "The results of this grammar test will determine whether or not you become a successful member of society," and "That little ache in your ribs means your heart and/or lungs are about to wither and/or fall out of your butt."

In the same way Pippa looked at her dark magic, I used to look at my anxiety with fear and not a little disgust. I had this thing I'd inherited that I had no control over. It could do awful things to my guts and my brain and it lurked in the back of every thought. I never knew when it would make an appearance. I constantly dreaded how much it would gleefully destroy before it became sated and returned to a calm-ish hibernation.

After a whole lot of talking to people who are trained to talk to other people, I started to realize that the anxiety wasn't a disease to eradicate or a problem to banish. Of course all our experiences are different and there is no way on this green Earth I'm going to put actual psychological advice in the "Author's Note" of a romance novel, but my own experience culminated in the discovery that once I looked at anxiety as part of what made me *me*, it didn't seem so bad. It would appear, it would force a different perspective, and then it would settle. For a long time, I felt broken, but this way of thinking helped me understand there's no "broken"; there's "able to visualize many, many outcomes in my head," and "wow I'm so good at packing for trips."

Pippa's journey obviously mimics that realization, although mine is thankfully far lighter on the necromancy.

My hope is that this journey resonated with you, and if not, then it provided an insight of sorts.

And if it didn't do that, then hopefully you at least enjoyed the sex scenes.

-Alexandra Alan

Acknowledgements

This book would not have been possible without a large assortment of people to whom I am eternally grateful. I'm only slightly terrified of leaving someone's name out (see Author's Note) but if I've left out a name, just know it's because I've forgotten it, not that I've forgotten you. I love you to pieces.

Lola, I would never have started writing this without our extended phone call where I literally hashed out the meat of this story. Thank you for your (almost) thirty years of friendship, giving it to me straight when I need advice, and coming up with this book's concept of familiars. The ending literally would not have been possible without you. I also love that you skip right to the smut scenes.

I was buoyed beyond measure by the excitement that came from Ariel, aided immensely by brainstorming walks with Maddy, and provided the knowledge of how many times I re-used words and messed up timelines thanks to Bryn. Jamie, your cheerleading kept my editing going. Chelsea, your enthusiasm for the things that fall out of my brain makes me want to keep letting things fall out of my brain. Cecelia, your support and encouragement had me believing I could even do this in the first place.

A huge and somewhat reluctant thanks to Jess. Your play-by-play texts gave me life, but you also had some wonderful feedback that resulted in reworking large chunks of this book. (Kidding about the reluctant part—you're the greatest, it's much better now thanks to you.)

Christa, you are an absolute editing genius and a wonderful writing buddy. Seeing your comments (and sweating emojis) in the margins let me know a section was going just the way I wanted it to.

Thanks to everyone in the All That [G]litters Discord chat. Katie Shepard and Tamara, thank you two so much for reading this in its infancy and providing wildly helpful feedback.

A huge thanks to Rebecca Baker for her legal firm knowledge and advice while I noodled on the very earliest version of this story.

Libertad, you made the most exquisite cover. I'm so happy for the Star Wars "I Just Had Sex" mashup you created over 10 years ago that never left my brain and inspired me to reach out and ask you to illustrate my books.

I'm truly grateful that none of my parents are the inspiration for the parents in this book. Thanks to my dad for being excited about my writing, even if it's not in his preferred genre; my stepmom for encouraging me to dream outside my comfort zone; and my stepdad for his reassurance and optimism.

And to my mom: thanks for spurring me to publish this. (Is "demanding" too strong a word?) I'm forever grateful for your boundless motivation and the fact that you've read nearly all the smut I've written and not judged me for it.

About the Author

Alexandra lives with some very strange cats and an assortment of wildly varied and anachronistic hobbies. When not writing, she works in academia and likes to pretend that she's found a use for her art degree. She has never met a bad pun she hasn't adored and loves to read and write books that make her heart race.

She loves to hear from her readers! You can find her on various social media platforms at @alexalanwrites or at AlexandraAlan .com.

Other books available now!
Standalone Novellas:
Going the Distance
Bound to Remember
The Art of Getting Off